The RIGHT MAN

MICHELLE MANKIN

ISBN: 9781795430555

Edited by Pam Berehulke at Bulletproof Editing
Cover design by Lori Jackson Design
Photography by Wander Aguiar from Wander Photography, Florian Tarpinian model
Formatting by Elaine York at Allusion Publishing, www.allusionpublishing.com

The RIGHT MAN

About the Book

Rush McMahon is one of the biggest rockstars on the planet. Handsome, talented, and famous, he has his choice of pretty women. After finishing another successful tour, he should be on top of the world. He pretends to be, but he's not. How can he be anything but miserable when his brother just married the woman he once loved?

Jewel Anderson is desperate and all alone in the world, except for her impulsive roommate Camaro Moltepulciano. She's hungry. The rent for her tiny apartment is overdue, and Cam just gave the last of their money away to someone less fortunate. Jewel has a heart of gold like her best friend Cam, but hearts can't be traded to pay for rent. Since both refuse to return to the homeless shelter where Jewel was almost assaulted, what can two nearly destitute women do?

Rush is a bad boy lead singer living a lie.

Jewel is a good girl at the end of her rope.

He is her last option.

She might be his only hope.

What happens when Rush and Jewel meet on a dark street corner in LA?

Can a chance encounter between two people from opposite worlds lead to happily ever after?

Prologue

"Tell me about Cinderella again, Gran," the little girl asked Alice as she reached to switch off the lamp.

"It's time for bed, sweetheart."

"Just one more time. Please." Jewel blinked her big golden eyes. "I'll go right to sleep afterward. Promise."

"All right." Alice's expression softened. Her granddaughter was the apple of her eye, and she could hardly refuse the child anything. Carefully, she tucked the ruffled pink comforter she had sewn for Jewel around her. "But how about a different love story this time?"

"Another fairy tale?" Jewel lisped through her two missing front teeth. She was about to start second grade, not yet ready to set aside the happily-ever-after endings of her favorite childhood stories.

"Much better than that." Alice smiled, and nostalgia warmed her heart. "A real love story. The story about how your grandfather and I met."

"Oh, goody." Eagerness bloomed in the seven-year-old's peaches-and-cream complexion.

"All right. Once upon a time—"

"That's how all good stories start," Jewel said with a knowing nod.

"Yes, you're right, and this is a good one. The very best." Smiling, Alice stroked her granddaughter's silky hair. This nightly ritual was her favorite part of the day. "Once upon a time, there was a fall celebration in our little town, and everyone received an invitation. I just had to go. You see, there was a handsome boy who had caught my eye."

"Granddad?"

"Yes, precious one." She patted the girl's small hand. "My best friend, Pauline, told me he and his friends were planning to attend. But there was one problem. I had nothing to wear."

"What did you do?" The little girl's auburn brows knitted together. "Did you wish for a gown from your fairy godmother?"

"Wishes are the seeds of desire within your heart. Sometimes to make them come true, you have to plan and take action. I knew Pauline's sister was my size, so I borrowed a dress from her."

"And you went to the dance in an enchanted carriage?"

"Nothing quite so fancy." Alice chuckled. "I went in a rusty old farm truck."

"Oh." Jewel frowned, and her bottom lip jutted out.

Drawing her granddaughter back into the tale, Alice waved a hand in the air as if to sprinkle stardust. "Nevertheless, the night had plenty of magic. Excitement buzzed in the air. Fireflies twinkled in the field like fallen stars. Streamers fluttered from the barn's rafters. The tables were laden with delicacies fit for any princess. I brought my mother's famous peach pie."

"That's my favorite!"

"I know, sweetheart. When I set the plate down, I looked up and immediately found him. Your grandfather stood so tall, head and shoulders above the rest of the crowd. So handsome in his crisp white shirt and pressed jeans, he marched straight to me. People cleared out of his way as if he had given them some silent command."

"And then what happened?" Jewel asked.

"He stopped in front of me and said, 'I'm Eli. I've seen you around town.' And I told him, 'I'm Alice. I've seen you around too. I like your blue eyes.' Then he said, 'I like your honesty, Alice,' and smiled at me, a smile so big and bright, it melted my heart."

"Did it hurt when your heart melted?" Jewel asked, her button nose scrunched.

Alice laughed. "No, dear. It means it felt warm and happy. So then your grandfather said, 'I have to confess something. I only came to the party tonight to see you. You're pretty and sweet, and I've been watching you and hoping to meet you for some time now.' Then he held out his hand, and I took it without hesitation. When his fingers closed around mine, I knew."

"What did you know?" the little girl whispered, her eyes as big and round as a harvest moon.

"That he was mine. That I was his. That he was gentle, kind, and everything I needed."

"How could you tell?" Jewel asked.

"Because his steady gaze was true, and his grip was sure. Because he was considerate. Because while we danced, he told me his plans for the future, and how he wanted me to be part of it. And then he asked me to marry him."

"After one dance?" The little girl's expression turned wistful. "Just like Prince Charming in Cinderella."

Alice nodded. "Your grandfather was a simple farmer, just like his father and his grandfather before him. The passing of the tobacco farm from one generation to the next was the only part of his life that resembled royalty. He worked hard from sunup to sundown every day to provide the necessities we currently enjoy: food, clothing, and shelter. But the very best thing he gave me was his love."

Cupping Jewel's cheek, Alice said, "Through that love came your mother, and then you. Carriages, castles, and crowns are fun to dream about, my darling, but having all that finery won't make you genuinely happy. Only real love will. Real love will stay by your side, through thick and thin. Real love will make the good times better and the bad times bearable. Use your head to find love like that, Jewel, and trust your heart to do what's right to keep it."

Jewel nodded. "I know."

Surprised, Alice chuckled. "Is that so?"

"Yes, Gran." The girl studied her grandmother for a moment. "I know because you've shown me."

"I hope so, sweet girl. I hope you don't forget, and that my example is enough. I hope you never have to learn the hard way about how difficult life can be."

"Like my mother?" Jewel's lip trembled.

Alice studied her granddaughter, surprised by the clarity of the child's perception. She'd mistakenly believed Jewel had been too young to remember the circumstances of her life before her grandmother had adopted her.

"Beauty is reflected in honorable actions, not pretty promises, not in what a person has or how they look on the outside." She took and squeezed her granddaughter's hand. "And the right man—a good man—is one who will look at you with love in his eyes. He'll listen. He'll be gentle. He will show he cares by the changes he makes in his life for you."

Alice smiled bravely, blinking back the tears that threatened at the memory of her Eli, and gave her granddaughter the best advice she could.

"A good man's arms, not a castle, will be the most perfect home you will ever find."

Rush

Naked and on my side, I was being worked over by three curvaceous women in the middle of my hotel bed. I weighed the supersize tits of the babe in front of me, not sure if they were fake or real, while the chick who pressed into me from behind ran her manicured nails around my nipples.

Guys who tell you that isn't a turn-on? They're fuckin' lying.

Tension built inside me as the third woman worked my cock. She knew what she was doing. Determined, she kept at me as I lengthened in her hand, not stopping even when I was distracted by a phone call from my drummer, Jack Howard, about another argument between him and my bassist, Benton Kennedy. My bandmates had been at each other's throats the entire week, ever since Ben had been busted having phone sex with Jack's wife.

I didn't get the constant competition between them. Maybe the rivalry arose from their different backgrounds. Jack had been raised in an abusive low-income home, while Ben had a privileged upbringing where his physical needs were indulged but his emotional needs were ignored.

But why poach another guy's woman? There was plenty of unencumbered snatch on the road.

Groupies at the venues. Groupies on the bus. Groupies at the pre-show hotel parties like this one. A never-ending surplus of them. They threw themselves at us constantly. The last stop on the tour tonight? No exception.

Apparently noting my inattention, the groupie behind me pinched my nipples at the same time the one down low fisted my rod like a super-tight cunt.

Refocused, I felt a tingle begin at the base of my spine. The chick crouched beside me shoved one of her basketball-sized globes into my mouth, and my body drew taut. Fake or real, tits were tits. I had a pair of fantasies to suck on, two pressed into my back, and two more shadowing my cock.

I swirled my tongue around the globe in my mouth and sucked its elongated nipple between my lips, then bit down. Fantasy Chick liked that a hell of a lot. She moaned, and the hand working my steel-hard cock sped up.

Finally, inevitably, it happened. Three bodacious babes, naked and writhing on my hotel bed with me? Yeah, that setup had the desired effect.

Despite a bump of coke and too much whiskey, I groaned low in my throat and let go. My spine stiffened as I released my load. Spurts of hot cum coated the pumping hand fastened around my cock.

"All right, darlin'," I said as I sat up.

Over and done, from the heights of make-believe to the depths of reality I crashed. Disappointment awaited me on the other side.

"That's enough. Hands off my junk."

As my dissatisfaction came roaring back, I didn't bother pretending I was interested anymore. Because I was an asshole. But also because I knew what this was, and so did they. I got a reprieve from the hubris of my own headspace, and they got bragging rights that they had done it with Rush McMahon, Black Cat Records' biggest rock star. An even exchange.

And now I wanted them gone. Their clashing fragrances filled the air, searing my nasal passages and making my eyes burn.

"Nothing personal," I said as I carefully swept Fantasy Chick out of my way.

The down-low chick was already on the floor retrieving her clothes. The ringleader of the trio, she seemed well versed with the *fuck 'em and leave 'em* drill.

"Pick up your cell phones in the other room on your way out," I said gruffly.

"What about our VIP passes?" the ringleader asked, her voice shrill and her calculating eyes narrowed.

"Those too." I whipped the rumpled sheet off the bed and tucked it around my waist. "My manager will see that you're taken care of. Go on. Move along." Shuffling them toward the door without allowing them time to finish dressing, I explained. "I gotta get ready for the show."

I clicked the door closed behind them and turned to press my back against it, squeezing my eyes shut as the weariness of the nine-month-long tour slammed down on me. I was so fucking sick of it. Night after night, day after day, it was always the same. Show, long bus ride, hotel, chicks, booze, more chicks, more booze.

"Be careful what you wish for, my boy." My father's words of advice rattled around inside my skull as clearly as the day he'd spoken them. *"Dreams are great things—unless they're misguided ones."*

He'd thought mine were misguided. The way I felt today, I certainly couldn't argue with his assessment.

Don't, I warned myself. *Don't you fucking feel sorry for yourself. You're Rush McMahon, on top of the world. Top of the charts. You busted your ass, and you made it. And now you have everything you ever wanted.*

Yet, as I opened my eyes and glanced around the opulent suite, I knew I had nothing I really needed. Nothing that mattered. And no one in my life anymore who truly understood how I felt.

I raked my hand through my hair. *Bullshit!* Introspection like this was a waste of time. It didn't change anything.

No, what was called for here was self-medication. At the proper dosage, it would suppress the brain's tendency toward focusing on unproductive matters while keeping it coherent enough to be functional.

With that goal in mind, I tugged the sheet tighter around me and pushed away from the door just in time to escape the rising sound of the irritated voices on the other side. Groupies never responded favorably to being forced to sign nondisclosure agreements.

No signature? No cell phone.

Yeah, I might feel like a loser at the moment, but I wasn't a fool. No way in hell was I going to let some random chicks I'd just fucked screw me over with a viral video.

Returning to the center of the room, I paused at the glossy mahogany table and grabbed the half-full bottle of Jameson I'd abandoned earlier. I lifted it into the air in a toast.

"Here's to you on your wedding day, darlin'. And here's to me, myself, and I—and the fuckin' success I am without you."

Fuck, that sounded lame. Apparently, banging groupies hadn't gotten my mind off anything.

Exchanging one rock star's vice for another, I brought the bottle to my lips and knocked back an unhealthy swallow. My throat warmed, and the chill inside my chest receded.

A pleasant numbness settled into my limbs as I snagged my cell from the charging cradle. I loaded some of my music and hit PLAY, needing some fucking sound to drown out the silence.

Whiskey in hand, I headed toward the balcony on a mission for some perfume-free air. I threw open one of the French doors and slipped through the gap.

The outside speakers crackled as they picked up the first track. My guitar chords streaked like a blazing comet through the darkness. It was some kickass ax work, if I did say so myself. And I did. Hearing it brightened my gloom.

I set the bottle on a cushioned lounger—not that I wouldn't hit it again or tag another chick later. I just had a better option for now.

With my own voice serenading me, I moved to the edge of the balcony to take in the view. Elbows propped on the iron railing, I surveyed the twinkling lights of LA from fifteen stories above.

Jack's drums pounded the melancholy from my chest. Ben's snaky bass groove further improved my mood. A breeze gently lifted the layers of hair at my brow, soothing me.

My lips curved. My twisted guts unraveled.

Liquor and drugs were only temporary fixes. Music was my preferred therapy. The lifeblood of my soul. The rhythm of my heart. My unshakable foundation.

Brenda had never fully understood that . . . or me. Like my dad, she'd thought my career was some post-adolescent phase. Even if I hadn't screwed up with her, she and I would have never worked.

On that depressing note of clarity, I finally noticed the cold of the stamped concrete seeping into the soles of my bare feet. The chill spread throughout my body, raising goose bumps on my skin.

Sighing, I turned away from the view. At the lounger, I bent and snagged my bottle before reentering the suite. On my way to the shower, I shook my head as an unmistakable ringtone stopped me in my tracks.

Shit. I walked back to my phone. My manager's disapproving image lit up the screen.

"Hello?" My gut tightened again as I braced for the inevitable lecture.

"You're not dressed yet, are you?" Bradley Marshall asked, sounding as stick-up-his-ass irritated as he usually did lately.

"No, man."

"Pre-show meet and greets are in ten minutes."

"I know. Gotta shower first."

"I'll bet you do. Hell, Rush, you probably need a hazmat unit to get clean after rolling around with that unholy trinity. The blonde had some video of you snorting coke off her tits. Must have taken it before we confiscated their phones."

"Uh, well . . ."

"I deleted it."

"Thanks."

"Not smart."

"I know, it's just—"

Brad sighed. "Yeah, I know. Today's been rough for you. But you didn't really think she was going to wait around forever, did you?"

"No, man. I lost her. I know the score."

A beautiful, caring woman like Brenda? I'd known it would only be a matter of time before some other guy came along who could give her what she wanted. Things I couldn't or wouldn't offer.

Fidelity. Reliability. A permanent home.

"You send her the flowers?" I asked. Red roses. Her favorite.

"Yeah, but I don't think it was such a great idea. Those aren't the kind of flowers you send somebody on their wedding day."

"I had to do something."

"You shoulda just called. Told her you're sorry you screwed up with her. Wished her well. If Randy sees 'em and figures out who they're from, it'll just piss him off."

"Too bad. My brother's marrying my ex-fiancée." I had been prepared for her to move on. It was who she'd moved on with that had blindsided me. "Doesn't anyone get that I'm the injured party?"

Brad snorted. "You stepped out on her."

"We were on a break! And she'd withdrawn from me emotionally long before that."

So did everyone else back home when I dropped the bomb that I was leaving college to pursue a career in the music business. Everyone except for Brad.

"Not an excuse," he said.

Brad didn't bullshit, just spewed the facts as he saw them. He always gave it to me straight, which was one of his best qualities. He had a lot of them—intelligence, loyalty, honesty. There were a lot of reasons he was my best friend, my only one these days. My bandmates didn't count. We enabled one another's dysfunctions.

"I know. I get it. I came clean with her and accepted the blame."

I raked a hand through my hair, and my agitated movement stirred up more noxious perfume. The fragrance stung my eyes again, making them tear up. It sure as shit wasn't the sharp shards of regret.

I had made my bed. Gotten laid in it before I ended it with her. But I was good now. Things were better. I'd moved on.

So, why did every step I'd taken since then feel like the biggest lie of all?

2

Jewel

"Shit," I muttered, waking to my alarm blaring. Rolling over, I fumbled for my cell. After swiping off the clock function, I frowned into the grainy gray twilight. I couldn't believe it was sundown already.

"Get a move on, Jewel, my precious gem. Nothing's worse than time that's wasted."

Gran's age-warbled voice was only in my mind nowadays, but hearing it echo in the lonely hallways of the past made tears prick my eyes.

"I miss you," I whispered to the painting of her that hung on the wall opposite my bed. Eyes a golden shade nearly identical to mine, though infinitely wiser, seemed to gaze back sympathetically. If only I'd heeded her wisdom. "I'm sorry, Gran."

Her serene expression radiated forgiveness because that was the way I wanted to read it. But there would never be any absolution. All that remained was the portrait. An amateur one. After all, it had been my hand that had painted it. The lessons to improve my craft that I'd hoped to take when I moved to LA had never come to pass. More practical concerns like food and shelter had quickly taken precedence over art and dreams.

Reminded of those pressing needs, I tossed aside my threadbare covers, bolted upright in bed, and threw my legs over the side. I needed to get ready. No one was going to wave a magic wand and make money appear.

Swallowing hard, I grounded myself by gripping the edge of the bed—the cot that functioned as one—in my apartment that was barely larger than a broom closet. A translucent scarf thrown over a light bulb didn't soften the harsh reality.

My current accommodations were a far cry from the comforts I'd once enjoyed inside my grandmother's foursquare home. Here, cardboard boxes served as tables. Plastic cartons stacked as shelves. Foil over the lone window curtained the light during the day.

My already sagging spirits sank lower when I noted the other cot beside me was unoccupied. The rumpled sheets provided no clue as to where my roommate had gone. She was probably gallivanting around doing who-knew-what as usual. Camaro Montepulciano had a kind heart, taking me in when I had nowhere else to go. She'd shown me the ropes. But she rode on the winds of her everchanging moods.

I let out a disappointed sigh, but I didn't fault her. Cam had her flights of indulgence; I had mine. Painting, mainly, though I only had the dregs of a few basic colors left to work with and no more canvases. No escaping through the strokes of an imagined reality today.

Feet on the floor, I firmed my frown into a determined line and got out of bed. I stood, my fingers curled into my palms. The embers of a once-bright hope flickered uncertainly inside my chest. Wishes couldn't fan them to a healthy glow, not when blanketed by so many suffocating regrets.

I closed my eyes, allowing myself a moment in the meadow in my imagination. A crown of common daisies on my head and a handful of them in my tiny grip. My grandmother beside me, her strong fingers wrapped around mine.

Gran had been my firm foundation when the world around me was shaken. It had been eighteen months since she passed, but her loss hadn't gotten any easier. For me, grief wasn't just a burden, it was a razor-sharp knife that had carved out a permanent cavity inside me.

Opening my eyes, I blinked through the sting of tears and ineffectively rubbed my hand over my aching heart before I shuffled to the shower.

Predictably, the hot water ran out halfway through, and I had to rinse my hair in a cold stream. Sliding the plastic curtain back, I stepped over the rim of the tub and placed my feet on the old towel that stood in for a bathmat. Ribbons of russet against my slim shoulders wept rivers that rushed downward over the slopes of my breasts. I grabbed a towel from the rack and draped it around my slender frame. It absorbed the excess moisture from my body, but it couldn't wipe away the pain.

At the cracked pedestal sink, I picked up the comb from the glass shelf and began the time-consuming process of running it through the long strands to untangle my hair. My empty stomach grumbled. I ignored it and the reflection of myself in the rusted mirror. I preferred not to acknowledge the hard-learned lessons reflected in my eyes.

Finished with my hair, I set aside the comb and returned to the adjoining room. Maybe I had a leftover packet of crackers in the bottom of my bag.

Crouching beside my cot, I removed the slouchy handbag I stored under it. I rummaged through the contents, looking for money and food, but discovered it was as empty as my stomach. Setting it aside, I pulled out the box that contained my clothes. Not the ones I was most comfortable in. The other ones.

My work clothes.

I laid out the lace and the silk on the bed. Seductive undergarments on one side. All the pieces to the costume that made up my outward persona on the other. It helped to compartmentalize the two aspects of my life. What happened to her, my alter ego, didn't happen to me. It was a lie, but sometimes I believed it.

Lingerie and outfit on, nail polish and makeup applied. I tucked my hair under a wig and arranged its platinum-blond pigtails around my face, avoiding looking at my heavily mascaraed eyes rimmed in kohl as I took a quick glance at my reflection.

The white oxford shirt had been too tame before I took a pair of shears to it, cutting off the sleeves and baring the midriff all the way to my bra. The red-and-black-sequined skirt I'd salvaged from the dumpster at Goodwill was so short, it revealed the racy crimson-and-black garters that held up my fishnet stockings. Black sky-high stilettos completed the look.

The whole effect was my artistic bent put to practical use. When I was done, my persona was part naughty Catholic schoolgirl and part comic-book villainess.

I tugged on a hooded jacket against the night chill and stuck out my tongue at my reflection before I left the bathroom. *This chick doesn't take anything seriously. She doesn't put up with shit, and she does what needs to be done.*

Shoulders back, spine straight, invisible armor against reality in place, I left the apartment. The musty corridor was deserted, thankfully, except for a half-naked man lying on the hallway floor. I stepped over him, and he grunted.

"Sorry, Terrance."

"It's okay, Jules." His wizened face riddled with pockmarks, he peered up at me through his good eye. "You going out?" The idea of that seemed to make him sad. He wasn't alone in that sentiment.

"Yeah." My gaze slid away. I had no food. The rent was overdue. I had no choice.

"There's always a choice." Gran's voice echoed inside my head again. Only she was gone, her bright, shining ideals carried off with her, leaving me alone with no one but myself to rely on.

"Watch out for Wanda," I told Terrance.

"She on the warpath?"

"If you mean is she on a mission to clear out the nonpaying residents who like to nap for free in the hall, then yeah, that's what she's on for sure."

"Shit." He sat up and reached for the oversized garbage bag that contained all his belongings. "Don't have no place else to go," he muttered.

"And there but for the grace of God go you." Gran's voice. And that small-town upbringing I'd run away from.

I sighed. I couldn't let him inside the apartment. But the shelter on Peach? I had a token for a bed. I'd gotten one just in case I had nowhere else to go.

Bracelets jangling on my wrist, I dove my hand into the pocket of my skirt. "Here." I offered the token to Terrance.

"You sure?" he asked, even as he stretched out his thin arm to take it.

"I'm sure."

I fought back the wave of trepidation and got my feet moving again. Traversing the remaining length of the narrow hallway, I pushed open the door to the stairwell. I glanced around inside it to make sure it was clear before I started down.

At the bottom, I pressed the bar to open the heavy steel door but jumped back when a diminutive black woman with an attitude as huge as the Hulk appeared inside the circle of light from the overhead motion sensor.

"Wanda," I said.

Shit. Shit. Triple shit.

I wobbled on my stilettos. My retreat was cut off as the door to return inside the building snapped closed behind me.

"Jewel Anderson, I thought I might find you here." In a business suit, her glasses sliding to the tip of her nose, Wanda raked her gaze over me. "Going somewhere?"

"Um, yes. I—"

"You conveniently forget that your rent is due?" She arched a brow.

"No, I'm just—"

"Sneaking around. Three days late." She clucked her tongue. "You'll pay the late penalty. I'm not floating you a zero-interest loan."

"I know you won't. I didn't expect you to. It's just that we're a little short this month."

"You two are always a little short. I should've kicked your sorry asses out the first time. Girls like you—"

"Not a single person is on a waiting list to move into your apartments," I said, my spine stiffening. "Tiny rooms. A/C and heat that's always fritzing out. No blinds on the windows. Hot water that barely works." I put a hand on my hip and lifted my chin. "And you don't know me or the type of girl I am."

Wanda scoffed. "Girl, I know everything I need to know about you. Cheap-ass hooker, blaming everyone but yourself for the predicament you find yourself in." She looked down her nose at me, and even though I stood a half foot taller than her in my stilettos, I was the one who felt small.

I didn't like her. I didn't like her at all. Even when the rent wasn't due, I avoided her.

"I'll have your money after tonight," I said, though my stomach churned on nothing but my bravado.

"You will, or I'll be evicting you first thing tomorrow morning."

Once she hit me with that ultimatum, she spun around. Her sensible heels clicked on the concrete as she marched the length of the alley. Probably off to her office to roll around on her stacks of cash and polish her broomstick.

Mean. Evil. Spiteful woman.

My eyes burned from within their kohl frame as I watched her go.

Don't cry, I told myself, curling my hands into fists and focusing on the bite in my skin from my nails rather than on my fear that my roommate and I would likely be on the streets soon.

I squeezed my eyes shut. I couldn't give up before I even tried. It wasn't just me. There was Cam to consider.

Reopening my eyes, I forced my body into motion, navigating the trash strewn in the alley. Crushed aluminum cans. Broken liquor bottles. I stepped gingerly between them, feeling as used up and empty as the abandoned items around me.

At the sidewalk, I slowed my pace and ducked into the shadows beneath the awning of an adult-clothing shop. I glanced over my shoulder. No sign of Wanda or anyone else watching me.

I let out a sigh and caught a glimpse of my reflection in the plate glass.

My eyes were wide pools of gold beneath dark auburn brows. If only they were an actual physical commodity I could pawn.

I slammed them closed. Fool's gold. They gave away too much. It was unwise to appear vulnerable outside the apartment.

Opening my eyes again, I narrowed my gaze and gulped in a deep, determined breath. Then I reached for the hood on my jacket and pulled it over my wig.

Be brave, I told myself, remembering another of Gran's sayings. *"Bravery isn't the absence of fear; it's the ability to keep going despite insurmountable obstacles."*

Bravery was my choice. One foot in front of the other.

My night was only starting; I still had to get on the bus. It would take me two transfers to get to the better-paying side of town. Further, I had to hope that I looked more tempting than the girls who had already set up shop over there.

If I didn't, I was fucked, and not in the way that would get me the money I needed to pay the rent.

3

Rush

"Rush. Rush. Rush."

The chanting of my name echoed in the cinder-block corridor after I left the stage.

"They want a second encore," Brad told me, as if I didn't already know.

"They can't always get what they want." I snagged the white towel a stagehand offered me and swiped it across my brow.

Narrowing my eyes at my manager, I noticed the chicks we swept past vied for his attention as much as they did for mine. Blond, blue-eyed, barely older than me, Brad was the manager of the ten-million-dollar-a-year Rush machine. He was also catnip to the backstage pussy that went for his Armani brand of boring boardroom predictability.

"Life sucks and then you die, right?"

"Rush." His tone was warning as he glanced up from his phone and the glow of platinum profits from tonight's sold-out show. "Not here." He lifted his chin to remind me of our audience. "Put a lid on the negativity."

He might have a point about the crowd. My PR rep, the stylist, and the visiting record-label VP had signed nondisclosure agreements, same as the groupies. While my staff was paid handsomely to keep their mouths shut whenever I shot off mine, I held no such sway with the ticket-holding masses.

"I'm not making apologies for how I am."

Brad frowned as we entered the dressing room. "You weren't always this difficult."

I brushed past him on the way to the bar. Out of deference to my company, I poured a tumbler of whiskey. Alone, I would have chugged it straight from the bottle. I threw back the socially acceptable portion, but the fire the amber elixir ignited barely registered. Ditto for the lingering adrenaline rush from the roar of the Staples Center crowd.

Get a grip, I told myself, staring at my reflection. The guy within the rectangular frame of bulbs surrounding the mirror looked a little too needy and wrung out. His brown hair was plastered to his skull, and so saturated with sweat, it appeared black. The eyes were the real giveaway. Twin portals whirled with a vortex of negative emotions.

"No more drinking." Brad snatched the bottle of Jameson from my grasp. "You know what happened last time you got trashed."

"I remember. No need to rub my nose in it." Sales had gone in the shitter after someone posted a video of me going nuclear on an overly aggressive paparazzo.

I had zero regrets. Asswipe had it coming for shoving his camera in my mother's face at the funeral. If my father had been the pillar of strength in our family, she was the pedestal. Only she had crumpled completely when they lowered his casket into the ground. Remembering that day and all that had been lost, the ground rumbled at a Richter-scale magnitude beneath my feet.

The betrayal of my ex-fiancée marrying my brother was a minor temblor in comparison.

It wasn't only that my father was gone, or that Brenda had moved on, it was that so much had been left unresolved with each of them. I knew my failure as a man was the common factor with each.

As the specter of that truth rose within me, my mouth went dry and my hands twitched. I needed another drink. No, I wanted to drain that entire fucking bottle of whiskey dry. And I knew what that meant. The narrow line I'd been walking with my drinking had gone well beyond a casual thing.

I ripped my gaze away from my reflection and glared at Brad. "Is my car washed and gassed up?"

I could see no other cure for what ailed me. I needed to get away before I did something ill-advised. Paparazzi were like a plague of locusts, ready to devour my mistakes, and talking heads were on standby to regurgitate the lurid stories for mass consumption.

He scowled at me. "Yeah, but do you really think you're in any condition to drive?"

"I need some fresh air."

"Rush, you've got interviews and the VIP meet and greets."

"You said we were through with all the bullshit after tonight."

"After tonight's *obligations.* It's not all about you. Your fans are what keeps the Rush machine cranking out the cash, and you know it."

"Yeah. All right. I get it."

I closed my fingers into tight fists, wishing they were gripping the leather-wrapped steering wheel of my Porsche instead.

"They get an hour." I could do sixty more minutes for him and for my bandmates who worked as hard as I did. But that was it. I was as sick of myself and the arrogant rock-star act as everyone else was. "After that, I'm gone."

"Everyone out." Brad barked the order to the media reps who had followed us into the dressing room. "Rush needs a shower." He cast his authoritative gaze around the throng within the claustrophobic ten-by-fourteen-foot space.

As usual, when he spoke, people listened. It was an innate ability he'd been honing since I met him in grade school and he convinced our headmaster that after-school suspensions were inhumane.

"Interviews will run according to the order on the sign-up sheet," Brad said, and the already rapidly emptying room cleared out even faster. Everyone hoped to be first in line.

When only my entourage remained, he addressed our small crew. "Thanks for all your hard work tonight. I'll meet you in the green room. For now, I need you to give us some privacy."

They filed out, and as soon as the door shut behind them and we were alone, Brad narrowed his gaze on me.

"Been on tour for nine months without a fuckin' break," I said quickly, recognizing the impending lecture gleaming in his eyes. "I gotta go off the grid before I go completely insane, man."

"I hear you."

He studied me a long beat. Whatever he saw turned his light blue eyes storm-cloud dark.

"I've got your back. You know I do. But you aren't the only one who's dead tired. If you go underground this time, I need you to stay underground, all right? I've been at the center of this whirlwind with you, and I'd like a breather from the chaos too. So, no aspiring actresses during the break. No models. And no more Rock Fuck Club chicks."

"You expect me to be celibate?" I raised my brows.

"As a priest."

"After the stunts we pulled in Catholic school, I don't think they'd allow either of us to become men of the cloth."

"Real wine swapped out for grape juice." His flattened lips twitched.

"Frogs and garden snakes in the sisters' lockers." I grinned. "They were prophylactic measures. Our stunts served a purpose."

"Kept those rulers off our knuckles after that, didn't they?"

I nodded, missing those days when we'd not only had each other's backs, but also confided everything to each other. Simpler days. Simpler lives.

Brad's expression turned serious again. "So, you headed to your condo in Santa Monica?"

"Yeah, after I drive around a bit. Clear my head."

"You mean go to a bar, pick up a chick, and get laid again."

"Probably."

"Your standards are appallingly low." He shook his head. "I'm going back home. I'll be reachable on my personal number if you need me."

"Bree giving you another chance?" I asked. He'd been practically domesticated by her.

Shit, I'd given up on that gig after my one and only failed attempt. Why settle for one woman when I could have however many I wanted each night?

"I hope she does." Brad's brow creased, and suddenly, he seemed less like the confident business manager and more like my geeky grade-school friend. He knew my issues as well as I knew his. The past year had been tough on both of us. But this girl mattered to him.

Giving me a serious look, he said, "Make this break count, Rush. I plan to. Get your head together. We've got from now through New Year's off, then we're back out on the road."

Stuck at a stoplight an hour later, I impatiently drummed my fingers on the steering wheel. The street sign seemed to mock me, probably because I'd seen it before. At least three times.

How the fuck did I end up circling back to the same corner on Wilshire?

I glared at my navigation display. Unreliable piece of shit. This wasn't anywhere near the hotel where my next hookup was waiting.

I zoomed in on the map. Maybe I could take Hollywood Boulevard around and then just cut back in at . . . *Fuck.* That route for whatever reason was all red. A parking-lot standstill. And I didn't know this part of town well enough to come up with an alternative.

My phone rang. The display switched off the map to reveal it was my mother calling.

My heart stuttered. Our communication was irregular, especially sparse since the funeral. Her phoning at this time of night led me to immediately anticipate a crisis.

"Hey, Mom," I said. "Is everything okay?"

"No, not really."

"Are you sick?" My voice lowered to a strained rasp. An out-of-the-blue phone call similar to this one had broken the bad news about my father. A massive heart attack. Gone within a matter of hours, before I could even say good-bye.

Had I come to terms with it? Had she?

Hardly.

"No, Rush." Mom's voice sounded a little strange, as if I'd caught her off guard. "I just had my yearly routine checkup."

"Okay. Good." Shaky, I steered the Porsche to a nearby curb. Since I was using the Bluetooth connection, I hadn't taken my hands off the wheel, but it was too distracting to drive while talking to her. "So, what's up?"

A quick glance out the windows confirmed I wasn't in the best part of town. Porn shop. A couple of skeezy-looking bars. A by-the-hour motel. I clicked the locks.

"I'm lonely. Sad. I rarely hear from you anymore. You're my boy, and I miss you."

Her voice hitched, and my stomach bottomed out as if it had been dropped from a height.

"Mom, I'm sorry. It's just been crazy busy . . ." I pulled in a breath, not knowing what the fuck to say. Even before the rift between us, I hadn't been any good at the emotional stuff. It wasn't the way I'd been raised.

Life had been rough growing up in the heartland. Dad had been a farmer and rancher, the family livelihood largely dependent on the Indiana weather. Our lives revolved around pragmatism and planning.

There wasn't any thought of getting in touch with our feelings, no understanding for a son who preferred to express his creativity through music. And certainly no neutral ground for reconciliation after I left them and chased after my unlikely dreams.

And now the man who had modeled the values of strength and silent stoicism was gone. Far beyond my reach. The chance for us to explore those feelings was taken with him.

"It's my first Christmas without your father," she said, and the reminder stole my breath. "The house is too quiet. Like a tomb with your brother and Brenda away on their honeymoon."

Randy had never moved away from home. The ever-dutiful son, he'd taken over the management of the farm after Dad died. But with my brother out of town, it wasn't surprising that Mom had reached out to me in a low moment.

I didn't much like the idea of her being all alone in the big empty farmhouse, miles away from the nearest neighbor.

Worry and guilt wrapped a tight band around my chest. I hadn't been out to visit her in months, not since the funeral.

"I was going through my old photo albums after the Johnsons stopped by to check on me," she said. "Do you remember the year Thunder climbed up the Christmas tree?"

"Yeah, Mom," I said, fighting back a smile. I'd forgotten about that cat. "He was just a kitten. He was so small, he looked like one of the ornaments."

"Yes, that was before he got fat and mean."

"He slept in my room at night. But he used to bring you mice whenever he caught 'em. He left them on the front doorstep so you couldn't miss them. I think he wanted your approval."

The cat. Me. I got the ironic parallel, but did she? Would she ever see value in the choices I made?

"Yes, I think you're right. He also used to lie in wait to pounce on anyone who walked by. Those claws of his were sharp." She sighed, her breath heavy with remembrance. "You were so attached to him. You got attached to all the animals, wanted to name them all. It's hard to send them to the slaughterhouse when you think of them as pets. I guess your father and I should've seen the writing on the wall."

Was she trying to say she understood why I left? Why I went my own way? Maybe even that she was sorry? Or was I just wishfully reading between the lines?

"Why are you really calling, Mom?" I said, putting it out there. "I haven't heard from you in months. I don't understand. You're going to have to tell me straight out what you need from me."

She sighed, and the line fell silent for a moment. "Just that I don't want there to be long stretches without us talking to each other anymore. That's all."

Jewel

"You look hot." My roommate clattered toward me at a precarious pace in her skyscraper heels.

"Thanks, Cam." I stamped a hand to my hip and posed for her as the bus door closed behind me, and she stopped and twirled to show me her backless dress. Her long black hair swished the exposed skin above her ass. "You're not so bad yourself."

"Digging the cartoon-character-slash-schoolgirl vibe." Her dark red lipstick framed an approving smile.

"Thought it might sell well with the older guys on this side of town."

"Sick bastards acting out their underage-girl fantasies. You're probably right." She unwrapped a piece of gum, split it, popped half in her mouth, and offered me the other.

"Appreciate it," I said as I took it.

"You're late." She narrowed her olive-green eyes at me. "You stop to take a client on the way over?"

"Nah." I shook my head. "Just another run-in with Wanda."

"Bitch."

"Yeah." I agreed readily, my empty stomach twisting. "You made your half of the rent yet?"

"Nope." She shook her head. Glossy ebony hair spilled over her delicate shoulders.

"But I thought you had most of it saved already."

"*Had* most of it." She slowly blinked her pretty eyes at me.

"What do you mean, had?" My stomach didn't just twist, it knotted.

"I gave it to Lori."

"Oh no." I squeezed my eyes closed for a second, but there was no shutting out the shitty reality.

"I had to." My roomie donned a pleading expression. "She was sick. She had the shakes and was puking her guts out."

"She's a heroin addict, Cam, and needs to go to rehab. She'll just use that money for another fix."

Bright pink neon lights advertising a triple-X show blasted my gaze. A reminder, not that I needed one, that the harsh world we lived in couldn't be remedied with kindness.

"You don't have your part either?" she asked.

I shook my head.

"We're fucked." Frowning, she touched my arm. "I'm sorry, Jewel."

"It's okay." Kindness might not change much, but I couldn't blame Cam for it.

I covered her fingers with mine. Even through the worn cotton of my jacket, I could tell her skin was freezing cold.

"Two softies is what we are." I gave her a warm smile. "I probably would've done the same thing. What are the odds we'd end up rooming together, huh?"

"You regret moving in with me?" Her crimson lips trembled uncertainly.

"No. And anyway, it was your apartment to begin with. Lucky for me, you took me in. I had no job. Barely any money after my boyfriend screwed me over. You took a chance on me. Rescued me." I squeezed her hand and frowned. "You're freezing."

I removed her fingers, unzipped my jacket, and shrugged out of it. Goose bumps erupted on my exposed flesh, and there was a lot of it, more than Cam revealed in her slinky slip. A guy in a passing car let out a piercing whistle and gave me a leering look, and then he was gone.

"Put this on," I said.

"I'm okay. It's seventy degrees outside. I'm hardly freezing."

"It's damp. There's a chill in the air. Take it." I shook the jacket at her. "I was just going to tie it around my waist, but it messes with my look."

"All right." She frowned at me, but put it on.

"You make *any* money tonight?"

I held my breath for her answer as we moved into our usual position by the streetlight closest to the curb. Best to flaunt our attributes in the light while we could. The longer we kept on making our living like this, the sooner we would wind up falling back into the shadows to hide the toll it took on us.

"Fifty bucks."

"That's something. Good for you."

"One blow job." Her brow creased. "That's hardly rent."

"It's a start." I bit down on my plump, often-abused bottom lip. "Maybe we can convince Wanda to let us pay what we owe in installments."

"Maybe," she said, but we both knew there was zero chance. No excuses. No exceptions. Wanda was a total hard-ass.

"Hey." Cam lifted her chin to point at a sleek sports car idling at the curb. "Would you look at that."

"What?" I swiveled to glance in the same direction.

"It's a Porsche 911 GT2 RS."

"I know what kind of car it is."

She raised a disbelieving brow.

"Okay. No, I didn't. You're the car expert, Camaro Montepulciano."

"Not an expert. Not like my dad."

"Yeah," I said softly. "But you have nearly every make, model, and spec memorized like he does."

A love for all things automotive was his one and only legacy to her. After she'd lost her job as a cashier in the auto parts store and her father discovered what she'd taken up as a second career, he completely shut her out. Yet she religiously read *Car and Driver* magazine every morning as though it were a devotional, just on the off chance that he might one day change his mind and welcome her back.

"Special silver-metallic finish," she said almost reverently as she drank in the sight of the expensive car. "Rear-wheel drive. Six cylinders. Three-point-eight-liter twin-turbo engine. Seven hundred horsepower. That baby can do zero to sixty in two point seven seconds."

"Sounds super sexy." I snorted, not as impressed by cars. "So, go get him."

"Nah." She shook her head. "You look way hotter than I do."

"Not true, but all right. I'll go over and take a shot, if you're sure. Though I better move fast, since I've probably only got two-point-something seconds to snag him if he stomps on the gas." I straightened my shoulders.

She shook her head at me as I took my first step. "Work your approach faster, roomie. He just put his blinker on. He's gonna get away. And that's $293,000 worth of sports car, before options."

In other words, if I played it right, I might make rent.

I picked up the pace, jogging inelegantly to the vehicle, and bent over to tap on the passenger window.

When the driver slowly turned his head, my heart that was hammering from my dash to the curb slammed to a complete halt as his gaze hit mine. I'd never seen eyes like his before, so gray, the shiny platinum finish of his Porsche seemed tawdry in comparison.

A long moment passed as I took in his features. Tousled brown hair a little long in the front, strong jaw, chiseled lips, straight nose. He looked me over in return.

"Hey, handsome," I said when he lowered the window.

I feigned confidence, though anyone who really knew me would have noticed that my voice was pitched a higher octave than usual. The potential for rejection with the initial approach always made me nervous. This one more than most. He was way too cute to be trolling the streets for a paid fuck.

"Want a date for the night?"

"You even legal, little girl?" he asked, his sable brows arching higher above his heart-stopping eyes.

Okay, maybe I had taken the schoolgirl thing a bit too far.

"Twenty-one last March."

Most guys didn't care about legalities. Was he a cop? I dismissed the idea immediately. Not likely. Not in a $300,000 car. Just cautious, probably. Another factor that made me wonder why he was cruising for sex.

I batted my eyelashes at him. "You wanna see my driver's license, honey?"

The guy gave me a bored look. "No, not really. Just wanted to acknowledge your tap on my window." Lifting a hand, he made a shooing motion. "You can step away from the car now. I'm not interested. Just pulled over to have a conversation on my phone. I mean, do I look like I need to pay a fucking prostitute to have sex with me?"

His rejection stung, making my temper flare.

I glared at him, spitting out my response without thinking.

"With manners like that, you couldn't possibly pay me enough to put up with you."

"Get your filthy little hands off my car, Harley Quinn." His gray eyes flashed fiery silver.

I planted my fists on my hips. "I'm not going anywhere."

Those eyes of his were second-place silver to my defiant gold. I wasn't an exotic half-Italian beauty like Cam, but his dismissal triggered my attitude. Attitude I couldn't afford, but I let it rip anyway.

"Get your statusy piece-of-shit car off *my* corner. I was here first." Holding my head high, I flicked a pigtail over my shoulder. My bracelets jingled my irritation as I strolled away.

Take that, rich guy.

He didn't immediately leave, and I didn't turn to see what he was doing, even though I could feel his gaze on me. Swaying my hips provocatively, I moved to the car that had pulled in front of his Porsche.

Locks suddenly popped behind me. "Hey, Harley! Wait up."

I spun around and froze.

He stood next to his vehicle, the streetlight bathing his sculpted form. The breadth of his wide shoulders split open the lapels of his black leather jacket. He wore no shirt beneath it to hide the view of his chiseled pecs and abs. His smooth, golden-tanned skin glistened in the light as he casually propped his elbow on the roof of his car. Narrow hips and long legs in low-slung jeans completed the compelling portrait.

A shiver that had nothing to do with the chill in the air rolled through me as I withstood a heavily hooded leisurely scan from him.

His verdict? I couldn't tell.

Mine? He was great—if you went for an incredibly handsome guy with arrogance stamped into every single cell of his flawless body.

"What do you want?" Not giving an inch, I narrowed my gaze, shooting haughty daggers at him.

"How much?"

My mouth went dry. There was no mistaking what he wanted.

Me. For a price.

My mind blanking, I licked my lips to moisten them. Sex with him? I shook my head, but the thought of it only increased the heat that had combusted within me.

Pulling in a deep breath, I forced myself to take a mental step back. Methodically, I sized him up like Cam had taught me to do, and discounted his looks and his body. It was the car and the value of his clothing that mattered.

"Two hundred," I said. "Cash."

"You're joking."

"I never joke about money."

At an impasse, we stared at each other. One heartbeat became one too many.

"You're wasting my time," I said, deciding for him, and moved toward the other car.

"All right, Harley."

I stopped and turned to give him a big smile, and he went completely still. When his smoldering gaze dropped to my mouth, my lips tingled from its intensity.

He whistled under his breath. "You should've led with the smile. I would've agreed to twice that."

5

Rush

My gaze was drawn to her pretty mouth as it gaped at my admission. It was wide, glossed in red, with a Cupid's bow at the top and a plush bottom lip. *Perfect.* I imagined tracing the lines of her mouth with my tongue, then I would lick the gloss off. Make a feast of her.

Her mouth was made for making love to as much as it was for expressing her mood. That amazing smile took her from beautiful to blinding. As surely if she'd flipped an internal switch, she went from intriguing to irresistible. That smile alone changed her from a possibility to a certainty in my mind.

My previous rendezvous was easy to dismiss. I had no interest in her at all anymore.

No, I wanted *this girl.*

I'd take those ruby-red lips wrapped around my shaft to start. Then I would peel away her clothes and explore every inch of her sexy body.

Taste it.

Feel it.

Take her, again and again.

In my mind, I traded the fire of our opposing wills for the heat of our mutual passion. I'd been imagining how hot it would be to fuck her from the moment she shot me down and turned her back on me.

As I hurried to open the passenger door, my already eager cock jumped when my arm brushed against hers, and my grip tightened on the metal handle. My pulse raced as fast as my imagination, and my nostrils flared as I watched her slip into the seat.

"Thank you," she murmured softly, glancing up at me through sooty lashes.

Her voice was low and throaty. I wanted to hear it and feel it when I had my cock buried deep inside her.

I noted that she seemed surprised when I opened the door for her. Yeah, well, I guess most of her clients just popped the locks and ordered her to get in.

Why the hell I was treating her like a date instead of a hooker, I didn't really know. Maybe it was my Midwest upbringing. Maybe it was my guilt for the flinch she hadn't been quick enough to hide after I insulted her earlier. Maybe it was her million-dollar smile.

Whatever. I didn't plan to fully analyze it. *Hell fucking no.*

"You're welcome," I said politely while taking a self-serving moment to fully enjoy the view. She was a looker, for sure. Long shapely legs, round ass, full breasts. She had an hourglass shape any guy would lust over, though she seemed a little undernourished.

Pressing her legs together and crossing them at the ankles, she settled in. Her demure behavior only added to my confusion as I shut the door.

Time to move things along. To get out of this neighborhood. To get *us* out of this neighborhood. It wasn't safe. Plus, I needed to get her alone to have my way with her. Anything I wanted with her, I could have. I was a paying customer, after all.

Her gaze followed me as I quickly rounded the hood. What was she thinking? She seemed genuinely into me. I wasn't totally clueless with chicks. I recognized the signs. Darkened eyes. Parted lips. But then again, maybe she was just really good at her job.

I yanked open my door with more force than necessary.

"Smiles cost extra," she said, her tone sassy as she flipped her platinum pigtails over the black leather headrest.

I lowered myself into the seat and glanced at her, noting the remnants of one playing on her lips. The stinging retort I had ready to deliver evaporated from my tongue.

She was damn cute. The supple red suede of her seat seemed to conform to her. More confusing than her behavior was the proprietary rush I felt looking at her beside me in my car.

I reached for my seat belt and snapped it into place.

"What? No comeback?" She let out a low, sultry laugh that affected me as strongly as if she'd wrapped her slender fingers around my cock.

"I'll keep that in mind," I said, then mentally cursed myself for sounding like a dumbass.

"You do that." Her small smile widened into a full-blown one that lit up her eyes.

Suddenly, she became the only thing I saw. Gone was the interior of the car. The rounded aviation-style dials. The polished chrome. The gold-and-red crest on the center of the steering wheel. Everything receded but her.

I ripped my gaze away from her. "You have a usual place?" My voice was overly loud, my grip tightening on the wheel.

She was staring at me again; I could sense it. What could possibly inspire such unnerving scrutiny? I desperately wanted to know.

"What?" she asked, and I couldn't resist.

I turned my head to take her in.

Her golden eyes widened, and she blinked at me in return. At a distance, they were striking, but up close, her eyes were fucking phenomenal.

Suddenly, I couldn't think straight. My cock twitched, so tight and uncomfortable that I had to make a conscious effort not to adjust myself.

I pulled in a deep breath. A necessary one, but a mistake that flooded my senses with her fresh peachy scent, a light fragrance that took me home, reminding me of the peach pies my mom used to bake.

Fuck me.

I cleared my throat, and when I spoke, my voice was gruff. "Where do you want me to do you, babe?"

"Oh. Yes. Um." She wet her lips, seeming caught off guard by my abruptness. "Don't you mean *me* doing *you*?"

"Yeah, darlin'." Oh, hell fucking yes. Now we had things refocused. "For sure."

Her gaze dipped to my lap as if to gauge the magnitude of that task. My already steely-hard cock hardened even more. Her gaze pinned to my lap, she made a low appreciative sound. My spine tingled as if she'd actually traced my sizable length.

"Where?" I asked, trying to focus and remind her of the issue of logistics. "This ain't happening here."

"There's a park nearby," she said.

"I'm not having you blow me in a public place. You want us both to get arrested?"

"No." She shook her head. Her expression clearing, she no longer appeared dazed. "But if you want to go to a motel, that's a different price structure. I have to consider travel time. Hookups like that tend to go over an hour. Plus, they . . ." She trailed off, seeming nervous.

For the first time since she'd gotten into the car, she glanced away from me. Her brow creasing, she stared out the windshield. Her focus seemed to be on the car in front of us, where a hooker with long black hair was bent over with her face near the open window, propositioning the driver.

I glanced at my passenger. Was the other hooker someone she knew? Or maybe the other driver was a potential customer she thought might pay better? Or had her attention wandered because of something else?

She licked her lips. Swallowed.

Was she scared to be alone with me? Given the direction of my thoughts, she probably should have been.

I cleared my throat. "I'm not doing a by-the-hour shithole place either." Motels like that were often a roach-infested health-code violation. I hadn't stayed in one since my first tour.

"Okay." She turned to face me, tilting her head as if she didn't fully get me.

I found it cute. She was more than cute, but I ignored that and all the other conflicting feelings I had regarding her. I needed to take charge and get the situation back on track to get what I wanted.

"The Chamberlain's close." I typed the hotel's name into my GPS.

Avoiding my eyes, she said, "I can't go in there."

"Why the fuck not?" My lips flattened.

"I just can't."

She frowned as if I'd insulted her again and crossed her arms over her chest. The movement lifted her tits. I bit back a groan as I imagined her holding them for me so I could suck on them.

"Well, we gotta go somewhere, darlin'." As a concession to the possibility that she might be frightened, I left off the *and fast*.

"*I* don't have to do anything," she said, her tone defensive. "Sorry to waste your time." She reached for her door handle.

Oh. Hell. No. I clicked the locks.

"What are you doing?" She glanced back at me, her eyes wide.

"You stay."

"Open the damn door." Her voice rose as if she were panicked. "That's my friend at the car right in front of us."

Ah. Realization dawned.

"I'll scream." She rooted around in the bag in her lap and pulled out a small cell phone. A cheap burner, for sure, but it would still work. A shadow passed through her eyes as she added, "I don't like being trapped."

Had she been trapped before? Had someone hurt her? That thought made me see red, and I reconsidered the way I'd handled the situation.

"It's okay, Harley." I clicked open the locks and raised my hands in a conciliatory gesture. "You can go if you want to."

Disappointment rose as she swiveled to the door and grasped the handle.

"But I'd like you to stay." I let out a breath. "Please stay."

When she froze, I realized it was the politeness that she'd responded to. I filed that away as something to remember.

She turned to glance back at me, her brows raised. Surprised, maybe? Apparently, she'd noted that I was a little arrogant.

"You're right. I don't use that word often. I rarely have to anymore," I muttered, and she tilted her head at me again. "Listen, I've had a particularly shitty day. One of the worst I can remember in a long while. I'm dead tired, but wired too. You ever feel like that?"

Slowly, she nodded.

"Then you know how it sucks. But I know one guaranteed way to feel better. You offered to have sex with me, and I'm willing to pay. If we can agree on a new price and a place, can we proceed?"

"I guess," she said hesitantly.

"So, will four hundred cover the extra commute time?"

Her nostrils flared as she stared at me. Seconds ticked by before she said, "Eight hundred."

My eyes widened. "That's a lot of money, Harley."

The chick had balls to ask for that amount, but I already knew I was willing to pay it.

"Done." I wasn't wasting fucking time on haggling. "So, we're agreed on price. Now on to location. Is it the Chamberlain in particular you object to?"

"No. Not really." Her gaze straight ahead, she narrowed her eyes as she watched her friend climb into the car in front of us.

"Hmm. Well, the rooms are nice, and I'm familiar with the staff. If I call them, they'll do everything they can to make sure my stay . . . our stay . . . is comfortable." I grabbed my phone from the center console. "Is there any special request you might have? Something I can have them do that might change your mind about going there?"

I hit her with my most sincere expression, and she stared back at me as if I were an enigma to her. Well, that went both ways. I couldn't for the life of me figure her out either . . . a girl who looked like a hooker but acted like an ingenue and smelled like a juicy peach.

"Could you ask them for a room near the entrance?" she asked softly.

"I could do that. Sure."

"Maybe one on the first floor?" She bit down on her lip as if uncertain of my reaction. "With a patio, if they have that?"

"All right."

The silver ring on my middle finger glinted in the light. A gothic cross, an homage to my upbringing. I spun the cross around to my palm so I didn't have to see it. I'd remove it before we got started.

It wasn't that the things I planned to do with her were anything I hadn't done before. Just that the way I felt right now—afraid to get busted, afraid she might throw on the brakes—it reminded me of my awkward teens and fooling around in the back seat of a car with a girl I really liked.

My hair fell into my eyes as I completed my task and returned my phone to the console. The call connected and rang over the car's speakers before someone answered.

"Chamberlain Hotel, West Hollywood," a woman said in a chirpy voice. "Manager Mindy Johnson speaking. Can I help you?"

"Yes, Mindy. This is Rush McMahon." I paused to glance at my companion. Did she recognize my name? She was studying me as closely as I was studying her. But there was no recognition in her gaze.

"Mr. McMahon. Yes, we haven't seen you since your last launch party. How are you?"

"I'm fine. A little tired from traveling. I've got someone with me, and we could use a room."

"Absolutely. The usual amenities?"

"Yes. Only I have a few additional requests. Is there a first-floor suite available? One near the front entrance? With a patio?"

"Let me check." A keyboard clacked in the background. "Yes. Only it's just a regular suite."

"Does it have a separate shower? A garden tub? A seating area? A fully stocked bar?" Basically, easy alcohol access and plenty of places to fuck her.

"Yes, all of that."

"Then that'll be fine. We should arrive shortly."

"We'll be ready for you."

"Your name is Rush?" the girl asked after I ended the call.

I nodded.

"Should I know you?" Her gaze narrowed.

"Most would." I assessed her. "However, you don't seem to."

"No, I'm sorry. We don't have a TV, and I'm not big on movies and all that stuff."

"Why not?"

"I'm not from around here."

"Obviously." I'd noticed an unfamiliar accent in some of her phrasing. "Most everyone in LA is obsessed with the whole entertainment industry. Are you against that kind of thing?" I asked. "Even music?"

"Not really against. Just not interested, I guess."

My lips curved. No built-in expectations or biases. I liked that she didn't know me.

"Gran wasn't keen on those things," she said.

"Gran?"

"My grandmother."

The girl's expression changed, closed off. There was something more, but she wasn't going to share it with me.

"So, the one hour? At the hotel?" Her lips moved for a few seconds as if she were doing some internal calculations, then she said, "I only take cash. You have it on you?"

"No."

"Cash up front. No exceptions."

"Pretty steep up front." I slid my gaze over her. "How do I know you're gonna be worth it?"

"I'm worth it." She blazed a confident smile at me.

"I'll be the judge of that. Soon."

Anticipation coursed through me. For the first time in a long time, I found myself not only engaged, but looking forward to something.

"You, sir, are getting a bargain since I'm not charging you for the first couple of smiles. From now on, the tack-on fee for those is a hundred each."

Her grin widened, and my brain short-circuited on the brilliance of it.

"I'm sure you know," she said softly, "that nothing worth having is ever free."

6

Jewel

From the corner of my eye, I watched him whip the car out of a slow lane into a faster one. Focused. Quick reflexes. Steady grip. He handled the Porsche capably.

Cam believed you could learn a lot about a guy by how he drove his car. If that theory held, there was a lot for a girl to like.

"So, your name is Rush."

"That's right." His eyes nearly obscured by layers of hair—expertly and expensively cut, I could tell—he gave me a quick glance before he returned his attention to the road.

I added *careful* to his attribute list. High on the list. In my profession, guys didn't always handle me with care.

"Is that a nickname for some reason?" I asked.

"Um, no. Not exactly. Brother Randy. Father Ronald. My mom has a thing for names that begin with *R*, I guess. Plus, I was born early."

He shrugged, then frowned as the car in front of us suddenly stopped. Throwing his arm in front of me, he applied the brakes. Hard.

Momentum slung me forward, then threw me back as my seat belt engaged.

"You hurt?"

When he glanced at me again, I was struck by several things at once. What a unique shade of gray his eyes were, and how they changed with his emotions—they were darkened in concern at the moment—and how his instinct had been to shield me from harm. I added *protective* to the list.

"Sorry." He withdrew his arm, and his hand brushed my breasts.

My cheeks warmed. I watched his grip tighten on the wheel, straining the leather. Was his apology for the contact or the braking?

"Hope the belt didn't give you whiplash," he said.

"I'm fine. Would've been worse if you hit him. Good thing you have quick reflexes."

"I do. Plus, I'm not one to miss an opportunity when it's presented to me." His eyes twinkled like the sun breaking through the clouds as he gave me the side-eye.

"So, not accidental contact, huh?" I raised a brow in his direction.

"Hell no." He grinned, completely unapologetic.

My breath caught. Being on the receiving end of his teasing made me feel warm and tingly. "So, that's how it's gonna be with you?"

"Me taking advantage every chance I get?" His grin widened. "That would be a *hell fucking yes*."

So he was one of those, a handsome troublemaker with a sense of humor. I liked guys like that. After following one to LA and learning well the hard lesson Landon had taught me, I was Teflon-coated now.

But deep down, I wasn't so sure my resistance could withstand this particular one.

7

Rush

She was prettier up close. A lot of eye makeup, sure. But I wore some myself onstage.

I knew what it was. Part of her act, like the clothes and the platinum pigtails. The icy blond didn't match the fire of her personality or her russet brows. The hair might be a dye job, or it might be a wig.

A lot of mystery surrounded Harley Quinn. But I liked mysteries. Kept a guy guessing.

"So, do you usually rap on the window of any random car that pulls up?"

"Why do you ask?"

"I could be a cop. Or a psycho." My lips flattened. "Don't you have any criteria to rule those type of guys out?"

"You asking for trade secrets?"

"Just wondering."

How many times it had been a cop, and she had spent the night in jail? How often had she ended up with a psycho? Was one of those the reason why the hotel setup scared her?

"Wondering why I picked you?" she asked.

"Sure." I'd take that. Seemed the other line of questioning wouldn't be allowed.

"The car." She made a face, and I laughed.

"Figured. Chicks say it's never the car, but it always is."

"Is that why you bought the Porsche? It is your car, right?"

"It's mine."

The Porsche was a reward to myself after years of barely breaking even until the multiplatinum album, which was a huge accomplishment professionally. But beyond my bandmates and occasionally my manager, there had been no occasion for anyone else to ride in my reward with me.

"You like it?"

"It's nice and shiny."

"That doesn't sound very enthusiastic."

"I tried to get my friend to go for you. She's into cars. She knew the make, model, the retail price tag, and the acceleration stats. *She* was very impressed."

Curious, I glanced her way again. "So, why'd you come over and not her?"

"She said I looked hotter than her tonight." She nibbled on her plump bottom lip. "But I think it's really that she feels . . ."

When she hesitated, I lifted my chin, wanting her to go on. "What?"

I was intrigued. Not only did I want to undress her, I also wanted to know what was in her head. Not a usual thing for me. But then, nothing about this night seemed usual.

Least of all her.

8

Jewel

"The brakes are super sensitive," Rush said to the hotel valet while I stood beside his shiny car and waited. "Be sure to park it so the doors don't get dented."

"I'll park it in VIP and put traffic cones around it. Same as always, Mr. McMahon."

"See that you do." Rush gave him a somber nod.

His wide shoulders back, his spine straight, he carried himself confidently, as if accustomed to having his orders obeyed. Even the breeze seemed to hesitate to lift more than a few strands of hair from his stern brow without permission.

Was his confidence an inherent personality trait, or was it a learned behavior due to his celebrity status?

Whichever it was, I counted myself fortunate that I'd been able to put him off when he pressed me earlier. There was no way I wanted to let him into my private thoughts and admit that I knew the real reason Cam had passed over a guy with a Porsche was because she felt sorry for me.

Studying Rush with narrowed eyes again, I racked my brain, trying to figure out if I'd seen him somewhere before. The area in front of the hotel was well lit, and my view of him was clear. He was handsome, for sure, but he didn't seem familiar to me.

I took another glance around as he continued to interact with the kid in the festive Santa hat.

Lush foliage surrounded the boutique hotel. A black-and-white striped awning at the center covered the entrance. Prickly shrubs framed the ground-level patios. Noting the sharp leaves, I gnawed my bottom lip. Those would hurt if I had to quickly shimmy through them.

Stop it, Jewel. If you need to get away, a couple of surface-level scratches will be the least of your worries.

I shifted my attention back to Rush and caught the valet's bright-eyed gaze skimming over me. His lips parted as his perusal lingered in the usual places. In my work gear, I was accustomed to male interest like his. On the street we'd left behind, guys barely old enough to drive slowed their vehicles to gawk at girls dressed like me.

"Eyes on me, Doyle," Rush said with a growl. "Focus on the task I've given you, not her."

Huh. I might be accustomed to the gawking, but my client wasn't. The valet's interest obviously irritated him.

"But isn't she cold?" Doyle's eyes widened. "She looks really naked . . . I mean, cold."

"Cold isn't a word I'd *employ* to describe her. But it's my *job*, not yours, to ensure that's she's plenty warm." Rush's sexy lips curved, a sardonic complement to the proprietary glint in his eyes.

I got the not-so-subtle hint. I was his. Bought and paid for during the hour he had me tonight. Not sure the kid got it, though. He continued to stare until Rush gestured at him impatiently.

"The car, Doyle," my scowling client reminded him. "Park it. Now."

"Oh yes. Right. Sorry." The valet's face turned tomato red. Dipping his head, he took the keys from Rush's outstretched palm and scurried to the driver's side of the Porsche.

"You ready?" Rush asked when he reached me.

"Sure." I pretended I hadn't noticed how fine he looked in his jeans. The faded denim clung to him in all the right places.

"Good. I'm certainly ready." He wrapped his hand around my upper arm.

His grip was as proprietary as his gaze, making my skin tingle. Not because his fingers were overly tight, but because of the jolt of adrenaline that zinged through me the instant his flesh connected with mine.

He felt it too. I knew he did. It was the reason we were here together, after all. Nothing personal, which would be wise for me to remember. Just hormones and chemistry at an agreed-upon price.

"You sure you're all right, Harley?" One brow rose as he watched me gulp in oxygen to fuel my escalating heart rate. "You sound out of breath."

"I'm fine," I mumbled, willing my pulse to slow.

"If you say so."

As he steered me up the walk, I hoped he attributed my breathlessness to my trepidation about the hotel. Entering the Chamberlain dressed the way I was would be embarrassing, not to mention humiliating if they kicked me out.

Was he interested enough to take me somewhere else? Or would he abandon me? If the latter occurred, which was more likely, I'd figure out a way back to the other side of town on my own. I was tough and resourceful. But I would lose the money I needed to make rent.

Distracted, I murmured a thank-you as he stepped aside and held open one of the etched glass doors for me. He was surprisingly solicitous, surprising in a number of ways, not the least of which was my response to him. So we had some chemistry. I just needed to remember that in addition to the things I found attractive, he was also arrogant and rude.

Inside the lobby, I paused and my mouth gaped open like the valet's. With its crystal chandeliers, and seating groups in velvet with polished chrome knickknacks, the hotel was more elegantly appointed than I'd expected.

"Let's check in." Watching me closely, Rush grasped my upper arm again and resumed dragging me along. The ring of my stilettos and the determined thud of my escort's boots on the marble refocused me, reminding me where I was, who I was with, and that this was only business between us.

"All right." I pulled in a deep breath to clear my head, but it only fogged it up again on Rush's woodsy cologne. Seductive and disorienting, like a naked plunge into an icy mountain stream, it had scrambled my equilibrium in his car too. Only—joy of joys—it was worse now with his touch amplifying the effect.

"Mr. McMahon." The front desk clerk greeted him warmly, but only gave me a cool, disapproving side glance. "We have everything ready as requested."

"Good. The location of the room is important to my companion."

Don't read anything into him following through. He wants what he wants from you. You gave him your parameters. It's not consideration or kindness on his part.

Not really.

But it certainly seemed like it was.

"Yes. And there's this." Reaching behind the counter, the clerk placed a thick envelope in front of Rush. "Now, for your suite. Will it be just the two keys? And the one night?"

After running two keycards through the programming device, she slipped them into a small cardboard folder before placing it in front of him. Apparently, his response to her questions was familiar enough to be a foregone conclusion.

Like me.

"Thank you, Mindy." He folded and tucked the envelope I suspected contained my cash into a pocket inside his leather jacket.

"The Wi-Fi password is the usual. But I wrote it inside the jacket sleeve, just in case, along with your room number," Mindy said. "Your suite is just on the other side of the lobby."

I shifted my weight from one spiked heel to the other. My feet hurt. I was cold. And I stuck out like a West Hollywood drag queen would at a Sunday church service back home. There was absolutely no chance I blended in with the understated finery around me.

"Down the hall." Mindy pointed. "The second door on your left."

"Perfect." Rush took the small keycard envelope and turned to me. "Why are you standing so far away from me?" His brows drawing together, he quickly closed the distance between us.

"I don't . . . feel comfortable here," I said, tugging ineffectually on the revealing hem of my skirt.

His gaze dipped, and when it rose again, his eyes were dark in a lustful haze.

"Can we . . . um . . ." I paused to lick my dry lips. Being on the receiving end of his interest, I discovered that I was a little hazy myself. Sliding the strap of my bag higher up my shoulder, I began again. "Can we go to your room?"

"Anxious to get started, huh?"

I was anxious for something, all right, but before I could come up with a response, a well-dressed couple stepped up behind us.

"Oh my." The woman gasped, stopping abruptly when she saw me. She clutched her brown-and-gold handbag to her chest as if she feared I would snatch it from her.

The man predictably leered.

"What are you looking at?" My spine snapped straight. I went from embarrassed to defensive the instant she wrinkled her stuck-up nose at me. As if I would steal. As if I would want a purse with her initials stamped all over it. And I did *not* smell bad. I'd showered before going out tonight.

"Arthur . . ." The woman sniffed, seeming affronted that I'd addressed her. "You didn't mention there was a *costume* party at the hotel. *Unusual* at this time of year." She made the word *unusual* sound as if it meant *trashy*.

"I'm a Christmas elf," I said, making up the lie on the spot. As I linked my arm with Rush's, I couldn't help but notice how incredibly hard his bicep was beneath my fingers. "My man likes seasonal-themed sexual play, which usually means spankings for me. I've been very naughty. But if I take my punishment like a good little girl, he might move me to the nice list."

I glanced at the woman's companion through my lashes, and he smiled at me. She noticed and stiffened, frowning at him.

"The nice list comes with his cock and cookies. I—"

"Harley." Rush interrupted me, letting out a strangled sound as if he were choking. "Come along, naughty girl. That's enough. Excuse us," he said to the couple, and tugged on my arm.

"What?" I tottered on my heels as he pulled me away. "She was rude. I wasn't finished."

"You're finished." Rush chuckled as we entered the hall.

My brows rose. Had that choking been him holding back laughter? Surprised, I stared at him. His silver eyes sparkled brighter than the polished chrome in the lobby as he grinned at me, making my stomach flutter.

"You have *some* attitude, Harley Quinn."

"I don't like people judging me." I pouted for a second before another thought occurred to me. "You're not mad at me?"

"Why would I be mad?" He gave me a puzzled look.

My gran would have been. I had a reputation in her small town for popping off.

"*Don't react, precious Jewel,*" she'd say. "*Starve those who insult you.*" In other words, take the high road and ignore them.

"I thought you'd be angry because of the way I acted just now," I said, getting straight to the point. "And doesn't the way I look embarrass you?"

"You have better manners than that stuck-up bitch back there." He ran an approving gaze over me and stepped closer. "And you look great. Your outfit suits you."

Befuddled, I sucked in another dizzying lungful of his cologne.

His eyes actively searching mine, he reached up slowly, as if afraid I would bolt, and carefully ran the back of his fingers down my cheek. "You're badass and pretty."

"I . . . thank you." I swayed on the unfamiliar ground beneath my feet. Clients, even the few regulars I had, never treated me like this. His approving words flooded my parched psyche.

"Not done yet."

"No?" I couldn't fathom it or him. Quickly, too quickly, the water of the unknown rose over my head like a river cresting its banks.

"Huh-uh." He touched my nose. "You're cute. Beguiling. And let's not forget, totally fuckable."

He was teasing me. Again.

And I liked it. *A lot.*

Stunned, I watched him insert his keycard in the door before I managed to blink away my confusion.

"You first." Holding open the door, he gestured to the interior.

"Okay. Yes. Sure."

I got my feet moving and stumbled inside. Behind me, he fumbled for the light switch on the wall while I cautiously stepped farther into the darkened suite.

"There we go," he said as the room suddenly filled with light.

The welcome glow of lamps chased away the shadows, illuminating a large bed on a riser on the right, a hallway on the left that I assumed led to a bathroom, and a sunken sitting area directly ahead with a couple of carpeted steps leading down to it.

"Nice enough?" he asked.

"Yeah, sure. A/C works great." I rubbed the sudden chill bumps from my arms. "Everything looks brand new." The bed linens were ice blue, the couch and easy chairs a deep sapphire, and the decorative accents mostly reflective chrome, like the lobby. "It's a palace compared to my place."

He had to know this was way better than anywhere I had ever been. So why even ask?

"Cold?" Placing his hands on my upper arms, he turned me to face him.

"A little." Meaning I was burning hot where his skin touched mine, and cold everywhere else. And nervous, so nervous, as he stared at me with his mesmerizing silver eyes. I'd been with countless men. But none had ever confused me the way this one did.

"I thought so."

His brow furrowed, he removed his jacket and carefully arranged it around my shoulders. The soft lining retained his heat and his seductive scent. Watching me with a tender expression on his handsome face, he untucked my pigtails and arranged them outside the collar.

Longing stirred within me, an emotion that had no place in a hookup for cash.

"Um, thank you." I gave him a furtive look.

Did he know how off-kilter he made me with his flattering comments and consideration? Staring at him didn't provide an answer to my question, only supplied me with more temptation. My legs wobbled as I took in his torso, left bare now that he'd removed his jacket.

Focus, Jewel. Focus. Not on his chiseled physique, but on doing what you need to do to it.

I gulped and gestured around us at the suite. "Isn't the point of all of this to be with me somewhere private? Not so you can give me your clothes, but so I can take off mine."

I reached for his jacket, planning to remove it from my shoulders. I needed to get things back on familiar ground, but he stopped me.

"Keep it." He placed his much larger hands over mine. My black sparkly polish contrasted with his bare, blunt-tipped nails. He had long, slender, artistic-looking fingers, and wore a silver gothic cross on his middle finger.

"I insist." He squeezed my hands.

I lifted my gaze and met his molten eyes. Transfixed, I stared. Warmth flowed through him to me. I was suddenly afraid . . . not of him, not really, but for myself and the knowledge that I liked his care and concern and the way he looked at me.

Far too much.

Childish dreams and wishes. The hope that being myself could make a difference to the right man. I had set those unrealistic expectations aside after returning from my grandmother's funeral to find Landon in our bed with another woman.

Rush's gaze flitted over my face, and the groove in his brow deepened.

"You seem to be in a hurry. Why don't we take things a little slower and move to the living area." He removed his hands, making me lament the loss of his touch as he gestured to the living area. "Let's sit and talk for a minute. Get to know each other a little better before we proceed."

"Why?" A cold wave of unease washed away the warmth. No longer transfixed, I was suspicious. I anticipated the worst, since unfortunately I'd nearly experienced it before by being caught unaware.

I quickly shifted my weight to the balls of my feet. Ready to flee, I noted the nearest exit and its proximity to him.

"Why the hell not?" He frowned. "You gotta run back to your street corner for some reason you haven't shared?"

His tone no longer kind, he watched me with a hard expression and narrowed eyes. Apparently, I wasn't the only one with suspicions.

"Don't tell me you have some other loser lined up tonight to fork over eight hundred bucks to fuck you."

"No." I lifted my chin. "Just you."

The inside of my chest burned. He thought he was paying too much for me. It hurt to be told flat out what you believed deep down to be true.

"You're the only asshole I have . . . had . . . on my hook tonight."

My eyes stung as tears filled them. He'd ripped open a raw wound. After being betrayed by someone I trusted, then being forced into prostitution to survive, I feared the damage to my self-esteem would never heal properly.

Nearly vibrating with emotion, I spat out, "Does it make you feel like a big man to cut me down because I didn't immediately do what you wanted?"

Stupid, Jewel. I clenched my fingers into fists at my sides. *You just lost eight hundred bucks because you're too proud and couldn't control your tongue.*

"What I meant to say was—"

"Don't filter yourself on my account," he said, cutting me off with a sharp gesture. "Got enough people kissing my ass." His gaze iced over with permafrost as it slid over me. "I have a list of things I want to do with you tonight, but you kissing my rear ain't one of 'em."

"All right." I bobbed my head, taking the reprieve he offered.

"Don't look so nervous. It doesn't become you, kickass chick that you are, shooting me down nearly from the first moment I saw you." He shook his head, studying me. "Speak your mind if you want to. You did it before, yeah? It's one of the many things that intrigued me about you."

"Oh." My mouth rounded in surprise at the revelation I wasn't sure he'd intended to let slip. "Okay, I guess."

"You're right. I'm used to having my way. I acted like an asshole. It's a habit, a bad one I fall into. But with you . . ."

He paused and rubbed the back of his neck. His defined pec and corded bicep rippled from his movements, and his abs tightened. It was distracting.

"Listen." His gaze no longer cold, but not as warm as before, he eyed me carefully. "I'm sorry. I didn't mean what I said. I thought you were being dismissive, and I snapped at you. Okay?"

The sincerity in his expression undid me. He was handsome, we'd already established that, and I was attracted to him. But even more appealing than his looks was his uncertainty about me.

Was it possible that what I thought mattered to him? Could he actually be afraid I might refuse him?

"Apology accepted."

"Thank you." He nodded once and gestured again to the seating area. "Now, will you come and sit with me?"

"Sure." I agreed readily, following him while telling myself not to be fooled.

Men could seem one way and totally be another. I had been down that path before. I was in my current situation because I'd trusted too easily and thought too highly of myself when I should have been wary.

Swallowing the bitterness from that hard lesson, I removed his jacket. Carefully, I folded it in half and laid it on the easy chair before moving to join him on the midnight-blue couch. With self-preservation instead of a jacket to cape my shoulders, I sat and perched stiffly on the edge of the cushion next to him.

"This is much better," he said.

I wasn't so sure, but at least I had my professional demeanor back in place.

"I'm going to borrow this." He took my hand without waiting for permission and stroked my fingers with his thumb. The calloused pad was rough against my soft skin, but not unpleasant. Far from unpleasant.

"I'd prefer we talk without any contact for a moment." I withdrew my hand, wondering what repetitive motion an actor might do to develop calluses.

Stop it, Jewel. Focus.

I couldn't allow myself to be distracted by mysteries regarding him, any more than I could allow myself to be seduced by his kindness or caresses. It was good for us to have a discussion. Cam and I had work rules that were important to maintain detachment. Only, I was having a hard time remembering them tonight.

"I'm not trying to piss you off, Harley." He frowned. "I just wanted to clarify some things. And maybe put you more at ease with me. I think it'll be better for both of us if you're not afraid of me."

"I'm not afraid." My spine straightened with the denial.

"Okay, if you say so." His expression said he thought my denial was bullshit, and he was mostly right. "I'm not exactly sure what your procedure is. I've never . . . you know . . . picked up a hooker before."

"I don't believe you."

"Strip clubs. Lap dances. Shit like that. But no one like you. Ever." His hair slid forward over his eyes, shielding them.

I couldn't get a definite read on him, but there was an edge of seriousness to his tone that made his words seem like a compliment. "You want to know if there's a certain protocol to follow?"

He nodded. "Rules. Dos and don'ts. Something like that."

"Not really." I shook my head. "You give me cash. I do what you want. I leave."

Don't get all misty-eyed again, I warned myself. *This isn't him being considerate. This is business. Do what you need to do. Stay in control.*

"You had the cash." His eyes narrowed to assessing slivers. "It was inside my jacket."

"Oh, right." I stood and went to get it.

"Don't trust me, huh?" he said, and our gazes met as I riffled through his jacket. "Go ahead and count it then."

"I have to," I said once I had the envelope open.

"I get it."

"No, I don't think you really do," I said. "You drive a Porsche. You stay in fancy hotels. You call people, and in ten minutes, *ta-da*! Cash appears. A large sum of it."

I hastily counted the bills. They were all there, sixteen $50 bills. I quickly put them in my bag, set it aside, and rejoined him on the couch.

"Did you just say *ta-da*?" His tone had that funny ring to it again, and he smiled.

With him so close, I could feel the warmth of his amusement. "It seemed the best word to aptly describe the way you snap out commands, and everyone gets in a dither to do what you want."

His grin widened. "Never heard a chick talk like you."

How could my complaints about his arrogance amuse him?

"Where did you say you were from again?" he asked.

"I didn't."

"Give me a hint." His tone turned coaxing. "The state, at least."

"Tennessee."

"Never been there."

I scoffed. "You must not get out of LA much."

"Oh, I get around, all right."

"Yeah. I'm sure you do." The signs that he was a major player were obvious.

"You have your cash now." He didn't seem to like my confirmation of the obvious. "So, the formalities are out of the way." His gaze broadcasting his intent, he placed his palm on the center of my chest, directly on my bare skin. "Is it time for me to get what I want, Harley?"

His voice lowered, he held me captive with his eyes. My heart thudded beneath his touch.

Slowly, he spread his fingers. "Without restrictions?"

"Yes." I nodded, and the motion moved his hand. The infinitesimal glide made my flesh tingle. My nipples tightened beneath the silk of my bra.

"I appreciate your permission," he said softly, and I preened with pleasure beneath his heated regard. "I like very much that there's nothing I can imagine that you won't do."

My skin burned where he branded me with his fingers. He slowly lifted his gaze and our eyes met. Gold and silver clashed.

His were dark gray like thunderclouds, and my heart raced beneath his touch like lightning.

I felt claimed, though he had given me cash. Claimed, though economics and reason clamored for my attention.

This was dangerous. *He* was dangerous.

But right now, in this moment, I didn't care. There was something about Rush McMahon. The care, the concern, the teasing . . . the way he treated me evoked hope. Risky, perilous, deceitful hope.

Stepping into that compelling light, I followed his lead. I angled my head one way as he tilted his in the other. In concert, our faces aligned. His eyes fluttered closed but mine remained open, and I held my breath as I watched his sexy mouth come closer to mine. Anticipation hummed inside me as the warmth of his breath feathered over my lips.

And just like that, even though I knew better, I gave in. I wanted to merge our mouths, fuse our lips, and mingle the very essence of our breaths. I wanted the fantasy.

The melody to a long-lost dream filled my mind, and I allowed myself to be swept away. Desire and desirability filled me, as did hope and faith. More than anything, I wanted to believe I deserved to experience those things again.

I knew, even as I reached for them, that they weren't for me anymore.

But that didn't stop me from longing to dance.

9

Rush

Forget going slow.

I was fucking her.

Right here. Right now.

On this couch.

But I was tasting those painted lips of hers first. I had to. Not kissing her was *not* an option. I had to know how she tasted. Had to see if my tongue in her mouth would make her moan. If her body would melt. If her strong spirit would yield to mine.

Not because I'd paid her, and not because she knew who I was, but simply because I was a guy and she was a girl and there was the allure of the unknown to explore between us.

"Rush . . ." She sighed.

I opened my eyes to see her expression reflecting the same sense of anticipation as mine. *Excellent*. She wanted what I wanted. No other consideration to interfere. It was about damn fucking time.

I gently framed her pretty face, and she pressed deeper into my hands, my name on her lips. Her with me. Us on the same page. *Fuck me*. I liked it. I liked it a whole fucking lot.

"Babe." Searching her gaze, I swept my thumbs across the satiny-soft skin of her cheeks. "Tell me your name."

I had to know. It was a travesty that I didn't know already. When her lips were nearly mine. When I was staring so deeply into her eyes. When just beneath the surface of her gaze glistened a treasure I had to have, a woman who seemed to want just me.

"What did you say?" Her breath warmed my parted lips.

"Never mind." I groaned from only a hint of her taste—peaches, wholesome and sweet. Which was impossible, but somehow in perfect harmony with the golden reward that glittered within her eyes. "Tell me after I kiss you," I said, my mouth almost on hers.

"No." A shudder ran through her as she pulled back and turned her cheek, making my lips miss their intended target.

I blinked in confusion as her hands wedged between us, and when she planted them on the center of my chest, I nearly scoffed. They weren't a deterrent. Only her word served that purpose. My eyes blazed as I registered the firm press of her fingers into my skin.

"What the hell? Can't what?" Disappointment harshened my tone. My gaze narrowed and my cock throbbed. Grasping her chin, I turned her head so she had to look at me. "You said there were *no* restrictions."

"There are none," she whispered, only she wouldn't maintain eye contact. Her lids lowered, and the blush on her cheeks deepened as if she were embarrassed, but I wasn't buying it. "No restrictions for you. It's just that it has to be . . . it needs to be me doing all the work, and you reaping all the reward."

Her lids fluttering, she lowered her voice to a sultry purr. "I'll make it so good for you, I promise. I'll fulfill every fantasy. You blow your load in me, on me, however you want. Just tell me your preference, and I'll see that you get there."

My cock liked all of that. Liked the sweetness and softness of her along with the dirty talk. But the other part of me, the greedy part that had gotten a glimpse of the golden prize? He was a more discerning fucker.

"I wanted to kiss you," I said, snarling like a petulant child denied a sugary treat. "Isn't that on the menu?"

"Is kissing me what you want, Rush?" She brought her hands to her breasts, shaping them like I'd imagined her doing since she first appeared at my window. "*I'll* kiss *you* if that's what you want. Because this is about *you*. You *paid* me to pleasure you, freeing you from worrying about what anyone else wants. Whether they like what you're doing. Whether they get off or not. It's best when you can just sit back and enjoy."

I wasn't so sure about that. For a long time now, I'd gorged on a continuous cycle of selfish enjoyment that reaped dissatisfaction.

But she distracted me as she shifted. Straddling my thigh, she unbuttoned her cropped blouse and plucked her tits right out of her bra. They weren't the biggest pair I'd ever seen, but they were the most perfectly formed. My eyes glazed over as she lifted the rose-tipped beauties to me.

"Suck on them, baby," she said softly, her voice still a purr. "If you'd like to, or I can play with them for you. I can take care of that. I can take care of all the work. I can take care of everything." Abandoning her breasts, she leaned forward and placed her hands on my chest. "Let me help you release all that tension you mentioned earlier."

As I held my breath, she danced the tips of her fingers lower. Skimming her touch over the ridges of my abdomen, she ignited a fiery trail of sensation that ended when she reached the waistband of my jeans.

"What are you doing?" My voice rumbled from deep inside my chest where my heart was already sprinting for the finish. "Why are you stopping?"

"Getting permission." She peered at me through sooty lashes while sweeping her fingertips along my length. "May I touch you here?"

"Yes." I groaned as she palmed me through the denim, my eyes already half-closed, my cock jumping eagerly in her grip.

"Good," she said. "Because I like touching you."

I glanced up, watching her face as she focused on unbuckling and unthreading my belt. She wore a look of intense concentration, her tongue emerging to moisten her red lips, and her bracelets jingling as she slowly unbuttoned my fly. I felt pre-cum on my shaft. It wasn't going to take much effort on her behalf. I was primed to explode.

Her mouth parting, she dove her eager fingers into the waistband of my boxer briefs.

"Can you lift up, please?" she asked, her breaths short bursts of air between her words. "I need to get these down. I want to see all of you."

I lifted immediately. I wanted that too.

"Oh my." Her eyes widened. "You're so big. So hard."

As she stroked me, her fingers skimming my velvety length, she moaned, and it all seemed so real. She looked up at me, swiping her pink tongue over her perfect teeth.

"Do you . . . Do you want me to suck you off? Or finish you right now with my hand?" Her voice was as seductive as the hunger on her face as her eyes met mine. "Because you're wet, baby. And I can go either way you wanna go in a situation like this."

She rolled her hips, grinding on my leg. Even through the denim, I felt the heat of her arousal.

"Finish it." I groaned as she gripped me. "Now."

I put my hand over hers. The ring was still there, but I didn't stop—I couldn't stop to take it off. Instead, I helped her jack my cock as I stared at our joined hands, mine large and masculine, hers dainty. The glittery black polish on her nails sparkled like dark magic as she glided her hand up and down my shaft.

"So good," I told her. "You feel so good."

"Faster, please," she said, since I was controlling the pace, and I eagerly complied. "Oh yes, baby."

Her nipples tight, her tits bouncing, she rode my thigh with abandon, matching the pace of our combined strokes on my dick.

"Your cock is so beautiful. So hot. So big."

Without breaking our rhythm, I glanced up at her face again. Her cheeks were flushed, and her expression was stark with need. She meant it. She was turned on.

Her eyes met mine. Unguarded, the allure within her gaze remained, only now the gold was molten.

"You're fucking phenomenal."

Her beautiful eyes were her tell. I wanted them on me every single time I fucked her.

"Say my name," I demanded.

"Rush, I can't . . ."

Only she already had.

I moved our hands faster, loving the feel of her delicate fingers sliding along my slippery length. Loved it even more when she threw back her head and moaned her release. She looked like a fucking goddess when she came, coming from doing me.

Watching her, feeling her, I stiffened in our combined grip, and then I was coming too.

Fuck, I wanted her name, but even not knowing didn't stop me from erupting all over our joined hands.

Jewel

"Here." Rush grabbed a few tissues from the box on the end table and shoved them at me.

"Thanks," I said, taking them and plummeting from the heights of a climax to a crash landing in practical reality.

"Climb off me, darlin'," he said, his voice low.

"Yes, of course." I dismounted his thigh and righted my clothing, glaring at the tissues as if they were responsible for me breaking the rules.

How long had it been since I'd found enjoyment with a man? Since the early days with Landon. And I'd never come with such abandon.

My cheeks warmed as I dabbed at the evidence of Rush's desire. The tissues didn't improve the situation; they only made a stickier mess of things. What I needed was a sanitizing wipe. I had a package of them in my bag. It was part of being prepared, like noting the exits, having a cell phone, and maintaining a safe professional distance between me and my clients.

I peered at Rush through my lashes as he stood and refastened his jeans, realizing that I didn't want to be prepared or anything at all that went along with my professional persona. Not with him. Instead, I wanted to let go, to be the me I'd been before my life had taken a turn where I had to worry about practicality, escape routes, and maintaining control.

"I'm gonna get cleaned up." Rush's hair hung down, shading his metallic gaze, but it didn't reduce the intensity as he stared down at me. "You're coming with me."

Without waiting for a reply, he reached out and plucked me right off the couch. With my upper arms locked in his firm grip, my feet hit the carpet, and I rocked on the heels of my stilettos. My uneven momentum carried me forward into him, and my palms landed on his rock-hard chest.

Heat blazed beneath my fingertips as I stared up into his eyes and registered the smoothness of his tanned skin and the tensed strength beneath it. One time with him hadn't been nearly enough. I wanted to do it again, and longed to take my time exploring and acquainting myself with every smooth, sculpted contour of his body. But before I could even think about acting upon that desire, he grabbed my hand.

"Where are we going?" I asked as he tugged me along with him.

"To the shower," he said on the steps. "Like I told you."

"But . . ."

"You wanna know if I'm fucking you in the shower?"

"Yes, because my bag's by the couch," I said at the entrance to the hall. "It has the condoms."

"I have one in my pocket."

"Okay," I managed to say before he shuffled me inside the bathroom. Caging me in from behind at the counter, he kicked the door shut behind him.

"What are you doing?" In the mirror, my eyes widened as he bracketed me in from behind with his much larger body.

"Getting the sticky off," he said, his gaze on the sink. Not noticing my fear, he turned on the water and took both my hands, plunging them underneath the room-temperature flow.

Breathless, I stuttered, "B-b-but can you please open the door?"

My fingers clasped in his, I bucked like a skittish colt inside the pen of his unyielding arms. His reflected gaze lifted, meeting mine.

"Oh shit. Hey." He stroked my wet skin with his thumbs. "Shhh, baby. Settle down. I'm not gonna hurt you. Didn't I stop earlier when you asked?"

"Yes." I cobbled together a placating smile. "Only . . ." I licked my lips. A memory of myself being backed into a corner by three large men blanked the reasonable part of my mind.

"What's wrong? Did someone force themselves on you?" His brows drew together.

"Almost." I swallowed to moisten my dry throat. "But my friend Cam stopped them."

"Them?" His expression hardened, and he tightened his fingers on mine. "Not cool."

"No. It wasn't."

"This happen while you were working?"

"No, before. When I was at the shelter." But that didn't stop me from being anxious every single time I got in a car with a stranger.

"You homeless, Harley?" The crease between his brows deepened.

"I was. I'm not anymore." Not yet, at least. Not once I gave Wanda the money Rush had given me tonight.

"Glad to hear that." He pulled in a breath and let it out. "And good to know you have a friend looking out for you. But even though she's not here with you, you don't have to worry. You're in control. Yeah?" His reflected eyes darkened in the mirror, and his expression seemed sincere. "Like before. You say stop, I stop. Okay?"

I nodded and released a relieved breath.

"I'll just finish washing our hands, and then I'll open the door. All right?"

"Okay. So you still want to fuck me?" I asked, pretending I didn't hear the plaintiveness in my tone.

Our time was nearly up, and I needed to check in with Cam. But with Rush's eyes on mine and his warm, solid presence behind me, I wasn't overly motivated to leave.

"Oh, hell yeah, I do." His sexy lips curved. "Right here in front of this mirror. I wanna watch you take my cock and come again like you did before. That was a hell of a show."

"You liked that?" I asked, tilting my head. Most guys were happy with the one-sided deal with them getting all the attention.

"You bet I did." His gaze darkened, now a slate gray. "I want that every time I fuck you."

"But . . ."

"But what?" His eyes narrowed as he opened the door and the alarm on my cell sounded in the other room. "What the fuck is that noise?"

"The timer on my phone. Your hour's up." I swallowed. "I have to go."

"I didn't get a whole hour." He frowned. "We were talking. Not fucking."

"You agreed to the hour. You wanted to go slow. I started the timer when we sat down. I always do. It's business. My friend will be expecting me to call her." I tried to shrug as if I didn't like being right where I was, and that it didn't matter to me one way or the other that I had to go.

"How much for the whole night?"

My eyes widened. No one had ever asked for more than an hour. "I don't know."

"Give me a number, Harley. What will it take to keep the timer off, and you focused on me and what we do together for the rest of the night?"

"Forty-eight hundred," I said after doing a quick calculation, starting with the eight hundred an hour and figuring there were roughly six hours left until morning. But basically, I just pulled the number straight out of the air, knowing he would never go for it. "Cash."

"Of course, cash. Done." He didn't even hesitate. "Now, how do we get this thing off?"

Bracketing me in again, he reached around me. As his long, slim fingers unbuttoned the first button on my blouse, his silver ring reflected the vanity lights. My breath caught as he undid the few buttons that were left without stopping. When he finally slipped his hands inside the widening gap, his skin a warm glide against mine, my heart hammered.

He watched me in the mirror, his breath coming faster. "I want to see those tits of yours again, baby, but I want you with me all the way again too, yeah?"

"How do you mean?"

"Turned on, revved up like the Porsche when I give it gas."

"I was. I mean, I am." I licked my dry lips.

"You like me touching you?"

He sucked in a breath as he framed and lifted my breasts in his hands, then skimmed his thumbs over the undersides. My breasts swelled within the cups of my bra and my nipples drew tight, the puckered tips pushing against the satin.

"Yes, I like what you're doing right now." My lips parted as his thumbs swept higher.

"What else do you like?"

The hard edges of his thumbs brushed my aching nipples. Fiery pleasure shot through me, a bolt that zinged straight to my core and weakened my knees. Drawing in a sharp, needy breath, I leaned heavily into him.

"I liked that," I said, my voice coming out husky.

"I could tell." His lips curved with satisfaction.

"I like your eyes. I like your mischievous smile too. It's cute."

He scoffed at me. "I'm not cute."

"You are when you grin and your hair falls forward. You remind me of a bad little boy caught with his hand in the cookie jar."

"You have a strange fascination with cookies. We might need to analyze that later." His tone was teasing. "But nothing about me is little, and I have something much better to feast on." As he squeezed my breasts, his grin deepened. "You have experience with bad boys?"

"Some." They were part of my rebellious youth, like shooting my mouth off.

"I like touching you and looking at you." His gaze rose to meet mine in the mirror as he lifted my breasts.

"I like . . ." I didn't finish. It was too telling to reveal how much of a turn-on it was to be praised.

"This needs to come off." He withdrew his hands. "I need to see all of you."

He moved his hands, skimming my blouse over my shoulders. Down my arms it glided, his hands urging its quick removal.

I lost his eyes for a moment, watching the white fabric flutter to the tile floor, but I quickly regained them—the silvery reflection of them, anyway. His actual focus was elsewhere. His fingers hot on the skin over my spine, I felt a release of tension beneath my breasts as he deftly unclasped my bra.

"Gorgeous," he said, staring at my breasts as he slid the bra straps down my arms, leaving me naked from the waist up.

I didn't watch the satin fall to the floor. My rapt attention was on his expression in the mirror, and the impact deep inside me of the approval I saw there.

"Rush." My voice was throaty, almost strangled, and he lifted his gaze to find me looking at him. "I need . . ." His hands. His touch. Us joined.

"What do you need, baby?" The handsome planes of his face were drawn, but his eyes were smoldering. "This?"

He framed my breasts in his large hands, awaiting my response. I shifted, arching to press them deeper into his hold while also backing my ass into his erection.

"Yes, and I need us . . . I mean you." I hastily corrected myself because there was no us. Only in the mirror, it seemed as though we were a couple.

I liked the way we looked together. He was so handsome, golden-skinned where I was fair. Chiseled where I was curved. Hard where I was soft, and strong, and yet he was so careful in the way he touched me. He was as solicitous as a lover when he had been opening doors, honoring my requests, and a myriad of other things.

"I need you too, darlin'."

I gasped as he flicked my taut nipples with his thumbs.

"That feel good?"

"Yes."

"Good. But I don't feel like being good right now." Watching me closely, no hint of a smile, he drew his fingers in a slow, deliberate path around my nipples. The areolas pebbled. "I feel like being very bad with you, Harley."

I moaned softly when he swiped the aching points.

"You wet?"

"Yes."

"Good. I'm hard."

"I know." I rocked over him. His cock seemed to strain for me. "I can feel you."

"You like what you feel?"

"Yes." Earlier, his cock had felt like a hot velvet rod in my hand.

"I like it too." He lifted my breasts and flicked the nipples. "Prettiest tits I've ever seen."

I would have argued, but the way his gaze was fixed on them supported his statement. He pressed closer, his thighs unyielding. His steely cock prodded the cleft of my ass. More wet heat dampened my core as I imagined how good it would feel to have him inside me.

"I want to touch you. Watch you while I fuck you. Would you like that?"

"Yes." That meant I got to watch him, see his eyes darken and his muscles tighten, see his expression as he slid his cock inside me.

"Are you ready for me?" he asked.

Keeping one breast to play with, he dove his other hand down the center of my body. I drew in a sharp breath as he skimmed my abdomen and then flipped up my skirt. A moan escaped that became a needy whimper as cupped my pussy in his capable hand.

"Mmm." My lips parted with pleasure as his skillful fingers glided over the silk of my panties, right to where I ached for them to be.

"You're soaked," he said.

"Yes, I'm ready. Please."

"You don't have to beg, Harley." Finding my clit, he lifted his gaze while pressing his thumb to the swollen nub.

"That feels so good." My lids fluttered as he strummed it, making me nearly incoherent with pleasure.

"Just tell me what you want. I'll give it to you."

"You." I licked my lips, experiencing a full-body shudder from his touch. "Your cock inside me."

"I want that too, pretty girl. Badly."

He suddenly released my breast, using both his hands to yank my panties down my legs. My breath sputtering, I stepped out of them while he unbuttoned his jeans and lowered his boxer briefs. His engorged member sprang free. My eyes grew wide as I watched him roll on a condom.

He caught my stare. "You've seen it before, babe."

"Yes, but I didn't consider the size then . . ." I lost my train of thought as he traced his palm down my spine, gently but firmly encouraging me to bend.

“Grab the counter, babe,” he said as he aligned himself. “Trust me. It’ll fit.”

“If you say so.” I let out a broken moan as he glided his cock inside me.

“*Fuck.*” He groaned when he was all the way in. His gaze in the mirror was as possessive as his grip on my hips as he withdrew slowly until only the blunt end remained, then plunged back inside.

“That feel good?” His voice was gravelly and deep. His cock was deep too, filling me perfectly.

“Yes.”

“Feels so fucking good.”

He pumped in and out, his strokes perfectly angled to increase my pleasure, and his grip on my hips tightened when he was completely inside me. Surrendering to him and the delectable sensations he evoked in me, I allowed my eyes to drift closed.

“Keep them open,” he murmured.

“All right.”

Pulses of ecstasy shredded my thoughts as he stared at me in the mirror while thrusting in deep and pulling out in shallow glides.

“You’re so hot, baby.” He thrust in. “So tight.” He withdrew. “So perfect.”

As he praised me, my clit began to throb in time to his thrusts.

“Harder, Rush. I need it. I need you, harder.” I gripped the counter.

His next plunge was so hard, he lifted me off the heels of my stilettos onto the tips of my toes.

“Yes, that’s it, darlin’.” He grunted his approval.

His hips slapped my ass as his controlled thrusts became wildly erratic. I was filled with his thick length, filled so full.

Pleasure, so much pleasure, rose within me. My scalp started to tingle, and I panted out each breath. His ragged breathing bathed the back of my neck with humidity. Mine fogged the mirror.

"Name, babe. Give me your name." His darkened gaze narrowed.

"Jewel."

I never gave clients my name, but I was unprepared for him and this undeniable pleasure. It spiraled higher and hotter as he pumped into me.

"Don't stop!" I begged, then screamed as he drove in deep. "Yes, Rush!"

It hit me then, bursting over me like a frenzied dance in a fiery rain.

"Yes! Oh yes!" I unraveled without caution, my shield obliterated, my eyes wide open, and his there to see all of me.

"Jewel . . ." He groaned. Stiffening, he buried his cock deep one last time and spilled himself inside me.

10

Rush

I pretended I was shaving, but I was really watching her in the mirror while she had her turn in the shower. I'd tried to get her to shower with me, but when she made an excuse about not wanting to get her hair wet, I let it go. I found myself letting go of a lot of things when it came to her.

Jewel . . . Even her name was amazing, and she'd knocked me completely on my ass.

My jaw dropped as she shimmied and stepped out of her sequined skirt. It was the last item to go. The removal of the stilettos and fishnet stockings before that had been better than any strip show I'd ever seen.

Fucking hell. I'd thought she was sexy in her clothes. Then I thought she was sexy half out of them. Then I decided I preferred her bent over the sink, climaxing around my cock.

But now I had a new favorite.

Totally naked.

She closed the glass shower door and caught me staring. I grinned at her within my shaving-cream beard.

"Fuck getting the hair wet." My arrogance resurfaced. I had paid, after all. Why shouldn't I get exactly what I wanted?

And what I wanted was more of her.

"I'm coming in with you." I tossed the complimentary razor on the counter, swiped the hand towel across my jaw to remove the shaving cream, and spun around.

"But my hair," she said. "And we need condoms."

Yeah, she read my intent correctly. I wasn't coming in to help her get clean. I was coming in to get dirty.

"Rush." She held up her hand, but that sparkly nail polish of hers wasn't a mystical deterrent. "Wait." Her eyes wide, she backed up as I stalked toward her.

I had my hand on the twist of the towel around my waist when I heard a shrill bell ring.

"What's that?" she asked, her gaze sliding over my shoulder.

"The doorbell," I grumbled.

"For a hotel room?" She frowned and took her bottom lip between her teeth.

"Yeah." The Chamberlain had them, one of the reasons the rooms here worked for me. "It's Doyle."

I'd arranged for him to stop by. A built-in interruption at about the hour mark, just like her timer. I didn't like my hotel hookups lingering too long.

"Who?" She cocked her head.

"The valet. I'll get rid of him and be right back."

I kept a tight grip on the twist in the towel, a towel I was glad was thick cotton. It hid the boner I was sporting thanks to Jewel with those tempting eyes of hers, her blinding smile, and a strength to shield her vulnerability. Everything about her, including her name, threw me for a loop.

I heard a clatter and a curse behind me. In the hall already, I paused and glanced back in her direction.

"I'm okay. I dropped the friggin' soap."

My cock gave an eager bounce as I imagined that scenario. Her shapely legs flexing and her sexy, rounded ass up in the air. I'd reached the door, but I wished I was back with her in the shower. Consequently, I cranked on the handle with more force than necessary.

Practically growling at the valet, I said, "What do you want?"

Doyle's eyes widened. I was usually relieved when he arrived.

"I brought your guitar, Mr. McMahon. You . . . you . . . said never to leave it in your car." The fluffy white ball on the end of his Santa hat trembled like the rest of him as he carefully placed the case containing my Martin on the carpet in front of me.

"Thanks, Doyle. You're right."

Making teens quake. I wasn't that big of an asshole, was I?

"I appreciate you remembering." I bent and picked up the case by the handle.

He stepped closer and whispered near my ear. "Do you want me to make the excuse about your manager calling the front desk so you can get rid of her?"

"Hell no."

"Didn't think so. She's . . ." He straightened, his attention wandering.

Her flowery scent wafted toward me even before I turned to follow the direction of his gaze. Wearing one of the hotel robes, Jewel was in the living room, bent over at the waist. Not for soap, but to pick up her purse.

"She's what?" I frowned at him, annoyed that I'd missed an opportunity to slide my hands all over Jewel's sexy slippery-wet body.

"She's really pretty."

"Yeah," I said. She was definitely that. I started to shut the door, wanting to have all that beauty for myself. I had zero interest in the valet or anyone else gawking at her.

"One more thing." Doyle stuck his foot in the door, preventing me from closing it.

At the end of my patience, I glared at him. "What?"

"You have a message. Here." He thrust a piece of paper at me.

I took it, grumbled my thanks, and crumpled the note in my hand. Behind me, I heard Jewel speaking in a low confidential tone to someone.

Closing the door on Doyle, I turned around and my brow furrowed. She had her back to me, and I took it as an affront. The rock-star entitlement thing was a difficult habit to break. Jonesing on way too much of my-every-whim-being-indulged adrenaline, I stomped straight to her.

"I'm fine," she said to whoever she was talking to on her burner phone. "Really."

"Who are you talking to?" My tone was sharper than I'd intended, making me sound like a jealous lover, but I didn't really care.

"Oh." She spun around. Her lips rounded, and her free hand floated to her throat as she scanned my face. "It's Cam. I . . . I needed to check in. We have a system."

"I get it." Not another guy. Just her friend, the one who seemed to look out for her. My anger faded. "Go ahead."

"Thanks."

For some reason, she smiled at me giving her permission. While I registered the megawatt impact of her amusement, she nodded to whatever her friend was saying.

"Yes, that's him. Yes, his voice is nice." She cocked her head while staring at me. "No, he's not too bad-looking."

My brows rose.

"He paid for the whole night, Cam . . . No. Not the Courtyard. He didn't like that idea, or the Park either. We're at the Chamberlain . . . No, really. It's not too pricey for him." She nodded again. "Sure, they were snooty about me." Her brow wrinkled. "No, he's not a psycho."

"Enough." I made a slashing motion across my neck with my hand.

Her friend had been reassured. She could talk to her later. This play-by-play was eating into *my* time.

"I gotta go." Jewel's gaze dropped to my guitar case, where I'd set it on the carpet beside her purse, and she frowned. "Take the rest of the night off. I've got rent covered. Okay. 'Bye."

She ended the call and dropped her cell on the coffee table.

"Sorry." Straightening, she wore a look of apology. "Cam likes to talk. She worries."

"She should." I raked a hand through my hair. What Jewel did wasn't safe.

"Is that a guitar?" she asked.

"Yeah." I refocused on her and not on the thought of someone hurting her.

"*Your* guitar?"

"Uh-huh."

She searched my gaze. "You're not an actor, are you?"

"No."

"Oh."

"You got a thing against musicians?"

"No. Sort of." She shrugged. "It doesn't matter."

She had that closed-off look again, and I didn't like it. I wanted the unimpeded view, her looking at me like she did whenever her guard was down. I would have paid more than the amount I paid to fuck her to get it.

"I think it does matter." I reached for her upper arms and drew her against me. Her supple curves conformed to me. She felt good in my embrace. Really good.

The crumpled paper fell to the table. It could wait.

"It's just something in my past." She reached up. Hesitantly, as if I might stop her, she smoothed my hair from my brow. "Like silk." She hummed a low sound as if pleased by the texture.

My already hard cock began to throb. That sound of hers coupled with the soft expression on her face as she continued to sift through my hair made me feel something deeper.

"We have better things to do than talk. Don't you think?" she said, practically purring in her sultry tone.

It was a total turn-on, but I knew she was redirecting me. She'd done it earlier, and that time, I'd allowed it.

But not now.

"What in your past?" I demanded.

She blinked in surprise. Her defenses seemed to waver.

"I wanna know," I said. "It's come up twice now."

And both times, it seemed to be a sensitive subject. But what the fuck did I know about treading carefully?

"Tell me." I swallowed, remembering something that had worked with her before. "Please."

"My mom played the guitar." She licked her lips. "She was a singer."

"Was?" I asked, softening my tone.

"She died when I was five. Her and my dad in a fire at the club where she worked. She stripped. He was the bouncer."

Jewel's eyes turned glassy, and she blinked rapidly to clear them.

"That was what she had to do to pay the rent. Her dream was to make a career with her music. Then she met my dad, and he made her a bunch of promises to further her singing career that he never followed through with. It didn't end well for them."

Or her either.

"It was a long time ago." Jewel shook her head, clearing the hurt from her gaze.

There was more to tell, but I didn't push. Not with her eyes wavering like a mirage.

"Sorry you asked, I'm sure." Her plush bottom lip trembled.

She seemed as uncertain about sharing personal information with me as I felt about handling the heavy emotional undercurrents between us. So *not* my area of expertise.

"I'm not sorry you shared." I stroked the back of my hand down her cheek. "I'm sorry you lost your parents, Jewel."

She leaned into my caress, accepting the comfort I offered, and something clicked into place inside me. She didn't seem to find me lacking.

No longer feeling uncertain, I let down my guard and shared something significant too. "I lost my dad recently."

"Oh no," she whispered. "I'm so sorry."

"We weren't close," I said quickly as her eyes welled with empathy.

"Does that make it any easier?" she asked, her shimmering eyes searching mine.

"No. Not really."

She nodded. I think she knew the answer before I'd given it.

"Your mom?" she asked.

"She's around. Back where I grew up in Indiana. We're not all that close either. She's not a big fan of my career choice. But she called recently. Tonight, actually. She was who I was talking to when you rapped on my window."

"Oh." Jewel cocked her head, studying me. "The wired feeling. Her call upset you."

"Yeah, it did." I schooled my expression, surprised at how well she put together the few pieces of information I'd given her.

I didn't tell her about the other stuff. About how the call with my mother and my ex-fiancée marrying someone else tonight seemed to underscore my feelings of inadequacy. She was keeping some things back. I was too. I didn't want her to think badly of me.

"You keep surprising me," I said softly. "You know that, right?"

She shook her head.

"Pretty. Sexy. Smart. Sweet. Who are you, Harley Jewel?" *Why the hell is a girl like her on the streets?*

Framing her face, I stared deeply into her eyes. She gazed back with the wide-open unimpeded view I was rapidly becoming addicted to.

"Just me." She licked her lips, drawing my gaze.

I lowered my head and closed my eyes. The peach scent of hers swirled around me like a dream.

A sharp groan suddenly pierced the shimmery curtain of unreality between us. For a moment, I thought it might have been me, expressing my desperation to finally taste her. But it was her.

Her gaze unfocused, she groaned again.

"I . . . don't . . . feel . . . well," she whispered through lips that seemed too pale.

11

Jewel

"I've got you, babe."

The ringing in my ears made Rush sound far away. One moment his lips had been coming closer to mine, and the next thing I knew, the room started spinning faster than my racing heartbeat.

"Okay." I wasn't up to arguing about giving him the control. "I'm a little woozy." I clung to as much of his taut biceps as I could get my hands around while trying to blink his handsome face into focus.

"You don't look so good." He walked backward, taking me with him. "Let's sit down on the couch a minute."

"Sure. All right. Sitting sounds like a good plan."

I assumed he would sit on one cushion, and I would sit on another. I assumed wrong.

He lowered himself onto the couch and pulled me with him . . . right onto his lap. I was woozy, but it was impossible to miss his solid thighs under me, the warmth of his body, and his woodsy scent.

"Um, what are you doing?" I asked as he pressed the back of his hand to my forehead.

"Checking to see if you have a fever." The *duh, don't be a dunce* in his tone was unmistakable.

"But I'm not sick."

"You almost passed out." He frowned at me.

"I did not," I said sharply, hating how petulant I sounded. "Let me off."

I wiggled in his lap, and he put his arms around my waist.

"Be still," he said. "You're too thin to be pregnant. Aren't you?"

"I'm on the pill. And I always use condoms. I'm not pregnant!" My stomach grumbled as if it were offended too.

"Whoa." His eyes narrowed. "Sounds like you need to be fed. Have you eaten today?"

"Define eating," I said, not meeting his eyes.

I didn't want him to pity me. I didn't want anybody to feel sorry for me. I'd once gone all day wearing my church shoes at school once because I thought the kids seeing me in my fancy shoes and not my regular ones would make them accept me, even though my feet had started bleeding after recess.

"Did you put *anything* in your mouth today?" he asked.

"Does half a piece of gum count?"

"Answer the question." He frowned again. "When was the last time you actually ate food?"

I couldn't remember. It was easier not to think about it. "The day before yesterday, maybe." At least, I think there had been food in the fridge then.

"Fucking hell! I'm ordering room service."

"At this time of the morning?"

"Babe." He arched a brow.

Oh yeah. I'd forgotten the Porsche, his celebrity status, and the way everyone scurried to do his bidding. When he touched me, all I could think about was him, and how he made me feel.

He shifted me on his lap and grabbed the phone from the end table.

"Mindy, this is Rush McMahon," he said into the phone as he gently stroked my arm. "Listen, I need some food delivered to my room ASAP. Can you make that happen?"

He tapped his leg rhythmically, and being on his lap, I bounced.

"Burgers are fine. Make it two. Fries and everything."

"I can't eat two," I whispered. "That's unnecessary." And wasteful.

"I'm famished too," he told me with his hand over the phone. "Not to the same degree as you, but I missed dinner. I had a meet and greet after the show that ran long."

"Oh." Obviously, the music thing was lucrative for him.

He returned his attention to the phone. "Thirty minutes will be fine." His leg tapped faster as he listened. "Yes, have them ring the bell and leave the food outside the door. That's perfect."

He ended the call and jostled me again as he returned the cordless phone to the cradle.

"You didn't have to do that. I'm okay, really." I swallowed my pride. "But thanks. I mean, I guess I could eat if you're eating too."

"You're welcome."

He loosened his hold on me and reached for my hair, rubbing the end of one of my pigtails between his thumb and finger. He didn't comment on it being soft like I had about his. Did he know it was a wig?

"I guess we've got some time to kill." I leaned forward, not wanting him to speculate about my subterfuge. He saw too much . . . I had given him too much of the real me already.

Placing my palms on his chest, I tried to refocus, to get back to me doing things to him and not the other way around.

Staying in control had always helped me compartmentalize the working part of my life. And his thick erection beneath me definitely had my mind on other things.

"I can think of something we could do." I slowly circled my thumbs around his nipples.

The copper-hued tips hardened, and he drew in a sharp breath.

"None of that." He grabbed my wrists and pulled my hands away.

"But . . ." I sputtered. He'd definitely liked it. I'd liked it too. "I want to touch you."

"Later," he said. "Difficult as it is to believe, I want to talk some more first."

"Really?" I studied him, not believing him for a second.

His cock was hard. His eyes were liquid smoke. His sexy body was drawn taut. All the signs were there that talking wasn't really what he wanted.

"You almost fainted," he said, as if I'd already forgotten. "I want food in you and your strength up before I fuck you again. And again. And again. Getting the picture now?"

My throat dried up and my mind freaked out as I imagined three more times with him. Slowly, I nodded.

"Why don't you tell me about your gran? It seems like she means a lot to you. Did—"

I shook my head vigorously and pushed hard, managing to get off his lap and my feet to the floor. He seemed so stunned by my vehement response that he didn't resist.

"No. I don't talk about her." I pulled the lapels of the robe together as if they could protect the wound in my chest. My eyes filled, and I struggled to keep my voice steady. "Not with Cam. Not with anyone anymore."

The memories and the pain from Gran's passing were all I had left of her, and those were solely mine.

"All right." His eyes shuttered, much like mine probably had.

Had I hurt his feelings? Did he really think I would share something so personal?

"I'm sorry if maybe I gave you the wrong impression." I gave him a tight smile. "I'm here for you to fuck me however many times you want, but the other stuff, my personal life, it's not on the table. If that's what you're looking for, I should just go. No hard feelings and all. You won't owe me any more or anything."

"Stay." His expression hardened. "You already agreed. We fuck." His tone was harsh, recoiling and snapping at me like a whip. "You can keep your secrets. I'll even go back to calling you Harley, if that's what you want."

I nodded, swallowing as he stood. He towered over me, strong emotion rolling from him in waves. Hurt or anger, I wasn't sure, but either way, it blasted me like a cold wind.

"Go ahead and take off the robe," he said through clenched teeth. "Might as well get my money's worth while we wait for the food."

Without giving me a chance to remove it, he yanked the belt off and ripped the parted cotton from my body. The robe dropped.

Naked, I shivered, but as his gaze dipped to take me in, I knew I was far from repulsed. He lowered his head. When his heated breath wafted over the sensitive skin beneath my ear, pleasure rippled through me.

"You're lying to yourself, Jewel, if you think all that's between us is business."

Rush

I stalked around her, so mad, I was practically shaking. But I was also extremely turned on.

Her golden eyes followed me as I circled her. Her nipples tightened and her thighs trembled. If I reached out and slid my fingers into the auburn curls at the apex of those long legs, the folds beneath would probably soak my fingers.

"There's no hiding from it, baby. You're attracted to me. I'm attracted to you."

Understatement of the century on my part. I was on fucking fire for her. My cock was a flagpole that tented my towel. I was pissed that she'd shut me down, twice if I counted the pullback on the kiss, and I certainly did. I so counted it.

Her lips were a prize I wanted, but I wasn't going for them now. She'd almost fainted when I tried to kiss her before. I wouldn't risk it. Yet.

But I was going to fuck her. I had a point to make.

"On your knees, on the carpet."

"Oh. Okay." Her amber eyes glowed, reminding me of a harvest moon.

She lowered herself. Her knees folded beneath her, she licked her lips as I stopped in front of her and whipped away my towel. She didn't need more direction. Thankfully.

I lost my breath as she grasped my cock by the root, and I bucked in her hands. Pre-cum slicked the blunt end. I was so ready to be inside her again.

Her mouth parted, she glanced up at me. Desire pooled in her gaze.

I nearly erupted from that alone. But there was more. For a moment, she gave me a glimpse of what I greedily wanted, and she'd decided to withhold from me.

All of her. I wanted it all.

She dropped her gaze and I closed my eyes, groaning as she took my shaft into her wet mouth. It wasn't a half-hearted effort. She took it deep.

"Jewel . . . Harley." I corrected myself, trying to remember I was pissed at her. "Yes, baby."

I curled my fingers around her slim neck, guiding her, then hissed as she licked the underside of my entire length. She made a mewling sound in response and kept at me. Relentlessly she sucked, alternating between massaging my balls and digging her nails into my ass.

Tension gripped my spine. Opening my eyes and seeing her on her knees, though, it just wasn't right. I pulled out. Her suction was so tight, the separation of her lips from my cock made a wet popping sound. Her lids fluttered open.

"On your hands and knees," I said. When she hesitated, I said sharply, "Now."

"All right," she whispered, and I caught a glimpse of hurt in her eyes before she complied.

"No one's ever sucked my cock so good. You've got me ready to blow." I grabbed a condom from her open bag. "But I wanna be inside you."

I wanted to be covering her. I wanted to smooth my hands all over her sexy ass. I wanted to feel her hot cunt squeezing me. Yes, I wanted the control, but I also wanted to feel her come.

I ripped open the package, rolled on the condom, and dropped onto my knees behind her. Spanning my hands over her back, I ran my fingers down the bumps in her spine and then caressed the perfectly rounded globes of her ass. When I found her entrance and dipped a finger inside her, she moaned.

"You're drenched, baby. You liked sucking me off?"

"Yes." She turned her head to look at me over her shoulder. Part demure, but all sexy, with her lips red and swollen from pleasuring me.

"You're a fucking goddess."

I lowered my body over hers, my tensed flesh gliding against her creamy soft skin. I felt primal. I wanted to rub myself all over her and mark her with my scent. My chest to her back, I reached around her and filled my palms with her bountiful tits.

"Oh, Rush." She let out a breath and then hissed as I pinched her nipples. "Please." She wiggled her ass backward.

"You want my cock, baby?"

"Yes."

"Stay still then."

Angling my body underneath hers, I took one nipple in my mouth and sucked on it hard. She let out a deep moan. I moved to the other tit, did the same, and nipped it.

"Rush, you're making me crazy." Her voice was a husky, turned-on rasp. "Please. You said earlier to tell you . . ."

Practically snarling, I choked out, "Earlier, you weren't holding back from me."

Repositioning behind her, I grabbed her hips and yanked her ass backward, letting her feel the blunt end of me. It was enough.

She whimpered.

"You want me," I told her, not asking. "Say it."

"I want you."

"My name." There's no way in hell I'd let up until I had all that I wanted.

"I want you, Rush."

"You got it, babe."

I surged inside her.

"Yes," she hissed, and I groaned my agreement.

"You feel so good. So wet." I stroked out and in, deep then shallow, watching myself pull out and then disappear inside her. "You make me insane." My balls were as tight as her cunt felt around me.

“Mmm,” she murmured brokenly.

She was so far gone. And so was I.

I began to hammer into her. Our flesh slapped together, and seconds later, she began to moan. The base of my spine tingled, and my balls drew up.

“Jewel. Fuck.” I was so fucking in over my head with her.

“Rush, Rush, Rush.” She chanted my name, spasming around me as I emptied myself inside her.

We came together in a hot, heated frenzy, and it was better than any standing ovation I’d ever received.

12

Jewel

When I stepped out of the bathroom after my second shower, the food had arrived. My stomach rumbled as the aroma of French fries, ketchup, and burgers wafted over to me from the coffee table.

I nearly wept. I was so hungry, my stomach cramped.

"Hey, you look a little wobbly," Rush said as he hurried to my side.

"Yeah, I guess I am." Wearing the robe again, I feigned a casual tone, but I curled my hand around his forearm, grateful for the strength he offered me to lean on, as well as for the food. "It smells delicious."

"Just a couple of plain burgers with condiments on the side. The fries aren't too bad. I sampled a few, and found a couple of brews inside the minibar."

Frowning at the two bottles, I said, "I don't drink."

"No?"

I shook my head. "My dad had an issue with alcohol, so I avoid it. You know?"

"That's not a bad plan."

Looking sheepish, Rush raked a hand through his hair. It just fell back into his eyes, but I appreciated getting a glimpse of the platinum of his eyes without his hair shadowing the sheen. Those eyes were like a mystical mirror, a mesmerizing conjurer that I had no countermeasures to resist. Compartmentalizing wasn't working. He'd made his point about that.

At the couch, he helped me sit.

"I'm not made of glass. I won't shatter."

Yet, as I said it, I glanced at the spot on the carpet where he'd fucked me so thoroughly, and knew it wasn't true. His being so kind to me made me feel fragile, made me vulnerable with him. My flimsy shield wavered, and my senses were skewed. My mind kept playing tricks with my heart, wanting it to think that the physical connection we shared meant more than it did.

He frowned down at me. "You okay? You went quiet all of a sudden." Taking a seat on the couch, he shifted to face me, his gaze searching. "I wasn't too rough?"

"No." I shook my head, a blush warming my cheeks. "You know it was good. You have to know it was good. It's just that I . . ."

Those magic eyes of his made me want to confess that I never climaxed with clients. It had always been just business before him. But I told myself that he didn't need to know.

"Just what?"

He stroked my arm softly, and my skin tingled where he touched me. I wanted to climb onto his lap again and melt into him. But my stomach saved me when it growled again.

"Sorry." His expression softened. "You should eat."

He stood. He was wearing his jeans, but unbelted, they rested much lower on his hips than before. Following the *V* that disappeared into the denim, I forgot the food.

"Babe," he said, giving me a stern look. "Eat." He glanced pointedly at the burger. "Is a soda okay with you?"

He sauntered toward the minibar. The way his jeans fit his ass made the short walk a distracting exhibition.

"Yes, soda's fine."

I leaned forward and grabbed a French fry. The wax paper beneath it crinkled. My stomach grumbled again the moment the fry touched my tongue.

"Oh my gosh," I said around the explosion of saltiness and fried potato flavor in my mouth. I covered my lips with my hand as I chewed. "This is so good."

"If you say so." He shook his head as he set two cans on the coffee table. "I think maybe it just tastes really good because we worked up a big appetite." Grinning at me, he reclaimed his seat.

I rolled my eyes, too busy shoveling food into my mouth to come up with a better response. I alternated humongous bites of the juicy burger with multiple crisp fries.

"Hey, slow down." His eyes narrowed in concern. "You'll be sick."

"You're right." I pulled back my hand from reaching for more fries and focused on chewing my current bite.

"Better." He nodded encouragingly as I continued eating, but at a more normal pace like him. "Do you wanna watch something on TV?" he asked, crumpling the napkin he'd used to wipe his mouth.

"No. Not really."

"Ah, the anti-entertainment thing." He studied me closely for a long beat, his speculation making me antsy enough to feel obligated to respond.

"Leftover biases from my small-town upbringing." I shrugged. "It doesn't make sense. It's not really gonna damn me to watch TV or listen to secular music."

After all, the selling of my body was a much bigger sin, ensuring my eternal damnation. Feeling foolish, I glanced away.

"What do you do in your spare time?" he asked, watching me closely and drawing conclusions. Accurate ones more often than not, I was discovering.

"I sketch, and sometimes paint when I can afford a canvas."

"You're a painter?"

"I try. I go to the park with Cam. She makes up stories about the people we see. I sketch them."

"What's Cam like?"

"Beautiful. A free spirit. A kind one. She took me in when . . ."

I glanced away and popped another fry in my mouth. The last one. But chewing and looking away from him didn't remove the weight of his stare.

"What do you do with your spare time?" I peeked back at him to find him staring at me as I suspected.

"Don't have a lot of that anymore. Touring keeps me pretty busy."

"You travel across the whole country?"

He nodded. "Not just this one. Europe. South America. Japan. Russia."

"Wow. That must be really cool."

"It's been a while since it felt cool. It's exhausting, actually. Isolating. Lately, I wonder if it's worth it." He trailed off, and his brow wrinkled.

"I get it." I put my hand on his. "Losing your dad makes you question everything you thought you knew before, right?"

"Yeah, that's pretty much it." He nodded once to confirm.

"You don't have to talk about it. We should pick a new topic."

"You lost your grandmother, didn't you?" he asked softly. "Recently, I'd guess."

"Yes." The food suddenly sat heavy in my stomach.

"We keep circling back to it, Jewel. Maybe if you talk about her, and if I talk about my father . . . Hell, I don't know . . ."

My eyes burning, I flattened my lips. "Will talking about it bring her back?"

"No, baby."

"Death is final."

What I had done and the choice I'd made leaving home without my gran's blessing had put a wedge between us that could never be removed. Her death made sure of that. My eyes flooded with stinging tears at the thought of the time with her I'd lost and could never get back.

I glared at him, but I was really only angry at myself.

"All right," he said. "Don't bow up at me again."

"It's not you I'm mad at. It's me." I swiped the wetness away from beneath my eyes. But not before he noted it.

"I'm sorry. I suck at this stuff, okay?"

"I suck at it too. Obviously." I cast about for some other topic to discuss and my gaze snagged on his guitar. "Do you ever play just for yourself anymore? Or does making music a career take that pleasure away from you?"

"Pretty insightful question." He shifted his attention to the instrument. "I think you're much better at this talking thing than me. Better at a lot of stuff, I'm sure."

He turned back to me and gave me a long searching look.

"Truthfully, I haven't played just for myself in a long while."

13

Rush

"That's kind of sad." Her pretty lips turned down. On my behalf. A more compelling sight I couldn't ever remember seeing, especially as I weighed her empathy against the magnitude of her losses.

"I feel like remedying that right now." Sensing that she would approve of me lightening the mood, I reached out and touched the tip of her nose. "Would you like to hear me play?"

"I would." Her eyes lit up, and her lips curved upward. "Please."

I was right. She retreated when I pushed too hard.

"Done." I swept my thumb across her lips. "Fair disclosure, babe. I'm doing this as much for myself as the potential to see another one of your smiles."

Her mouth framed a sweet one beneath my hand, and my soul surged with satisfaction.

I got up, set the case flat, clicked the latches, and withdrew the guitar. She was watching me during the entire process. I could feel her perusal, and I liked having her watching me. I liked her company, her attention, and every privileged glimpse she gave me into her life. I liked it all, a hell of a lot.

I returned to the couch, and she scooted backward to make room for me and the Martin.

"It's a pretty instrument," she said, folding her legs underneath herself and leaning her head back on the couch as I strummed a few chords and adjusted the tuning.

"Shiny like the Porsche, huh?" I said, unable to resist teasing her for not being interested in cars, entertainment, or music.

"It's a solid-top Martin?"

"Yeah." Surprised by her guess, I stilled, my fingers paused on the strings of the performance-grade acoustic.

"My mom had a similar one. She pawned it, but my gran got it back by paying for it in installments. It was one of the only things she bequeathed to me. Not sure why. Forgiveness for me pursuing a dream away from her like my mother? Or because it was the most expensive thing she thought I'd be able to carry away with me?"

"Maybe both," I said, and her eyes glassed up like polished gold. "It's probably vintage. Worth more than you probably imagine. I'd love to take a look at it sometime."

"Maybe," she said softly.

I let that noncommittal reply go. There was no maybe about it . . . I was going to see her again. I was also getting everything I could from her in the time that remained. This, whatever it was, wasn't ending when I gave her the cash I owed her in the morning.

My lips were lifting at those determined thoughts when I noticed her fingers tapping on her thigh in perfect rhythm to my tune.

"Is that a song of yours?" she asked.

"Not a song. Just chords."

"Do you write your own music?"

"Yeah, mostly. My bandmates help sometimes."

"Oh, you're in a band?" She yawned.

"Yeah, a pretty popular one."

"That's nice." Her eyelids drooped, making her appear a lot more sleepy than impressed now that her stomach was full.

"A lot of people think it's more than nice," I said without taking offense. I liked that she didn't have an inkling about that part of my life, but deep down I also registered some unease too. I was pretty accustomed to my celebrity status getting me what I wanted with women.

"No. I meant the chords you're playing are nice. Soothing."

Less than a glowing endorsement of my music, and yet I smiled. It was refreshing not to be told everything I did was amazing.

"Hey," I said softly. "You aren't getting sleepy on me, are you?"

"A little." Worry tightened her lax features.

"That's okay. Rest a little while I play. Only I'd prefer you rest here," I said.

I opened my arms, and she immediately scooted closer and laid her head on my chest. I liked that she didn't hesitate, and my earlier surge of satisfaction was a blip compared to the sense of rightness I felt with her in my arms.

"You make a much better cushion than the couch," she murmured. Placing her small hands on my chest, she tucked them under her chin and peered sleepily up at me through her thick lashes.

I hummed and strummed. It was a little awkward playing the guitar and holding her, but the reward was worth it.

She sighed. "I like your voice."

"Thank you, baby."

"You should sing." She yawned again.

I didn't tell her I did sing. That I was the lead singer and founder of the band. It really didn't matter here.

Eventually, her eyes closed and her delicate features relaxed, leaving her expression peaceful.

I didn't speak again for a long time. Instead, I watched her sleep.

As I watched her, I played. The chords became music, the humming became words, and those words became the beginning of a new song.

Jewel

Shit. Shit. Triple shit.

I'd fallen asleep. And so had he.

Light from a crack in the blinds beamed into my eyes like an accusation. It was time to go, and yet I didn't move. Rush asleep was something to savor.

His hair tumbled over his closed lids. The strong lines of his face relaxed. His sexy lips parted, the darkness between them a tempting seam that I longed to slip my tongue into, but to kiss him would surely be the next step into certain madness. Foolish, so foolish, the thoughts I'd allowed to flourish inside me.

I eased up carefully, intending to disengage from temptation, but found my hand within an inch of the hair over his brow that I longed to smooth back one last time.

Resist, Jewel. Don't make this harder by lingering.

I got off the couch and started clearing the dinner remnants. My movements would likely wake him, but I had to ask for my money soon anyway. It was humiliating to have to ask, to draw attention to what this was and what it wasn't, but necessary.

Strictly business? It didn't feel that way. But it most certainly would return to that when I brought finances into the mix. The spell would be broken.

"Hey, you," he said.

Over on the couch, he stretched, and I swallowed hard at the play of his smooth skin over sculpted muscle.

"What are you doing?"

"Just cleaning up," I said, not meeting his gaze as I turned away. His body was one thing to resist but his eyes were another, and mine would reveal too many telling emotions.

Sorting through the stack of trash in my hand, I tossed recyclables into the appropriate bin and tried not to think about how difficult it would be to salvage the current situation. I stiffened as he came up behind me.

"You don't need to do that," he said, his morning voice deep and rumbly. Wrapping his strong arms around me, he lowered his head and nuzzled my neck with his stubbled jaw.

"Apparently, I do," I said, my reply hoarse. It was hard to speak, let alone sound coherent when I had such a big lump in my throat, cutting off the oxygen supply to my brain. "I think you forgot this."

I spun out of his arms and thrust the crumpled note the valet had brought last night into his hand.

"Thanks." He studied me a moment before dropping his gaze. "You're right. I had forgotten."

He unfolded the paper, and as he scanned it, his brow creased.

"Everything okay?" I asked, grateful for a distraction.

"It's just my boss. The CEO of my label." He rubbed the back of his neck. "I'm gonna have to call her."

"Of course." I nodded. "I understand. Duty calls for me too. I need to go."

I dropped my gaze and stared at my toes. Unfortunately, that also gave me a glimpse of his. Sad how I even found his masculine feet sexy.

"Do you think you could, um, pay me now?"

He didn't respond. But I could feel him staring, and the vibes radiating off of him weren't cool.

"Jewel, look at me."

I lifted my gaze, and his eyes immediately scanned mine.

"I don't want you to go."

Hope tried to leap from my chest to his. Terrified by it, I grabbed it by the neck and quashed it with reality.

"I *have* to. Cam's expecting me." I swallowed my pride, trying not to wince at its bitter taste. "I need the money. My rent's due. I know I fell asleep; we both did. But the time's gone now, and I can't stay any longer."

"I put the cash in your bag last night while you were sleeping."

"Oh, okay. Good." I tried not to frown. What he'd done had made sense, made it easier to get me out the door in the morning. "Thank you."

I backed away and retrieved my purse, noting wistfully how it looked right leaning against his guitar case.

"Well, I guess this is good-bye." My chest tight and my throat burning, I choked out, "It was nice." I slid the strap onto my shoulder and risked one last glance at him.

"It was better than nice," he said, his eyes like coals. They burned with strong emotion, yet his expression was blank.

"Thank you." My heart wanted to read so much into the compliment. "I liked getting to know you."

"I liked that too." He was watching me expectantly, almost as if he wanted me to say something more.

I shifted my weight from foot to foot. *Go, Jewel. Move. Take the compliment and leave before the situation turns awkward.*

"Good luck with everything. Your mom. Your music." I tore my feet from where they were rooted on the carpet and hurried for the door, but he stopped me.

"I want to see you again."

"You do?" I spun around.

"Today. After I square things with my label." He pinned me in place with his gaze, then ripped the hope right out from under me. "I assume the same hourly structure applies."

"Yes." Disappointment sliced me in two.

What did you think he was going to say? This started one way. There's no changing it into anything else.

"Okay. Sure." I should have said no. But I was weak, and I needed the money. Cam and I both.

"Can I have your phone?" He moved closer, his scent flooding my senses as he narrowed the distance between us.

"Sure." I ducked my head, dug in my purse, and handed him my cell. Our fingers brushed, sending a tingle up my arm. My thoughts spun as I recalled how amazing it felt to have him running his hands all over me.

He tapped at my phone, then handed it back to me. "I put in my personal cell. Text or call when you're free, and I'll come get you."

"Okay. But you can't pick me up."

"Why not?" He gave me a puzzled frown.

"I wasn't in my neighborhood when I met you. Your Porsche on my side of town wouldn't be good. Unsafe for you and trouble for me. I'll come to you," I said firmly.

14

Rush

"I apologize for not getting back to you sooner," I said, hoping I sounded appropriately contrite.

Holding the phone with one hand, I raked the other through my hair, and I swore my fingers stirred up Jewel's peach scent, which definitely stirred up other parts of my anatomy. Although it was enjoyable earlier, it was distracting now that I was being called on the carpet by the CEO of Black Cat Records.

"You are not the only artist under contract with my label, Mr. McMahon."

My libido flatlined at her cutting tone. "I realize that, Ms. Timmons."

"Then I expect you to behave in a manner that exceeds rather than misses my expectations." Clacking came from her end of the line, probably her manicured claws on her computer keyboard, lining up some other musician to torture. "My early morning is already filled. I was going to eat lunch at Taix with someone, but he can wait. I'll see you there before. Eleven sharp."

"The French place on Sunset Boulevard?"

"Yes, and don't be late. We have lots to discuss. And having to cut my personal time short to accommodate you doesn't put me in a conciliatory frame of mind."

She ended the call, and I exhaled heavily. Fucking hell, Timmons was a ballbuster. I didn't like dealing with her at all, and usually let Brad run interference for me.

I set my cell on the coffee table. Twisting my ring around and around on my middle finger, I thought about calling him, but really, all I wanted to do was sit here and think about her. *Jewel.*

Not entirely true. I actually hadn't stopped thinking about her. And I wanted to do more than think. Much more.

But I'd almost blown it and let her get away, hoping that maybe she might want to stay of her own volition without it being just business between us. Obviously, I was an idiot. Out of touch. I'd been with so many groupies, a paid fuck felt like something real.

It had been an hour since she left, and I'd felt every minute as a loss.

Sure, I'd taken care of the basics. Showered. Scarfed down a full American breakfast. Gotten dressed. And I'd done it all alone, like I usually did on a break. After months of sharing a tour bus with the guys, I usually relished some "me" time. But since the door closed behind Jewel, I'd never felt so alone.

Did she eat?

She had money now. She could buy a lot of breakfast with the money I'd given her. But on the other hand, had I just made her a target by giving her so much cash?

Her part of town sounded dangerous. I didn't like the idea of her returning to it without protection.

I picked up my phone again. Checked to make sure I hadn't missed any calls, and that my ringer was on and the volume was turned up.

No calls.

Why the hell hadn't she called yet?

Oh yeah, douche. You just gave her a wad of money. Do you really think she's gonna hurry back?

I certainly hoped she would. She'd hooked me, both with her smile and that indefinable something in her eyes that seemed just for me.

But, really, beyond the money . . . what did I have to offer her?

Jewel

"Don't do it," I said, gasping for breath. "These are my tight jeans. I can't laugh anymore." My sides were going to split from the endless stack at IHOP *and* Cam's impressions of Wanda as the Wicked Witch of the West.

"Come, my pretties," my roomie said mischievously just as I took a sip of water, a mistake that shot the liquid straight out of my nose.

"Cam . . ." I whined, dabbing at my face with a napkin. "Really. No more."

She grinned. "Okay."

I didn't trust her, but I smiled. I couldn't help it.

He wanted to see me again. For cash.

I knew what it was. I wasn't stupid.

But the rent was paid. We'd stocked our fridge, stashed away the leftover cash, and eaten pancakes until we were stuffed. Today was an infinitely better day than the one before it. I was going to take it, and with Rush, I was going to live in the moment.

At least, that was the plan. It sounded doable in my head, but I knew the reality of walking the talk would be a lot harder.

"I'm stopping." Her green eyes narrowed. "But only so you can finally give me the deets. Spill. No more putting me off."

"What do you want to know?"

"Well, for starters . . ." She leaned forward, her elbows on the table and her chin on her hands. "How deficient is he?"

"He's not deficient, Cam."

"Get out! He paid you for the whole night. Beaucoup money for it, and he's actually good in the sack?"

"I came. Every time. Even when we were just fooling around."

"No!"

"Yeah."

"Your face just went all soft." She pulled back slightly, her eyes wide. "You like him."

"Yeah."

"Fuck."

"Uh-huh." My elation faltered.

"You're still going to see him again?"

I nodded, and my chandelier earrings tickled my neck. "It'll be okay."

She gave me a sharp look. She didn't believe me either.

"It's a limited-time thing," I said, not sure if I was trying to convince her or myself. "He's a musician. He tours all over the place. His interest has a built-in expiration date."

"Hold up. He's a musician who drives a Porsche. That's not your average nightclub-performing starving artist. What's his name?"

"Rush McMahon."

"Rush McMahon!"

Mortified, I shushed her as several patrons turned to look at us.

Her eyes ridiculously wide, Cam scooted closer to me in our half-circle booth and lowered her voice. "Rush McMahon sold out the Staples Center last night, Jewel."

"Oh." My eyes grew as wide as hers.

"Oh my God!" she exclaimed. "And I so gave him to you. This is a huge fucking deal. He's as rich as that guy who owns that internet-streaming company."

Confused, I gave her a blank look.

"Samuel Lesowski. You know, the producer who's in that big lawsuit with his daughter." When I merely shook my head, she waved a hand, dismissing the comparison. "Well, rich like that, but Rush is also mega hot."

"Yeah." I got the hot part.

"He's a major player too. If we had a data plan to surf the internet, I'd show you."

"Here you go." The waitress, a tall thin girl with close-cropped blond hair, had returned with our change.

"Thanks." I pulled out a five for her and pocketed the rest.

"You're welcome, honey. Hey . . . did you say you met Rush McMahon?"

I shrugged. "Sort of."

"Wow," she said, her voice all breathy. "Was he nice?"

Arrogant, sure. But nice?

I nodded. "Definitely."

"Cool. I love his music. But lately he's been caught saying stuff . . ."

"What kind of stuff?" I asked.

The blonde glanced over her shoulder. The restaurant was mostly deserted. "Let me show you."

She slid in beside me and opened YouTube on her phone. My heart raced as Rush's image filled the screen.

"He has his own channel," I whispered.

Two million subscribers. Six albums.

She clicked on one of the videos, scrolling too fast over an image of Rush onstage. He was wearing jeans, no shirt, his hair plastered to his head as he sang, a black electric guitar slung low across his hips.

"Um," I said, about to ask her to scroll back so I could hear him sing, but his voice suddenly blasted through the speakers.

"Life sucks and then you die, right?"

"Ah, he's not exactly a diplomat," Cam said, rolling her eyes.

"He lost his dad recently." When the words slipped out, I covered my mouth.

"Yeah," the waitress said, not looking up from her phone. She'd moved on to checking her emails. "And his ex-fiancée got married to his brother last night."

"What?"

The blonde looked up. "You really don't know anything about him, do you?"

I shook my head. Apparently not. He'd left out a major detail.

"Shoot. Well, I'd better get back to work." She got up, took a step, then turned back around. "Hey, did you at least get a picture with him?"

"No."

"Too bad. Candid pics of him are rare. He only does them in the meet and greets now."

As soon as the waitress moved away, Cam turned to me.

"So, start over from the beginning." Her eyes sparkled with excitement. "I want to know everything."

I'd just finished programming Jewel's contact info into my car and pulled away from the Chamberlain when my cell rang through my car speakers. The display showed Jewel calling, and I grinned. She'd called. *Finally.*

"Hello," I said.

"Hey, it's me. Jewel."

As if she needed to clarify. I would recognize her sultry voice anywhere.

"Hey, Harley girl. Whatcha doing?"

"Freakin' out a little."

"You told someone you were with me last night." The little bubble we'd enjoyed outside of reality burst. It was inevitable this would happen, but I'd hoped it wouldn't happen so soon. "Your roommate?"

"Yes, and a waitress at the IHOP overheard. Not about what really happened, just that I'd met you and didn't realize who you were."

There was a lot of crap about me out there, some true but most not. Jewel's opinion of me would surely go in the shitter if she caught wind of even half of it.

"There's a lot of talk out there that goes along with the life I lead," I said, trying to get ahead of it. "So I give the world a show. That's the guy they want."

The truth was, everyone ignored any evidence contrary to what they wanted to believe, so I no longer tried to deny anything.

"Yeah? Like it's who you have to be to pay the rent."

Jewel's words gave me pause. There were similarities between what she did and my own career. But she did what she did out of desperation; my basic necessities were met and then some. So why did I continue doing something that made me unhappy?

"That guy I am onstage is a part but not all of me." I exhaled as I turned a corner, both literally with the Porsche, and figuratively in our conversation as I gave it to her straight. "I liked that you didn't know him."

Being with her seemed easier, simpler, like I could be myself, or like I had a chance to be someone different. At least, it felt that way.

"How long were you on the internet?" I asked, but what I really wanted to know was how much she'd seen and if I could dig myself out of it.

"Not long."

"Okay, great. What exactly did you see? Can you give me some specifics?" Could she hear the rising panic in my voice?

"You onstage from last night."

"Not my best performance." But not too bad. I hadn't stumbled or passed out. "And?"

"Not much else. Just how big your following is. How many albums you have. A video someone recorded with you saying how life sucks."

It could have been worse.

My new high-priority short-term goal? Keep her off the internet.

"Oh," she said, "and I heard about your fiancée."

Fuck. So now Jewel knew what a loser I was. Sure, I could have any woman I wanted, but not the one I'd wanted to keep.

"I'm so sorry, Rush," she said softly, sounding sincere, but her sympathy was a balm I didn't deserve. "I know how a betrayal like that feels."

"What?" I nearly crashed into the car in front of me.

"I didn't come out to LA alone. I was with a boyfriend. He . . . we were together for a while, but when I got home from my grandmother's funeral, I found him with someone else." She sighed, a deep, jagged-edged exhale that sawed through the center of my chest.

"He was an idiot."

"I don't know. Maybe if . . ."

"I've been with you, Jewel. Trust me. He's a first-class fuckup."

"Okay, if you say so." She didn't sound convinced.

"Where are you?" I wanted to comfort her, almost as much as I wanted to beat up the idiot who had hurt her.

"On the bus, actually. On my way to the Chamberlain. I wasn't sure where you wanted me to meet you. I just assumed . . ."

"Shit." I couldn't swing back to get her. If I did, I'd be late meeting Timmons, and I couldn't risk that.

"Can you get off? Transfer to Sunset. I've got an appointment with my boss at Taix, and I can't be late. She's already pissed at me. Could you meet me there? I'll tell the maître d' to expect you. We could have lunch together afterward. The food's good."

I was so excited to see Jewel again, I was babbling. There was more to explore between us, but I couldn't go there. Not yet.

Get her. Hold her, I told myself. *Then be very careful to make the most of every opportunity she gives me.*

15

Jewel

When I got off the bus, I almost thought I was at the wrong place. The name above the beige-and-brown chateau-style building was right, but the long line of half-naked girls waiting outside made it seem more like the street corner where I'd first met Rush.

"Is this where we check into the restaurant?" I asked a brunette in a leather bra and fishnet stockings as I stepped into line behind her.

"It's where we wait for our turn to meet Warren Jinkins and Rush McMahon."

I figured it was something like that. "Who's Warren Jinkins?"

"You don't know who War is?" Her brows rose as I shook my head. "The lead singer of Tempest. One of the baddest boys in rock music, and the hottest until Rush came along. He's inside with his girlfriend, so he's probably out for a possible hookup, but Rush is fair game. He chose three girls from a lineup at his hotel last night, if you believe the talk in his fan chat room."

Rush had been with someone before me last night? Three other someones?

Foolish, Jewel. Getting your hopes up. Forgetting your paid-for role. Believing your night with him meant something.

"I wouldn't waste my time, if that's why you're here." Sizing me up in my jeans and tee, she blew and popped a pink bubble. "A guy like Rush would never pick you."

"Why's that?" I asked as she gave voice to my fear.

"Your clothes, for one." She squinted her thickly mascaraed eyes at me. "Your hair. Your flip-flops." She ticked off item after item she found lacking. "You're not even wearing makeup, are you?"

I was, though only a little mascara and lip gloss.

"You look all washed out. Like you just rolled out of bed and threw on some old clothes. Sorry, hon." She patted my arm, obviously noting her harsh comments had hit their mark. "Just telling it like it is. Keeping it real."

I thought of myself as a pretty laid-back person, but this chick pushed all my buttons. Narrowing my eyes, I said, "Real, meaning you're being a bitch."

Her jaw dropped open, and her gum tumbled out and hit the sidewalk.

Throwing her words back at her, I said, "That's me telling it like it is. Keeping it real." I took a step away from her.

She reminded me of the girls back home. Knowing what my mom did for a living, they'd never accepted me. Part of the reason I left was because I'd wanted to live in a place where no one had built-in biases against me.

"But I was only trying to help—"

"Untrue." I lifted my chin. In my work clothes, I was better prepared for cruel treatment. Bringing my shield up, I fired back. "What you were trying to do was get rid of someone you saw as competition."

I had more to say, but my words were drowned out by screams. I found myself swept forward in the line.

When the crowd parted and I saw Rush, the anticipation that had made me feel like an overloaded electrical socket all day returned. Underneath the portico to the building, he stood as tall and handsome as ever, wearing the black jacket from the night before, a tee, and faded jeans. His slate-gray eyes passed over me without recognition.

Hurt, I stopped, planting my feet to hold my position. The tide of women that he seemed to control surged around me and continued to flow to him.

Rush's gaze moved back and his eyes went wide as he swept a slower glance over me. His lips lifting into an approving grin, he strode straight to me. He ignored the women in his way, touching him, calling his name, and snapping photos.

"Jewel," he said, breathing out my name like I actually was a rare and precious gem. "You're here. I've been watching from inside, but I didn't see you." Grabbing me by my upper arms, he pulled me into him, his gaze roaming my face and hair. "Red. I should have guessed."

"Just brown with reddish highlights," I said with a shrug.

"You'd argue with a post and insist it was a stick in the ground." His grin widened. "The color of your hair is as complex as you are."

He took my hand, placing it on his forearm, and tucked me into his side.

"Stay close." He gave me a firm look, and that's when I noticed we were surrounded. "We're going inside."

The crowd pushed and jostled us as we moved together as a unit. There were some bottlenecks. Some women shouted derogatory things at me, and some he had to turn his shoulder into to get by. But eventually, we made it inside. The quiet inside the foyer was startling after the chaos outside.

"Sorry about that." He turned me to face him. "You okay?"

"I'm fine."

"Good. I'm glad."

"I could've made it inside by myself." I glanced at the maître d', who was watching us from behind his glossy black podium.

"You're such a badass, you probably could have. But I wasn't taking any chances." Rush's brow creased. "Listen, I gotta go and make nice with my boss. I'm late, and she's guaranteed to be pissed. I'd introduce you, but I don't want to subject you to that. Can you wait for me here?" He gestured to a bench that reminded me of a church pew.

"Sure." I started toward it.

"Anything you need, you tell Jean."

"Jean?" I asked.

"That's me, mademoiselle." The maître d' looked up from his reservation book and lifted his finger.

"Okay, I will," I told Rush. When he hesitated, I shooed him away. "Go on."

"Don't leave."

I smiled. "I won't. Promise."

His approving nod told me my word meant something to him. I liked that, and was thrilled that he didn't want me to leave.

After he disappeared, I sat down and took in my surroundings more carefully. But the red tile floors, the potted plants, and Jean making phone calls to remind dinner patrons of their reservation times didn't hold my attention the way Rush did.

Dropping my gaze to my lap, I picked at the frayed threads over my right kneecap and wondered if he thought my outfit made me look washed out. He certainly had seemed pleased to see me, and he'd smiled after looking me over. That worry aside, I moved on to speculate about Rush and his boss.

"Excuse me."

A woman's voice interrupted my musings. I looked up to discover a beautiful blonde standing in front of me.

"Can I sit here?" She gestured to the empty spot beside me.

"Absolutely." I nodded and scooted over to give her more room.

"Thanks." Setting a pretty pink clutch on the bench beside her, she sat down and started bouncing her legs. "Oh, shooty-shoot." She let out a long sigh.

"Is everything okay? It's none of my business, but if there's something I can do to help, I'd be happy to try. As long as it involves me staying here," I said, remembering my vow to Rush. "I promised him I would stay right here."

"You're sweet." Her brow scrunched. "I'm okay. Just impatient. This is taking longer than I expected."

Something about her seemed familiar, but I couldn't quite figure it out.

"Is the *him* your boyfriend?" she asked as I studied her.

"Not exactly."

"Ah. You must be in the beginning stages, then. I could never accurately describe what War and I were to people at the start of our relationship."

Rush and I didn't have a relationship, but I didn't correct her. I was too intrigued by the rest of what she'd shared. "You're with Warren Jinkins?"

"Yes." She wiggled her left hand, where an enormous diamond solitaire sparkled.

"You're engaged to him?"

"Yes." She smiled. "I've been dying to share with someone. He's breaking the news to his boss now. Even though she's in a chilly mood."

Suddenly, I knew where I'd seen her before and who she was. "You're Shaina Bentley from *Pinky Swears*."

"Yes, I am." She nodded. "Only I'm not really on the show anymore. It's actually in syndication. I've gone on to doing movies."

"Oh, well, I loved it. It was on one of the few channels my gran allowed me to watch when I lived with her."

"I'm glad you enjoyed it." Her brow crinkled again. "My manners are horrible. I should've introduced myself before. I'm Shaina. What's your name?"

"Jewel. Jewel Anderson."

"Nice to meet you, Jewel. And you're here with . . ." Her eyes widened as she guessed. "Rush?"

I nodded and blushed as she did a double-take. "I know I'm not his usual type." Or at least I wasn't dressed like one now.

"Who told you that?"

"One of the women outside."

"Those aren't sisterhood supporters."

"Yeah." I snorted. "I got clued in when one slammed me for my appearance."

"You look cute. Your earrings are boho. Your jeans fit nice. And your tee, well . . ." She smiled. "It's different in an endearing way. I've never seen anything like it."

"My gran made it for me." It was a little snug now. She'd given it to me when I was in high school, but there was no way I'd ever give it up.

"Sounds like she's a wonderful grandmother."

"She was."

"Oh no. Is she gone?"

"Yes." Tears filled my eyes.

"I'm sorry." Shaina scooted closer, pulled out a travel packet of Kleenex from her clutch, and offered me one. "Here."

"Thanks." I sniffed, dabbing at my nose with the tissue she'd given me. "I'm okay."

"I can see that you are. And I can also see that Rush is a lucky guy." She gave me a firm nod as if it were decided. "I saw him in the other room with Mary. He kept glancing this way, because you're here. And your attention keeps wandering his way too. It's intense. I remember those days. Actually . . ." Her frosted-pink lips curled upward. "It's still that way, to be honest. I think when it's the right one, it always is. You just get better accustomed to dealing with those feelings."

As she inclined her head to the room where Rush was, a handsome guy with dark brown hair and eyes only for my companion strode our way.

"Let's roll, sweetness," he said.

"Hold up." Shaina stood and gestured to me. "Jewel Anderson, this is my fiancé, Warren Jinkins. She's dating Rush."

"I'm not." I shook my head.

"She is," Rush said as he walked up.

The two men exchanged a glance, then War grinned at me.

"Better go with it, babe. As the front man dictates, so it shall be. It's in our DNA." War gave me a chin lift that made me feel like I'd been accepted into some kind of inner circle, then turned his attention to his fiancée. "Shaina, as much as I'm enjoying meeting your new friend, I'm gonna have to pull you away. Your man needs some alone time with you."

"All right." She gave him a blinding smile, then turned to me. "Jewel, I've got a project in LA that'll keep me here a while. If you need anything, if you want to talk about anything"—she directed a pointed glance at Rush and slipped a card into my hand—"you can call me. Anytime. That's my private cell number, but don't hesitate to use it."

As she turned and slid her hand into War's outstretched one, I noticed how many rings he wore, and how different the two of them appeared on the outside. She was dressed in a fussy pink couture skirt and jacket, and he was in a plain black tee and jeans. And yet as they walked away, they moved in unison as if they belonged together.

"I see you won over Shaina," Rush said.

"I don't know . . ."

"You did. I run into her whenever War is around. Tour stops. Events. That kind of thing. Never seen her give her private number to anyone. Her agent's line? Yeah. Her cell? Never."

"Oh. Well. Cool." I kind of wished she would have stayed longer. I glanced at the hallway she and War had entered. It was empty now.

"My boss wants to meet you."

"Come again?" I turned to Rush, my brows high.

"Let me put it this way. She thinks I'll pay more attention to her if you're beside me."

"Oh." My mouth rounded in surprise.

"Mary Timmons is the CEO of Black Cat Records and feels like she has to control everything. They call her the ice queen. There's no warning sufficient for her, and I apologize in advance. You'll soon see why."

My hand firm on the small of her back, I steered Jewel through the crowded dining room toward my boss. Strangely, I breathed easy, though this wasn't going to be a pleasant meeting. Not if it continued the way it had started.

"Hello." Mary inclined her head to Jewel as she took her seat in the chair I pulled out for her.

"And you are?"

"Jewel Anderson." Her gaze flicked to me as if to get direction for how to proceed.

The hell if I knew. I shrugged to convey my ineptitude as I returned to my original seat on the ice queen's right.

"I believe I am the one speaking to you, young lady, not Rush."

Jewel's pretty eyes rounded. "My apologies."

Damn, she was beautiful. Gorgeous coppery-brown hair cascading to her slim shoulders. Wide, expressive brows. Golden eyes. Light complexion. Minimal makeup that complemented her delicate features. Clothes that clung to her sexy shape, not fancy ones, but she looked comfortably unforgettable.

The night before, her wig and makeup had masked everything. Right now, all I wanted to do was bask in her glow and stare at her. And that desire was obviously something the boss lady had picked up on.

"Apology accepted." Mary tilted her head. "I'm pleased to meet you."

"Same."

"That's nice of you to say. I'm not sure what Rush has told you, or what the nature of your relationship is exactly, only that he seems to consider time in your company of higher value than my own."

Whoa. Absolutely true.

"Given his distraction, I saw no harm in having you sit in with us on a discussion regarding my current displeasure with him. Perhaps you might be of some help for me with him in that regard."

"I don't know about a lot of what you said." Jewel licked her lips, and even in this business setting, my cock jumped at the memory of how her mouth felt on me. "But I don't think you should expect assistance from me when I don't really know you at all, and my loyalty is to him."

"Well said." Mary tucked a strand of her short brown hair behind her ear, and her gaze narrowed. "I will say that I value loyalty among my close friends, and based on how you have conducted yourself thus far, I look forward to us getting to know each other better. However, for now . . ." She returned her determined gaze to me. "Back to the top item on my list. Your recently completed tour."

She flipped open a file folder on the table beside her empty plate. After perusing rows of facts and figures I suspected she had memorized, she lifted her gray gaze and squinted disappointedly at me. "Do you know how much money we lost?"

"I have a fair idea." Brad had kept me informed. "I told you before those dates were booked that my band needed a rest. Then after . . ." I paused, not sure how to proceed. Talking about my father with Jewel was one thing, but discussing his death with my boss was another.

"I'm not unsympathetic to the circumstances, Mr. McMahon. If I weren't, I wouldn't have asked to see you personally. I believe in you and your talent. These expenses can be offset by the revenue from your last album, which continues to perform quite well, despite the continuing deterioration of your reputation. But it could be better. You could do better."

Sitting back in her chair, she tugged on her black suit jacket and steepled her fingers.

"I have some mandates and a couple of suggestions." She peered at me over her hands. "Mandate one: No more public intoxication. Mandate two: No more negative outbursts in public. Mandate three: No wasting my studio time."

"I haven't wasted—"

"You have. I've listened to every track personally, and they're all subpar."

Yikes. "Now, wait a minute—"

"No more waiting. From now on, you pay the studio expenses out of your own pocket, Mr. McMahon. I think once you do, you'll quickly learn the value of being focused and on task when you bring in material to be produced."

Damn. Nothing I said was going to help at this point, so I just kept my mouth shut. She nodded when I no longer protested.

"Now, on to suggestions." She pulled in a breath, and I braced. "I suggest trashing everything and starting over."

Mary had never held back on critiquing, but on the other hand, she usually approved of what I presented. Was every track for the new album that bad? I honestly wasn't sure. I'd been pretty trashed when we recorded most of it.

"I think you need a new direction, and I suggest you dig deep to find it. In the past, you've relied heavily on an antiestablishment theme. It's a popular message but not very original. It's not where you were at the beginning of your career, and quite frankly, I don't really believe it's where you are now. In other words, your heart's not in it, and an artist whose heart's not in his material is a fraud."

Fuck. This was worse than I expected.

Her lips thinned as she skewered me with her gaze. "Ultimately, that's why I'm disappointed with you, and you should be disappointed in yourself. You and your fans deserve better."

Her gaze flicked to Jewel. "It was interesting to meet you."

Mary stood, and when her attention moved to the entrance to the dining room, her stern expression softened. "My lunch date has arrived."

Curious, I turned my head toward the entrance. When I saw who was standing there, my eyes widened.

Her arch rival, Charles Morris, the CEO of Zenith Productions.

16

Jewel

"So that's your boss?" I said, watching Mary as she crossed the room, weaving gracefully between the tables.

A striking and well-put-together woman of about fifty, she turned nearly as many heads as Rush had on his trek. She was attractive and confident. I could appreciate those qualities at a distance. Up close, I'd mainly concentrated on not being gobbled up alive.

"That's her, all right," Rush said. "And that's Charles Morris."

Mary joined a man her age with striking blue eyes and close-cropped gray hair. He wore a suit as elegant as hers, and given the way it draped across his wide shoulders, it had to be a custom fit. Murmuring something that made her dark expression lighten, he lithely spun the exec into his arms and steered her out of the dining room.

"Wow." I turned to find Rush much closer than he'd been before, his arm now resting along the back of my chair. "You weren't exaggerating about her."

"Nope. She's a very powerful woman in a business mostly controlled by very powerful men. I get the reason she's the way she is, and I actually like her. But don't ever tell her. I like the way she gives it to me straight. What the hell use is someone handling my career if they just tell me what I want to hear?"

I nodded. I could understand that. "And Charles Morris is?"

"The CEO of Black Cat Records' biggest competitor, Zenith Productions. If Mary signs a rising artist, he goes after a bigger one. They both tried to sign me. They've been rivals for as long as anyone can remember. But there are recent rumors."

Rush seemed to lose his train of thought, and so did I as he took a long strand of my hair and stared at it as if in wonder at the color, the texture, or both. Rubbing it between his fingers, he murmured, "Silky soft."

"The rumors?" I said, recoupling the train of our conversation somehow, though my voice was breathy.

"Something about a shared past. A tragic one, but I can't recall the details."

With one finger, he traced the strand upward, his gaze following his progress. My entire body tingled as he brushed the shell of my ear and tucked the piece of hair he had captured behind it.

"I love your hair, especially with it loose around your shoulders like this," he said, his voice an intimate rumble.

"Thank you," I whispered.

His gaze lifted and met mine with a jolt I felt throughout my entire body. "You knocked me on my ass when I saw you outside. So unexpectedly pretty. So unassumingly beautiful."

My cheeks heated. "You don't have to compliment me."

"I do. Why shouldn't I give it to you straight?"

Again, I met his gaze, and this time it stole my breath. "Because . . ."

Because this was temporary. Because if I'd knocked him on his ass, he'd done the same to me. Because he could get back up and go on with his life, but I was afraid it wouldn't be so easy for me. But I couldn't tell him that.

"It was all there last night. The smile. Those eyes. Your soft skin. Perfect tits. Ditto on the ass and legs. Amazing, all of you. But dimmed until now." He shook his head as if in disbelief.

I smiled. Huge. "You make me feel beautiful."

"Good." He took my hand, stroking my skin with his thumb. "I like you with me, Jewel. But there's one thing I don't like."

His expression firmed, and I felt a frisson of fear.

"You leaving."

Confused, I shook my head. "I'm not going anywhere."

"You did this morning. And I didn't like it." His lips flattened. "We'll talk more about that later." He lifted his gaze, releasing me. "The waiter's on his way with the first course. I went ahead and ordered for us."

"All right." My lips puckered into an embarrassed grimace. "I wouldn't know what to order anyway."

"Have you ever had French food?" He hooked the leg of my chair with his foot, dragging me closer, and his armrest bumped mine. This close, his warmth compelled me, and his woodsy scent messed with my equilibrium. *He* messed with it.

"No," I managed to reply.

"Well then, you're in for a treat. I've had it all over the globe, but Taix is the best."

He grinned, and the force of his happiness settled somewhere deep inside my chest. The room spun, and then it hit me. That brilliant smile of his did more than just mess with me.

Rush McMahon completely rocked my world.

Rush

Watching Jewel eat was seductive. The dabbing of her lips with the white linen napkin. The swiping of her tongue across them. The moans of pleasure that escaped. My cock leaped with eagerness each time she did one of those things. Hell, it twitched right now at just the sight of her taking a sip of her coffee.

"I can't believe you used to work here." Her head tipped to an inquisitive angle, and the shards of coppery metal dangling from her delicate ear skimmed her regal neck.

I longed to press my lips to her soft skin, wanted to trace the stretched tendon between her neck and shoulder with the tip of my tongue. Would her lids lower? Would she shiver? Would she sigh my name? Did she have any idea how much she tantalized me?

Lost in my thoughts, lost in her, I imagined a cascading wind sound accompanying the movement of her earring. Jack could duplicate it with chimes. The sound would fit well as the background for the bridge in the song I had started.

"How long ago was that?" she asked, oblivious to my thoughts.

"A long time ago."

Hardly any of the same staff remained from those days. But it still felt more like coming home to eat a meal here than it did to sit around the formal dining table at the farmhouse. To me, home was more a place where you knew you were always welcome than it was anything else.

"And you never waited tables?"

"No way. Just bussed them. I would never be able to remember what everyone ordered without writing it down. I love great food, but I'm shit at the finer details, knowing what wine goes with what and all. I just like what I like."

I gave her a pointed look.

"Back then, I could barely cover my portion of the rent on the dump the guys and I lived in. Working here, I was guaranteed a good meal. Most days it was the only one I got. I held on to this job even after I got the advance from Black Cat. I only let it go when they booked us our first tour."

"I can relate to that." Her brow creased. "Do you think maybe . . . I mean . . ." Her cheeks turned pink. "It might not be appropriate, but do you think they might have an opening I could apply for?"

Fuck. I was such an insensitive ass. Jewel could certainly use a job like I'd had here. She was living the hand-to-mouth existence I had back in the early days of my career.

"Would you like me to introduce you to the owner?"

"I'd love that."

"Done." I lifted a finger to snag our waiter's attention, and he hurried over.

"Would you like the check, Mr. McMahon?"

"Yes, I would. But I'd also like to introduce my companion to Gustav. Is he in his office today?"

"No, monsieur. Sadly, he's not. He's out of town until the day after tomorrow. Would you like me to give him a message?"

"I'll scribble one on our receipt. I know he enters those himself."

"That he does." The waiter set the leather folder on the table beside me. "Whenever you're ready."

When he deftly reached for my empty plate and then shifted to retrieve Jewel's, her hand shot out to stop him.

"Not yet." She smiled prettily at him, evoking an irrational surge of jealousy in me that she'd frivolously shared such a treasure with him. "There's a tiny bit of creme brûlée left."

"My apologies, mademoiselle." He backed away.

Jewel turned her smile to me, and all was forgotten. "Do you think it would be bad manners to lick the bowl clean?"

"It might be." My gaze dropped to her lips. "But that's something I'd like to see." I scanned her face, enjoying the view before stopping on her eyes. "But better than watching what you can do with your tongue, I'd much rather experience it."

"Rush . . ." She breathed out my name again like she thought I was a gift.

But it was her. *She* was the treasure.

The way she looked at me. The way I felt with her. Every moment made me feel like a thief for paying her so little.

"Anything I want?" I asked. "Is that offer still on the table?"

"Yes. You know it is." She lowered her gaze, and her creamy skin bloomed like a blush rose.

"Good. I have more than a few ideas about that."

Sensing the weight of Jewel's gaze on me, I scrawled a quick note to Gustav, thanking him for the delicious meal. I mentioned Jewel's interest in a job there and gave myself as a reference. Then I dropped the pen, pushed back my chair, and stood, suddenly very anxious to get going.

"Can I have your hand, pretty girl?" I asked her, offering mine.

Nodding, she took my hand. A surge of emotion swept through me at the sight of her slender fingers resting within mine.

I closed my hand around hers. *Mine.* That word blazed through my mind.

First on my list was a kiss. I had to taste her lips. Then I was having her every way I could imagine, in every room in my condo.

It would take longer than the day I suspected she'd set aside for me. But if we ran over the twenty-four hours, I'd just schedule with her for more. I didn't want anyone else to touch her. I'd pay her whatever it took for exclusivity.

But deep down, I suspected there wasn't enough money in my entire bank account to have what I really wanted from her.

17

Jewel

In the passenger seat, I watched Rush. His expression focused, his thigh flexed as he gave the Porsche a little gas to inch it forward. He was a much more compelling sight than the bumper-to-bumper traffic on the freeway.

Correction. He was a more compelling view than any other I could recall. And the more I knew, the more I wanted to know about him.

"The temperature okay?" he asked, but didn't turn his head to look at me since he was driving. He was careful on the road. Careful with the passenger beside him.

"It's fine."

"You sure?" He glanced at me to confirm, his hair falling over his eyes and shadowing his gaze. "You were cold last night in the hotel."

"I was, but I was wearing a lot less clothes then."

"Your lack of clothing is definitely not something I'll ever forget." When he returned his attention to the road, he grinned, giving me a side view of the upward curve of his sculpted lips that made my stomach flutter. "But I gotta say my favorite outfit on you is none at all."

"Why am I not surprised?" I said, hiding my smile.

"What's the story behind your tee?" he asked, catching me off guard with a straight question after the sensual teasing. "It's very original."

"My gran made it."

"Oh, Jewel. I'm sorry." He seemed to sense the sudden mood switch, or maybe my fingers flexed and gave me away, threaded together with his.

"It's okay," I replied automatically, and tried to extract my fingers from his mood-barometer-sensing ones.

"Don't pull away just because I stumbled into a sensitive subject." He tightened his grip. He'd only let go of my hand once since the restaurant. Apparently, he wasn't going to do it again anytime soon.

"Do you wanna tell me about your father?" I asked, turning the question back on him.

"You withdraw or lash out whenever I hit on a sensitive subject." He sounded exasperated. "C'mon. Don't be defensive. We weren't talking about him. Tell me about her. She obviously supported your painting if she made you that T-shirt. That's pretty cool. I didn't have that kind of support in my home."

"You mentioned that, and I'm sorry I snapped at you. It's just that . . ." I pulled in a breath and let it out, giving him the truth. "The memories I have, the good and the bad, they're all I have left of her or my parents."

Rush nodded. "I understand. With my dad, before he passed, all I could focus on was the bad. My bitterness that he didn't understand me blinded me to the rest. But with him gone, I remember those other things."

"What other things?" Swiveling to more fully face him, I covered our joined hands with my other one, trying and failing not to feel so much emotion when I was connected to him like this.

"How he would work so hard on the farm, out at sunrise, home in the late afternoon with his clothes covered in dirt, exhausted. Yet he would smile whenever he saw me."

"That's nice."

"It was. If I was shooting hoops behind the garage, he would join me. If I was at the kitchen table working on math problems, he would help me. He never made me feel like I was putting him out. It was later, when I took my life in a direction he didn't understand, that things became strained between us."

"I'm sorry."

Rush glanced at me and his lips lifted, but his smile didn't reach his eyes. "I'm not gonna tell you it's okay. Because it's not. It sucks. I can never fix the breach between us. He's gone, and he's not coming back."

"I know." Tears filled my eyes. "I know exactly how you feel."

"I suspect you do." He let out a breath and flicked on the turn signal. "So, tell me some good stuff about your gran. Telling me won't take them away from you. It breathes life into the memories you cherish, right? Like now that I shared about my old man, you have that picture of him inside you too. It's something we can both share. Yeah?"

I nodded, feeling the tight bands around my heart loosen. "There was a lot of good stuff with her. She took me in when I was little. She'd just lost my grandad, but she made my coming to live with her seem like I was giving her a gift rather than being a burden."

"That's pretty amazing."

"*She* was amazing. She didn't get mad when she caught me drawing on the kitchen walls with my markers. Instead, she took me to the hobby store and bought me paints in every color, moved my bedroom furniture to the center of the room, covered it with tarps, and told me to paint the walls however I wanted. 'The world is your blank canvas,' she told me. 'Make it whatever you want.'"

"Like your shirt says."

"Yeah." I sniffed, blinking back the tears that threatened. "She was always saying beautiful, encouraging stuff like that. There's a huge hole inside me with her gone. I miss her."

"I bet you do, Jewel. I bet you do."

Rush

"Well, this is it." I gestured for Jewel to enter my home ahead of me, and started to apologize as soon as I shut the door behind us. "It's small. Minimalist decor. Don't expect too much."

She didn't reply at first. Her flip-flops snapped as she quickly passed by the dramatically curved entryway into the combination kitchen-living-dining space where she stopped.

"This is gorgeous."

"Thanks." I didn't tell her how much her approval meant, or how I'd been holding my breath, waiting for her verdict. "I've been on the road six months. I didn't want to stay in a hotel another night." There was so much more to me bringing her here, but I downplayed it.

"Stop apologizing. Flat-screen TV on the wall. Fireplace. Comfy leather couch. Shag rug. Glass fixtures. Teak accent tables. Dark hardwoods unifying it all." She spun in a circle, taking it all in. "It's eclectic. Modern. Masculine. It suits you."

Stopping where she'd started, she faced the glass doors that slid open to a four-hundred-square-foot ground-level patio.

"I've only seen part of it, but I can already tell that part is way nicer than the Chamberlain. And then there's that to seduce you." She gestured at the view. "The Pacific Ocean right at your doorstep. An unrestricted view." She swiveled to look at me, and I was immediately given an infinitely better one. "This place must've cost you a fortune."

It had. But when I'd first stepped inside, it felt right. "Luckily, it came furnished and was newly remodeled."

She shook her head. "I'm thinking I undercharged you." Her lips lifted slightly. "I might need to bring back the per-smile fee."

"Hold up there, Miss Opportunist." I moved closer, drawn to her levity, attracted to her in a way that I'd never experienced before. "I have a ridiculous mortgage."

I reached out and ran the back of my hand down her arm. I had to touch her, had to convince myself that this was real. That she was real and here inside my condo.

"I'll be eighty by the time I finally pay it off."

"Only eighty, huh?" She lifted her head from watching me stroke her skin to tilt it at the patio. "Can we go outside?"

"We," I put emphasis on the togetherness, "can go anywhere you want. Here, let me open them for you." I unlatched the doors and slid them apart. Standing aside, I gestured for her to precede me.

"You're such a gentleman. Thank you." She slipped through the gap I'd created and moved straight to the glass half wall that overlooked the beach.

I was hardly that, but I shrugged out of my jacket, tossing it onto one of the easy chairs, and followed her, my strides intent.

My arms banded tight around her slender shoulders as I drew her backward into my embrace. She could still enjoy the view with her back to my front, but I had to be connected to her while she did. Her chest expanded as she pulled in a deep breath.

"I don't know how you ever manage to leave," she whispered as if the moment were sacred. Or maybe that was the way I read it, because to me, that was exactly how it felt.

"It's not easy. This is the one place where I feel like I have some peace. Where I can be still. Where I can be myself."

She pulled in a quick breath but didn't speak.

Did she get it, the underlying significance of what it meant for me to allow her into my private places? The passenger seat in my car. Here in my personal sanctuary. No other woman had been in those places except her.

"I love it here." She let out a sigh, relaxing into me, leaning her head on my shoulder. The sea breeze combed through her thick gleaming hair like I'd longed to since I saw her outside Taix without the wig. But for the moment, I had what I wanted.

Her.

18

Jewel

"Baby." Rush gently spun me around in his arms.

My eyes were misty. Did he know why? Did he sense how quickly I was falling for him? In that moment, I thought maybe he did.

He stilled, his metallic gaze linking me to him. But what did I have to bind him to me?

I didn't move, didn't breathe, didn't even think as he slowly lifted his hands. Sliding them into my hair, he framed my face. Lowering his head, he breathed out my name as if it were a plea . . . or a prayer.

"Jewel."

His fingers tangled in my hair as he brought our faces together and pressed his lips to mine. Warmth like the clouds parting to reveal the sun replaced the emptiness inside me.

This. This was the kiss I'd avoided last night. So much for being in control.

I reveled in it, in him, in *now*. Rich waves of luxurious sensation lapping at my skin, my entire body tingled as he moved his mouth ever so softly against mine.

"Open, baby. Let me taste you."

I parted my lips willingly, surrendering to my desire, and he slipped his wet tongue between them.

A bolt of heat shot through me the moment his tongue touched mine, and I let out a moan. He groaned in reply, and the vibrations from his pleasure zinged straight to my clit.

He shifted closer and I melted into him, feeling his hard cock against me, right where I ached. He stroked my tongue with his, and my legs began to tremble. When he did it again, I could swear I felt the ground quake. I began to suck on each thrust and curled my fingers around his forearms.

"Wrap your legs around me." He released my mouth to whisper, trailing kisses across the curve of my cheek. "Baby, baby, baby." His warm breath tickled my ear. "Hop up. I'll catch you."

When I jumped, he was ready, his large hands a ledge, his fingers digging crescents into the underside of my ass. I twined my arms around his strong neck, clinging to him as if my life depended on maintaining the connection, and maybe it did.

He brought our mouths together again, fanning the heat between us to an intense flame. Higher and hotter, deeper and deeper, I fell under his compelling spell. The catalyst for the madness was his deep, drugging, demanding kisses.

On one level, I realized he was moving, that the roar of the waves faded behind me. His kiss consumed me as his strides took us back inside, down a hall and into a large bedroom. His steps were fast, his goal as certain as his lips were.

Devouring me. Eating me alive. Swallowing me whole.

Suddenly, I was sliding down the long, sculpted length of his body. He ripped his mouth from mine as my feet touched the floor. Swaying, I stared at him. His hair was disheveled from my impatient fingers. His gaze was wild, his muscles visibly tensed.

Without warning, he pounced. Grabbing my tee by the hem, he yanked it over my head. My hands shaking, I fumbled for his belt buckle while he reached behind my back and unhooked my bra, then whipped the straps down my arms and tossed the scrap of lace aside.

My nipples honed to points in anticipation. I wanted my breasts crushed to his hard chest. I wanted to score his smooth skin with the tips. I wanted to feel the weight of his body bearing down on me, but to get that, I needed him naked. I wanted to see all of him, wanted to experience all of him. But he wasn't done with my mouth.

He plunged his hands into my hair, bringing our lips back together again. While he drove me crazy with his lips, teeth, and tongue, I unthreaded his belt and released the top button of his jeans.

"More. Need more." He growled out the words, tugging urgently at my hair to get me to part my mouth wider.

He kissed me like he was drowning and needed to gulp air from my mouth to breathe. I kissed him back just as desperately, giving him all the oxygen I had.

I clung to him as the room tilted and my mind spun.

Without releasing my mouth, he moved me across the room until we reached the mattress. I dropped onto the bed, and he followed me down. Our descent into further insanity was completely under his control, so I surrendered to him. There was no other way.

His gaze intense, he peeled my jeans off my body. I had no idea where my flip-flops were. I only knew that one moment I was partially clothed on his bed, and in the next, I was completely naked and so was he.

"I can't go slow." With his hands propped on the mattress on either side of my shoulders, he swept a devouring glance over me.

"I don't want you to go slow."

His eyes flared, the color of smoke, fueled by out-of-control desire. Moving his weight to one arm, he curled his chiseled lips upward as he reached between my legs.

"You're soaked." He growled the words approvingly, gliding his fingers along the slick skin on my inner thighs. "All this wetness for me."

My breathing hitched when he deftly parted my curls and swirled his thumb in a slow, deliberate circle around my needy clit.

"Rush." Fiery sensations blazed through me, and I started to shake. "Please."

"I'm right here, baby."

He spread my thighs apart and moved between them. As I watched, my breathing choppy, he grabbed a packet, ripped it open, and rolled a condom on. After positioning himself, he slid inside me, filling me with his hard length. Stretching me with his thickness. Covering my quivering body with his steady strength.

I ran my hands all over him, everywhere I could reach. Greedily, I explored his chiseled contours and smooth skin as he pumped his hot, steely cock in and out of me. No shallow fucks this time. Just deep and deep and deep.

"Baby," he choked out. "You're burning me up. You feel so good."

"You feel so right inside me."

Every guy had been wrong before him. All of them.

Did he get it? Did he guess the truths that I couldn't speak? I'd been lost before he found me on that street corner.

I grabbed his ass. It was so taut. And it felt so good to feel him flexing as he pounded his cock inside me.

"Yes!" I shouted. "Yes! Yes!"

Each thrust was perfect. Every single stroke jolted my clit and me with electrical current.

"Rush!" I screamed his name as my climax raced toward me at the speed of lightning streaking across a stormy sky.

"Jewel! Baby!" He hammered into me, then stiffened. "Fuck!"

His fevered eruption catapulted me to a place where everything we'd ever known disappeared. It was only the two of us alone in a remade universe, fractured particles forged by our passion into a new whole.

19

Rush

I pulled out, my heart still hammering, and my jaw dropped as she immediately turned and slipped away from me.

"Mind if I use your shower first?" she murmured.

"Of course not." My brows dipped as she quickly scurried from the bed. "Anything you want, baby," I added softly, lost in the show of her sexy ass and hips swaying as she padded to the master bath across the hall.

She didn't acknowledge me. Had she even heard me?

The shower door creaked, and the water came on.

Probably not.

Turning to the side, I disposed of the condom in a nearby wastebasket, then came up onto my elbows and stared at the spot on the bed where she'd only just been. I reached out and laid my hand on the wrinkled sheet. It was still warm.

My spine still tingled from coming so hard. And within my chest, a very strong emotion was careening around that I didn't want to process alone.

I think better with her in my arms. Turning that thought over in my mind, I sat up and threw my legs over the side as another realization hit me. *And I need her back inside them.*

My cell rang, and I sighed. I wanted to ignore it, but it was display side up, revealing the caller's name. *Brad.* With no other choice, I slid my cell the rest of the way out of the pocket of my jeans and answered the call.

"Yo."

"Why didn't you tell me she threw out the entire album!"

With the phone clamped between my neck and shoulder as I stepped into my jeans, I cringed as he blasted my ear. I'd been anticipating his call and his displeasure. Only with him and Bree and the holidays, I hadn't been anticipating it quite so soon.

"She's right," I said carefully. "It sucks."

"It wasn't *that* bad."

"It wasn't good either."

"You get that the entire cost of recording a new album is coming out of your wallet?"

"Yeah."

"Yeah? Is that all you can say? What the hell's up with you?"

"How do you mean?" I stared at the open door to the bathroom as the water shut off and the shower door creaked again.

"I've been dropping hints about those tracks since they were laid down. You nearly snapped my head off at the mere idea that I didn't think they were up to your standards. Why the change? Where's the real Rush McMahon? This can't be you. You almost seem . . . amiable?"

"I haven't been that bad."

"Oh yeah, you have."

"I met someone."

"Last night? She must be a miracle worker."

She was a miracle, all right. A miracle I didn't deserve.

"A groupie?" he asked.

"No." I ran a hand through my hair and gave it to him straight. "A hooker."

I held my cell away from my ear as he released a string of expletives at top volume.

Jewel took that inopportune time to reappear, a fluffy white towel draped around her breasts. She stopped in midstride, her bare feet seeming to snag on the hardwoods.

She'd heard me. I saw the flash of hurt in her gaze before she dropped her chin and moved to the pile of her clothes on the floor.

"Are you insane!" he shouted. "Did you get a nondisclosure?"

Her hair a reddish-brown curtain hiding her face, Jewel slid on her panties.

"No, I didn't," I said carefully. "It's not like that."

"What is it then, Rush? You tell me. Because I'm thinking the major amount of cash that we're going to have to fork over for new recordings is going to be nothing compared to the amount we're going to have to flush to make this mistake go away. *If* we can get her to go away without bleeding you dry. What did you do with her? Did she video any of it? Does she have anything she can blackmail you with?"

That pleasant careening feeling came to a sudden stop inside me.

Am I being played?

I knew what I felt, but as I watched Jewel pull on her clothes, I suddenly wasn't sure.

"I'll have to call you back."

"She's there with you now," he said flatly.

"Yes."

Dressed, Jewel lifted her gaze, and her eyes met mine. Shadows swirled in them like the tempest swirled within me.

"Listen, I need to go."

"Have you paid her yet?"

"Last night. Not today."

Her hair an auburn halo around her delicate shoulders, Jewel shifted from one foot to another. She didn't look like a hooker. She looked young, beautiful, and uncertain.

Unable to take my eyes off of her, I said into the phone, "I'll talk to you later."

"Get her to sign something, Rush. Pay her. Get a receipt."

I ended the call while he was still shouting instructions.

"I should get going," she said, her eyes glassy and bright.

"Do you want to go?" My lips flattened. Brad's cautions echoed in my brain.

She dropped her gaze. "It's late. Cam will worry."

"That's not an answer." I tossed the phone on the bed, rejecting caution as I moved toward her. Gliding my hands up her arms, I felt the shiver that rolled through her. "Baby, look at me."

"What do you want me to say?" Her chin rose, her eyes pools of liquid gold. "I *am* a hooker. We have an agreement. I provided a service. As soon as you pay me, I'll leave."

"Jewel." My fingers flexed on her skin. "There's more."

"There's not." She shook her head, and the wetness in her eyes shimmered. "You said it right on the phone. I am who I am. Don't make it complicated. Don't . . ."

Her voice cracked, deflating the anger that had risen within me at her rejection.

"How about this? I pay you, and then you stay for a while. You just being you. Me being just me. Without money being between us."

Light eclipsed the shadows. Her unshed tears evaporated. And the shutters that had been hiding her true self flew open as she gave me a fleeting glimpse of what I wanted.

Her.

All of her.

Jewel

His stormy eyes intense, he asked, "Sound good?"

It sounded dangerous. And yet I found myself agreeing like a naive fool.

"Yes," I whispered.

He yanked me against him, sealing our unlikely agreement with a searing kiss. No tongue, no teeth, just his firm resolve overwhelming my uncertain compliance.

His cell rang again.

"Shouldn't you get that?" I asked, frustrated at how the real world didn't want to give us a break.

"I don't want to. It's not a ringtone I recognize. I've got what I want right here. It can wait."

"Okay." I breathed out the word, searching his eyes and finding only sincerity within them.

I twined my arms around his neck. Lifting me onto my toes and using his grip on my upper arms, he returned his mouth to mine. I surrendered to him and the persuasion of having his lips moving across mine.

Only the ringing started up again.

His fingers tightening, he broke the kiss and set me from him. "I'd better get that. It's my private number."

"It's okay." I rubbed my arms, trying to erase the chill bumps that had suddenly erupted on my skin without his warm hands.

"Hello," he said, and his brow creased immediately. "Yes, this is he. And you are?"

In the pause that I assumed was a reply on the other end of the line, his eyes rounded.

"Yes, she is. Yes, she's fine. No, I haven't harmed her. Hold on, she's standing right here, wondering who I'm speaking to. You can ask her yourself."

He thrust the phone at me, and his lips twitched.

"It's your friend. She seems kind of worked up."

"Jewel Serena Anderson," Cam screeched into my ear. "Why aren't you answering your phone?"

Oh. Shit.

"I think I left it in the car, along with my bag."

"I'll get it for you," Rush said, and I nodded.

"That's not cool." Cam's tone was full of disapproval.

It wasn't. Unwise decisions littered the floor all around me. "I know."

"Are you really okay?"

"No. Yes. Mostly."

"What the hell does that mean? What's going on? You've been gone for hours."

"I met his boss. We ate lunch. He brought me to his house. Well, his condo. It's on the beach. In Santa Monica. It's gorgeous." I was rambling, not letting her get in a word. Because I knew the ones she would say would crumble my compliance.

"Not a hotel?"

"No."

"His boss?"

"Yeah. We met her at the restaurant where he used to bus tables. He put in a good word for me to apply for a position. It's a nice place. Food's included as a benefit of employment. It's not too far from us."

"A job like that's not going to come close to paying the rent, honey."

"I know."

"And you have a record."

"I know." Deep down, I knew it was impossible. I sank onto the bed.

"Girls like you and me, we're not girlfriends with our clients."

I nodded without speaking.

"You know it won't work out."

But my heart wanted what it wanted.

"Just a little while longer, Cam," I said as Rush returned.

He set my purse on the teak dresser, and he lifted a wad of bills to show me he was keeping his end of the bargain. I nodded numbly, watching him tuck them inside.

"A little while longer," Cam said, "and it's going to hurt more when you wise up and end it."

"Yes, I know." I was going to be obliterated. I could already feel tiny fractures opening up inside my chest, just thinking about how it would be.

"Or he ends it. It's worse when it goes that way." She spoke from experience . . . experience I had been around to witness. I had to shoulder a month of rent alone after she'd gotten her heart broken.

"I can't . . ." I coughed, trying to clear the tightness from my throat. "I already agreed to try."

"Oh, Jewel."

"I love you, Cam." What I didn't say, she knew. I was going to need her every bit as much as she'd needed me after she let her feelings blind her.

"I love you too. And I'm here."

"I have my phone back now. I'll talk to you soon."

"In the morning?"

"Yes. If he wants me to stay the night," I said, glancing at Rush, and he nodded. "I'm staying the night." Ridiculous how my heart soared because of his simple nod.

“Okay. Tomorrow it is. But, Jewel, just to remind you in case you’ve forgotten, you’ve got regulars on the calendar. The money Mr. Rich and Famous gave you is only gonna stretch so long with only one of us working. Christmas is our busiest season. Makes up for the slower times.”

My throat completely closed. Be with someone else after Rush? Just the thought made me want to hurl.

“Noted.” I dropped my head.

“Do what you feel you have to. I support you. Friends forever goes with the territory without it needing to be said.” Her tone softer now, Cam said, “Just be careful. Don’t let this go on with him too long.”

20

Rush

"Hey, pretty girl."

I sank onto the bed beside Jewel. She looked so worried, a concern that matched mine. But knowing we were both scared, would that be enough to keep this from becoming a mistake for both of us?

"What can I do to make you smile?"

"You're not responsible for making me happy, Rush."

"Maybe not, but I want you to be happy. How can I do that? Tell me, and it's done." I might not have the answers to how this might end up, but right now, all I wanted was to see her smile.

"Saying things like that." Taking my hand, she turned it over and traced the lines on my palm, seeming to give my question serious consideration before she answered. "Meaning what you say the way I can tell you do and following through is a very good start."

"That's too easy."

"Maybe." She let out a sigh. "But maybe it's easy because that's just you."

"That's so not me. I'm a selfish, entitled, narcissistic bastard. I told you that when we first met."

"I remember. But you're not that way with me anymore, or you hardly are."

"I'm trying to be on my best behavior because I don't *want* to be like that with you." I swiveled to more fully face her, jostling her in my bed. "When I come here, it's a relief to leave all the rock-star bullshit on the other side of the door."

"I think that's the key with me, and you too. Just being ourselves. The other stuff that tries to intrude, let's set it aside and not worry about tomorrow." She stared deeply into my eyes. "In this moment, right now between the two of us, there's an eternity to experience."

"Who said that? Your gran?"

"No, just me. But it's the me I am because of her influence. The better parts. The parts that seem to rise to the surface naturally because you're gentle and kind to me."

She swept her thumb across my palm and turned my hand over to tap the cross on my ring. The brush of her skin ignited a light within my chest that had gone out after my father died.

I wanted Jewel again, no surprise there. But we'd just done that.

Our bodies worked exceptionally well together. I wanted—I *needed*—to work on bridging the gaps that separated us emotionally. That was the great unknown.

I'd probably fuck it up, but if I got it right, I might succeed with her.

"So, the here and now. What would you like to do?" I asked her.

"I don't know. What is there to do?"

"We could go to the beach. It's too cold to swim, but we could roll up our jeans and dip our feet in the water."

"That sounds nice." She gave me a small but genuine smile.

It wasn't that big smile I'd gotten from her before, but a tiny light inside me blazed brightly with satisfaction anyway.

Maybe I could do this. Maybe I wouldn't fuck it up with her after all.

"Then let's do it." I stood and held out my hand, and she placed hers within mine.

"Do you wanna have a shower before we go?" she asked.

"Nah. I'll just get sandy out there. We can take a shower together after." I tucked her into my side and headed for the door. "You've been to the beach before, haven't you?"

"No."

I gave her an incredulous look. "You're kidding."

"There's no beach in Tennessee."

"But when you came out here . . ."

"There was never any reason to go. Landon wasn't the beach-going type."

"Was he the douche?" The hand I'd placed on the small of her back curled into a fist.

"Yes."

"What was he like?"

"He didn't want to have to work hard for anything. And he didn't have time to do anything except what he wanted to do."

"You forgot he was a total idiot."

"No, I didn't forget that." Her lips twitched.

I steered her through the sliding doors, locked them after we were through, and gestured to the stairs down to the sidewalk.

Jewel glanced at me. "What was your fiancée like?"

Unprepared for the question, I stumbled. Sharing about Brenda was like walking through a field of land mines.

"I'm sorry," Jewel said. "It seemed natural to ask, but it's none of my business."

"No, it's okay. She just . . . she had an idea about how our lives should go. I had another."

"You were on different pages."

"We were on different planets." I pulled in a breath as we crossed the sidewalk, and let it out when my toes sank in the sand. "She wanted me to stay in our small town, take over the family farm, raise kids."

"What did you want?"

"She was my first and only girlfriend. Before I left for college, I thought I wanted those things too. Then I got a taste of the world outside Pendleton, Indiana, and I've never wanted to go back since."

It was a shame, really. The rift between my parents and me had destroyed most of the nostalgic feelings I could have had toward my hometown.

Jewel gave me a curious look. "How did your music come into it?"

"It was more a symptom than a cause. We grew apart long before I started having success in the small clubs around the college. I didn't see it at the time, but looking back, I realize the farm-family agenda was her dream, her way or the highway. Given an ultimatum, I chose the latter."

And then there was the fact that I'd strayed. Brenda and I had been on a break at the time. But the way I'd done it sucked.

I didn't want Jewel to know I was a total idiot like her ex, so I reached out and picked her up by her waist. The girl was too easy to lift; she needed to eat more. I had an idea about dinner, but for now, I spun her in a circle and then pulled her down with me to the sand.

"Enough talking about the past." I sat her on my lap and nuzzled her neck.

She giggled. "Your whiskers tickle."

"Ah, a weak spot to exploit. Where else are you ticklish, I wonder."

"Nowhere." She jumped up and scampered toward the water.

"I'm thinking that's not true. Get those hems rolled up. I'm gonna give you a tour of the beach. The 411 on the 90401. Then when your guard's down and you least expect it, I'll find those secret tickle spots and I'll exploit them." I wiggled my fingers, and she grinned at me.

"You can try," she said, a challenge in her voice. "But to get to them, you have to catch me."

Jewel took off like a flash, and I stood there in awe, watching her run away. Her hair streamed like a sunset-hued banner behind her. Her tinkling laughter drifted back to me on the wind.

She wasn't worried anymore.

She was having fun.

I was having fun.

So I'd stumbled over a few unexpected questions about past relationships. I hadn't done all that bad if I could still make her laugh after that.

Grinning, I jumped up and broke into a jog after her, pretty damn pleased with myself. After all, I'd made Jewel happy without even really trying.

And her happiness?

It made me happy too.

Jewel

Rush caught me by the waist, lifted me into the air, and threw me over his shoulder in a fireman's carry.

"Don't you dare toss me in the water." I beat my fists against his back, having a fair idea now why his skin was so tanned. He obviously went all over the place with his shirt off and didn't think anything of it.

Me?

It was all I could do to string two words together when presented with his half-naked body.

"Stop hitting me, and I might consider putting you down." He feigned a release, and I slid down off his shoulder and into his ready arms. He grinned at me as a wave splashed into him from behind.

"I'm stopping. I surrender." I lifted my hands into the air.

"I changed my mind."

His gaze dropped to my mouth, and my lips started to tingle. Then my whole body shimmered with warmth when he pressed his mouth to mine.

But he didn't stop there. He traced my lips with his tongue and slipped it inside my mouth so I could taste him—a dash of lemon and sage from lunch, but also something uniquely Rush. His taste was incredibly addictive, just like he was.

"You're all wet," I told him when he ended the kiss and set me down on the sand.

"I bet you are too." He arched a brow.

I nodded, my cheeks burning.

"Love this." Framing my face in his large hands, he brushed his thumbs over my rosy skin.

"It's silly."

"How so?"

"For my face to turn red as if I'm an innocent when you tease me."

"What you think is silly, I think is beautiful."

"If you say so." I turned my head, but he captured my chin.

"I do. It's becoming, really. Demure, and I get it now because of your upbringing. You're also capable, because of all you've endured. Caring, because that's just your nature." His eyebrows waggled playfully. "Naughty too. I like it when you let it all go and talk dirty."

A laugh burst free. "I'll bet you do."

"I like you, Jewel. Wouldn't change a fucking thing."

Those words gave me pause, and I stilled for a moment.

"Take that," he said, "and file this moment away for eternity."

I nodded, planning to do just that. I'd commit to memory everything about this day. The walk. The teasing. The kiss.

And the other part, earlier today? The coming so hard in his bed that emotion had leaked from me and sent me scurrying away to hide it?

I wouldn't file that away. I would hold it close to my heart, a treasured reminder to myself that no matter how this went with him, I was all those things he had said. He treated me as though I were. I'd felt it profoundly when we were joined together.

"Hey, you still with me?" He searched my face as if trying to read my thoughts, and he might get them. In such a short time, he'd gotten very good at reading me.

"I'm with you." My stomach grumbled, deciding to make its presence known.

"The beast has spoken." His lips curved. "Will you eat sushi?"

"Never had it."

"It's really good. They have rolls and ahi tuna poke bowls at a takeaway place up ahead off the boardwalk. Are you willing to try some?"

"I would try anything with you," I said honestly, giving him something to make him pause too.

"Ah, darlin', you should never give me an opening like that. To do all the things I've thought of to do with you would take more than a single day. It would take a lifetime."

21

Rush

We returned to the condo and ate outside on the porch, listening to the waves and not talking much. She asked how I met the guys in the band, and I gave her the simplified version. How I'd put an ad in Craigslist.

I asked her how she met her roommate, and she explained about the rescue at the shelter. I sensed there was more beneath the surface of her brief answer, but we'd covered a lot of heavy territory today. By mutual but unspoken understanding, we kept the conversation easy and light.

"So, what's your verdict on the raw ahi tuna?" I glanced at her empty bowl.

"Loved it." Her chair was so close, her knee touched mine. "Not something I should make a habit of liking, though, at eighteen fifty a bowl."

"Beachfront prices. It's probably more reasonably priced inland."

"Probably." She smiled as I covered her hand with mine and softly stroked her knuckles with the pad of my thumb.

"Mmm," she murmured. "I like how you do that."

"What?" I was staring at her again. The glow of the sun had set her hair ablaze.

"Touch me whenever I'm close, like it's a compulsion. And you do it so rhythmically too. It's soothing and seductive."

"That's my plan." I grinned at her. "Only not really. I just can't help it. If you're near, I want to be connected. If it's soothing to you, it's that to me too. Rhythmic? Guilty as charged. I'm a musician. Seductive? Hell, I'll take credit, but if anyone is under someone's spell, it's me under yours."

She leaned in and pressed her mouth to mine. Her lips were lush and tasted like peach nectar.

It was a soft, brief kiss. The first she'd initiated, and sexy as hell. She started to move away, but I slid my hand around her nape and held her in place so I could capture her lips and take the kiss deeper.

When I finally pulled back, she looked a little dazed.

The hushed peacefulness of the evening fell over us as gently as the ocean breeze. We held hands, watching the sun go down, and when it was gone, I got up and flicked on the switch to ignite the gas fire pit. I grabbed a folded blanket from a nearby basket, shook it out, and draped it around her shoulders.

"Aren't you going to be cold?" She glanced up at me, her eyes reflecting the flames as I smoothed the blanket around her.

"Not for long. We'll share." I gestured to the oversized cushioned lounger facing the water. "Come sit with me."

I held out my hand to help her up. She took it and clutched the blanket to her chest with the other. After I lowered myself into the chair, I scooted back to rest against the cushion and spread my knees wide for her.

"Sit here." I patted the empty space I'd created.

She sat down and I did the rest, pulling her back into my chest.

"This doesn't seem fair," she said after a moment.

I didn't know what she meant. It felt pretty fucking good to me. "What doesn't?"

"Me with the blanket. You out in the cold."

"I'm fine. Really." I sifted my fingers through her hair, imagining the silky softness of her fiery locks falling around my cock.

"Let's share."

She shifted, rocking her sexy ass over me, and my cock thickened. I suppressed a groan.

"Help me." She offered the ends of the blanket. "We can snuggle under it together."

Snuggling was no longer all I had in mind.

"Baby, I—"

She turned and tilted her head back to peer up at me. "No one can see what we do underneath here."

Not needing another hint, I lowered my head and took her lips. I let her worry about the blanket and propriety. While kissing her, I peeled her tee up, and only released her mouth briefly to whip the shirt off. Tossing it aside, I recaptured her lips, thrusting my tongue inside her mouth and unclasping her bra at the same time.

She moaned into my mouth while I slid my fingers over her soft skin and filled my hands with her lush tits. Strumming her tight nipples with my thumbs, I kissed her like there was no tomorrow, only today, only now, and she kissed me back with equal abandon.

Fucking phenomenal.

"Rush." She gasped, pulling her lips from mine, and spun around to face me. "I need you. I want you." She moved to straddle me.

"Not here."

Fucking cameras were everywhere. I didn't give a shit about me, but I didn't want anyone else to see her naked. Yanking the blanket over her, I pulled her to my chest, straightened with her in my arms, and stood to take us back inside.

"Hold on tight," I told her. "Hands around my neck."

As she clutched my shoulders, I walked us through the open doors, then closed and latched them.

"Mouth," I grumbled irritably, resenting every obstacle that kept me from the prize. She lifted her face, and I leaned over to sip fruit-flavored nectar from her perfect lips.

My intended destination was the bedroom, but I didn't make it there.

Releasing her mouth, I lowered her to the floor and unfastened her jeans. She hissed when my fingers skimmed her pussy as I removed her panties. Breathing hard, I stared at the naked beauty of her as I unbuttoned my jeans and kicked out of them and my boxers.

Afterward, I stalked straight to her, and with my hands on her shoulders, walked her backward into the closest wall.

She knew what was up. Me. My cock bobbed, aimed at her pussy.

"Stay," I told her.

I raked my gaze over her before bending to remove a condom packet from my jeans. Rolling it on, I stared at her while she watched me. My naked goddess beside the flat screen in my living room.

"Baby . . ." In awe, I knelt before her and placed both hands on her thighs. Gliding my palms over her legs and her silky skin, I grasped her hips and ran my nose through her curls, inhaling deeply.

"Rush." She trembled in my hands.

"I have to taste you." I made a tight frame for her pussy and swept the curls aside with my thumbs.

She gasped and plunged her hands into my hair, pulling at it as I found and rolled my tongue over her. I lapped at her sweet little clit, saturating my tongue with the thick gloss that covered it.

"Rush." Her fingers tugged urgently as I circled and sucked. "No more. Please. No more."

I licked her one last time, savoring her taste that was similar to her mouth, only richer and riper.

Rising quickly from the floor, I dove my hands into her hair and captured her mouth, letting her see how good she tasted. I didn't hold back. I wanted her to know how much she excited me. Just as turned on, she moved her hands frantically across my back and purred her appreciation.

"Hop up, baby," I murmured against her kiss-swollen lips. Grabbing the rounded globes of her ass in each hand, I squeezed. "Now."

She jumped. I positioned myself and glided inside her smoothly. All the way, until I was buried as deep as I could go. My lips finding hers parted and willing, I fucked her mouth with my unrelenting tongue, and pounded into her sweet pussy with the blunt force of my ruthless cock.

No finesse. No control. I hammered her with my desire, and she returned my fervor.

Her arms leveraged on my shoulders, she bounced on my cock. Her tits put on a hell of a show as she rode me using my hair as her reins. Up, I surged inside her, driving deep. Down, she plunged, impaling herself.

Hot. Fast. Quick.

My balls drew tight. My spine blazed.

Into her slick heat, I thrust one final time, and then I was coming. Hard. She followed, her body shuddering in my hold as her pussy spasmed around my cock.

Her pleasure prolonged mine. Making it more. Making it shared.

Making it mutual.

22

Jewel

"That feels so good." In the shower, I leaned my wet head on his strong shoulder. His fingers tugged rhythmically as he sorted through the strands to ensure he'd rinsed out all the suds.

"Never had anyone wash your hair?"

"No." Never had any man put his mouth on my clit either. Never tasted myself from a lover's lips.

I'd thought I was jaded, that I'd seen and done everything since coming to LA, but with Rush I was discovering that wasn't the case. He made everything seem brand new.

Right, even.

His fingers underneath my hair, he lifted and brought the waterlogged mass of it to my back, then glided his hands over my front, up and down over the slippery slopes of my breasts, and then back and forth more lightly across the peaked nipples. His movement stirred up splashes of spray and renewed desire.

We'd already had sex against the wall in the living room and then another time in the shower. Yet it wasn't enough. Not nearly. There was an insatiable craving building just beneath the surface.

But I couldn't indulge that craving. Because I couldn't keep him.

Rush turned me around gently, his fingers curling around my shoulders. He blinked at me, his lashes wet, and his eyes narrowed as they searched mine. "Don't go in the morning."

"I can't stay."

"Why not? Is being here with me such a bad thing?"

"No." Turning my head away, I squeezed my eyes shut.

Don't let him see the truth. Don't speak it, I told myself, and yet I did.

"It's because it is that good." I opened my eyes, and his satisfaction blazed back at me.

"So say yes."

Didn't he see the cost, the pieces of my heart I would lose, and the potential revenue? I had another day, a week maybe—if he wanted me to stay that long—before it would come to a critical point. The money he'd already paid me could cover my expenses for a little while, but not indefinitely.

Pressure built inside me. I longed to stay, but it was safer and more practical to go.

I stared at him, my eyes burning, knowing the answer I should give. But the words that slipped from my lips came straight from my heart.

"Yes. Yes, I'll stay."

With a sigh of relief, he pulled me into him, and my soft curves yielded to his hard planes. Lowering his head, he crushed his lips to mine.

Rush made slow, tender, beautiful love to me again while the water pelted our bodies and washed away the tears that escaped my eyes. Afterward, he dried my body and then his with a towel.

Naked, but warm with him holding me, I felt boneless as he carried me to his bed. He laid me on the cool sheets, then came around to climb into the other side of the bed. Drowsy, I watched him with infatuated eyes, taking in his long and lean body, handsome and compelling face, liquid-silver eyes.

Shifting to his side, he lifted his arm, and I scooted backward into him, loving the way he tucked me to him. His cock, hot and temptingly hard, pressed against my ass as he wrapped his strong arms around me.

His breathing leveled out, and he dozed off almost immediately. It was just that easy for him. But me, I stayed awake for hours, racking my brain for some way that I wouldn't lose in the end.

When dawn lightened the pitch-black of night to shadowy gray, I finally drifted off, but I still didn't have an answer.

Rush

The feeling I got waking with her in my arms, knowing she'd agreed to stay without money being between us anymore? Nothing in my life had ever made me feel better.

In fact, everything seemed better. The sun streaming through the blinds was brighter. My heart lighter. My mind sharper. And there was an insistent tune playing like a soundtrack inside my head that I longed to scribble down.

But as Jewel stirred beside me, stretching her slender arms above her head and dislodging the sheet from her tits, I had a more overwhelming compulsion.

"Good morning," I said, lowering my head as she cracked open eyes more beautifully golden than the sun.

My cell blared, stopping me before I could act on my compulsion. She turned her head toward the sound, and I pressed my lips to her cheek.

"Fucking hell," I said. The kiss was nice, but it was only a start. I wanted to skim my mouth over every single inch of her body.

Sighing, I shifted in bed and snagged my phone, intending to shut the damn thing off, but I changed my mind when I saw who was calling and how many text messages I'd already missed.

"Hey, Jack, is everything all right? What's going on?"

"I'm gonna kill him. This time I'm really going to. Honest to God, I really will."

"What'd he do?"

"He had sex with my wife."

My grip tightened on the phone. "The phone thing was a lark. He gets bored easily. You know how he is."

"Yeah, believe me, I know."

"He doesn't take anything seriously."

"He seemed really serious in *my* bed last night with *my* wife."

Fuck. "The reconciliation with her is over then?"

"Oh yeah."

Thanks, Ben. Way to completely screw over the group.

"She was the best thing that ever happened to me."

Uh, maybe not the best. Jack had shared shit with her that Ben and I both knew, but rather than help him navigate the pain of his past, she preferred to use it to exploit him.

"Where are you at right now?" I glanced at Jewel to find her gazing at me, her eyes wide. She was fully awake now.

"On my way to his house to strangle him."

"No you're not. Do a U-turn and come to Santa Monica to see me."

"You're not gonna talk me out of it."

"I'm not gonna say I won't try. What kind of friend would I be if I didn't intervene when I knew you were on your way to commit murder?"

Jack snorted. “I’m replaceable. You’ll find another drummer.”

“Not true. I was floundering as a musician until I met you and Ben.”

“Maybe.”

“Maybe you’ll come by?”

He sighed. “Yeah.”

“I’ll get some coffee going,” I said, then clicked off the call and tossed the phone aside.

Jewel turned over and scooted to climb out of her side of the bed, but I snagged her. Tugging her by the waist, I pulled her back into my arms.

“I had other plans for the morning,” I growled into the side of her neck.

“I know you did,” she said, and turned her head to kiss me on the lips.

It wasn’t much of a kiss, just a chaste press of her mouth to mine. But with her naked, that kiss did insane things to me.

Pulling back with a small smile, she said, “Don’t apologize.”

When she wriggled out of my hold, I let her go, mourning the loss of her nakedness and the opportunity to fuck her.

Jewel yanked the top sheet from the bed and draped it around herself. “You’re being a good friend.” She gave me an approving nod and left the bedroom with the sheet trailing behind her.

Was I? I leaned back against the upholstered headboard and gave that some thought.

A good friend would have spoken up and done more to prevent Jack from marrying the bitch in the first place. Ben wasn’t the only one she’d put the moves on, but I’d been wrapped up in my own apathy at the time. My give-a-shit meter was on empty after my father’s funeral.

Singing came from the other room, and my ears perked up. It was Jewel. Some type of gospel hymn, not a pop tune, but she sang it incredibly well.

Amazed, I shook my head. Jewel was full of surprises. Every time I turned around, I found more about her that I discovered I liked. More to fill the empty spaces inside me.

Jewel

Rush was handsome, undeniably good-looking. I'd been downplaying his looks when I first set eyes on him because guys who drove cars like his and looked like him weren't for girls like me. Still weren't for me, long term.

But Jack Howard, the drummer in Rush's band? He was cute and approachable, the type I would normally go for.

Short brown hair. Soulful matching eyes. Board shorts. Muscle tee. Flip-flops. Trying to look Cali cool, he had a lean surfer physique, but his skin was too pale to pull it off.

His dark eyes followed me as I skirted around the dining table. He acted like he wasn't checking me out, but he so was as I returned from the kitchen with the carafe to fill the coffee mugs for both men.

But his interest didn't make my heart flutter. He didn't give off an arrogant vibe that said *I'm going to rock your world and leave you reeling*. It was more *let me rock you to a steady beat*, though his own world seemed more than a little unbalanced at the moment.

"Where did you say you and Rush met?" Jack asked. Again.

Rush scowled at him. "She didn't. I didn't. It's none of your business. And keep your eyes to yourself." He grabbed my hand and took the carafe from me, then placed it on the table. "Leave it, darlin', yeah?"

"Maybe I should come back at another time." Jack's gaze flicked first to me, then Rush. "You seem pretty busy."

"We are, but you made it seem like a life-or-death matter." Rush frowned. "So, which is it?"

The sudden loud slam at the front of the condo startled me, and I moved closer to Rush's side. He put his arm around me.

"Where the hell is he?" a deep voice roared.

Heavy footsteps echoed in the kitchen before a tall man with wavy ebony hair and emerald-green eyes appeared. He hadn't taken the longer route through the living room. Like Jack, he seemed well acquainted with the layout of the condo.

His eyes narrowed at Jack. "Thought I'd find you here."

"You fucking bastard." Shoving back his chair, Jack launched himself at the other man, but the punch he threw was dodged. Pivoting on his heel, he reared back to deliver another.

"Cut this shit out!" Rush shouted.

Pushing himself between the two men, he grabbed Jack's shoulders and gave him a hard shake. Red-faced, Jack glared past Rush at the newcomer, who seemed strangely calm when confronted with Jack's fury.

Gesturing at Jack, the black-haired man hung his head and said flatly, "Go ahead and hit me if it'll make you feel better."

"She's my wife, Ben. I should kill you." Jack spat out the words, struggling in Rush's hold. When Jack closed his eyes for a second, then held up his hands in surrender, Rush let him go but stayed close.

"You should thank me for doing you a favor." The newcomer, Ben, slid his hand through his inky-black hair, pulling it off his forehead to reveal a brooding brow and high cheekbones, the perfect complement to his cleft chin.

My eyes wide, I stood at the other end of the table, watching the drama unfold.

Rush hadn't shared what was going on. Not that I didn't think he wanted me to know, just that there had only been enough time for me to get coffee started and for us both to get dressed —Rush in his jeans but no shirt, as usual.

I only knew what I'd overheard from the phone call. That Jack wanted to kill someone. Now I knew who and why.

"How the fuck do you figure that?" Jack's brown eyes narrowed to slits.

"Because I'm the best friend you got, and I told you before you put that ring on her finger that she was bad news. She put the moves on every guy in the band. I put her off. Rush put her off. But she just kept coming at me."

"I don't believe you." Jack said the words, but doubt seemed to flicker in his gaze.

"You do. You showed me the pics you found on her phone."

Jack's shoulders slumped, his expression bleak. "You could have turned her away."

"I did the first half dozen times. But she caught me at a bad time."

"Meaning you were drunk."

"Meaning I'd had a few drinks and thought she had a few too many too, so I drove her home . . ." Ben's green gaze landed on me as if seeing me for the first time. "Who's the hot chick?"

"She's with Rush," Jack said.

"Hi, I'm Jewel," I said, wanting to speak for myself. Rush had introduced me to Jack, but the drummer seemed unable to remember my name.

"Well, hello there, baby." Broadcasting player vibes, Ben started toward me, but Rush put a hand on his chest to stop him.

"Stay away from her." Rush's snarl made the fine hairs on my nape stand on end. "She belongs to me."

"Really?" Ben slowly raked his hooded gaze over me. "That's never happened before." His lips curled into a sensual grin as he glanced back at Rush. "Sure you won't consider sharing?"

"Absolutely not." Rush stepped away from Ben and touched my arm. "Babe, do you think you could step out on the porch? Give me and the guys a moment. We've got some private stuff we need to work through."

"Oh. All right." I couldn't help the hurt that seeped into my tone. "I was actually thinking of going to get us something from the bakery we passed by last night. I'll just get my purse and get out of your way. Take your time. You can come find me when you're done."

Of course he didn't trust me with the inner workings of the band. Why should he?

As I left the room, I heard Jack ask again where Rush had met me, but I didn't hear the reply. Grabbing my purse from the dresser, I moved quickly to the sliding glass doors, not trying to overhear the conversation, but unfortunately, I did.

"She's just a hooker," Rush told his friends.

I froze for a moment, then forced my feet to carry me through the doors. The brisk ocean breeze whipped away the flash of tears that rushed to my eyes.

Rush

"She's not an undercover reporter. She won't tell anyone what she heard. Chill, man."

"You sure?" Jack didn't appear convinced. "Maybe she's just pretending to be a hooker. You remember that chick Carter Besille sent backstage to spy on us."

"Positive." I nodded. After the fiasco with the talk show host, we started to get nondisclosures signed before we fucked anybody we didn't know.

"Well, okay." Jack seemed to relax.

"When you're done, can I have a go at her?" Ben's gaze moved to the door, but Jewel was already gone. Thankfully.

"Keep mentally undressing her like you were, and I'll fuck you up."

Inexplicably, Ben grinned.

"No joke, man." I shoved him, but he didn't budge. Ben and I were equally matched physically, but I'd wipe the floor with him if he tried anything with her.

"About damn time." His grin widened.

"What the fuck?"

"Didn't like Brenda any more for you than I liked Carrie for him." He hooked a ringed thumb at Jack. "At least your fiancée wasn't a cheater, but I never did like the way she made you twist in the wind."

I huffed out a sigh, hating to have to remind him. "I stepped out on her—"

"Yeah?" He shook his head. "Seemed like more of a gray area, if you ask me. But she kept at you afterward. Tightening and tightening the screws."

"Now, hold on."

"No, man. About damn time you stopped wallowing in guilt. But I'm not totally getting why you wanna get up in my face about some hooker."

"Her name is Jewel. She's a sensitive woman with feelings, not a new plaything for you."

"All right." Ben nodded as if I'd confirmed something. "What Jewel truly is remains to be seen. But for now, we've got this loser to sort out." He gestured to Jack, who glared at him, and pulled out a chair.

"Pass the fucking coffee. It's too early in the morning for this." I glanced back at the sliding doors, wishing I were with Jewel and not dealing with a crisis with the guys. "But since we're here, we might as well iron some stuff out. I met with Mary yesterday. She rejected everything we turned in for a new album."

"No way." Wincing, Jack scrubbed a hand over his short brown hair, and dropped into a chair on the other side of the table from Ben.

Joining them at the table, I said, "I agree with her. We have an entire new album to put together on our break, and we're paying for it. But first, we gotta fix this stupid shit with you two."

"It's not stupid," Jack mumbled.

"It's stupid if we allow it to mess us up," I said firmly. I'd let this go on too long. I needed to lead the band, both on and off the stage.

Ben nodded. "Rush is right."

"Maybe," Jack said, his expression somber. "But you gotta know you crossed an uncrossable line."

"I do whatever it takes to keep either of you softhearted losers from being played." Ben's expression remained as steady as his Fender groove.

"How about this? Ben agrees to keep his dick in his pants from now on." I gave Ben the death stare, letting that hang. We had a test of wills for a moment, but when he eventually nodded, I turned to Jack. "And you agree not to murder Ben."

Jack's eyes narrowed.

"This time around," I said, and with that clarified, he nodded.

Thank fuck. No blood spilled and no one is going to jail.

"On to the new album," I said, deftly changing the subject. "I might have a decent single for it already. But I need a good drumbeat and some rhyme for my phrases."

"I'll anchor whatever you need." Jack, my drummer, nodded.

"Lay the phrases on me," Ben said. "I'll see what I can do."

"Great." I reached for my cell to share with them what I had.

24

Jewel

I sat at one of the pub-height tables at the bakery with an uneaten Danish in front of me. Feeling numb, I stared through the windows at the ocean, not seeing it as a picture to paint like I normally would. My heart ached, missing the hope I'd felt walking the shoreline with Rush only the night before.

Just a hooker.

I knew it, knew how this would play out. Yet it seemed I was always determined to learn my lessons the hard way.

Needing to talk to Cam, I pulled my cell from my bag. She picked up on the first ring.

"Hey, girlfriend. Whatcha doing?"

"Checking in," I said.

Picking up on my somber mood, she said sharply, "What's wrong?"

I sighed. "It's already happening."

"Oh, Jewel. I'm sorry." She didn't need to ask. We were sisters cut from the same cloth, only she was one lesson ahead of me. "Need me to come get you?"

"You don't have a car, Cam."

"I can ride the bus, same as you."

"No need. I know the way." *The way backward.*

"You don't sound good. It really won't be any trouble."

I dropped my head into my hand, lowering my voice as I stared at the table. "It'll cost money. We'll need to be careful. I . . . it'll be a while before I can go back on the street."

"Who are you talking to?"

Startled, I looked up to find Rush standing stiffly a few feet away.

He glowered at me, his jaw clenched tight. "You're not going back on the street."

My heart pounding madly, I sputtered, "S-sorry, Cam, I gotta go. Rush is here."

"He sounds mad."

"Yeah, apparently. I'd better see what's going on."

"Call me back."

"I will." I ended the call and set the phone down, then gestured to the stool opposite me. "Have a seat."

"Don't feel like chatting, Jewel. I wanna know what the hell you're doing."

"Just talking to my friend."

"About going back to hoo—" He stopped short and glanced around, seeming to realize he was in a crowded place and that people had turned to watch us, probably recognizing him.

It had happened when we were out last night. But after an initial double-take or a request for a photo, most people went about their business, seemingly used to a celebrity, probably lots of celebrities, living among them. It was the tension radiating off him that made this morning different.

"You're not going back to work," he said again.

"Today, tomorrow, a week from now, what's the difference?"

"The difference is how you come apart in my arms."

"I . . ."

"You usually climax when you're working?" he said in a low voice, cutting in precisely, like he steered his Porsche.

"No." I shook my head. He might as well know the truth of it before I took off.

"Didn't think so." His expression softening, he moved closer. His warmth and his woodsy scent dredged up memories, stirring desire that now caused pain.

I wasn't ready to give him up.

"You tell any of them your real name? Or share about your gran?"

"No." My throat closed up, and I coughed to clear it. "But I shouldn't have told you."

"Why the fuck not?" His eyes flashed, reminding me of cloud-to-cloud lightning. "Did I ever treat you in any way that made you think you couldn't trust me to be careful with you, to betray your confidence?"

I glanced away.

Rush edged closer. His legs brushed mine, then his chest touched my shoulder just before his fingers glided softly over my skin. Capturing my chin, he turned my face to him.

"Did one of my guys say something that upset you?"

I shook my head, barely able to think straight with him touching me. All too soon, I'd be gone, without him. Tears threatened at the thought.

"Was it me? Did I say something?" he said softly, searching my eyes.

"Only the truth," I whispered, hating to admit it.

"And that is?" His jaw firmed.

"I heard you tell them what I am."

"No, you didn't." The crease in his brow deepened. "What you are defies a simple description. I told them about what you did for a living prior to our agreement. And I only shared because Jack was worried you were undercover and might leak info about us to the press."

My eyes widened.

"Yeah." He let out a breath. "Jack has an imagination. Plus, the guys and I have had some fucked-up dealings with chicks wanting to latch on to use us. But I didn't tell them your occupation to hurt you. I'm sorry if it did." He stroked my skin with his thumbs, soothing me with the back-and-forth movement. "They would find out eventually anyway."

"How?"

"I wanted another day before I laid my cards on the table. Thought if I had a little more time, it might be easier to convince you. But here we are already, so here goes." Staring earnestly into my eyes, he said, "I don't want you to stay just for today. I want you to consider staying longer, until we figure things out between us."

My heart soared and then just as quickly plummeted.

"There's nothing to figure out." I shook my head, dislodging his touch, and his expression hardened. "This isn't us dating, Rush. It's us capturing a moment in time. We can put off the reality of your world and mine for a few days, maybe a week. Then I have to go back to my life. I have a roommate, responsibilities, and bills to pay."

"I'll pay your expenses."

"I can't accept that. We might as well go right back to the hourly payment structure."

Understanding dawned. His expression changed, turning as bleak as my mood.

I'd thought I was sad before, but the mood was closer to tragic now that both of us were clear at the beginning about how it all would end.

Rush

I wanted to yank Jewel close and never let her go. How could she basically say good-bye without giving me a chance? I couldn't accept it. I wouldn't.

I saw her point, and I respected it . . . and her. But I wasn't convinced that this only played out with both of us losing.

We were from different worlds; I got that. But what she didn't take into account was that mine had some advantages, and I was going to use them.

"All right. I'll take a week. Is that what you can give me?"

"Yes." She nodded.

"Then call Cam back. Tell her how it is."

"Okay." She picked up her phone.

"But know this." I cupped her face with my hands, my unsettled soul soothed by touching her. She allowed me an unhindered view through those golden windows to the heart that I coveted. "You're completely mine during that time."

"You can't own another human being, Rush."

She was right. Even when I was paying, I only got what she'd been willing to give.

"I want all access," I said firmly, willing her to agree. "Your time. Your body. Your heart."

Something flashed in her gaze in response to the last and most important clarification. Something so blazingly bright, it made the treasure of her accepting me for myself in the beginning seem like pocket change.

"Do you agree?" I lifted her chin since she'd lowered it, disappointed that her golden eyes no longer glittered, their brightness dulled. Maybe I'd only seen what I wanted to see—a reflection of my own desire.

Did she suspect why I wanted it all? How very close my heart was to being hers? How easily she could crush me if she walked away?

"I agree."

"Good." Relief filled me. If she was beside me, anything was possible. Trying to lighten the mood, I gestured at the uneaten pastry in front of her and asked, "Are you gonna eat that?"

Her voice flat, she said, "I'm not that hungry."

"You're gonna eat it," I said, deciding for her. "Every single crumb, while I get in line for egg sandwiches for both of us."

I moved away, not far, half the length of the bakery. Waiting in line, I watched her pick at the Danish. *Stubborn girl.* I'd get after her when I sat back down.

Jewel wasn't used to someone looking after her, but she had someone now. And she'd find out that I meant business about her health and safety, about a lot of things.

I slid my cell from my pocket, scrolled to recent calls, and tapped Brad's number. He answered on the first ring.

"Everything okay, Rush?"

Not now, but it would be. "Why you always gotta ask that first thing whenever I call you?"

"Because nine times out of ten, when you do, it means I've got trouble."

"Not this time. This time I've got a job for you that I think might make somebody's life brighter."

"That sounds interesting and different for you. How?"

First, I had to find out where they lived, and I doubted she would tell me. "Jewel Anderson."

"Come again."

"That's the name of the girl I picked up. The one who's staying with me." *The one who made the inside of my empty condo feel full.* Well, turnabout on that was fair play, or at least it was in my mind.

"Pretty name."

"Wait till you see her," I muttered, looking at her. "She's twenty-one. She has a Cali driver's license. I don't have the exact birthday. She says she lives in a real bad part of LA. She has a roommate named Cam."

"Why are you telling me all this?"

"I want you to get an address for her."

"You stalking her?"

No, I was staking my claim, wanting her in my bed and everywhere else I could get her. Show her that we could fit together well in every part of my life.

"Not stalking her the way you think. I want you to get inside the apartment."

I wanted her friend secured so at least Jewel didn't have that weight on her mind. I preferred her thoughts to be all about me.

"Rush," he said, the warning clear in his tone. "I can pull a lot of strings with you being who you are, but keeping you out of jail, keeping *me* out of jail for breaking and entering, isn't one of them."

"It's not breaking and entering when you put stuff into the apartment instead of taking it out."

"What am I putting inside it?"

"Food in the fridge, for starters. Furniture as needed. Whatever it appears that they don't have, I want them to have."

"In a bad neighborhood?"

"Yeah. She won't take my money, Brad." *Christ. What were the odds I'd pick up a hooker with principles?* "I'm going to do this."

Since it was for her friend, I suspected Jewel would accept my help. Sure, she would give me grief, but too bad. This was only the beginning of me pressing her, and I was going to press fucking hard.

25

Jewel

"I don't need new lingerie." I came to a halt and dug the rubber soles of my flip-flops into the boardwalk.

"Jewel." Rush gave me an exasperated look. "You could probably keep wearing the bra you have on and go without underwear. I definitely wouldn't mind knowing I could have easy access under your clothes, but I think you might be uncomfortable."

"But . . ." I gnawed on my lip as I glanced at the hot-pink striped awning above the shop he was trying to drag me into. "It looks expensive."

"You gave me grief about eating this morning, and then about the couple of outfits I bought you at the surf shop. The least you can do for me after I endured all that is let me see you model some of those sexy things." He gestured to the display inside the window, then gave me an arch look.

"I don't know." He wasn't making it easy for me to hold my ground on this one. Wearing sexy things while Rush watched me? An excited thrill shot through me. *Um, yes, please.*

"A guy can buy lingerie for a girl he's interested in." He ran his hands down the length of my arms, making my skin erupt in chill bumps from his electrifying touch. "And I'm *very* interested in you."

"Fine. I'll do it."

"Good." He grabbed my hand.

"Never knew guys liked shopping as much as you do," I grumbled.

"I like *doing it* with you." His silver eyes sparkling wickedly, he grinned.

"Oh, brother."

"Not thinking brotherly thoughts toward you."

I smiled. "Lame."

"Nothing's lame that makes you smile," he said, holding the door open for me.

I stumbled over the step into the shop, and he was right there to steady me, his sure hand firm on the small of my back.

The actual physical stumble was minor, but inside, I staggered majorly.

Rush had crumbled the world I had known before him. He made me feel cared for, like my smiles were worth every effort. Like my spending time with him was an incredible gift.

"Can I help you?" the saleswoman asked, sliding her reading glasses to the tip of her nose. Her pinched expression made it seem she thought it unlikely we could afford a single item in her store.

Familiar with attitudes like hers, I instinctively whirled around to go somewhere else, but only ran into Rush's solid immovable form.

"Yes, you can help us." Rush looked straight over my head to her. "Everything you have in her size in black, I want her to try on."

"But—"

"Do you know who I am?"

The woman shook her head. Her gray hair was so tightly wound into a bun, not a single tendril came free.

"It's not important." Rush's expression was fierce. "*She's* important."

He framed half of my face in his hand and stroked my cheek with his thumb. I was grateful once again that he'd sent the rest of our purchases ahead to the condo, so his hands were free to do whatever he wanted to me.

"Her name is Jewel. I want you to treat her like a queen. I would set my credit card down on the counter, step back, and let her choose what she wants, but I find that I'm in a more *discerning* mood."

Releasing me, he withdrew a black American Express card and set it on the counter.

"That being the case, I'm going to go to the dressing room with her to watch her take every single item off the hanger and try it on for me before we approve it for purchase."

"Absolutely. Yes, sir." The woman glanced at the card. Her eyes widened, and she immediately moved from behind the counter and started flipping through the closest rack.

"Do you think she knows my size?" I asked Rush as he urged me toward the pink-striped dressing-room curtain at the back of the store.

"Don't really care if she has to expend a little extra effort figuring it out."

"Ah." My mood lightened with understanding.

Rush's lips twisted into a smile. "Now you get it."

"No." I glanced back at the saleswoman. "But she does." I tapped my chin while he took a seat on a velvet-upholstered stool in the center of the large dressing room. "You know what?"

"Huh-uh."

"The rock-star entitlement thing?"

"Yeah, what about it?" His gaze narrowed.

I gave him a big smile. "It's not such a bad thing when you're on the winning side of it."

Giving me a saucy glance, Jewel slowly slid the curtain closed. Each lingerie set sexier than the last, she was killing me. But what a way to go.

"You can leave now." I gave the saleswoman a dismissive look as she entered to drop off another armload.

I'd lost track of the number of items Jewel had tried on. It was difficult to do math with my pulse roaring in my ears, and my cock so hard and extended, it practically hobbled me.

"Don't you need me . . ."

I didn't need anything from anyone else. Everything I wanted, Jewel had.

My voice raw with want, I said, "I can take care of everything from here."

Fuck waiting, I had to have Jewel now.

"All right . . ."

Since the saleswoman appeared confused, I spelled it out. "You work on commission?"

She bobbed her head.

"I'll add an extra twenty percent on top of whatever I spend when I purchase everything that has fit Jewel so far." He gave the woman a pointed look. "But only if you leave us alone, lock the door to the shop, and put on some headphones or crank up the music in the shop really loud until we come out."

"Oh." She blinked her widened eyes at me. "Absolutely. Take your time."

I didn't reply. This wasn't going to take a lot of time.

I stood, took two steps, and whipped back the curtain on Jewel as the woman scurried out.

"Rush." Spinning around, Jewel crushed a silken robe to her tits while peering at me through lowered lashes.

"Don't even play coy with me. I've been in fucking hell since you showed me the first bra."

"What if there are cameras?" Obviously, she'd noted the escalating signs of my deteriorating self-control.

"There's not." My nostrils flared as I caught a lungful of her peachy scent. "I already asked."

"Then come here." Her lips curling, Jewel dropped the robe. It puddled on the carpet as she crooked her finger at me.

I swept a heated glance over her. She had on a set from my favorite designer. Every single Avery Rose piece that Jewel had tried on, she'd looked amazing in. The lace seemed to mold to her curves. This set, like the others, featured a silver-studded band beneath her tits, and adjustable side strings on the thong.

Gorgeous, practical, and so coming right off.

"I want your hands on me, Rush," she said, tracing her tits and hips with her fingertips. "And your cock inside me." She passed a palm over her pussy and fluttered her lashes. "Please."

"Done."

Stepping forward, I swept her hands above her head and walked her backward into the mirrored wall. Lowering my head, I captured her lips, feasting on her mouth, devouring her sigh, and slashing her tongue with mine. She arched her hips against me, wiggling impatiently.

"Patience," I murmured, breaking the seal between our lips. My hands flexed tighter over hers. "You've been teasing me for an hour. It's all I can do not to loosen those strings and sink my cock right inside you."

"Do it." Daring me, she went up on her toes, peppered my stubbled jaw with kisses, and nipped my chin. "Why wait?"

"Because I need to do this first."

Releasing her hands so I could get mine on her, I ran them through her silky hair, along the smooth skin on her jaw, down the graceful column of her neck until I reached those glorious tits of hers. She arched them fully into my hands as I framed them.

"So pretty," I said, my voice husky as I stared down at my bounty. The flowery pattern on the thin fabric was tantalizing, revealing just a hint of her dusky nipples beneath. I swept my thumbs across them.

"So good," she said on a moan.

My cock jumped, in tune to her need.

"Are you wet, baby?" I slid a hand down to her pussy.

"Yes." She rocked beneath my possessive hold.

"You can be wetter."

I propped a hand on the mirror for balance as I lowered my head and fastened my lips around her nipples through the lace. The dampened mesh drew tight over peaks that scored my tongue as I lifted them one by one and lapped them.

"Beautiful, babe," I said, praising her as she writhed in my hold.

"You're beautiful." She stared at me, her lids lowered, her mouth parted. Her broken breaths made my cock impossibly harder.

"Guys aren't."

"But you are."

I didn't argue. I was busy, lapping at her and swirling my tongue. I bit down on her nipple, knowing it would make her breath catch, and it did.

"There's a condom in my bag." Moving her hands through my hair, she tangled her fingers in it and tugged impatiently.

"The one in my pocket is closer."

I pushed off the mirror and released her breast to take it out. She was already unbuckling my belt, but she was too slow.

I pushed her hands aside, flicked open the button, and yanked the denim and my boxers down.

"Fine." Jutting her bottom lip out in a pout, she reached for the strings at her hips.

"Oh no. I'm doing that."

"Then give me the condom." She took it, and I worked on the strings while she rolled the rubber on.

Then things got crazy frantic. The sight of her loosened thong sliding down her shapely legs and the feel of her delicate fingers gliding along my length seemed to unleash a beast inside me.

Hooking my foot around her calf, I tripped her. She toppled. I cushioned her fall to the carpet, and then I was on her.

Kicking the scrap of insignificant lace aside, I covered her body with mine. Grabbing her hands, I pinned them above her head with one hand and spread her thighs open to position myself between them with the other.

She was so wet, her thighs were slick with her essence. I wanted to lick my way to the fountain, but there wasn't time. Not for me. I had to be inside her.

"Please, *please*, Rush." She thrashed back and forth in my hold.

"I got you, babe."

When I entered her, she bucked. Knowing she was going to scream, I covered her lips with mine and swallowed her passionate cries.

My spine burned. My cock stiffened. Driving deep, I roared her name in her mouth, coming just as explosively as she did.

Impossible to stop it. No way to control the fall. I only knew that if I went over the edge, she had to come with me.

26

Jewel

"I'm starved, darlin'," Rush said when we returned to the condo. "What's for dinner?"

"Are you serious?" I raised a brow as he spun me in his arms. He made me feel like we were dancing, emotionally and literally.

He swayed me rhythmically by my hips to a tune only he seemed to hear. The two bags of lingerie slid from my fingers to the entryway floor, and my hands landed on his solid chest.

"Well, yeah. Practicality calls." He leaned back and raked a hooded gaze over me. "You're sexy." His grip on my hips tightened as if he was remembering how I'd looked in the lingerie made him lose control. "You're hot. And you're the only woman I've ever wanted to spend time with after I got off. But do you really not know how to cook?"

"My gran tried to teach me, but she gave up after I nearly set her kitchen on fire."

"Good to know." His eyes widened. "Well, practicality's overrated."

"Lucky for me."

"I'm the lucky one." The teasing lilt disappeared. "Lucky not to have driven past your corner and missed meeting you."

"Stop." My eyes burning, I swallowed hard. I'd already contemplated the good fortune of that encounter.

"Stop what? Telling the truth? Stop finding more things to like about you? Stop the timer you've insisted on setting from winding down?"

I sniffed, blinking hard. "Stop saying stuff that makes me want to cry."

"Okay, no more things that make my girl cry."

"I'm not yours."

"You are when you're with me. And my opinion is the one that counts. Shush." He pressed a finger to my lips. "You have places you insist on drawing lines—well, this one is mine. *You* are mine while I have you." His lips lifted. "Nod if you agree."

I nodded, and he removed his finger. "Do I have your permission to order dinner to be delivered?"

His lips twitched. "Any chance of spontaneous fires with you holding a handful of takeout menus and my cell?"

"Not if you separate me from the matches."

"Follow me then." He started for the kitchen. "I'll show you where the drawer is that'll keep us both from starving."

He moved to the fridge, pulling out a beer for himself and a soda for me while I glanced through the menus.

"Pizza okay?" I asked after sorting through our choices.

"Pizza's great."

He took a seat at the dining table and pulled a chair out for me. I sat beside him, and he slid me his cell. After I called and ordered a large pizza with the works, he seemed dubious about it being enough for the two of us.

"I really don't eat that much," I said.

"Barely eat at all, you mean. That's not cool, babe. We walked a lot today, and we fucked a lot. Burned a lot of calories."

He hooked my chair leg and turned me to more fully face him. "I dig your curves. Don't want you to lose 'em because you're not taking care of yourself."

"I eat when I'm hungry."

"You eat when you have food." He frowned.

"How about you? There's a lot of liquor in the kitchen, but not a lot of actual food." I slid my gaze over him. "I like the way you look too, you know. Takes calories, the right type, to have muscles like you do."

"I hear you." His eyes narrowed.

"Don't dish it out if you can't take it."

"Message received."

Changing the subject, I said, "Your boss said something about public intoxication."

Rush pulled in a deep breath and released it. "Her points were valid. Been spiraling for a while, Jewel. Because of my dad, mainly. But also with Brenda marrying my brother. And one other thing I didn't see until you pointed it out."

"And that is?"

"Music's my place to process. I've just been going through the motions, cranking out songs that don't mean shit to me. I'm not gonna do that anymore. Not planning to tune out the emotional stuff. I'm gonna try to make sense of it."

"That's wise."

"That's because of you."

I shook my head. "But I didn't do anything."

"You really listen to the things I say, and are a great sounding board for my thoughts. You might not approve, but you don't act judgy with me either."

"I've had enough judgment pointed at me to last a lifetime."

"I bet you have." He picked up a strand of my hair, wrapping it around his finger with the gothic cross. "I think you're too hard on yourself. Maybe we both lost our way. I think I wasn't the only one spiraling. You might've forgotten some important things too."

"Such as?"

"That you matter. That you should just be yourself. That you're uniquely beautiful." His expression tightened. "Perfect is an unattainable standard. In fact, it's fucking boring."

"So, is Jack going to be okay?" I asked from within the circle of Rush's arms.

He stopped strumming his guitar. We were on the lounger together, me between his legs, and the instrument balanced on my lap. I immediately missed the vibrations.

"I'm sorry. Maybe I shouldn't have asked." I should have remembered that the band had triggered the tension between us earlier.

"It's okay, darlin'. You can ask me about the guys. You can ask me anything. All right?"

I swiveled to peer up at him. Sincerity blazed from his eyes. The breeze lifted his hair off his brow, which was a pity, really, because I would have preferred to have sifted through the thick layers myself.

"I hope that might be a reciprocal thing between us."

I nodded, and he gave me a soft smile that did amazing things for his eyes.

"Jack's a good guy, but he often overcompensates. He made excuses for his wife that she didn't deserve. It was only a matter of time before their marriage fell apart." Rush blew out a breath. "I was waiting her out, letting her dig her own grave. But Ben, well, that's not his way."

I had seen that. Ben was shockingly direct. "Are you guys going to be okay? Were you able to work things out?"

"We're solid. We get mad, and then we get over it. Until the next blowup. But there's usually a long break before the pattern repeats itself."

Rush set his guitar to the side on a stand, just like the one he had in every room in the condo. He picked up a pencil and scribbled down several phrases, then flipped the page when he was through and placed the steno pad back on the side table.

"You're filling that up fast," I said.

"I'm feeling inspired."

He picked up the guitar, set his cell to record the chords, and once again I was safe, his warm body behind me and his instrument on my lap. But I felt even warmer than before because of what he'd implied.

"Are you saying that I inspire you to write songs?"

"Haven't written anything in a long while, baby. Well, besides the shit my boss rejected. I put a damn good tune to paper the first night we were together, and another couple of contenders tonight that I'd like to run by the guys soon."

When he started strumming, I turned to face the ocean again. It was a perfect end to a practically perfect day.

Listening to him play, I sighed with contentment and watched the large waves. They lifted, turned over, and crashed as they hit the sand, then gurgled as they flattened and withdrew from the shore.

The sunset's oranges and pinks tinted the water. Far way, the waves appeared tranquil, but near the beach they were agitated. Like me underneath my calm, it seemed as though the waves sensed their impending demise. Reaching up to a sky that was beautiful and bold but that couldn't catch them, they tumbled back to earth and broke apart as they hit the packed sand. A foamy last breath exhaled at the shore.

My fingers twitched. I needed my brush in my hand, wanting so badly to capture the beauty stretched out in front of us before it dissolved.

With Rush and me too. All of it.

His arms around me. His guitar. Even the sound of his music had color, shape, and texture in my mind.

Guess I'm feeling inspired too.

I snuggled closer, deciding to savor the moment rather than focus on my fears. And then he made the moment even better, sensing my need and offering to fill it.

"We're going for some paints and canvases for you tomorrow. There's a shop up the road that has brushes and everything. If I'm going to be creating for pleasure, you should be too."

Tears welled in my eyes at his intuition and thoughtfulness.

"I can try." That was all I could manage to choke out with my throat suddenly so tight. "It's very nice of you to think of it."

"Nice is you, not me, Jewel. I want you to be happy while you're here, and comfortable. To have pretty things to wear. Food you like. We should go to the grocery store after the art store. You made a good point about the lack of food in the house."

"All right." A warm tear spilled down my cheek and onto his arm before I could swipe it away.

"Are you crying?" He set down his guitar, hooked his finger under my chin, and lifted it, turning my head so he could see my face. "You are. I'm sorry. What did I do?"

"Nothing. Everything." Wanting to be honest, I gave it to him straight. "It's been a long time since anyone's worried about me. I mean, Cam is wonderful. She's a great friend. But she and I are in survival mode most of the time. It takes two of us to make ends meet." My lips trembled. "Necessities are prioritized, not comforts. Not paints, and certainly not being happy."

Rush was quiet so long, I thought maybe he hadn't heard me.

"You're very brave, Jewel. Resilient. Tough." His voice was gravelly, as if his throat was tight too. "But I hope you know you don't have to be while you're with me."

The hand-to-mouth life Jewel described so matter-of-factly made me both sad and proud at the same time. That she remained who she was despite all she'd been through was amazing. Her situation made my problems seem minor.

"Let's go to bed," I said.

"It's early."

"I wasn't planning on sleeping."

"Oh yes. Okay."

"Up, darlin'." I released her. "As soon as you move, I'll follow."

And wasn't that the story for me with her. We were so in sync already.

I thanked whatever lucky star had steered my car to her curb that night, and wished upon it to show me the way to keep her beyond the week she'd granted me.

Jewel set her feet on the concrete and turned to offer me her hand. I took it readily, not that I needed it to stand, but I wanted her and everything she had to offer. That was what I wanted to show her. Not in a hotel. Not against the wall. Not in a dressing room. In my home. In my bed.

I closed and latched the doors once we were inside. Returning my guitar to the open case on the couch, I closed it, but didn't bother latching it. Not tonight. I had better things to do with my time.

My hand on the curve of her back, I led her down the hall and turned us into my bedroom. The sheets remained rumpled from the night before. Every visible reminder of her in my space brought me satisfaction.

"Would you like to have the bathroom first?" I asked.

Earlier today, I'd insisted on buying toiletries for her. While we waited for the pizza to arrive, she'd set them out on the bathroom counter. I liked seeing her things next to mine.

"Sure. But why don't we get ready for bed together?"

"I want to go slow with you tonight, Jewel. Once you start undressing, I don't seem to have much control."

"Control's overrated," she said, giving me a teasing glance through her lowered lashes.

"Not this time. Wash your face. Shower. Put lotion on, brush your teeth, whatever you normally do to get ready for bed. Then put on that robe from the shop. All right?"

She nodded, padded to the dresser, and withdrew the black silk from the drawer I'd cleared out for her to use. It had seemed to mean something significant to her, just like seeing her things around the condo did for me. She'd certainly gone misty-eyed about it.

Ignoring the burning in my own eyes, I watched her leave the bedroom, cross the hall, and disappear inside the bathroom. When the water came on, I stood in the center of my room, my hands fisted at my sides, trying not to think about her being naked in the shower.

I scanned the room, looking for something to distract me. Her purse on the dresser reminded me of the task I'd given Brad. Quickly, before she returned or I could change my mind, I found her wallet and snapped a quick pic of her driver's license.

I was seated on the bed, texting the photo to Brad, when she reappeared.

My mind blanked as I took her in—her skin freshly scrubbed and dewy from the shower, her coppery-brown hair wet, the silky robe clinging to her damp curves.

"My turn. I'll be right back." I tossed my cell on the bed. Her *okay* followed me as I left the room.

The humidity from her shower hit me as I unbuttoned my jeans, and the peach scent from her body scrub made my cock hard. I stepped into the stall, took the fastest shower in human history, wrapped a towel around my waist, brushed my teeth, and returned to the bedroom.

"Hey." She tilted her head, her eyes searching mine for a long moment. Something intense seemed to be working behind hers. "You didn't shave."

"No. I was in a hurry."

"It's okay. I like the roughness of your stubble against my skin."

Those softly spoken words were all it took. In a heartbeat, I joined her on the bed. It wouldn't be until later that I would realize she'd moved my cell to the nightstand.

She twined her arms around my neck, and I wrapped mine around her waist. Staring down at her, I clutched the silk at her hips, drew her closer, and lowered my head.

Kissing her was the dream it always was. Her lips were plush, her tongue as eager as mine, her taste sweet and seductive. I locked down the lust as she whimpered into my mouth and pressed her curves against me.

She broke the kiss. Surprised, I peered down at her.

"Rush, I'm not sure what you had in mind exactly, but slow isn't what my body says when you kiss me like that."

"What does it say?" I reached for the studded tie on her robe. "Can I have a look?"

Having a feeling I knew and anxious to see my hunch verified, I untied the sash and parted her robe. The gap revealed the slopes of her tits and the pretty coppery curls of her pussy. But it hid too much. I reached up to slide the silk off her shoulders, but she seemed to sense what I wanted, shrugged, and the robe fluttered to the floor.

"Your mouth says *kiss me.*" I framed her face and pressed my lips to her parted ones. "Your tits say they ache to be touched." I moved my hands, skimming my fingers over her creamy skin, then lifted and shaped her breasts. "Your nipples say *pinch and pull.*" I twisted and pulled.

"It burns. In a good way." She gasped as I did it again, her lids lowering to watch me.

"Your hips say *grab me.*" I yanked her to me. "And your pussy says *pound your cock into me.*"

"Yes!"

Jewel released my towel and reached for me, curling her fingers around me and sliding them down to grasp me at the root. "Take me where you want to go. Fast or slow, I'm with you. I . . . I love the things you do to me." She lifted her head, opening her eyes to me, baring her soul. "No man has ever made me feel the way you do."

"Baby." I captured her lips to kiss her.

She kissed me back, her fingers curled around me, pumping me until I couldn't take any more.

"Jewel . . ." I groaned, removing her fingers. "Slow down." Breathing hard, I pressed my forehead to hers.

"Sorry. But when you kiss me, I get so wet, I throb. And I ache for you."

Needing no more encouragement, I urged her to the bed and pressed her down on it, then lifted her legs to my shoulders while she grasped the sheet beneath her. She was so flexible, she folded herself in two. Swiping my thumb through her curls, I found her wet and swollen. Standing next to the bed, I slowly pushed my cock into her, enjoying the sight of her taking every inch of me.

"Move, Rush." Her fingers twisted the sheet. "Move, please."

I pulled out to the tip, then pushed back in. Repeating the pattern, I alternated between watching her face and seeing myself disappear inside her. "I'm going to fuck you so hard, baby."

When she wrapped her legs around me, I moved her body halfway across the mattress, then climbed into the bed and pounded into her.

"Yes." She panted and grabbed my ass.

Covering her body with mine, I slid my hands under her ass to deepen the penetration. I thrust into her, and she begged me to take her deeper.

So I did.

Again and again and again, I pounded into her, reveling in my oncoming orgasm and recognizing the signs of hers building as well.

Her nails dug crescents into my skin. Her lips parted. Her eyes fluttered closed. When her body finally spasmed around me and she moaned my name, I threw back my head.

Losing and finding myself with her, I roared her name in return.

27

Jewel

Rush sent me ahead to the shower, telling me he'd scoop up our discarded clothes.

As I was rinsing off the soap suds, I noticed him standing naked in the bathroom doorway, his arms crossed over his chest. He was as focused watching me as he had been rinsing the shampoo from my hair. Tender and sexy, he was a tantalizing combination of both.

"Come join me." I touched myself, then brushed my fingertips across my lip, pleased to see his already hard cock bounce in response to my tease.

He pushed away from the doorjamb, strode straight to me, and yanked open the glass door. Stepping inside, he dove one hand into my hair, and with the other, grabbed me by the hip to draw my body into alignment with his.

He lowered his head and kissed me. Hard. After letting me catch a breath, he kissed me again, long and slow, grinding his cock against my stomach.

"Rush." Spellbound, I gazed up at him. My hair was wet again, drops of water dampened my lashes, but between my legs, I was wetter still.

"Turn around." He spun me and placed his palm on my lower back. "Bend."

When I complied, he reached around me and found my clit, then swiped his thumb over it. Heat shimmered beneath his touch.

As I felt the blunt end of him probing my entrance, I stiffened. "Condom."

"I left packets in here, hoping . . ."

His voice was raspy, the acoustics in the shower magnifying it like a concert hall. My pulse certainly throbbed in concert to the desire he orchestrated.

After quickly sheathing himself, Rush glided inside, perfectly filling me. Gripping my hips firmly, he moved me along his length, in and out as he stroked deep. He started out slowly, sliding in to fill me, pulling out to tease. Building the heat, making me burn, making me ache for release.

Touch by touch, he mastered me. Weighing my breasts in his hands. Tugging my nipples. Kissing me, alternating between my mouth that he ravaged with his firm lips and his wet tongue, and sucking on the sensitive patch of skin between my neck and my shoulder.

Stroke by hot stroke, he took me higher and higher, hotter and hotter.

"Rush, oh, Rush." I sobbed his name.

"Jewel . . ." My name rumbled from his lips, resonating in the stall and deep inside me. "You feel so good."

"Yes! Oh, yes!"

My scalp tingled. My legs trembled. Anchored to him, pleasure centered where we were joined, I cried out as heat swept through me. He groaned and stiffened inside me, sending me over the edge in a complete freefall. Knowing as I surrendered, that he had me.

Already.

I was completely his.

I woke up in the darkness, tangled in Rush's strong arms. His sculpted front to my back, his heavy thigh was thrown over me. He had me pinned to him, but he needn't have bothered. I wasn't going anywhere. Not yet, at least.

I was in trouble, big trouble. I'd foreseen this from the beginning, but knowing hadn't stopped the inevitable.

I shifted from within the cage of his embrace. His cock was velvet, hot and hard against my bare hip as I flipped over. It imprinted every inch of me with tingling desire.

"Hey there." His gray eyes smoldered through his lowered lids. "Having trouble sleeping?" he asked in a deep rumble.

"A little." My gaze dipped to his half-parted lips. I licked mine to wet them.

"Jewel . . ."

I looked up to find his eyes narrowed, and his mouth on its way to mine. I lifted my head, shortening the distance. "Yes."

I pressed my lips to his. Warmth bloomed between us that I felt deep inside my abdomen. All it took was his mouth touching mine to make me hot, to make me wet, to make me ache for him. Actually, all it really took was him saying my name like that. Infusing it with so much desire.

I shifted, coming up on top of him, straddling him. His cock hard and hot against me, I kissed him. I licked my way into the seam between his lips and stroked my tongue to his. Shallow licks at first, then longer, deeper, more penetrating ones. The way I wanted to him to fuck me.

"Babe . . ." He let out a groan when I broke the kiss. "You're killing me."

"Not yet."

I stretched out my arm and slapped my hand on the nightstand. After grabbing a condom packet, I tore it open with my teeth and rolled it on him.

"Incredible," I murmured, a tremor in my voice as I fisted him.

"Jewel. Fuck!"

I didn't let him catch his breath. Removing my hand, I impaled myself on him. Then I had to pause. To savor. I pulled in a quick breath as his smoky gaze met mine.

"I . . ." I licked my lips, unable to formulate words for how good it felt to be connected to him. Pressing my palms to his chest, I lifted onto my knees and then lowered myself, sinking inch by inch onto his cock until he was as deep as he could go. "I love the way you feel inside me."

"I love being inside you." Reaching for me, he framed my breasts in his hands as I lifted and lowered myself again.

Shallow, then deep, I rode him while he played with my breasts. Until each swipe of his thumbs on the hardened tips made my breath catch.

"Baby." He lifted his hips, meeting my next downward plunge, and sent heat spiraling outward from my core. "You're so slick, so wet, so hot."

He suddenly sat up, startling me. Keeping us connected, he flipped me over. Now I was on my back, and he was on top.

"No!" I protested, a little twinge of disappointment inside my chest. "I wanted to be in charge."

His voice tight, he said, "I can't take any more." Propped on his arms, his biceps taut, he plunged deep into me.

"Rush . . ." I exhaled, no longer caring that he was on top.

"My turn, darlin'." He gave me a sexy half smile and pulled out, the movement achingly slow.

As the hard edge of him dragged over my clit, a hot bolt of desire shot through me. But before I could catch a breath, he pushed in deep again.

"Yes." My eyes fluttered closed, and his heated exhale bathed my lips before his mouth crushed mine.

Using his lips, teeth, and tongue, he kissed me deeply and fucked me slowly. With my arms wrapped around him, my legs crossed at the ankles, I lifted my hips into each stroke. Our passion-slick skin slid together. Heat blazed as bright as a fire each time he glided all the way in.

"Rush . . ." I tightened my limbs around him on his next deep stroke. "I'm going to come."

"Me too, Jewel. Oh, baby."

His groan sent me over the edge.

I shuddered as he stiffened, and even through the condom, I could feel his heat. Warmth washed over me, wave after wave. So hot. So good. So right.

Could he feel it too, feel the difference this time?

I was no longer holding back. I was giving him all of me.

Rush

The dawn's bringing a new day ruined my languid morning mood. I stopped stroking my hand down the creamy soft skin along her spine.

Was this day two already on the week she'd promised me? Only five more days . . . Could I change her mind so quickly?

"Why did you stop?" Yawning, Jewel rolled over to face me. "I like waking up to you touching me."

My gaze tripped on her sleepy smile. I forgot about my trepidation as she reached for me.

"Hey, sunrise girl." I traced her lips with my thumb.

When she looked at me and smiled, I forgot everything. In this moment, I was the center of her world, and she was the brightest star in the universe within my arms.

"Get them all." Unable to resist touching her a moment longer, I placed my hands on her shoulders. Warmth and rightness settled deep inside me as Jewel leaned back into me and tilted her head to look up at me.

"I don't need all of them, Rush. Paint supplies are expensive. That's too extravagant."

She was the extravagance, but I didn't tell her that. It was too soon. I had to prove to her what we could be—what I could be for her—if she would just give me a chance.

"We'll take one of each." I turned to the salesman who'd been dogging our heels since we walked in the door. "And every single canvas you have. Sketchpads. Charcoal and colored pencils, watercolors too."

Jewel had said acrylic was her preferred medium, that it was easy to work with and dried fast. But I wanted her to be prepared for whatever creative mood struck her. And I wanted what she needed easily accessible so she would never have to be far from my side.

Once we'd scheduled the art supplies for delivery to the condo, we climbed into the Porsche. As I slid the key into the ignition, I turned to look at her from the driver's seat.

"Babe, have you ever had any formal training for your voice?"

Her golden eyes wide, she shook her head, making her silky mane shimmer as it brushed her shoulders. Electricity shot through me as I remembered how her hair had felt brushing over my cock when she'd wrapped her lips around it.

"Why do you ask?"

"Heard you singing two mornings in a row."

"Sorry. I just felt like singing." Her brow scrunched, and her gaze went past my shoulder as her eyes glistened. "I haven't felt like it in a long time. Like I could connect to that part of my life." She swallowed and gave me a tight smile. "Probably not the stuff you're used to hearing."

She wasn't fooling me. Jewel was trying to downplay what she'd shared, but her voice was weighted with emotion.

"Not lately. No," I said. "But I grew up in the Catholic church and went to an affiliated school. I'm not religious, but I'll always have my faith." I twisted my ring on my finger before cranking the ignition. "So the hymns aren't unfamiliar, and you sing them really well."

"Um, not hardly." She crinkled her cute nose. "My gran was front and center, soloist in the choir. My mom too, before . . ." She paused, her perfect white teeth catching her plump bottom lip.

"You mentioned you weren't interested in entertainment." Filling in the blanks, I said, "I guess music is in that category for you too. Is that because of what happened with your mom?"

She nodded.

"That's a shame."

Jewel's eyes lit up. "I like *your* music. Your voice. When you sing, I see colors in my mind that I want to paint."

She was deflecting, but this time I'd let her. "Are you saying I inspire you?"

"Yes." Leaning her head back, she turned and smiled at me.

"Good to know, since the feeling is mutual." I took her hand and placed it on my thigh, pressing down to let her know I wanted her to keep it there as I pulled out of the parking space.

"Where to next?" she asked, her expression soft as her gaze skimmed my face.

"Mind if I swing by the guitar store before we get groceries?"

"Don't mind at all. I'd love to see your eyes glaze over like mine did with all the options inside the paint store."

"It's an hour's drive inland," I said, but she shrugged off my warning.

"I like watching you drive. I mean, I'm sure the scenery will make the time go by fast." She was teasing me. Her eyes glittered like polished gold. "The view along the road will be interesting too. And seeing you try out a new guitar."

"Norman's is a rare-guitar shop. It's hard to resist getting my hands on an instrument that one of my idols has played. But, Jewel . . ." I brought her hand to my lips and pressed a kiss to her knuckles. "You're much harder to resist than any of those."

28

Jewel

I pretended I was joking, but I really did enjoy watching Rush while he drove.

Wisps of his brown hair hanging in disarray over his platinum eyes. His handsome profile, his strong jaw firm as he focused on the road. His muscular thigh flexing under my hand as he alternated between braking and accelerating. Me beside him like I belonged there.

"Are you comfortable?" he asked, glancing at me as he slowed to a stop at a red light.

"I'm good."

"You sure?" He swept a concerned look over me. "That dress seemed like a good idea at the beach, but it's sparse on material. You've got chill bumps on your legs. I can tone down the A/C." He reached for the controls.

"Not necessary," I said to stop him. "You aren't wearing a whole lot more."

He had on his jeans, a black Gibson guitar tee, and flip-flops. If we were back on the beach, he'd probably have ditched the shirt, but the guitar tees seemed to be a staple item in his wardrobe like my art-themed ones. That was basically all he'd had inside the drawer he cleared for me.

I gave him a small smile. "It's a hyperawareness of you that's making my skin tingle. It's not the cold air. It's from having my hand on your thigh."

"Babe." His voice rumbled low as his gaze dipped to the gathered bodice of my sundress, making my nipples immediately preen to points.

"That too," I told him, knowing that the thin cotton and the tight fit revealed what he did to me just from a single glance. "Every time you flex your legs, it reminds me how good it feels when you drive your cock deep inside me."

"Jewel . . ." His Adam's apple bobbed as he swallowed. "Not here. Not on the freeway. It's too dangerous."

"You're right." I took my hand off his thigh, and the dark look he gave me almost made me return it.

His cell suddenly rang, the noise startling inside the quiet cabin. The center dash display read MOM CALLING. He glanced at it, and his entire body tensed. It rang again, and when he didn't move, his tension became mine.

"Aren't you gonna get that?" I asked.

"Yes, of course." He tapped the display to accept the call. "Hey, Mom."

"Rush." His mother had a nice voice, but she sounded out of breath.

"Are you okay?"

"Yes. Most likely."

The car lurched as Rush's foot seemed to slip, and he hit the brakes unnecessarily.

"Hold on. Can you hold on?"

"Yes, son. I'm at home. Sitting in the living room on the house phone."

"I'm not. I'm driving, but I'm pulling over now."

Now he sounded out of breath too. Blinker on, he took the next exit ramp.

"Why aren't you at home?" she asked.

"I'm out with a friend."

"Jack?"

"No." Rush slowed the Porsche at the stop sign.

"Ben?"

"No."

"A girl?"

"Yes."

"Is she with you right now? Can she hear me?"

"Yeah, Mom." He raked a hand through his hair while scanning both sides of the road. "I can't find a place to pull over."

"There." I pointed at a car dealership just off the freeway. "Up ahead on the right."

"Thanks, Jewel."

"Hello, Jewel," his mom sang through the speakers.

"Hi, Mrs. McMahon."

"You sound sweet. I love your accent. Where are you from? Where did Rush meet you, at one of his concerts?"

"I'm from Tennessee."

Rush pulled into the dealership and steered into a spot. He put the Porsche in park and cut the engine but left the accessories running.

"Oh," his mom said. "I don't remember that being on his tour schedule."

"It wasn't," Rush said. "I met Jewel here in LA."

"Why didn't you tell me you met someone when I called?"

"I met her right after you called."

"You seem very comfortable with her for someone you just met."

"I am, Mom. That's because she doesn't just sound sweet. She is sweet."

I smiled. Rush was so distracted, he didn't seem to be measuring his words.

"But you can't just call and start grilling me and my girl after scaring me half to death. What's going on?"

"Right. I'm sorry. It's just good news for you to be with someone. After Brenda, I thought you'd never move on."

"Mom," he said, pinching the bridge of his nose. "Focus."

"Sure. Well, the routine tests they took during my physical were normal. But I keep having dizzy spells."

"Dizzy spells? What the hell, Mom! You didn't say anything about that when I asked specifically about your health."

"Don't raise your voice to me, Rush Patrick McMahon. I assumed it was just low potassium. I've had that before, and I didn't want to worry you. More importantly, why didn't you tell me you have a girlfriend?"

"It's a new development." He flicked his gaze to me and pressed a finger to his lips.

I got the message. He didn't want me to contradict him, and I wouldn't. In a dream world, I would be his girl—gladly. In a heartbeat.

I reached for his hand and removed it from his mouth, then brought it to my lap and squeezed it reassuringly.

"So, Mom." He exhaled a shaky breath. "The dizzy spells. What do they think is causing them?"

"It could be seasonal allergies, or it could be just stress. It's probably nothing, but you know how thorough Dr. Shannon is. And I know how upset you'd be if I didn't tell you."

Silence filled the cabin. Rush's fingers tensed, and the lines deepened in his face. "I appreciate that. But I'm sure everything will be fine."

"Yes, I'm sure it will be. But, Rush, could you do something for me?"

"Yes, anything."

"Say a prayer."

"Done."

"And could you come home soon to visit? It's been so long since I've seen you."

His hand flexed in mine. "I start the tour soon. Maybe . . ."

"I know you do, but could you come sooner? During the break? It's only a few hours on the plane."

"And a long drive."

"Please?"

"Yes." Rush glanced at me. Shadows darkened his gaze.

"For Christmas?" she asked, her tone plaintive.

"I'll do my best, Mom."

"That's all I ever ask. Thank you."

"You're welcome."

"It really means a lot to me."

"I know it does. That's why I'm doing it. Listen, I need to go. I have work stuff to do. Studio time to try to rearrange on short notice." He sighed. "But I'll figure a way to make it happen."

"Thank you, son. Good-bye."

"'Bye, Mom."

I stared at Jewel after I ended the call, and she held my gaze, her pretty features pinched with concern. I was comforted by her presence, even with all the uncertainty swirling around inside me after what my mom had shared. And that wasn't the only uncertainty that weighed heavy on me.

"Do you think you could extend your week a little longer?" I hurried to clarify, sensing Jewel was about to refuse. "Just until I get back from Indiana."

Her eyes filled, and she shook her head.

"Then come with me."

"Rush, I can't."

"Why not?"

"It wouldn't be right." She glanced away.

"Why wouldn't it be?"

She blinked hard, then her eyes met mine. "Because this is temporary. I don't want to give your mom the wrong impression."

I clenched my jaw so tight, my teeth hurt.

"We have a few more days," she whispered.

That wasn't enough to change her mind. I knew it wasn't. Not with her so focused on the expiration date.

"All right." I lifted my chin, withdrew my hand from hers, and turned the ignition.

I avoided her eyes as I backed out of the dealership. We were both silent, lost in our own thoughts as I took the next entry ramp onto the freeway.

I wasn't sure what was going through her mind. Mine was racing as fast as the Porsche was speeding. I wasn't used to being refused, and I didn't like it, especially from her. But I wasn't giving her up. I'd just have to accelerate my plan to convince her to stay.

Problem was, I didn't have a plan. Just the vague idea to use the privileges that came with my status. And I was afraid that wouldn't be enough.

I reached for her, and she took my hand. Her skin was like ice. I glanced at her as I exited the freeway. She was staring out the windshield, her bottom lip between her teeth. She seemed tense.

"Maybe we should go back to the condo," I said as I squeezed her hand. When she was in my arms, she was all mine and I could read her better.

"What?" She turned to look at me, blinking slowly as she refocused. "And skip the guitar store?" Her thickly lashed eyes narrowed. "When I had my fun, and you haven't had yours? When we're almost there?"

She shook her head, luxurious waves of rich brown streaked with copper billowing around her slim shoulders. With time running out so rapidly, I wanted to catalog every detail.

"No way," she said. "I want to see you in your happy place. Imagine you there when . . ." Her lips flattened, and she swallowed. "I like being a part of your regular routine. I don't want you to change anything for me." She gave me a stubborn look, which I returned.

What she didn't realize was that everything had already changed because of her. But how could I convince her?

"All right, baby." I withdrew my hand from hers, but only to get both hands back on the wheel to turn it. "Norman's next. I'll make some calls. My boss to see if I can get her to settle for an incomplete album. Then the guys to see where we can set up some studio time on short notice. Then we're going home."

I turned to sweep a determined glance over her.

"I'm getting you naked. Then making you come. Over and over again."

29

Jewel

The guitar store wasn't much to look at from the outside, just a corner shop in a nondescript strip mall. But inside, it was different. I'd never seen so many guitars in one place before. On the wall. Lined up in rows in their stands on the floor. And seeing Rush's reaction to them was priceless.

"Hey, McMahon." A skinny guy approached us wearing an orange Cal Jam concert T-shirt and dark thick-framed glasses.

Rush set down the mahogany guitar he'd been reverently running his fingers over. "Yo, Dwight."

The two exchanged a typical guy greeting, bumping shoulders and then clapping each other on the back.

"Haven't seen you in a while. How'd the tour go?" Dwight's eyes narrowed behind his lenses as he turned to scan me from head to toe. "Who's the babe-a-licious?"

"I'm Jewel." Forcing a smile, I extended my hand, finding myself a little irritated by the way the guys in Rush's circles seemed to assume I couldn't speak for myself.

Dwight took my hand, but he didn't shake it. Instead, he brought it to his mouth and kissed the back of it like we were in an old black-and-white movie. "*Enchanté*, gorgeous."

"Dwight." Rush glared at him. "Cut the bullshit and back the fuck away from my girl."

"Can't blame a guy for trying." Dwight's brows lifted above his glasses' thick frames. "Not typical to see a hot babe in the store. Last hot redhead was Avery Jones." Then he turned his inquiring gaze to me. "You play, beautiful?"

"Um, no. And my hair's brown, not red." But my interest was piqued. "Avery Jones, the guitarist for Brutal Strength, she comes in here?"

"Every time she's in town."

"Wow. Is she as nice as she seems?"

"Nicer."

"Babe." Rush gave me an incredulous look, raising a single brow. "You didn't have any clue who I was, but you know Avery?"

"She's on the covers of all the fashion magazines. I thumb through them on slow nights . . . at work." Pivoting on the subject, I said, "She's unforgettable with her red hair and those green eyes. She does a lot of charity stuff. She seems cool."

"She's way cool." Dwight nodded and turned back to Rush. "Avery snagged the vintage EVH you were looking at last time."

"The signed one?"

"Yup."

"Shit." Rush's sculpted lips twisted. "You got any new inventory I haven't seen?"

"Hmm." Dwight pushed his glasses up his nose. "You still on a hunt for a signed Dylan?"

"Always."

"Bob Dylan?" I asked.

"Who else?" Rush turned to squint at me. "You see him on the covers of fashion magazines too?" He was obviously teasing me, but he still seemed a little insulted that he hadn't been on my radar as a recording artist.

"Not on a magazine." I shook my head. "But my mom met him once and played a set with him. She won a radio-sponsored lyric-writing contest. He played her song on her guitar, and she had him sign it after."

Slack-jawed, both men stared at me.

"The guitar your gran left you?" Rush asked.

I nodded.

"Holy shit."

"You interested in selling?" Dwight edged closer, his interest palpable.

"No. Never." I shook my head. "It's all I have left of her or my gran."

"Drop it, Dwight." Rush took my hand, obviously noting my distress. "What else you got that might interest me?"

"Well, no Dylan. But I've got a Pat Smear Martin."

"What year?"

"From 2007."

"I'd look at it. Sure."

"Swell. But you'll have to wait your turn." He hooked a thumb over his bony shoulder. "Bryan Jackson's trying it out."

Rush turned to look where Dwight pointed, and then cursed. "Fucking Tempest guys."

I turned too and recognized Warren Jinkins and Shaina Bentley from the French restaurant. They were inside a glassed-off room with a guy with short brown hair who held a shiny black guitar. Even from across the shop, I could see he knew what he was doing. His fingers flew over the strings.

"They've been in there a while," Dwight said. "Bryan seems to have taken a liking to it."

Sensing us watching, or maybe just catching our movement, Shaina turned and smiled at me. She touched War's shoulder, and he turned too and lifted his chin. Rush returned the greeting.

Bryan's fingers stilled as he noticed us. But it was Shaina who popped open the door and came hurrying over.

"Jewel. Hey." Her smile widened to blindingly bright. "I was just telling Bryan about meeting you."

"Oh yeah?"

"She was," War said.

The lead singer for Tempest came up behind her wearing a T-shirt and jeans, which seemed to be the requisite guitar-shop attire for guys. Unlike the others, War wore a rolled bandana around his head to hold back his shoulder-length dark brown hair. Shaina looked preppy by contrast, wearing a pink-and-white striped tee and solid powder-pink shorts.

The guitarist joined us after pulling Dwight aside and exchanging a few words. Up close, I could see that Bryan had light gray-green eyes, almost as uniquely striking as Rush's.

Both Tempest guys checked me out. Not with an interested eye like Dwight had, but speculatively.

"You made an impression with my sweetness," War said, but his fiancée interrupted.

"Genuine kindness. It's rare enough around here," she said with a grin. "Anyway, I was wanting to get your number to call and invite you over to my place, you and Rush." She turned her green gaze to the man beside me. "What do you say?"

Before he could answer, she switched her attention back to me, her hands clasped together to her chest. Her diamond engagement ring sparkled as brightly as her excited gaze.

"Would you come? We could barbecue out on the deck. Well, my dad could man the grill since War's not a chef. He could be in charge of popping the beers. War and Bryan disappear for hours whenever they're together. While the guys jam in the garage studio, you and I could get to know each other better."

"That's nice of you. I don't know, though." I glanced at Rush.

I liked Shaina. A lot. I just wasn't sure about War or Bryan yet. But one thing I was sure of. I only wanted to spend time with Rush.

"You have a recording studio in your backyard?" Rush asked War, his brow furrowed as he raked a hand through his hair.

"Not my backyard, her parents'. It's a second-story add-on to the garage apartment Shaina and I share when I'm in town and she has work stuff in LA."

"You recorded the Tempest unplugged stuff there?"

"Sure did."

"Timmons endorsed it?"

"Eventually." War blew out a breath. "After a little sweet-talking by my rhythm guy. She wasn't sold on the idea of an acoustic interpretation at first."

"It's a cool concept," Rush said. "Lots of bands are doing it."

"She thinks it's been overdone."

"Not if it's good like yours."

"Thanks, man."

"Truth." Rush looked a little uncomfortable, glancing between War and Shaina. "Hey, feel free to say no, but I'm in a bind time-wise for turning in a project Timmons is pressuring me about. Do you think me and my guys could maybe borrow your studio for a couple of hours?"

After exchanging a glance with Shaina, War nodded. "Abso-fucking-lutely. My drummer's out of pocket, so we got shit-all to do as a band at the moment."

Shaina clapped her hands with delight. "Bring your bandmates. We could make a party of it. What time would you be free to come over?"

"Well . . ." Rush gave me a hot look that sizzled. "Is nine too late? I wanna check out that guitar Bry was looking at. Then I'm having *alone time* with Jewel."

War grunted. "Sounds good to me. I wanna have some time to fuck my woman too." He pulled Shaina close, brushing her long blond hair aside so he could kiss her neck, and her eyes darkened.

Bryan rolled his eyes, and War and Rush grinned at each other. Apparently, *alone time* was guy code for *fucking your babe*.

I didn't object. I was totally on board with that plan.

Rush

"Plays like a dream."

Bryan hit me with that information as I started toward the practice room with Jewel in tow.

"Figured it does." Its original owner, the Foo Fighters' guitarist, was known to be a discerning collector.

"But I didn't pass on it." Bryan grinned. "I bought it."

"Bastard."

When he chuckled, I gave him the one-fingered salute with my free hand. He returned it before ducking out of the shop with War and Shaina.

Tugging, I pulled Jewel into me. "You make friends easily, babe."

Tipping her head to keep me in view, she blinked her golden eyes as I moved both my hands to the small of her back. "Shaina's easy to like," she said, deflecting the compliment.

"She is. But so are you." A pink shade similar to the former teen star's outfit colored Jewel's cheeks.

"Thank you."

"Just calling it like I see it. So, you wanna stay here and have Dwight give us the hard sell on shit I don't need to buy, or do you wanna go home with me and get naked?"

"Home. With you."

She smiled, and my heart did that thing in response that I was coming to expect it to do. But though expected, I didn't think I would ever get used to it.

As I stroked my hand through her hair and leaned in to kiss her, my cell rang. "Fucking hell!" I exclaimed, releasing Jewel. "It's my brother."

Her eyes fluttered open. Looking dazed, she watched as I dug my phone from my pocket.

"Is Mom okay?" I asked. A call from Randy was unexpected enough to make my gut knot. He was supposed to be in Hawaii on his honeymoon with Brenda.

Randy snorted. "I know as much on that front as you do. Just got off the phone with her. Unlike you, I check in with her every day when I'm not here."

His jab hit its mark. The lightness I'd experienced just a moment before because of Jewel faded.

"She told me she talked to you." Randy's voice tightened. "Said you're coming for Christmas."

"I'm going to try," I said, setting him straight. "I—"

"Don't."

"What?"

"She doesn't need you." Another jab, a harder one. "I'll be there. You'll only make things worse."

"How?"

"You fuck things up, Rush, and I pick up the pieces. That's the pattern."

"Like with Brenda, huh?" I fired back, going straight to pissed. My brother had that effect on me.

"You shouldn't have sent the flowers. They upset her. You've got no clue how to handle a woman."

"And you do?"

"Better than you. Obviously."

I pulled in a breath, my gaze snagging on Jewel's soft expression. Instead of moving away, she stepped closer. Reaching for my hand, she pried open my clenched fingers and pressed her much smaller palm to mine. As she entwined our fingers, the anger my brother so easily stirred up in me faded.

"Mom invited me. I'll be there," I said firmly.

"Fine." That one word, delivered like a bullet, ended the call.

Good-bye to you too, brother.

I hadn't heard from Randy since he broke the news to me about him and Brenda. It was no big surprise that them being together hadn't smoothed things between us brothers.

I slid my phone back into my pocket and reached for Jewel with both hands. Pulling her close, I kissed her, and my troubled soul and emotions settled. As she molded her body to mine, my heart melted.

For the first time since I found out Randy was marrying Brenda, I felt relief—rather than sadness—that she was with someone better suited to her.

Peace. Serenity. Warmth. I'd never felt those things with my former fiancée.

Yet despite everything that was up in the air, I felt all of those things right now with the beautiful woman I had in my arms.

30

Jewel

"Rush, no more." I gasped out the words. With my legs over his shoulders, all I could reach of him was his hair. Urgently, I tugged on it. "I want you inside me."

He merely growled in response. With his lips on me, the vibrations made it impossible to hold back any longer. So did the fact that he kept at me and wouldn't stop.

His tongue swirled in a perfect circle. Near, so near, but not where I ached the most. Lightly, teasingly, he stroked his tongue over me.

"Rush, oh . . ." Moaning, I lifted my hips, straining for it.

"Baby, I'm right here," he said and pressed his lips to my clit.

His kiss released all the tension within me. Unwound, I cried his name as I came apart.

Once my spasms faded, he rearranged my languid body and climbed over me.

I reached up and framed his face, my arms trembling. Dazed from pleasure, I stared at him with his weight planted on his hands, his biceps flexed. He looked amazingly proud—he had every right to be—and he was so handsome. I fought through the stab of pain at the thought of how soon I would have to give him up.

"You are *very* good at that." Forcing my mouth into a smile, I swiped my thumbs through the wetness of me remaining on his lips.

"It's you. I want to taste you, hear you moan, know that your focus is all on me and what I'm doing to you."

"It is, and it was." My focus would always be him. In the entry hall. Behind the couch. On the couch. In the shower. On this bed. We'd been relentless since we returned to the condo.

I searched his eyes, noting how shadows dulled the silver, even more than since we started. Time was running out, and we both knew it. Was the gold in mine just as tarnished?

I lifted his hair from his brow, following my movement as I combed through the rich dark strands with my fingers. Savoring the satiny texture and the thickness, I gulped around the tightness in my throat. When my gaze returned to his, his anxiety seemed to match mine.

"Can you? Would you? Could we do it again?" I asked.

"I could. I would. I don't think I can stop."

His eyes flashed, the silver dazzling, the intensity within piercing my soul. He lowered his head and sipped from my lips as if they were the best he'd ever tasted.

His kisses were like none I'd ever had. From long, sizzling explorations to short, sweet, surface-skimming pecks, each pulled me further under his spell, making me more his. Every single one a reminder, as if I could ever forget that there would never be another like him.

My hands moved, memorizing every inch of him. The breadth of his shoulders. The firmness of his arms. The strength of his spine. The curve of his ass. Smooth, warm skin stretched over sinewy steel, somehow made malleable beneath my questing fingertips.

As his mouth glided across the round of my cheek, he lifted his body and stretched out his arm to the nightstand for a condom. The stack of packets was diminishing fast.

He rolled it on too fast. A quick glimpse was all I got. The breadth, the width, the steely length of his cock—it was an erotic image that filled my mind with heat a moment before he filled my body with it.

Whispering dirty words in my ear, he told me how hot, how tight, how wet I was while he slid out and drove back inside me. Long, slow strokes, then quick, short ones that skimmed the surface of my need. Deep. Then shallow.

The world seemed to fade away. Nothing existed but him and me, and the ebb and flow of our bodies in unison.

My hips lifted to meet each thrust. His voice in my ear encouraged me to let go, then demanded as the heat inevitably built. The fire between us was an insatiable blaze. The moment he drove deep and stiffened, I surrendered, flying like he was, yet consumed by the flames.

I wrapped my arms and legs around him as if they could bind him to me. But I knew deep down, there would be little of me left but ashes in the end.

“Can’t I have a peek?” I asked her from my spot on the lounger.

“No,” she said.

Behind her new easel, all I could see of Jewel was the top of her head and her calves and bare feet.

I frowned. “I let you hear my music before it’s completed.”

“That’s different. It’s already beautiful. All I have so far is just blotches of color and indistinct shapes. Those will change as I fill in and add to them."

"A song's a lot like a painting."

"How so?"

"It's nothing inside my head until I give it sound, like your blank canvas until you select a color and pick up your brush and give it form. I strum and sing my imagination into being. You paint it."

Her brow creased in thought, she stepped out to look at me. "That's pretty deep. And true."

My eager gaze swept over her. She'd been behind that easel for almost an hour. Her hair loose in waves, her earrings dangled to her shoulders, she was wearing a thigh-skimming white dress covered by a black smock, but I well-remembered her curves and how she felt beneath all those layers.

"I love listening to you create, and being out here with you on your patio." She turned to look at the ocean. "The sunsets are the prettiest I've ever seen."

"Yes, they are," I said, but I wasn't looking at the waves. I was watching the sun set fire to the copper in her hair.

"You've been playing the same chords over and over tonight." Her gaze back on me, she tilted her head in an unspoken question.

"Sorry. Sometimes the sound comes straight out of my head just right. Other times, I have to keep repeating it until I figure out what's missing."

"I totally get that. It can be frustrating. When you know how it should be, but you don't know what to do to get there. Maybe you're even afraid that you'll never get there. That what you need—I mean, what you see or hear in your head—is too beyond your ability to create."

Was she talking about creating? Or did she mean something more? Was this about us?

"That's exactly it." On all counts.

The song felt like one of the best I'd ever written. She was the best thing that had ever happened to me. But did I have the skill to do the song justice? Did I have what it took to keep her from slipping away?

"You can do it. Don't give up. Otherwise you've already lost." Her expression soft, she laid her brush beside the paints and closed the distance between us.

I set my guitar in the stand and tugged her onto the lounger with me, arranging her between my legs. She leaned back into me, her sweet peachy scent filling my lungs, her warmth filling my heart.

"You were smiling earlier," she said. "I'm sorry you've hit a roadblock. Maybe when you get the guys with you at the studio, it will click."

"Maybe." I wasn't so sure.

"I feel lucky to be here with you."

She felt lucky? No, I was the lucky one, being here with her.

"I like your sound. Next to piano, the acoustic guitar has always been my favorite. And your voice, it's so rich and smooth and so sexy when you lower it to sing. I want to listen to all the songs you've already recorded."

"Thanks, babe." I squeezed my arms tighter around her. The platinum status of the last album paled in comparison to the way her praise made me feel. "But I'm not sure you'd like my old stuff."

"Why not?"

"It's hard-core rock. I abandoned the softer stuff early on in my career. It wasn't selling."

"That makes me sad."

"In the beginning, I played for myself. That playing for pleasure you mentioned the first night we were together? That was me. Music was a compulsion, something I had to do, something inside me that had to come out. That did well in the small clubs around campus. Then I came out here. After I got together with Ben and Jack, it got bigger than me, and I got caught up in chasing after the wrong things. Somewhere along the way, I lost my voice, my desire, the passion that started me on this journey in the first place."

But with her I felt like I'd rediscovered it.

Jewel gave me a smile. "If what I've been listening to is any indication, I'd say you've found your voice."

"I feel like I have. Yes."

"I'm glad," she whispered. "But it's getting late. We should probably go."

"I don't want to leave just yet." My arms tightened around her.

"Neither do I." She settled back into me.

I pulled her close and inhaled the fruity scent of her hair, both thrilled and terrified that I hadn't just rediscovered my muse.

I'd found much more.

31

Jewel

"I'm so glad I ran into you and that you could come tonight." At the party, Shaina took my hands and squeezed them.

"I'm the one who feels fortunate," I said. "It's lovely out here."

The backyard was a lush, palm-tree-filled oasis that spilled downhill from the main ranch-style house to a former garage that had been transformed into a two-story apartment. We were sitting on loungers on the deck behind the house, our legs stretched out in front of us. Light from the twinkling lights strung over our heads reflected in her pretty eyes.

"Lovely because of who you're with, I imagine." Shaina inclined her head.

I followed the direction of her gaze. Rush was on the other side of the deck, talking with War, getting a quick rundown on the inner workings of the studio sound system. Beer in their hands, Bryan, Jack, and Ben were nearby. Shaina's parents had excused themselves and gone inside after dinner.

“Yes, because of him.” My lips lifted into a smile as Rush’s eyes met mine.

“It happens fast,” Shaina said softly.

“What does?”

“Falling in love. Though I think the descent is faster than gravity. Or it was with me and War.”

Startled, I shook my head. “I’m not.” Yet as I stared at Rush, I had to admit to myself that was a lie. I had fallen. And it had happened before tonight.

“How did you meet him?”

“It was a chance encounter,” I said, not meeting her eyes. Vagueness seemed the way to go.

“So was mine, or that’s the way War sees it. But I don’t believe in chance. I believe in fate.”

Loving Rush felt like fate. It felt inevitable.

Shaina gave me an apologetic smile. “I’m sorry if I’ve overstepped my bounds. I just feel comfortable with you, like I’ve known you a long time. And . . .” She blew out a breath. “I guess I’m a little lonely too. I lost my best friend.”

“Oh no.” I would be crushed without Cam. “I’m sorry.”

“No, not that way.” Her somber expression lightened. “Alex found his significant other. With the wedding planning coming together so quickly, and his film career taking off, he’s totally busy. I’m happy for him. So happy, but I miss him.” She squeezed my hand, then let it go. “I miss talking to someone one on one. Hanging out. Feeling connected to someone in a similar situation. Being with a sensitive front man isn’t easy. You have to share them with their muse, their bandmates, and their fans.”

“It certainly isn’t easy,” I said. And she didn’t know the half of my difficulties.

“I hope you feel you can talk to me. That you can tell me anything. I’m very good at listening and keeping secrets.”

"I appreciate you. And the offer. It's still new." *And soon to be over*. "I don't feel like I can share yet."

I gave Shaina a small smile.

"But I can use all the friends I can get. My closest one is . . . well, we're separated right now too. But I'll see her in a few days." In a few days, Cam would likely be all I had left.

"Is she in the same field as you?"

I nodded.

"What do you do exactly? I forgot to ask. I just assume everyone here in LA is in film."

"Yeah. I'm in acting too." Pretending to be someone I wasn't. Selling my body for cash. Deceiving myself into believing I was doing the right thing, stealing this moment in time with Rush.

"It's a tough business."

"It is."

"Sucks the soul out of you. The casting auditions. The rejections."

"It does."

"Some days I feel like I just can't do it anymore. But then there's War." She turned her head.

The Tempest front man was watching her. His eyes followed her constantly. Hers drifted to him just as often. The connection between them was intense.

"Trying to break into top-tier roles is exhausting. He believes in me more than I believe in myself most days."

"That's special, that kind of support."

"When you meet someone special, someone who connects with you and who understands you and your passion, that's someone you should hold on to." She took my hand again, squeezed it, and smiled. "Whether it's a new friend like me, or . . ." She lifted her chin toward Rush, who was headed our way. "A possessive front man."

"We're headed into the studio." Rush scooped me up into his arms.

Smiling knowingly, Shaina excused herself and got up to rejoin War.

"All right," I told Rush. "I'll just stay out here and wait for you to finish."

"I want you to come with." His expression was firm. But behind him, Jack and Ben didn't appear as thrilled about me trailing along.

"I don't know."

"You brought your sketch pad, right?"

"Yes." I hefted my strap further up my shoulder. "It's in my bag."

"It's tedious, the recording process. Overdubbing chords." He gestured to Ben. "We sometimes argue over minutia with the lyrics."

"Sometimes?" Ben arched a brow.

"A lot of times. But only because it's important to get it right." Rush returned his full attention to me. "I think better when you're close. When I can see you."

"I'll come." I glanced at his bandmates. "If they feel like I'm a distraction, I'll leave. Fair?" I posed the question to everyone.

"Fair," Jack said, a grudging respect in his eyes, respect I didn't think I'd earned, though I was glad to see that less trouble brewed in the soulful depths of his gaze tonight. "Rush has been MIA as leader for a while. Gotta say I've missed that side of him professionally, and even more as his friend. He told us that's from your influence. I like that for him."

"But I haven't done anything . . ."

"Just encourage and listen," Rush said, reaching out to stroke the back of his fingers down my cheek. The cold metal of his ring contrasted with the warmth of his caress.

"He's the one who makes me feel like my thoughts matter, that I matter." I searched his eyes, hoping he saw the truth of my words and the magnitude of what it meant to me to have his appreciation.

"That's Rush, all right." Ben studied us closely. Well, mostly me. There was no respect in his gaze. Only speculation. "Let's do this. Time's a-wasting."

Wasn't it ever?

Stealing a moment? Yes, I could do that.

Holding on to that moment and making it last? Impossible.

Time hurried on, slowing for no one. Not for me. Not even for a rock star. The tighter we tried to grasp and hold on to it, the more tenuous it became, and the faster it seemed to slip from our hands.

I could feel Jewel watching me through the glass. It was difficult to concentrate when she was so close but so far way.

Did she feel it? My increasing desperation to keep what we had? I wanted to grab her, take her back to the condo, lock us both inside, and never let her go.

"First three tracks are solid." Ben moved in front of me, blocking my view of her. "This one's missing something."

"Yeah." Holding my Martin near my body, I shifted to look at Jewel. On the couch, she had her ankles crossed demurely, like the first time she dropped her ass into the passenger seat of my Porsche. Only her head was bowed, and her reddish-brown hair curtained her face. Whatever she was drawing absorbed her.

"It'd help if you focused on what the song needs instead of her."

I frowned at Ben. "If I knew, it'd already be on the track."

"Does she know this song is about her?"

I shook my head, glancing over to make sure the mic connection wasn't open to the other room.

"She got under your skin fast."

I didn't respond. The truth was, she was deeper than that already.

"Not smart." Ben shook his head. "What do you know about her?"

"All the important stuff." That she was smart. Loyal. Kind. Sweet. Beautiful.

"Enough background to know she's not playing you?"

"She's not a groupie, Ben."

"Neither was Jack's ex."

Jack's head shot up. "Now wait a minute—"

"You know you're worried too," Ben said. "We talked about it on the way over here."

"That was before I spent time with her. She's all right."

"You're not the best judge of women, though, are you?"

Jack's eyes narrowed. "Fuck you, Ben."

"What's your point?" I glared at my bassist. "Get it out. Speak plain." I was so done with this conversation.

"Be careful. Don't let on how twisted up she's got you. Don't give her the upper hand."

Would caution keep Jewel? I didn't think so.

"Message received. Topic closed." I gave Ben a firm look and swiveled to face Jack. "Give me the beat again."

"All right." He clacked his sticks.

I strummed the chords, put my lips to the mic, squeezed my eyes shut, and sang, imagining Jewel in my arms.

And then I heard her voice, echoing me on the chorus. *"Whatever I want you to be. Whatever I need you to be. You're so right for me."*

My eyes flew open and I stopped playing to slice my hand through the air at Ben. He stilled too. Behind me, Jack had already clued in.

"You write those words to go with the song?" Ben asked me.

"Yeah, basically, but not from her perspective."

His eyes widened. "That's your missing piece."

"I know." My gaze was fixed on Jewel. She didn't even realize we were all watching her.

"Get her in here," Ben said. "Her inflection is perfect. Don't let her overthink it."

But I was already on the move, pushing through the door of the studio enclosure directly to her. "Jewel!"

She glanced up. "Are you done?" Her gaze flicked to the guys.

"Not exactly, but almost. Can you come in the booth with us for a moment?"

"Why?"

"That little chorus you were singing—"

"I'm sorry," she said quickly. "It just came out. I was trying to be quiet. Did I mess up the track?"

"No, you might've just fixed it. Could you put down your drawing and let me record you? I think those words are the missing piece."

"The song sounded so good in the studio," Jewel whispered after our shower that night as I stroked a damp tendril off her brow.

"You, babe. It sounded good because of you," I said softly. Facing me in bed, lying on her side, she was naked but for the sheet tucked around her, the low lamplight from the nightstand caressing her dewy skin. "Your part was the perfect piece to make the song complete."

Much like she was the missing piece that made my life feel meaningful.

Needing to be closer, I slid my thigh between her shapely legs instead of flipping her onto her back and thrusting my hard cock inside her welcoming heat again. I'd had her several times since we returned to the condo, my need for her relentless. Actually, it had been relentless since the first time she smiled at me. But she was worn out, her eyes heavy and drowsy, her body relaxed.

My desire intrinsically interwoven with hers, I told myself to temper the urgency until she rested. But that was difficult to do when there was a driving need within me to have her, to join my body to hers, to prove to her how good we were together.

"I just echoed your lyrics," she said, her voice sleepy.

"You did more than that." I glided a fingertip across her cheek, marveling at the softness of her skin. Why was she so reluctant to accept my praise?

"Ben. Jack. You." Her pretty golden eyes searched deep within mine. "You three are the musicians. It was like being inside a dream to be part of your creative process."

"Misguided dream, maybe."

"How so?"

"That's what my dad called my musical ambition."

"He probably didn't understand it."

"It felt like he expected me to fail." I'd never voiced that thought out loud to anyone.

"Did he get to see you succeed?"

"Yes." But by that time, the damage had been done between us. Stubbornness in his heart to admit he was wrong, resentment in mine that he hadn't supported me in the first place. "The differences between us seemed so huge back then, but now . . ."

"I know." She slid her hands out from under her chin and cradled my face. "The love is what you remember, and the lost opportunity to bridge that gap."

"Yes." I exhaled heavily. "That's it exactly."

"I understand." Her eyes warm, empathetic pools, she ran her fingertips lightly over my skin.

"But your gran was supportive of your art."

"She was. Only the way I went about pursuing it was wrong."

"How do you figure that?"

"Leaving her. Moving out to LA without her blessing." Shadows crept into Jewel's gaze. "And . . . I never got the chance to tell her I was sorry. That I loved her. That if I could do it over again, I would have done things differently."

"Yeah. I feel that same way about me and my dad." I pressed a soft kiss to her trembling lip and pulled back to look at her, relieved to see my affection had cleared some of the regret from her eyes.

"If your dad were here, he would tell you he loves you," she said firmly. "Even though your dream wasn't his dream, you have to know that he was proud of you and what you've accomplished."

"I wish that were true."

"'Wishes are the seeds of desire in our heart,'" she said softly, her gaze reflective. "My gran said that. You have to believe he's proud and act upon that belief. I certainly am proud. I got chills listening to you, watching you work, hearing the playback in the studio. You're amazing."

My heart soared from her praise. "Overdubbing the instrument and my voice makes me sound like a professional," I said, trying to downplay it.

"It's more than that, Rush." Her gaze shone with conviction like the sun at midday, allowing no shadow. "You were born to be a performer. If you'd had more time with your father, he would've acknowledged that. You would've made things right with him. I'm sure of it."

"You think so, huh?"

"I know so. You're not the type to give up on someone you care about. I've seen that in action with your bandmates and their troubles, and with your mom. You make the world a better place with your music. Your lyrics. Your voice. Your emotion."

God, the things I felt with her. My cross ring winked in the light, as if to give some kind of heavenly absolution or blessing. A seed of hope formed, filling my chest with a fullness rather than the emptiness that had lived there for so long, with warmth where there had been only cold. It grew, glowing, because of her.

"Thank you, Jewel."

I brought my hands up to skim them over her features. We were mirror images. She framed my face. I worshipped hers.

"For nothing. I was truly impressed."

"Hold that thought." My mouth curved into a smile as I threaded my fingers into her hair. "I like you being impressed by me. I want to savor this."

"I'm far from your only fan." Her lips lifted.

"Your opinion matters." My serious tone reflected how very much that was true.

"Yours matters to me too."

I nodded, accepting that, and tapped her nose. "So you'll show me your painting."

"Not yet. Not until it's finished." She treated me to a full-blown smile, a million-wattage glow.

I traced the warm satin of her lips with my thumb. She grabbed my wrist and opened my hand to press a gentle kiss to the center of my palm. Desire roared inside me, vibrating my rib cage like a tuning fork. I wanted her so badly.

All of her.

"Do you think I might be able to prove to you that one moment can lead to a next for us?" I held my breath, needing to know there was a chance for me to succeed with her. I'd failed so utterly with Brenda. And it had never mattered with her the way it mattered with Jewel.

She sighed, not meeting my eyes. “I wish it could.”

“Jewel.” My heavy exhale lifted her hair. “You couldn’t be any better for me. When I look in your eyes, I see a better me and a brighter future. I’ll take that wish and make it reality,” I said, my words a solemn vow.

32

Jewel

Reluctant to leave his arms, I slipped out of bed quietly, not wanting to wake him. It had been so late when we returned to the condo after the party, later still before we actually went to sleep.

Rush's hair was disheveled, both from rolling around in the covers and my fingers running repeatedly through the strands. Still sleeping, he looked serene, the way I felt singing backup with him in the studio. Strangely, I hadn't even been nervous. His holding my hands had taken away the awkwardness of my voice being recorded.

His handsome features were relaxed now, and his sun-kissed golden skin contrasted with the starkness of the white sheets. Staring down at him, I longed to retrace the chiseled contours of his body again, even though I'd done so only hours before. I longed to sketch him like this too.

But I needed to call Cam. I'd been checking in with her, but only briefly, and I could tell she was irritated with me. I slid my phone from my purse and slipped out to the living room, counting ten rings before she picked up the call.

"Hello?" She sounded out of it, even though it was near noon. "What's going on?"

"Late night?" I dropped onto the leather sofa, worrying my bottom lip. I didn't like the idea of her going out to work without me nearby for backup.

"Yes, but give me a moment. I need to pull up the blackout shades. It's too dark in here. If the phone hadn't lit up, I never would have found it. Hold on." The line went silent.

"Okay."

A few seconds later, she picked up the phone again. "I'm back. I'm so glad to hear from you. Do you have time for a *real* conversation today?"

"Where are you?" My eyes narrowed. We had foil covering our windows, not shades.

"Our apartment."

"We don't have blackout shades, Cam."

"We do now."

"I don't understand."

"What do you mean?" She sighed. "I need caffeine. Lots and lots to try to figure out this conversation. Hold on. I'm gonna whip up an espresso with that fancy machine."

"What fancy machine?" I asked, but she didn't hear me. The phone clattered as she put it down. Then I heard an unfamiliar whirring in the background.

What the hell?

"I'm back. With my cute little Lavazza-stamped cup and saucer."

"Do I have the right number? Is this really Camaro Montepulciano?"

"Yes. And yes."

"And you're in our apartment? With blackout curtains?"

"And a brand-new espresso machine." She took a slurp of her coffee. "It does other drinks, but I haven't figured out all the settings yet."

Frowning, I asked, "How did you afford those things?"

"He didn't tell you? His manager said you approved everything."

He? That meant Rush.

"What is everything, Cam?" My stomach started to churn.

"A new fridge that actually works, full of food. Fresh fruit. A juice maker. A computer, a flat-screen TV with a remote. Furniture. Twin beds. End tables. Pretty crystal lamps. A dresser. A mirror. iPods. A Beats sound system. A box of pepper spray canisters and a box of condoms."

As she paused for a second to take a breath, my mouth opened and closed, but nothing came out. I had absolutely no idea what to say. Didn't matter, because she picked up steam again.

"Those last two were add-ons I didn't ask for from his manager. He was a bit of an ass, I have to tell you. He insisted on me doing a FaceTime thing with the new iPhone he had delivered to show him the apartment. Twice—once before, and then after all the deliveries started. All of them. Spaced out. The last one was just before I went to bed, at three in the morning. He said something about not wanting anyone to see what was going into our apartment. He called me his Christmas project. Calls himself 'Mr. Claus,' and he calls your boyfriend a lot of choice things I'm not going to repeat. Because . . . holy fucking shit, you hit the jackpot with that one."

"Rush did this?"

"Of course he did. Didn't he tell you?"

"No."

But now the picture of my driver's license I saw on his phone made sense. I assumed he was running a background check on me, and I'd been waiting for the hammer to drop on the results of that investigation. There was more to be ashamed of than just the few overnight detentions for soliciting undercover cops.

"Are you mad?" she asked, but I didn't know what I was yet.

"Did he . . ." I swallowed and pulled the lapels of the robe together, suddenly feeling queasy. Had the days I'd given him not been the gift I'd meant them to be? Had I been paying with my body all along? Was this not at all what I thought it was?

"Did he give you money too?" I held my breath.

"No."

I let out a relieved exhale. "Okay. Good." I glanced in the direction of the bedroom.

"Was he supposed to? I thought—"

"I thought so too," I said quickly, not letting her finish. My head pounded behind my eyes. Lack of sleep, sure. But I felt like the rug had been pulled out from under me. "I need to talk to him."

"Babe, you okay?" Rush stumbled into view. "I heard you talking."

His voice rumbly, he looked sleepy, yet strangely alert, sweeping his gaze over me as he padded closer on bare feet. He was shirtless, his jeans half-buttoned and hanging low on his narrow hips. Definitely no boxers under there.

"It's Cam. I called to check in with her. I didn't mean to wake you. But apparently, Christmas came early to our apartment."

"Ah. That was fast." His brows rose as he studied me. "You don't seem happy."

I shook my head at him. "Cam." I sighed, refocusing on her. "Rush is here. I'll call you back."

"You keep saying that, but I'm still waiting for a conversation between us that lasts more than five minutes."

"Soon, I promise."

"I hear ya. All right. Good luck. And, Jewel?"

"Yeah?"

"Don't be too hard on him. For what it's worth, I think it was a real sweet thing to do."

She hung up, and I lifted my gaze to Rush. Tears flooded my eyes.

"I can never reimburse you for something so extravagant."

His brow furrowed. "I don't expect you to pay me back."

"Was I paying for those things all along?"

"Fuck no." He didn't just look alert now. He looked angry. "I just wanted—"

Awareness hit, unfurling humiliation within me. "You feel sorry for me."

"No. I feel the opposite."

He came closer. From my position on the couch, I stared up at him. As a warm tear spilled down my cheek, he dropped onto the couch and reached for me, his long fingers curling around my upper arms as he gently moved me closer.

"I don't understand."

"I admire you, baby." His silver eyes searching mine, he framed my face with his hands and gently wiped away the tears that slid down my cheeks. "Who you are as a person. How you are. Even giving me grief right now, when I was only trying to do something nice. I wanted to take away some of your worry while you were here with me. I wasn't trying to buy anything."

"My heart's not for sale," I said firmly, willing my voice not to tremble.

"I know it's not." He frowned. "I'm sorry I did this all wrong."

"What are we doing, Rush?"

I pulled his hands from my face. Staring down at them, I had to set aside the shivery way I felt at the memory of him running those skilled fingers all over my skin.

The pressure of more tears rapidly built. I shouldn't have agreed to this. It already hurt so much, and it was only going to get worse.

"I should go."

"You promised me a week." His words snapped through the air like a whip.

Trying to be strong, I met his gaze. "We don't even have a week left."

"Today and tomorrow." His expression was inscrutable.

"Why do you want me to stay?"

"Because of the way you tremble when I kiss you. Because of the way you burrow into me in your sleep. Because when I don't screw up, I can make you smile."

"Rush . . ."

"Stay. Give me a little more time. *Please*."

I closed my eyes for a second, trying to be strong, but I couldn't deny him anything. Not after how kind he'd been to me. "All right."

"Thank you."

He yanked me into him, his arms clamped so tightly around me that I could barely breathe. He acted as though I'd given him some kind of priceless gift, when in reality, I was only delaying the inevitable.

My phone rang while I was sitting on the edge of the bed, distracted, and not just because Jewel was currently in the shower without me. My mind in a whirl, I kept running through scenarios to keep her, then discarding each one because I knew they wouldn't work.

I scooped up my cell from the nightstand without glancing at the caller ID. "Hello?"

"I forwarded your plane ticket to Indy to your email," Brad said.

"Thanks, man. Appreciate it."

"Any more news from your mom?" he asked, his tone concerned.

"No."

"No news is good, I'm sure. She's always been healthy. Don't worry," he said, knowing me well.

"Hard not to."

"I know. I'd be the same about my mom."

He would be. His mom was the sweetest. She loaned me the money for a bus ticket to LA when I decided to quit college.

Brad's voice brightened. "Good news on the Christmas project you gave me. The last delivery was completed early this morning."

"I know."

"Her roommate told her?"

"Yeah."

"Camaro Montepulciano. That girl's a piece of work."

"How so?"

"Smokin' hot, but exasperating attitude. Fought me at every turn."

Sounds familiar.

"Nice thing you did for them."

"Jewel doesn't see it that way."

"Why the hell not? You ever see the inside of that apartment?"

I barely registered his question. My focus was elsewhere, across the hall where the water was still running. Jewel had been in there a while. Steam billowed out into the hall. I put far too much stock in the fact that, even though she hadn't invited me to shower with her, she hadn't closed the door.

"I don't even think it's a real apartment." Incredulity raised his voice. "It's barely big enough to fit two twin beds side by side.

Only a single bulb dangling from a wire in the ceiling. Brackets and old shelving on unpainted drywall. The one window they have is barred and nailed shut. The refrigerator didn't even work." He sighed. "Are you listening to me?"

"Yeah." I raked a hand through my hair. "I suspected it was bad."

"Bad doesn't cover it. And the inside is Taj Mahal compared to the outside. Drug paraphernalia in the hall. Homeless people sleeping in the stairwell. One of my delivery guys got robbed. Another one got shot at."

"Fucking hell." I rubbed my pounding temples. Jewel couldn't go back to that. But how could I stop her when I didn't have the power to keep her here?

"She really isn't hitting you up for any money?"

I huffed out a laugh. "She almost left when she found out about all the stuff I had you do."

"Incredible."

"She is."

"You're into her," he said after a pause. When I didn't deny it, he switched subjects. "Hey, I listened to the songs you sent over late last night. Good stuff."

"Thanks." It was high praise, coming from him. Brad was nearly as exacting as the ice queen of Black Cat Records.

"I'll send them on to Timmons today."

"Already?" I wasn't sure I wanted her frosty displeasure dampening my creativity at this point in the process, especially with all that was up in the air with my mom and Jewel.

"You need her approval. It's a radical departure from your last album. I like it, but she's your producer. She's got to sign off on it."

I sighed. "Sure. I know."

"Your girl has a nice set of pipes. Perfect foil to your voice. She's a little rough, but unpolished works for that ballad. Can I make a suggestion?"

"Fire away."

"Make the part with you two in combo a progressive bridge: *Could be the one. Is the right one. Will always be the one.*"

"That's perfect."

"That song feels big." The line went silent for a few seconds. "This thing with you and her, is it like that?"

"It's exactly like that."

"I was going to hassle you about getting a nondisclosure from her."

"No releases." If I did that, I'd lose her for sure.

"So, what are you going to do about her?"

"I don't know, man."

"Go with what feels right."

Good advice, usually. It's what he told me about pursuing a career in music.

But this was different. Bigger.

33

Jewel

"Who were you talking to just now?" I knotted my robe tighter as I stepped into the bedroom.

"Brad. My manager. One of my closest friends. The guy who sent all the stuff to your apartment because I told him to."

"Did you tell him to come get it and take it all back?"

"No." Narrowing his eyes, Rush stalked toward me. His jeans were buttoned now, but he still hadn't put on a shirt.

I curled my fingers into fists at my sides, focusing on my nails digging into my palms and not on how sexy he was.

"It stays." His expression turned as steely as his gaze. "All of it."

I shook my head. "I can't repay you."

"I don't expect to be repaid, Jewel. It was a gift. It's Christmas."

"You bought me the clothes. The paints. The scales between us are already unbalanced. You can't refurnish my entire apartment."

"Is that what you're worried about? The scales between us?"

I nodded.

"This isn't about economics. It's about me as a man and you as a woman. You're too good for me. They're already unbalanced." Directly in front of me now, he reached for my hands and tugged me into him. "Look at me, Jewel."

His hard body aligned to mine, I had to crane my neck to keep his handsome face in view.

"The things I have, the things I can afford to do because of my job . . . they don't mean shit if I can't share them with someone I care about. And I care about you. Don't you get that?"

"But—"

"You gonna throw at me again the way we started?"

"Yes, I—"

"The fact that we haven't been together very long?"

I nodded.

"Do you think every story starts like a fairy tale?"

"No." I shook my head. My gran had been the last in our family to have a beginning like one of those.

"How long do you think is long enough to know how you feel about someone? A day? Two days? A week? Because we don't have that amount of time. You won't give it to me." His square jaw firmed. "But after spending night after night, day after day, hour after hour in your company, I know how I feel."

"How?" I whispered.

"I feel desperate, Jewel. Desperate to keep you, no matter what it takes."

"I don't—"

"You've backed me into a corner with your restrictions." His eyes flared.

"I didn't mean to."

"I want to wake up with you in my arms. I want to spend my days talking to you and making you smile, my nights making love to you. I don't want to miss a single sunset without you beside me to share it."

"I want that too. But—"

"No buts. Let's do it. What's stopping us?"

"I'm me. You're you. You leave in two days. I go back to . . . to . . . doing what I have to. There's no happy ending for us."

"There's none because you won't consider it. What are you afraid of, Jewel?"

"You. Us." And being left behind. Falling short. Feeling abandoned. "Picking up the pieces afterward . . ." Like I did after losing my parents, Landon, my gran. "I've done it before, but I just don't know if I can do it again."

"Baby, I'm not going anywhere that you can't come with me."

"You say that now. But what about tomorrow?"

"When I change my mind about us, you mean?"

"Yes."

"I'm not that dipshit who abandoned you."

"I don't think you are, or I wouldn't be here with you. But I need more time to be sure."

"What's more time going to tell you that you don't already know about me? I'm just a simple guy underneath all the rock-star trappings, a little more clueless about relationships than most. But I know this is real. The way I feel . . . the way I think you feel about me. We work together."

Amazed and confused, I blinked up at him. "You want me to just go where you lead. To follow you wherever and throw caution to the wind. And you want me to make that decision right now."

"Yes."

"No." Tears sprang to my eyes. "I can't. I'm sorry. Today, tomorrow . . . yes, you have all of me, all I have to give. That was the original deal. That's the way we can go on if you still want me to stay until the end of the week."

Rush

I pulled in a breath, trying to rein in my temper. "You're afraid?"

"Yes, I'm afraid. Those rock-star trappings of yours are luxuries to me. Food. Shelter. Safety."

"I realize that."

"From a distance, maybe, imagining my pitiful existence from your ivory tower. But that's my life."

Stunned and frustrated, I stared at her. Jewel didn't trust me. She was rejecting me because of how rich I was, yet the truth was I was poor . . . at least, when it came to the things that really mattered.

I backed away from her, the first time since I'd met her that I didn't want to pull her closer.

"Should I go?" Her eyes were wet, and her bottom lip trembled.

"Give me a minute, darlin'."

I couldn't look at her right now. This amazing woman was everything I wanted, but she didn't want me. Trying to hide my emotions, I turned my back to her. Yet even turned away, my eyes were drawn to her, drinking in her reflection in the mirror above the dresser.

Before I could look away, her eyes met mine in the mirror, reflecting my own anguish and desperation. One of her arms stretched out toward me, and I couldn't resist her. I spun around and quickly eliminated the short distance between us.

"I can't think straight when you talk about leaving." I took her hands and wrapped them around my neck, moving my body close to hers. She was warm, and she molded perfectly to me. "Give me those days. I'll take everything you have to give. I'll consider that time a greater gift than anything I could ever give you."

Her golden eyes widened as if with wonder. She was so beautiful, she took my breath away.

"I want to do right by you, Jewel." I reached up and lifted a tendril by her face, tracing one of the ribbons of copper fire in her hair. "The last thing I want to do is hurt you."

34

Jewel

"Where are we going?"

I sneaked glances at Rush as he steered the Porsche onto the highway after pulling away from his condo. Only a few moments earlier, he'd abruptly informed me that we were going out.

The news disappointed me. I'd wanted to spend the remaining time we had left in the condo, just the two of us, but that was an unrealistic dream. He had things to do before he went to see his mom, and I needed to stop clinging to him.

Yet, with less than forty-eight hours left, all I wanted to do was touch him. Unable to stop myself, I placed my hand on his thigh.

He took one hand off the steering wheel and pressed it over mine. "Keep it there."

"I plan to." I lifted my chin.

Yes, I needed to start the process of letting him go, but I couldn't seem to bring myself to do it. Not just yet. Not until I was forced to. All of me—that was the deal, until the very end.

Rush smiled at me. "I have a surprise for you."

"I'm not big on surprises." I thought of the load of gifts with Cam at the apartment.

"You'll like this one."

"Are you sure?" I gnawed on my lip and looked out the window, noting the change of freeway.

"I'm sure. But I can't tell you in advance. Do you want me to ruin the surprise?" He flicked on his blinker and took the next exit.

"Is it work related?"

"No." He zipped around turning traffic to go straight at the end of the ramp.

"Is it an errand for your mom?" I asked as he did a U-turn under the next underpass.

"No."

I saw the sign then. I hadn't noticed any on the freeway. Not the hidden signs he couldn't see to reveal the desires of my heart regarding him. The one outside the car—a literal sign for our destination.

He glanced at me and grinned at my awed expression. "For you, Jewel. Surprise."

"The Getty Museum? You brought me to the Getty Museum?" A huge smile on my face, I bounced in my seat. "How long can we stay?"

"It opened ten minutes ago. We have the entire day."

"But the band, the album," I said. "Your music. Your mom."

"They can wait. Today and tomorrow, it's just you and me."

Rush parked the Porsche in the garage. We entered the station and rode the hover train up the hill just like all the other visitors. When we disembarked, he stopped for a few fans who recognized him and graciously signed a few autographs. Once he was done, I grabbed his hand and dragged him up the steps to the welcome rotunda.

"Hurry!"

He chuckled, tugging on my hand to slow me down. "We have until five thirty, Jewel."

I gave him an annoyed look, and he lifted his hands in surrender.

"Okay, okay, I get it. It's like you at the art store all over again."

"Um, no," I said, stopping once we were inside. Beige Italian travertine beneath my feet, glass all around, and a sweeping staircase to the upper level beckoned. Spreading my hands wide, I gestured grandly. "The paint store is where you go to dream. This is where you see dreams come to life."

"Dreams, huh?" He came forward, an intense look in his eyes as he traced my smile with his finger. "I'm touching one right now."

"I don't think you're allowed to touch the ones displayed here," I whispered, my chest too tight to speak louder. Talking about dreams reminded me of our conversation in bed last night, and his vow to make our wish into a reality. I so wanted to believe in that.

"That's okay for me. They don't tempt me the way you do."

"Thank you for my surprise." I was mesmerized by his thoughtfulness, his words, the seriousness in his gray eyes. *By him.*

His expression brightened with his sudden grin. "I have a few ideas on how you can thank me later."

"Such as?"

"Naked. Multiple poses. Like art, but interactive. Plan on it taking hours."

I shook my head at him and smiled.

"I love that smile." He grabbed my hips and pulled me into him. My sundress, a pale yellow one with daisies that reminded me of the ones in Gran's meadow, swirled around my calves. "Let's get this dream thing started. Yours first, mine later."

"Slow down, babe." I tugged Jewel to a halt in front of the fountain. "Let's get something to eat before we do the sculpture garden."

Doing her was more what I had in mind. Only knowing how much she would love this place had convinced me to ditch my original naked plans for the day. Well, not a plan, exactly, just a desire to take her again and again, hoping to show her how much she meant to me.

"I'm not hungry."

"You are." I shook my head. "That beast that bays when you go too long without eating is scaring the other people in the museum."

She stared past me in the opposite direction of where I wanted to take her, a perfect metaphor for our relationship at the moment.

"Let's go this way." I curled my fingers tighter around hers and hooked my thumb over my shoulder. "I've got a little private picnic set up for us over on the lawn."

"That sounds nice." Her expression brightened, outshining the California sun. "Lead the way."

Oh, if it could only be so easy with her and me.

"C'mon," I said. "It's this way."

You can do it, McMahon. I wasn't normally one for pep talks, but unfamiliar territory called for extreme measures. *You've reasserted your role and your vision for the band. You can do it with her too.*

Only I was afraid I couldn't. With the guys, I had a history. With her, I only had a total of a handful of days.

When we turned the corner around a waist-high hedge,

she stopped and her mouth dropped open. "Wow. You can see all the way to downtown from here."

I forced my gaze away from her pretty face to take in what she saw. "You could from a lot of the vantage points inside the museum, but you were too busy looking at dreams to see what was outside the glass."

I'd been just as guilty lately, but in a different way. I had been too busy being dazzled by her to realize what I had. What I feared I could lose.

She tilted her head, scanning my face, seeming to consider my words, maybe even able to peer into my head to hear my thoughts. "The blanket, the food, chilled sodas, when did you have time to arrange all of this?"

"While you were sitting on that viewing bench staring at the Van Gogh."

"An amazing painting."

"It reminded me of you."

"How so?"

"The white iris."

Frowning, she shook her head. "I'm not pure."

"You're beautiful. You stand out, like a diamond among the more ordinary gems. I'm not interested in ordinary."

She searched my eyes. "Thank you," she said softly.

"Don't thank me for telling the truth. Sit." I gestured to the blanket. "Let's eat. And you can tell me what your favorite things have been so far."

I served the sandwiches and replenished her glass with ginger ale while she spoke around mouthfuls and sips. She was so animated, so excited, her face practically glowed. She was mesmerizing and more beautiful than any woman I had ever seen.

I wanted to clasp her to my chest. I wanted to lay my heart at her feet, then lay her out on the grass and make love to her.

I wanted to have her in every way a man can have a woman. Then I wanted to do it all over the next day, and the day after that.

I settled for pulling her between my legs when she was finished eating. The other would have to wait. Not too long, but just not quite yet. I didn't want to scare her.

"Mmm." She dropped her head back to my shoulder as I sifted through her hair. "That feels so good."

My cock lengthened, and I glanced around, considering. The hedge sheltered us somewhat from the vantage point of the museum, but I couldn't have her here. There were too many people nearby. Too many potential interruptions. Once I started, I wouldn't be able to stop.

"Rush?" She peered up at me.

I didn't get a read on her intention until she turned around to face me, straddled me, and hiked up her dress.

"I'm not wearing any panties." She put her palms on my chest, and my heart sped up until it was pounding in anticipation.

Incredulous, I stared at her. "You've been walking around all day like that?"

"Yes." The corners of her wide, pretty mouth tipped up.

"Naughty girl."

I lowered my head and took her lips, gliding my hands up her creamy thighs under her dress. Heading directly for the center of her, I swiped my thumb over her pussy, and then her clit when I reached it.

"You're wet, baby," I said softly against her lips.

"I'm that way whenever you put your hands on me."

I hissed as her hands skimmed me, lowering the zipper on my jeans. I circled her again with my thumb, sliding her wetness over it. When she tugged at my hips, I lifted my ass so she could pull my jeans and my boxers down. Thinking quickly,

I arranged her skirt to cover what we were about to do, thankful it was so long and wide.

"Condom," I said gruffly.

"I have one." She fumbled under the makeshift tent of her skirt, and I twitched under her fingers as she rolled it on me.

"Oh, babe."

I groaned and grabbed her sexy ass. One delectable globe in each hand, I lifted, positioned, and brought her down on my cock. She put her hands on my shoulders for balance, and I lifted my hips off the ground to go deeper.

Up, I thrust into her.

Down, she plunged.

Anyone who drove up the road to the museum and saw our movements would know what we were doing.

"So good, Rush."

Sunlight streaking through her hair, she stared at me, her eyes bright. Her lips parted and her breath caught as I thrust again inside her.

"You're so pretty." I gripped her ass tighter, thrust into her harder, and she accommodated me beautifully.

"I'm so close . . ." Her fingers dug into my skin as she ground her pussy onto me.

"Give me whatever you got, babe."

I lifted, and she lowered to meet me. Crashing together, our connection was electric. Our rhythm sped up, but our breathing was ragged.

"Jewel." My pulse scattered. Her name was an impending storm.

"Rush . . ." She moaned, throwing her head back. The storm had arrived for her as well. It swept away both of us. "Oh, Rush."

I watched in awe as her release hit her, feeling her spasm around my cock, and then mine slammed into me too. "I love you, baby."

It burst over me, the knowledge like a fountain. My heart overflowing with love for her, I hammered into her. Again and again, no holding back.

He put his lips on my neck, pressing them to where my pulse was still racing.

My soul soaring on his words, I came again. He took my mouth with his to cover and swallow my cries.

“Rush.” I framed his face with my hands as I came tumbling back to earth.

Still gripping my ass under my skirt, he stared at me, his expression as possessive as his hold on me.

“You’re not leaving.” His gaze was fierce. “Do you understand me?”

Unable to deny him, I nodded. “I’m not leaving.”

After all, where would I go? Wherever I went, wherever I was . . . with him or without him, I would always be his.

35

Rush

On the patio beside me in our usual evening position, Jewel stood at her easel, prattling on excitedly about the museum. I was on the lounger with my guitar, still tinkering with the melody that felt huge. Not just because it was good, but because it was about her. She was staying.

"Aren't you going to let me see what you're doing?" I'd been listening to her speak, but I really didn't understand half the technique and brushstroke shit she was talking about.

"Stop pestering me. It's a present for you. I told you already, you'll see it when it's done." She shifted her weight from one shapely leg to the other, barely visible beneath the large canvas on the easel. "But it's not like the ones we saw today. I've never had any formal training."

"You're making it for me, so I'll love it. The way I love you."

We hadn't discussed my declaration, and she hadn't reciprocated it. Notably, but that was okay. She was staying, so I had time to convince her. Apparently, I needed every bit of that time.

How long would she agree to remain if she didn't feel the same way?

"Rush." She stepped out from behind the mystery painting just as my cell rang.

"Hold on." I held up a finger, glancing at the display with a sigh. "It's my brother." Holding the phone to my ear, I said, "Yeah?"

"They're taking Mom to the hospital."

"What?" Ice water flooded my veins. "Why?"

"She had a dizzy spell and hit her head. She was still woozy when the neighbors checked in on her, so they called an ambulance, then they called me. I'm trying to get back stateside, flying standby. We were scheduled for tomorrow. Since you're closer to her, can you—"

"Yes." Instantly setting my animosity aside, I would have agreed to anything. After all, this was our mother. "If I have to get in my car and drive to her, I'll do it. I'll call you back as soon as I figure out the best way to get there. Text me the neighbor's number."

"Already have."

My phone bleeped.

"Safe travels," I told him.

"You too." He rang off.

"What's going on? You're shaking." Looking worried, Jewel sank down on the lounger beside me.

"My mom's on her way to the hospital."

"Oh no." Her eyes wide, Jewel curled her fingers around my hand.

I swallowed, focusing for a second on her, on her sweet gesture of comfort. It helped me to harness the panic galloping through my veins. "I'm calling Brad."

"Hello?" My manager picked up immediately. "What's going on?"

"My mom's in an ambulance. I need to get home to Indiana. Fast."

"Oh no. Is she okay?"

"I don't know, man. Just get me there, all right?"

"I will."

"I gotta call the neighbor. See if they can tell me what happened."

"It'll be okay, Rush."

I wasn't so sure. It hadn't been for my father.

"Hang in there," Brad said. "I'll call you back when I switch your flight, and I'll meet you in Indy as soon as I can. You okay to drive a rental after you land?"

Before I could respond, Jewel covered our joined hands and stroked the side of my palm with her thumb.

"Can I come with you?" she whispered. "I won't intrude. But I can drive if you need me."

My gaze locked with hers, I hit Jewel with the raw force of that need. I needed her now more desperately than ever.

"God, yes. I need you."

Jewel

Since the phone call, everything felt wrong. Rush was understandably distracted, and I was worried for him.

It only got worse after we landed in Indianapolis. Every bit of news he received along the way was more upsetting than the last. His mother's status had gone from "we're keeping her overnight for observation" to "we need to talk to the family" after the first test results came back.

I insisted on driving when we got our rental car, and Rush didn't argue. Clutching his phone like a lifeline, he slumped in the passenger seat staring out the window, but there was nothing to see except dark, empty fields in the distance. With his uncertain expression, he barely resembled the confident man I'd come to know over the last several days. Proof of how far I'd fallen for him, I now considered endearing what I'd first viewed as arrogance.

"Get off here?" I asked as we passed the city limit sign. He knew the way. It had pretty much been a straight shot along the interstate since the airport. But I couldn't remember the street for the hospital.

"Yes." He nodded, his features strained. "There's a visitors' parking lot up ahead." His voice quavered. He wasn't just worried; he was barely holding it together.

"It'll be okay." I reached for his hand as soon as I parked the car and cut the engine.

"It wasn't with my dad." He stared at the brightly lit four-story county hospital. "By the time I got to the hospital, he was already gone."

I felt his pain. I never got to say good-bye to my grandmother. "You talked to your mom on the phone. You said she sounded good."

"Yes, but that's her, Jewel. She's always been the strong one in the family. You'll see how she is shortly."

He opened his door and got out. I did the same and locked the car, then handed him the keys as we threaded our way between the rows of cars.

When we reached the revolving-door entrance to the hospital, he stopped short, and I looked at him in confusion.

A tremble ran through him. "She'll need me to be strong."

In deference to the climate, he was wearing jeans and his black leather jacket with a long-sleeved shirt. I wore my freshly washed jeans and art T-shirt plus an Indianapolis-emblazoned hoodie he'd bought for me at an airport gift shop. It was cold outside, but more worrisome to me than the chill was the tension I could feel in him from our clasped hands.

"I've watched you being strong. You've been coordinating information between everyone for hours. You can do this."

He nodded to me, moved his hand to my back, and we walked in together.

My gaze went to her as soon as I entered her room. It was like a punch to the chest to see my mom looking so pale, lying helpless in a hospital bed, tethered to blinking, beeping equipment.

"Rush." When she breathed out my name, her eyes filled with tears, turning her gray eyes silver.

"Mom." My throat tight, I blinked hard as my eyes burned like hell.

Tiny, barely five one, she appeared even smaller to me somehow. Her brown hair had turned mostly gray since the last time I saw her, and it didn't escape my notice that she'd lost a significant amount of weight.

She reached out to me with her left hand, since the right one was hooked to an IV.

My heart pounding, my chest tight, I moved straight to her. The words I hadn't been able to speak to my father before he passed had been lodged inside my throat for hours, and now they burst free.

"I love you, Mom." I bent and pressed a kiss to her soft cheek, and she took my hand.

"I love you too, sweetie."

We stared at each other, not acknowledging the wetness on our faces.

"It's going to be okay," I told her firmly. It had to be. "I'm sorry I've been away so much. After we get you through this, I'll fix that. I'll make a break in the upcoming tour schedule to spend time with you." I'd make Mary Timmons understand. If she didn't, I'd get another label.

Mom gave me a quavering smile. "I'd like that."

"Done."

"Who's the pretty young lady with you?" She peered around me. "Is this Jewel?"

"Hi, Mrs. McMahon." Jewel gave her a little wave and stepped forward. "I'm sorry you're not feeling well, sorry to intrude. Rush was just so worried about you. I didn't want him to be alone."

"Moira. Call me Moira." Mom returned her gaze to me. "She's worried about you. She came all this way to support you. Don't let this one get away." Her words were as firm as mine had been about her getting better.

"I don't plan to."

"Good." She closed her eyes. "I didn't think . . . What I mean is . . ." She opened her eyes, her gaze no longer glittering with emotion, but determined. "We need to talk to the doctor."

"I know. I was hoping we could wait for Randy and Brenda."

"They mentioned an operation in the morning."

"Yes." I didn't know they had already told her.

"I'd like to talk to the doctor now, if you don't mind."

"All right. I wanted to spend some time with you first, but I can go find him." I started to slip my hand from hers.

"I'll get him," Jewel said, her eyes bright. "Just tell me his name again. You stay."

So supportive. So sweet. If I hadn't already been certain, the way she'd been so solid at my side since I got the news would have sealed it.

"Dr. Shannon, dear," my mom said softly before her eyes pinched shut.

"Are you in pain?" I asked.

"A little."

Jewel and I exchanged a glance. "A little" coming from my mom meant she was hurting an awful lot.

"I'll hurry," Jewel said, seeming to read my mind.

As soon as she left the room, my mom spoke again. "I like her."

"I like her too."

"Only like?" Mom opened her eyes. Even in pain, she hit me with her interrogating expression, the one that always made me cave.

My throat tight, I swallowed. "I love her."

"Does she know?"

"Yes."

"But?"

"But what, Mom?"

"Your dad proposed to me after two dates."

"You want me to propose to Jewel?"

She nodded.

"I can't. It's complicated."

I didn't notice at first that Jewel had returned with Dr. Shannon. My eyes met hers, and they seemed troubled. She glanced away.

At the time, her response reinforced my impression that I had to proceed slowly with her. The key to the condo I wanted to give her as a Christmas present needed to wait until she gave me the words I had given her.

Later, too much later, I would realize my mistake.

He loved me, just not that way. A woman with a past like mine? Of course I could never be marriage material.

Don't be greedy, Jewel. Just be what he needs.

My eyes stinging, I said, “I’ll wait in the hall.”

Dr. Shannon gave me a nod. “That might be best.”

I slipped out. But before the door shut, I heard the diagnosis.

A cerebral aneurysm.

I didn’t hear the prognosis or the statistics following surgery. Rush explained it all to me later, so emotionless and withdrawn, as if he were a million miles away rather than right beside me.

It wasn’t encouraging news.

36

Jewel

"No. It's okay. You should stay here with her overnight." I gnawed on my lip. "I'll get a hotel room."

Rush frowned. "You're not staying in a hotel by yourself."

"Why not?"

"You'll stay at the house."

"But—"

"Stop giving me grief," he snapped. "Can't you see I have enough stress right now?"

"Yes, of course."

He'd been harsh, but I understood. When I got the news about my gran, I hadn't been able to even think straight on the bus out to see her. So worried. So alone. Then arriving too late.

I reached for Rush's face to comfort him, wanting to let him know he wasn't alone.

"There you are," a booming voice announced.

My hands fell to my sides, and I turned my head.

A tall blond with an authoritative manner strode toward us. "How is she?" His ice-blue eyes swept over me quickly before he focused on Rush.

"She's putting on a brave front."

"Typical Moira."

"Doc Shannon says it's a large aneurysm that has to be treated surgically. They're bringing in a specialist from Indianapolis to perform the surgery. He's supposed to be the best, but I want better odds than they're giving me."

"I'm sorry." The blond put his hand on Rush's shoulder. Both men were equally matched in height. Both drew the attention of the mostly female nursing staff in the corridor. "What can I do to help?"

"I'm staying at the hospital. There's a pullout single in her room. Can you take Jewel to the farmhouse, and stay with her until Randy and Brenda arrive?"

I wanted to stay with Rush, but I suppressed my hurt feelings. If my being somewhere else was what he preferred, it was what I would do.

"I'm sure they can drive her back in the morning," the blond said. "But if they can't, I'll do it."

"Thanks, man."

"No problem." The blond man turned to me. "Jewel, hey. I'm Brad, Rush's manager."

I knew he was more, but he didn't add that he was also a close friend. The omission added to the sense of isolation I couldn't help but feel.

"You sure you don't need anything?" I asked Rush. "You haven't eaten since the plane." And he'd only had something then because I refused to put food in my mouth if he didn't.

"You're sweet to worry about me, baby." He moved close. "Get some sleep. I'll see you tomorrow. I love you." Hands cupping my face, he lowered his head and kissed me.

It was a good kiss. One that told his friend that I was his and how he felt about me. When he ended it, I wanted to say the words back.

I wanted to—it was the way I felt—but I didn't. Not here. It wouldn't be right.

No, the first time I said those words to Rush, it needed to be private. Memorable. Like when he had told me.

I would never forget how it felt with him inside me, telling me he loved me.

"You're pretty," Brad said, but there was a twist to his lips that made it less than a compliment.

"Thanks." I sat stiffly beside him on the leather passenger seat of his rental car.

"He needs more than that."

"I know he does."

Tears threatened at Brad's words, but I blinked them back. He was right. Rush needed better than me.

Glancing at me, Brad frowned. "You need to toughen the fuck up if you plan to stay around."

I gasped at his sharpness. "I'm not weak."

"Didn't say you were." He gave me a quick side glance as the car jolted over a pothole in the unpaved dirt road. "Rush is a celebrity. This is going to be big news."

"His mom being sick?" I pressed my hand to my stomach, nauseated at the thought of Rush having to deal with media attention right now.

"Yeah. It's not cool, but that's the way it is. And you, with your profession, are gonna be like gas on a flame."

"No one knows."

"Yet. It's only a matter of time. You have a record."

"Does he know?" I gnawed my lip.

"About the solicitation?" he asked, not mentioning the other, though he gave me a searching look. "No. I didn't think his knowing would change anything. And he's got enough to worry about right now. I'll shield him as much as I can. The rest is up to you."

Staring straight ahead at the road, he switched topics.

"Reporters can't go inside the hospital. I'll make a statement and keep Rush away from the TV and off the internet. My loyalty's to him." He gave me another glance that felt like a warning. "But you're going to have to help and learn fast to fend for yourself. The media aren't your friends. Just say 'no comment' and don't engage them. Understand?"

I nodded.

"Good girl. Maybe he did all right with you."

Brad turned the car onto a gravel driveway leading to a two-story farmhouse with a wraparound porch. Large trees were planted on either side of it, and I wondered if Rush had climbed them as a boy. When the car came to a stop, I pulled in a fortifying breath.

Apparently in manager mode now, and no gentleman like his friend, Brad didn't open my door after he climbed out of his side of the car. His long strides sure, he headed straight toward the house without looking back.

I got out and followed him.

"Come on." Already on the porch, he held the screen door open for me and unlocked the front door.

"Sorry." I picked up my pace. "I'm still a little stiff from the plane." And the stress, but I didn't share. The media weren't the only ones I needed to be wary of.

"Living room." Inside, he gestured to where we stood. Plaid sofa, two easy chairs, all faded and worn. A Christmas tree in the corner with a couple of presents beneath, reminding me of the one for Rush I'd left behind. "Bedrooms are upstairs. His mom's room is at the back. His brother's opposite. Rush's room is on the right, the one with the guitar and Dylan posters."

"Got it."

"Kitchen's through there." Brad pointed at a pass-through on the other side of the living room. "Knowing his mom and the neighbors, it's likely well stocked. Get yourself something to eat. I'm gonna let Rush know we're in, and I need to make some calls."

"All right." I couldn't eat, not with my stomach in knots. But I could make sandwiches or something. Keep myself busy. Away from Brad.

"Jewel?" he said, and I stopped. "Randy and Brenda will be here soon. Rush texted they just arrived at the hospital."

"Okay." The knots in my stomach tightened.

"Randy and Rush don't get along."

"I know."

He nodded. "Well, he's not your problem. She is."

I gripped the edge of the kitchen sink and forced myself to take deep breaths. I couldn't let on that she upset me.

But none of my gran's lessons were sticking. Instead of starving Brenda, I kept feeding her ammunition to zap me with at every turn.

"There you are," the beautiful blonde said as she breezed into the kitchen, wearing a navy two-piece business suit and heels. I was dressed more appropriately for the casual farm setting in my jeans and tee.

"Did you need something?" I pasted on a smile, trying to ignore how her perfume made my eyes burn. Had she bathed in the stuff?

Brenda wrinkled her nose. "Not if you're making it." She hadn't been a fan of my sandwiches.

"I'm just tidying up. Then I'm going up to Rush's room."

Her sapphire-blue eyes narrowed. Every mention of Rush's name from my lips seemed to trigger her temper. "Do you have permission to be in his room?"

"Brenda." Randy stepped into the kitchen.

He had brown hair and gray eyes like Rush's, but that was where the similarity between the brothers ended. Randy's nose was too large, his lips too full. With his long legs, short torso, and thin frame, he reminded me of a terrier. The way he trailed along behind his wife reinforced that impression.

"Jewel is his girlfriend." Frowning at his wife, he scratched his ear, like a terrier with possible mange and bad taste in women. "She's welcome here."

"This is *my* home." Brenda stomped her foot. "Not his."

I winced. A hotel would have been so much better.

"He's my brother. This is a family matter."

"She's not family."

"Listen," I said. "I can—"

"You stay. That's what he wants. My brother always gets what he wants." Randy sounded whiny and looked beaten down.

"I don't want to be any trouble," I said. Moira was Randy's mom too. He had to be wracked with worry like Rush. I felt bad for my derogatory inner commentary. "It's an upsetting time for everyone."

"That you're making worse," Brenda said, her eyes narrowed like a cat's.

I curled my fingers into fists. "Again, I can leave."

"Can you give us a minute?" Randy said to me, waving a dismissive hand in the air. "Rush's room is—"

"I know where it is. Brad told me."

"All right then." Randy gave me an imperious look.

Relieved to escape, I slipped past them. Their raised voices chased me into the living room and up the stairs. Stepping into the first room on the right, I closed the door, successfully shutting them out.

Sighing, I leaned my back into the wood and wished—not for the first time since Brenda and Randy arrived—that I had left with Brad to return to the hospital.

My eyes watering, I glanced around the room. Twin bed beneath one of the windows. Bookshelves with trophies. Guitar case by a Dylan poster.

Looked like I had the right room.

I forgot to feel sorry for myself as I took a closer peek at the photos of Rush on the wall. In them, he looked very young with his hair shorn short, his expression guileless, and his stance unsure. He was cute, but I preferred the current version—more mature, cocky, and with his hair falling in his eyes.

Then I saw a grouping of photos that appeared to have been freshly dusted. Rush and Brenda. He'd been happy, grinning adoringly at her, his arm slung around her shoulders. With a bow in her hair and a virginal smile, she had ruled his world.

Deflated, I sank onto the bed. I used to be a girl like her. The type of girl you married.

My cell dinged. I pulled it out of my pocket, hoping for Rush, but it was Cam.

"Hey," I said.

"Hey, where are you? The connection is terrible. I don't hear the ocean. You sound like you're in a tunnel."

"I'm on a farm in the middle of nowhere."

"Did you go back to Tennessee?"

"No, I'm at Rush's family's house in Indiana. His mom's in the hospital. She has a cerebral aneurysm. Her surgery's in the morning."

"When did this happen?"

"Earlier today, I mean yesterday. It's late here."

"Is he okay?"

"He was all right when I left him. Mostly." I frowned.

"Why are you there if he's at the hospital?"

"He's staying in her room. It's a single bed."

"A single can fit two. It'd be cozy, but then I think cozy's what you two are."

"Yeah. He took me to the Getty Museum yesterday, Cam. He told me he loves me."

"Whoa." She was silent a moment, the ramifications of it hitting her. "That how it is for you too?"

"Yes."

"And you're there with who and why?"

"His brother, who's barely tolerable, and his sister-in-law, who's also Rush's ex-fiancée. The woman is a she-bitch straight from the pits of hell."

"She giving you shit?"

"Oh yeah."

"She's jealous. She's still into him."

"Definitely."

"Give her shit back. Channel a little of your Harley attitude."

Sighing, I said, "I don't belong here, Cam."

"How do you mean?"

"This is wholesome Hometown, USA."

"You're worth more than any of that whacked group. Don't be a kicked puppy. If Rush is what you want, kick that she-bitch back."

"His mom's sick."

"So do it diplomatically. But get your ass back to that hospital. If he's your man, stick by him."

37

Rush

"Jewel." I rubbed sleep from my eyes, thinking I was dreaming. "What are you doing here? What time is it?"

"Two in the morning, or somewhere around there. At least, that's what time it was when the Uber guy dropped me off."

"We don't have Uber in Pendleton."

"Well, I'm sorry to disagree," she whispered over the beeping of my mom's monitors. "But I called Brad, he used his app, and it worked. So here I am."

She shifted on her feet, looking adorable, sweet, and unsure of herself. I'd never been more relieved in my life to see anyone.

"You were supposed to stay at the house."

"I don't belong there. I belong with you."

And so she did.

I threw back the thin piece-of-shit blanket and moved to the far edge to make room for her on the pullout. Looking more relieved than I felt, she unzipped her hoodie, dropped her bag on the floor, and set down my old guitar. I was surprised to see it, but then again, not so much.

I smiled as she climbed into the pullout with me.

"This is much better." She tucked her body to mine, placing her hands on my chest.

I wrapped my arm around her. "It is. Worlds better."

With Jewel here, I didn't feel like I was flying through space untethered.

I pulled her closer, anchoring myself to her. "Was Randy an ass to you?"

"Brenda."

"I'll take care of her in the morning. I'm busy now." I kissed the top of Jewel's head, inhaling deeply. Peach aromatherapy, my preferred healing balm.

"How's your mom been?" she asked softly.

"Resting well now." I stroked my fingers up and down Jewel's arm. "They gave her something to relax. We talked for a while until she fell asleep."

"You did? What about?"

"Stuff we hadn't discussed in a long time." Things that had comforted and unsettled me. It felt a lot like tying up loose ends. The surgeon's talk of survival odds had probably rattled her too.

"Such as?"

"Her and my dad. How they felt about my leaving college." I stopped stroking, and Jewel looked up at me.

"That must have been tense."

"At first." I resumed the mindless motion. Focusing on the creamy softness of her skin made the details easier to retell. "Emotions were always high on both sides. They wanted one thing for me, and I wanted another. They saw my taking a different path as a rejection. I never realized that before, but I can relate to it now. I don't do well with rejection."

She nodded.

"Yeah, I guess that's pretty obvious." I gave her a wry look. "Anyway, she told me how proud she was of me for my success, for striking out on my own and keeping at my dream until I made it what I wanted it to be."

"Is it what you want it to be?" In the low lighting, Jewel's eyes appeared to be bronze as they searched mine.

"That's the question, isn't it?" It's what I'd been contemplating long after my mother fell asleep. "I think I was closer to it when I started out. But it could be that way again with the right focus, if I'm true to myself and my vision for my music. You helped me realize I wasn't doing that anymore."

I brought up my hand to frame half of her pretty face.

"I need the right people with me to support my dream and share my success. I'm fortunate to have a few. Brad. Jack. Ben. And now you."

In truth, she was the top one. I wanted to tell her how important she was and how much I needed her in my life, but it was too soon to lay that on her.

"Thank you." Her eyes darkened, shadowed with emotion. Whether she was happy or sad, I wasn't sure. With my mom in that hospital bed, everything felt tenuous.

I wanted to force the issue of Jewel's feelings. I also wanted to turn back the clock and fix things with my mom and dad before so much time had been lost, but life didn't work that way.

You got some chances. You lost others.

But it had hit home tonight that I needed to make the most of every single moment I was given with the ones I loved.

I drifted off to Rush stroking my arm, and woke later to the soft murmur of voices. Harmonized voices. Rush's deep compelling one, and his mom's softer emphatic one.

"She's awake." Moira's eyes, so like his, met mine.

"Good morning," I said uncertainly, sitting up and glancing around for a clock. Without a window in the room, it was difficult to tell the time.

"It's not quite morning." Rush came around his mom's bed and bent to kiss my cheek while holding the acoustic guitar I'd brought from his room close to his body.

"Why are you up? Is everything okay?" Given the circumstances, and on so little rest, I felt discombobulated.

"Mom wanted to talk." Rush returned to her side, and when she reached for him, he took her hand and squeezed it. "Well, she wanted to visit with you and me before everyone else gets here."

"But why the guitar?" I tossed my hair out of my eyes and crossed my legs.

"My girl seems to know I process better with it in my hands. Guess having one in every room in the condo gave it away. Or she just assumed my guitar is like her and her paintbrush."

"Rush told me you like art," Moira said.

"I do."

"Something you two have in common."

"Yes." I hadn't thought of it that way, but she was right.

"He told me about your grandmother. I'm sorry," she said softly. "You loved her very much."

Tears filled my eyes as I nodded. "She was my entire world."

"I'm sure she felt the same way about you."

"Before I left." I dropped my chin.

"Distance doesn't change love." Moira turned to look at her son. "Neither does a difference in goals. Not if you remember to love each other."

Rush gave her a small smile. "I love you, Mom."

My heart hurt at the glance they exchanged. It was buoyant with affection but weighted with apology, regret, and worry as well.

"Could I take a picture of you two?" I asked. "I'd like to sketch you together. I can work on it in the waiting room, then give it to you as a gift when you come out of surgery."

"How thoughtful." Moira gave me a sweet smile. "I'd love that. Two beautiful gifts. Light and love in unsettled places. Like the lyrics you were sharing with me, son."

"Yes. Jewel brings out the best in me." Rush stared across the room at me. My eyes burned from his statement while his blazed bright.

"That's all your father and I ever wanted for you. All any parent wants, I think. For their children to be the best they can be."

Rush leaned in to kiss her cheek. He reached out to brush away her tears, a tender caress, and as she looked up at him with adoration glowing in her eyes, I snapped a picture with my phone. They were so beautiful in that moment, I was afraid to breathe for fear I'd ruin it.

But then it got better. As was Rush's way, he sensed an unspoken need and filled it.

Straightening, he lifted the guitar and strummed a soft chord. The sound flooded the room with his dream, replacing the uncertainty with a son's hope and a mother's love.

Hey, feel the breeze blow
Soon don't you know
It grows to a wind
Life rushes along
A bittersweet song
Beginning to end

Hope bring me home
Love lead the way
Back to the ones that matter

Don't let my life
Go silently by
Make my words really matter

Time comes at a cost
All moments lost
Are never repaid
So spend your hours wise
Without compromise
Don't be afraid

Hope bring me home
Love lead the way
Back to the ones that matter
Don't let my life
Go silently by
Make my words really matter

Don't think you can wait
And leave it to fate
Say what you need to say
Before it's too late

Hope bring me home
Love lead the way
Back to the ones that matter
Don't let my life
Go silently by
Make my words really matter

"She's the right one, Rush," Moira whispered, glancing at my face, which was as wet as theirs.

He smiled at me. "She sure is."

38

Rush

Later, in the coming days and weeks when I had nothing to do but reflect, I'd look back and see clearly how everything had unfolded.

Beauty first. A bridge mended with my mom. The opportunity to introduce her to the woman I loved.

Then darkness crept in, at first only shadows.

When Randy and Brenda arrived at the hospital, I had a terse conversation with them about the way they'd treated Jewel. Then I had a moment alone with Brenda out in the hall.

"You'll treat her with respect and consideration at all times, Bren, or you'll answer to me."

Brenda's eyes narrowed into defiant slits. "That's asking too much. How long have you even known her? Randy says only a few days. How could you bring a stranger into our lives right now?" Her expression softened, and she touched my arm just as Jewel stepped out of my mother's hospital room. "She doesn't belong here."

Brenda had directed her last comment at Jewel, then swept past her to reenter my mother's room.

Jewel stepped closer, sadness dimming her eyes. "They need to shave Moira's head."

I would realize later that Jewel had misinterpreted my response to Brenda's touch. That at every opportunity, my ex would do everything in her power to widen the misunderstandings between Jewel and me. But in that moment, I'd been too worried about my mom.

"Your mom's acting like it's not a big deal," Jewel said. "But I can tell she's scared. Could you hold her hand?"

"Of course."

I stepped back inside my mom's room, pretending to be stoic. But inside, my heart broke at the sight of my proud mother's eyes glistening with unshed tears as one by one, long locks of her hair fell to the floor.

The anesthesiologist visited briefly, followed by the surgeon. Then, before she was wheeled into surgery, my mother said a quick prayer aloud while she held one of my hands and Jewel clasped the other.

Jewel

"How long has it been?" Rush asked me again, his escalating tension putting me more on edge.

"Half an hour." I patted the seat beside me on the worn waiting-room couch. "Stop pacing. Sit." I couldn't touch or comfort him while he prowled the length of the twenty-by-ten-foot room.

"All right." He dropped down beside me. In the chair across from us, Brenda frowned as he took my hand and placed it on his thigh.

“Any news?” Brad returned from the cafeteria, carrying a tray with steaming paper cups filled with coffee.

“She hasn’t gone back yet.” Rush glanced at the wall monitor that reported each surgery patient’s status. “They still show her in prep. Why is she still in prep?” His muscular thigh bounced to a nervous rhythm beneath my hand.

“They said it might take a while,” Randy said.

“I know, it’s just . . .” Rush jumped to his feet as the surgeon entered the waiting room, and mumbled, “It’s too soon.”

I rose with him, sensing something was wrong. Both needing comfort and wanting to offer it, I reached for Rush’s hand and squeezed.

“McMahon family?” the doctor asked, lowering his surgical mask.

“Yes, I’m her son. What’s wrong?” Rush’s voice was terse as he stepped forward, his fingers sliding free of mine. “Something’s wrong. Why aren’t you with her?”

“I’m sorry.” Behind the lenses of his glasses, the surgeon’s eyes revealed his sorrow. “Her aneurysm ruptured before we could take her back. We lost her in the prep room.”

Gasps of shock came from everyone, including me. My heart kept beating, but every beat was dulled by dread.

“No. No. No.” Randy sagged against Brenda, his eyes wide and disbelieving. He seemed to withdraw, as if to pull his sharper emotions inside himself to prevent anyone else from getting cut, and also to privately process his pain.

His wife didn’t say a word. Appearing stricken as well, Brenda threw her arms around him, burying her face in his neck, looking after her husband for once instead of lusting after his brother.

“If you would like to come back with me,” the surgeon said gently, “I can escort you.”

“No.” Rush shook his head. “No, I don’t want to go back. This isn’t right. There’s been some kind of mistake.”

My heart cracked as he struggled to comprehend what couldn't be denied.

Rush blinked hard, staring unseeing for a moment, then he glared at the doctor. "You were supposed to fix this!"

"I'm sorry, Mr. McMahon." The surgeon glanced between Rush and the rest of us, his expression weighted with regret and helpless frustration.

I tried to reach for Rush's hand again to lend him my strength, to give him something to hold on to, but he backed away from me.

"I don't believe you." Rush's voice was raw from strain. "I want to talk to another doctor. Get me another doctor." He glanced around wildly, as if looking for someone—anyone—to refute the surgeon's claim.

"Rush." Brad stepped forward. "Calm down. Let me help you."

He put his hand on his friend's shoulder, but Rush shrugged it aside.

"I didn't . . ." Rush's voice cracked. "Didn't have enough time with her."

"I know you didn't."

"We just reconciled. I didn't get to say a proper good-bye. This can't be right."

"You got to see her. You talked to her." Brad shook his head sadly. "But it's terrible, I know."

"You don't know anything!" Rush roughly brushed aside his friend's second attempt to comfort him. "Don't fucking touch me!"

"Settle down, Rush." Brad spoke quietly. "This is a hospital."

"If it's a hospital, why didn't they fucking fix her!" Rush shouted, his eyes wild, his movements agitated and frantic.

"Let's go outside—"

"No."

Rush took a swing at his best friend, but Brad dodged the blow.

Spinning from his momentum, his expression anguished, Rush kicked at a chair that was suddenly in his way. When it toppled over, he snatched it up and slammed it into the wall. It broke into jagged pieces that matched his ravaged expression.

"Rush!" I cried out his name as tears slid down my cheeks.

I couldn't stand to see him like this. He was drowning in his grief, waves crashing over his head. He was going under, couldn't breathe for the pain, and I knew how it felt.

"Don't, baby." He shook his head as I moved toward him. "Stay back. I don't want to hurt you."

"You won't," I said softly, approaching him as carefully as I would a wounded animal. "Just let me hold you."

When I reached him, he sagged as I wrapped my arms around him.

"Jewel." He dropped to his knees, his legs seeming to collapse beneath his burden, and I went with him. "This is all wrong."

He buried his face in my chest, and I felt and heard the sob that racked his much larger frame.

"I know. I know. I'm here. I'm right here."

I wouldn't give him false platitudes, wouldn't tell him he'd be okay, because he wouldn't. I knew from experience that his life would never be the same. But I would help him, would do whatever it took to get him to a point where the pain was bearable.

For now, my job was to be there for him so he wouldn't be alone. And I was.

As he said good-bye to his mother at the hospital.

As we returned to the empty farmhouse.

As preparations were made for the funeral.

39

Rush

"Where's your side piece?" At the small table in the kitchen, Brenda peered over her cup of coffee at me.

"Still sleeping." Frowning, my eyes dry after days of weeping and exhausted further by preparations for a funeral that felt all wrong, I trudged slowly toward the carafe on the counter.

"You two were so loud last night, we could hear you on our side of the house. I imagine she must be worn out. The way you go after her, it's disgusting. Your mom just died." My ex watched me with the intensity of a predator, an intensity that seemed to increase as each dark day passed.

"Loving her isn't wrong."

It was none of Brenda's business what Jewel and I did in private. Yet, was it love on Jewel's side? She'd never returned the sentiment. My ex had unerringly found a weak spot, a concern that had been nagging at me.

My grip tightened on the carafe handle. I knew I was probably making things worse by using sex to lessen the pain.

It was less than Jewel deserved, but touching her reminded me of life rather than death. Jewel understood, and she never turned me way. But how much longer would she stay?

"It's comfort," I said. "Not that you would understand that kind of thing. There's no give with you. Just disapproval and condemnation."

Brenda's bitterness was a jarring contrast to Jewel's sweetness. I counted myself fortunate that she was my brother's problem to deal with, and not mine.

"Comfort you pay for. It's your money, I guess."

"What?" I spun around.

She slid her iPad across the table at me, revealing an image of a driver's license photo with Jewel's face.

"What's that all about?" I asked, feigning ignorance.

I knew Brad had been shielding me, which made me appreciate him now more than ever. But it was only a matter of time before word got out about Jewel. Only a matter of time before she left me.

Was it only her kindness that brought her to Indiana with me? And was it only for pity that she remained?

"She's a hooker, Rush."

"*Was* a hooker."

Brenda gave me a smug smile. "You sure about that?"

"Morning, all." My brother entered before I could respond, but the seed of suspicion had been planted. "The viewing's today."

"Not something I'm gonna forget." I took a seat across from Brenda and stared into my black coffee. It matched my dark thoughts.

"You gonna have her with you?"

"Jewel?" I asked.

He nodded.

"Of course I am."

My brother's face twisted into an ugly mask. "You're going to make our last good-byes to our mother a media circus."

My grip tightened on my mug. "I can't control what they do, Randy."

"You can think of someone else but yourself for a change. They want pictures of you and her together. If she's not there, it'll be a lot easier on the rest of us."

I needed her there, a hell of a lot more than I needed either my brother or his wife. "Easier for you, you mean. I'm not the only one being selfish, am I?"

"You prick." Randy bared his teeth, and Brenda put her hand on his arm.

"Morning." Jewel walked into the kitchen and took in the scene. Her brow creased beneath her tangled hair. "Everything okay?"

My fingers had pulled and twisted her auburn hair during the night. Before my world had turned upside down, I'd savored its silkiness. Been gentle with her. Been more cognizant of her needs.

Guilt churned in my stomach, along with the coffee and my darker emotions.

"As if you really care?" Brenda spat the accusation at Jewel. "How much is he paying you to be up with him all night?"

Jewel took a step back, her cheeks turning pink. "I . . . he doesn't . . ." She glanced at me, her pretty mouth turned down with hurt, and her eyes bleak.

"The press broke the story," I said gently.

Her eyes widened. "Oh, I'm sorry."

"It's not your fault, baby. What they do. What others think."

"That's sweet. But not realistic." Randy shook his head. "But then, that's your manufactured world of make-believe." He lifted his chin to Brenda, and she stood. "Think about what I said, Rush. If not for us, think about her."

"Think about what?" Jewel shifted nervously from foot to foot, the hem of my shirt skimming her upper thighs.

"Nothing important. Come here."

I opened my arms and she stepped into them without hesitation. As soon as I had her in my grasp, my churning emotions settled.

Unfortunately, that brief interlude of peace didn't last.

Jewel

Rush was still by the window when I returned from taking a shower that evening.

I quietly closed the door to his room and tossed my damp towel in the hamper. Either hearing me or seeing my reflection in the glass, he stretched back his arm to me. Padding quickly across the wood floor, I took his hand and he reeled me into his side.

"What took you so long?" he asked.

"The hot water takes a while to heat up."

"Not that long." He lifted a brow. "I know this old house like the back of my hand. Know every branch on this tree. I chose a wrong one once, and when my mom caught me sneaking out, she grounded me for a month. Plus, your skin's cold, so 'fess up."

"I ran into Brenda in the hall."

His brow furrowed. "This hasn't been pleasant for you. I'm sorry."

"I can handle her. Don't worry about me. I'm worried about you. Today was hard."

"Yeah." His gaze drifted back to the front yard, and he stiffened.

"It's supposed to help, the viewing and talking to others about what she meant to them."

He didn't speak for a long moment, and when he did, his voice was gruff. "She did so much in the community I wasn't even aware of."

My voice wobbled as I said, "'Be a woman who serves behind the scenes. The joy's in the giving, not being recognized for it.' My gran used to say that."

"You've suffered loss too. And I've neglected you."

He touched my hair, the first non-desperate touch in days. It gave me hope. Maybe my being here was making a difference.

"Your mom was a special lady. I'm glad I got to meet her."

"I'm glad you did too. You're giving like my mom, you know."

"No." I shook my head firmly.

"You've supported me, comforted me. You're a loyal, caring friend to Cam. Why can't you see the good I see?"

"I've made too many mistakes."

Rush pressed his lips to my hair. "I don't believe in scales for redemption like you seem to. Doing something bad doesn't erase all the good things you've done. Most of the time, good deeds shine brighter in bad circumstances."

"Like the words in your song."

"Like you."

But he didn't know. Wanting to hold on to him and his good opinion a little longer, I hadn't told him everything.

"My white iris. My beautiful gem. I love you, Jewel." He turned to me and slipped his hand beneath the oversized shirt of his I was wearing. Grasping the hem, he lifted it over my head. "So pretty."

In front of the window, I stood nude in a patch of moonlight, and yet I didn't feel self-conscious. How could I with him looking at me like that?

When I placed a palm on his sandpapery cheek, he covered it with his, then moved it to his mouth. Pressing a warm kiss to the center of my palm, he made my scalp tingle. Then he sent shivers throughout my body when he touched the tip of his wet tongue to my skin.

"Kiss me, Rush," I said, not too proud to beg. I was always so hungry for him.

"Not yet." He put my dampened palm on the cool windowpane. Moving behind me, he lifted and pressed the other one there too. "Keep them there."

"It's snowing," I said, feeling like it was a sign. A Christmas gift from above.

No one had felt like celebrating the holiday after his mother had passed. But could the flurry of white be his mom and my gran telling us to keep on living our lives with their blessing?

I shivered as Rush nuzzled the side of my neck.

"Are you warm enough now?" He pressed closer to me from behind, and I realized he'd removed his boxers. His cock was hard against my ass, hot and already sheathed.

My mind blanked. Forgotten were blessings from above, sorrows, all of it. Nothing mattered but him.

Wriggling my ass slightly, I said, "I could be warmer with you inside me."

"Done." His palm glided down the length of my spine before he used both hands to spread my thighs apart.

"Rush . . ."

I pulled in a breath when he positioned his cock at my entrance. I was already ready, needing him as much as he needed me. As the days had passed, my desperation often matched his. I wanted to make the most of every moment, afraid of what would happen after the funeral.

I was afraid for him. Afraid for us.

He loved me. But what if love wasn't enough?

"Now," I said. "Please."

"Kiss first."

Eagerly, I turned my head, and he captured my lips and plunged his wet tongue in my mouth, even as he drove his hard cock inside me. In and out, tongue and cock in rhythm, he made me crazy. I whimpered into his mouth, throbbed around his cock.

He broke the seal between our mouths. "Open your eyes, baby. See how beautiful you are."

"I see us."

In the glass, we were beautiful together. He looked at me with a rapturous expression, and it stayed that way as he moved inside me.

"You're so perfect." He cupped my breasts in his capable hands. "So hot." He strummed the tightened tips with his talented fingers. "So sexy," he said, paying homage to my body with his.

I came undone on his next deep stroke, struggling to keep my eyes open so I could savor our reflection in the glass. I held the image in my mind of how we looked in that moment, our bodies worshiping each other, and memorized another of him coming.

It seemed in that moment that anything was possible.

40

Rush

I picked up my ring from the bathroom counter after my turn in the shower. Sliding it on, I turned around and Brenda was there. Right there.

When she turned and shut the door, I got a really bad feeling. My ex and me alone, and me wearing just a towel . . . it definitely wasn't a good thing.

"What are you doing?" My eyes narrowed in suspicion, I tried to move past her, but she blocked my exit out of the narrow space.

"Trying to talk some sense into you." She came closer. Steam and my unease hung heavy in the air.

"You've got nothing to say that I want to hear."

"What if it's about her?" She placed her palms on my chest and stroked her thumbs through the droplets on my skin.

A long, long time ago, her touch would have turned me on. Now it just nauseated me.

"You're jealous of her." Calling it like I saw it, I pried her hands from my chest. "Does Randy know you're in here with me? I mean, fuck, he's just right down the hall."

"What does it matter? We have a history, Rush." She glanced up at me through lowered lashes, but her eyes didn't seem sexy to me anymore. Just calculating.

My stomach churned.

"Step aside, Brenda, or I'll move you aside."

"Don't be like that. You're making a mistake with her. She's a prostitute. She's been with lots and lots of men, hundreds maybe. I can't even imagine it. Can you?"

The churn in my stomach increased at the thought of Jewel with anyone else. Ignoring it, I shook my head.

"Do you really think she's into you?" Brenda flipped her hair over her shoulder. "I've heard you throwing the words at her, but she doesn't say them back. Is that your arrangement?"

"What do you know about it?" My entire body tightened, my arms at my sides stiffening and my fingers curling into fists.

"You're being naive. All those years on the road, but you have no one who really knows you. No one who really cares. No one who loves you."

Brenda reached for my face, and I captured her wrist just as Jewel opened the door.

Jewel's eyes rounded, gold pools of misunderstanding. "I'm sorry. I left my hairbrush." She backed out, turned away, and retraced her steps to my bedroom.

"Cut the bullshit, Brenda." I tossed her hand back at her. "Stay away from me. Stay away from Jewel. Stop trying to cause trouble."

As I pushed past her, Brenda huffed and crossed her arms over her chest.

"You've already got trouble."

I paused in the hall, halfway between the woman I wanted, and not far enough away from the woman I was glad was out of my life.

"You're too nice for your own good," Brenda said to my back. "Too trusting. She's taking advantage."

As I walked away, praying she'd shut the hell up, Brenda raised her voice.

"What do you really know about her? Open your eyes. She is what she is, what she'll always be. Girls like her never change."

Sitting on the edge of his bed with my phone in my hand, I jumped when Rush pushed open the door.

"Hey," he said. "Didn't mean to startle you."

"Hey," I said listlessly, staring down at Cam's contact on my phone. I missed my best friend and had been about to call her, needing to do something to distract me from the ripping pain inside my chest from seeing Rush with Brenda.

I tossed my cell onto the comforter. He glanced at it, something flitting behind his eyes I couldn't get a read on before he looked up at me.

"You talking to somebody?" he asked, almost sounding suspicious.

"I was going to call Cam."

"It's late."

"She's up. She works late."

"She does, doesn't she?" His gaze narrowed. "I thought she was taking a break from that. You too."

"She can't." That pain inside my chest became a side-splitting case of guilt.

I'm a selfish, terrible friend.

I ducked my head. "I've been gone longer than I expected."

"You need to get back."

"Yes," I whispered. It was dangerous for her to go out alone. But I couldn't leave Rush, not yet. He still needed me. Worried about the odd note in his tone, I added, "But not yet."

I stood and went to him, telling myself not to be jealous of Brenda. He didn't want her. He had just been with me in front of the window.

Holding my breath, I put my hands on his chest, watching my fingers glide over his tanned skin. His muscles were tense, but his breathing grew heavy as my hands dipped lower. He stopped me just before I reached the knot in his towel.

"Not right now. Let's go to bed. I'm tired." His fingers tight around my wrists, his eyes searched mine for a long moment.

He looked sad. Of course he was sad. He'd never stopped me before, but his mom's funeral was tomorrow.

I told myself that's what it was, but I was afraid it was more.

Reluctantly, I slipped out of bed, leaving Jewel curled up beneath the covers. My mind was too unsettled to sleep.

How much time did I have left with her? Had I made the end come quicker, clinging to her so tightly? Had I declared myself too soon? Even worse . . . was I only seeing in her what I wanted to believe?

Padding softly across the room, I stepped out into the hall with my cell in my hand. At the bottom of the stairs, I called my best friend.

"Rush, what's going on? Is everything okay? What time is it?" Brad's voice went from sleepy to alert.

"I don't know." About the time, if everything was okay, about anything.

My mom was gone, and I was likely going to lose Jewel. Hell, I might not have ever really had her. The things I wanted, the people I loved, the ones who I thought loved me, they seemed difficult to hold on to. Was there something wrong with me, some fatal deficiency in me that kept people from staying?

"Do you want me to come over?" he asked.

"No," I told Brad. "Stay at the hotel. Go back to bed. I'm sorry I woke you."

"It's all right. Talk to me."

I tilted my head back, staring at the ceiling. "She's going to leave me."

"Jewel?"

"Yes."

"I was afraid this would happen," he mumbled. "Did she tell you tonight?"

"Not in so many words."

I raked a hand through my hair, moving through the living room and stopping in front of the big picture window to stare out into the dark night. The snow had stopped, leaving the front yard dusted in white. It looked pretty now but it would melt, leaving dirty puddles when the temperature rose.

"Do you want her to stay?" he asked.

"Yes. Hell yes."

"Then tell her."

"I have." In all the ways I could think of. "Many times."

"I don't know what to tell you. I'm not exactly an expert with women."

"Could you talk to her?" I asked. "Feel her out for me?"

I turned away from the window, glancing around the living room, and I could almost hear their voices, Mom's and Dad's. Him yelling at me to get my muddy shoes off the coffee table, and her soothing his reprimand. Voices of the past, now only distant echoes.

If it weren't for Jewel by my side when I lost my mom, I would have slipped back into my old ways of coping with stress—drinking, disparaging everything, pretending nothing mattered when everything did.

Silence stretched out on the line. I was asking too much. It wasn't up to Brad to solve my personal problems as well as my professional ones.

I sat on the couch and dropped my head into my free hand. "Maybe I got it wrong with her . . ."

Brad let out a long sigh. "I'll talk to her."

"Thanks, man. I appreciate you. I don't tell you enough."

"You don't need to. It's understood."

"Love you, man."

"Same here."

Jewel

"What do you want?" I frowned as Brenda entered the Sunday-school room where I was waiting for Rush. The service hadn't started yet, and he thought I'd be more comfortable waiting here rather than sitting in the church pew with her.

We'd all arrived at the church together for the funeral service, inside limos with tinted glass so the press couldn't take pictures of us. A swarm of them had gathered outside the building, milling around, waiting for a chance for a juicy interview or a heart-wrenching photo. Brad was on the phone, complaining to law enforcement about the press, his voice stern on the other side of the thin wall.

Handsome in his dark suit, but looking more like a lost puppy than a rock star, Rush had just left the room. His ex-fiancée's popping in so close on his heels put me instantly on alert.

I smoothed the hem of the ill-fitting black taffeta dress his manager had bought for me. Since leaving the hospital,

Rush and I had mostly stuck to the farmhouse. The little town of Pendleton was overrun with paparazzi, trying to capture a picture of me, him, his grief.

Brenda should go. She shouldn't be here.

Somber organ chords made the room vibrate.

"Rush isn't here," I said. "He went to greet people, along with your husband."

"I wasn't looking for Rush." Her eyes narrowed like they always did when she looked at me. "Though he does have a habit of disappearing at the most inopportune times."

"What does that mean?"

"Did he never tell you why we split up?"

My heart pounding, I shook my head.

"He fucked someone else while we were together. He gets bored so easily."

I blinked at her, then shrugged one shoulder. "Maybe you just weren't what he needed."

Was I still what he needed? After all, he'd been acting differently with me since last night.

Brenda lifted a brow. "And you think you're what he needs? A whore? A thief?"

I staggered slightly, her blow hitting its mark, and she saw.

She gave me an evil smile. "You didn't tell him, did you?"

Refusing to respond to that, I took a deep breath and stared at her, scrunching my fear and despair into a little ball and burying it deep inside.

Her grin widened. "Did you think because your grandmother eventually dropped the charges that there wouldn't be a record?" She clucked her tongue. "What will Rush do when he finds out, I wonder?"

I didn't know, not for certain. Which was why I hadn't told him.

Brenda's smile disappeared. "When you're with someone like Rush, nothing ever stays secret. I didn't just find out he cheated on me . . . I got to see the explicit pictures in the tabloids. Everyone got to see the pictures, even my parents and all my friends."

Did she want me to feel sorry for her?

Wanting nothing more than to curl into a ball and cry, I threw my shoulders back and firmed my voice. "Get out."

"I'm going," she said, yet she lingered. Peering around me, she glanced at herself in the mirror and removed a tiny smudge of scarlet from the outer edge of her mouth.

My blood?

She'd certainly gone right for my jugular. With stunning accuracy, she'd zeroed in on my biggest weakness—

My doubt that someone like me could ever have someone like him, even temporarily.

Rush

Where was Jewel? And where was Brad? It was time to go in.

Seated in the front pew, Brenda kept turning her head and giving me looks that contributed to my unease. At the front of the church, a glossy ebony box contained my mother's body. I didn't need any more stress. I was already reeling, unable to wrap my brain around it.

Grief had stages. Rationally, I knew that I was in shock mixed with a ton of denial. I knew it by the way I avoided looking at that casket. I knew it every time I deflected Jewel when she tried to get me to talk about the good memories of my mother.

But knowing didn't help me. I felt like I was spinning out of control. Jewel was the only one who stood between me and the whirlwind.

When I went to look for her, I ran smack into Carter Besille in the vestibule.

"How'd you get in here?" I glanced over his head, unable to deal with the sleazy talk-show host right now.

The son of a bitch has a habit of showing up at the worst possible time. Where the hell is my manager?

A bright light blinded me from my left. When my vision cleared, I realized Carter had brought a cameraman along with him.

"Get the fuck out of here before I have you arrested. This is a funeral."

My throat tightened. It wasn't supposed to be like this. My mother shouldn't be gone right after we'd reconciled, right after she met Jewel. We should have been in this church for my wedding, not her funeral.

"I only need a moment of your time," Carter said. "Just give me a statement. My people have been calling your people. We need a comment on the pictures from the hospital. They're really quite moving. You with your guitar, your dear sweet mother in her hospital bed."

"What pictures?" My body tensed.

"The ones Jewel Anderson texted to me. Didn't you know?"

"She wouldn't do that."

"But she did." He smiled. "For the right price."

A lump formed in my throat. "How much?"

"Twenty thousand. We started at ten, but she's a negotiator, that one." He tilted his frost-tipped blond head. "She drive a hard bargain like that when you picked her up off the street?"

My mind spun. It couldn't be.

"She looks so sweet, but then again, maybe that's the attraction. The dichotomy. It must've taken half a dozen texts back and forth for us to finally agree on a price."

I remembered Jewel holding her phone last night when I returned from the bathroom, and my blood ran cold. Wanting nothing more than to slam my knuckles into Carter's smarmy face, I had to hold my fists at my sides, trying to control myself.

Ignoring the danger he could be in, Carter just kept talking. "The behind-the-scenes exclusive is going to make her a fortune."

"No." I shook my head, unable to believe it.

"She agreed. It only takes one consenting party to avoid most sticky legalities, so here I am."

Carter's eyes glittered with excitement, much like they did after that debacle with the band. Grooves of glee creased the flesh-colored lipstick around his mouth, which contrasted eerily with his spray-tanned skin.

"Did you think she was something more than she is?" he asked. "You look shocked. You do realize what she does for a living? That she's not a trustworthy person. That there's no line she won't cross. She even stole money from the woman who raised her."

"No way." I shook my head. "I don't believe you."

"Her arrests are public record. Even the one for theft, though the charges were dropped. I have the texts with her right here." He turned the screen of his phone around so I could scan his message log.

Blood rushed in my ears. Everything was there, just like he'd said. Emotions slammed through me . . .

Betrayal. Anger. Hurt. Disbelief.

Needing to see Jewel, I pushed past him, turned the corner, and strode down the hall. I knew he followed. The cameraman too. But I didn't care.

Furious, I shoved open the closed door to the room where I'd last seen her. Last kissed her.

Jewel was inside, but she wasn't alone. Brad was with her, standing extremely close. When the door slammed against the wall, he dropped his hands from her arms and they jumped apart. Her face was wet. She'd been crying.

It was all very surreal. But one thing I knew for sure.

They both looked guilty.

"What the hell's going on?" I roared.

"It's not what you think." Brad backed away from Jewel, holding up his hands.

I had to give it to my manager, he caught on quickly to my read on the situation. Jewel seemed slower. But she was an actress of a higher caliber than I could have ever guessed.

"Are you two working together? Or is she screwing you too?"

Jewel gasped, but seeing Brad's hands on her made me snap. I stalked toward my former best friend, grabbed him by the lapels of the expensive suit my money had paid for, and shoved him into the nearest wall.

"Calm down, buddy," he choked out, his Adam's apple crushed by his tie and my fists at his throat. "You got this wrong."

I shoved him away from me. "Should've gotten that waiver. I know. You told me. My bad."

Then I turned to her.

Jewel blinked at me in confusion. The camera's light was bright on her face, blinding her the way she'd blinded me. It seemed right.

She held her hand above her eyes to shield them. "Please tell me what's going on, Rush."

I hit her with the full force of my glare, making her flinch. "I know, Jewel. I know about the pictures and the agreement you made."

She shook her head, that beautiful mane of coppery-brown hair. "I don't have an agreement with anyone except you."

"As if that was worth anything. A promise from a hooker."

Her face drained of all color. Seeming unsteady, she reached out for the back of the folding chair beside her.

I couldn't seem to let it go. The doubt. The fact that she was always trying to leave. That she'd never told me she loved me.

“Why didn’t you tell me you stole money from your grandmother?”

“I wanted to.” Jewel didn’t seem surprised that I knew. Instead, she looked resigned. “So many times, I wanted to tell you. But . . .” Her lips quivered. “I was young. Landon was leaving town, and she told me I couldn’t go with him. I loved her, but I hated that town.”

“Excuses.”

“Yes, I know.” She dropped her chin. “I paid her back. Landon hated the way I scraped and saved to pay her back. But it doesn’t matter. Wrong is wrong, right? She’s gone. I’ll never know if I had her forgiveness. Not that having it would negate what I did. Those scales, you know.” Her voice quavered. “There’s no taking the weight of the wrong away.”

“Did you sell photos to Carter Besille?”

Her eyes widened and filled with tears. “What photos?”

“I’m not a fool. I saw the texts.”

“I don’t know what you saw.” Trembling now, she hugged her arms around herself, so tragically beautiful in her black dress.

So *seemingly* tragic. I hardened my heart. I had to.

I’d been played. Every warning about her replayed through my mind. All of them were right.

“You won’t admit it?” I asked.

A single tear slid down her face. “I didn’t do anything except love you.”

I was such a sucker for her, even now, it was hard not to look at her and believe her.

I made a harsh disbelieving sound. “It’s over, Jewel. You got what you wanted. No more financial worries. Us at the end. And I got what I deserved for being a fool.”

“Brad . . .” She turned to him, and that was the final straw for me.

"Get out."

"I think you're making a mistake, Rush." That came from my manager.

"Yeah, well, you're the expert at cleaning up mistakes for me." I barked out a scornful laugh, not sure who I was more pissed at. Him . . . or myself. "So take my latest one, and the two parasites she invited here, off the premises. Make sure they stay away. All of them. And then maybe I won't add you to today's list of mistakes."

42

Jewel

Cam wired me money to get a flight back to Los Angeles.

In a daze, wearing my taffeta dress and no coat, I noticed fewer stares than I would have expected. A crushed girl in a funeral dress . . . who wanted to take that on? No one, not a single person, attempted to engage in conversation with me.

Sure, Carter Besille attempted to contact me many, many times. He had my cell number. The pictures of Rush and his mother were from my phone. The texts from me supposedly demanding more money, they were all there. The trail pointed to me. I was guilty in Rush's eyes.

Except I hadn't done it.

And where was the money Carter had paid?

I didn't know, though I was pretty sure I knew who'd set me up.

Back home in the apartment, I crawled underneath the covers in the bed Rush's money had bought, and Cam tried to get me to talk to her. Hourly at first, in the beginning. Hourly, in those early days, I thought about calling Rush.

But would he even take my call? And if he did, what could I say that would convince him to believe me?

Days passed. Weeks.

I went through all the stages, grieving for the love I'd briefly had and then lost.

My body ached. My mind reeled. My heart hurt. The blackout curtain on the window made it difficult to tell when the sun was up or down. The world continued to spin. Time rolled on, though it felt like my world had ended.

During all that time, the same thoughts ran on repeat, torturing me, stealing my sleep, making it impossible to work, to eat, to be a friend, to have a life.

Our arrangement . . . all of me, without holding back.

A deal I should never have struck . . . had struck me in the end.

Loving him had left me in pieces. Predictably.

I didn't try to forget. I couldn't forget. I replayed it all in my mind, punishing myself for being such a fool.

No processing. No moving on. No painting.

No escaping through dreams. After all, dreams were for the deserving.

And all I had left were what-ifs.

Rush

I stayed in Indiana for a while. Every day, I returned to the cemetery, a ritual that helped me cope.

Brad redeemed himself keeping the photographers at bay during these visits, at first hiring off-duty cops for security. Then, as media interest to see me at my lowest waned, it was just him and one bodyguard. They remained at the cemetery gate while I sat on a stone bench beside my parents' grave markers.

I didn't have much to say to them. I didn't talk about Jewel, couldn't talk about her. But I did talk about the past.

"I'm sorry, Dad," I told him. "Sorry I never got to tell you I loved you. Sorry I wasn't a better son."

When time ran out with my dad, so many words left unsaid, all that was left was regret. Alone in the windswept cemetery, I didn't hold back the tears. They slid down my face, the only warmth to be had in that cold place.

"I miss you, Mom." I stared at her fresh grave through wet, blurry eyes. "I miss you both."

Apologies were my constant refrain. It all became very simple what was most important. Love and the absence of it when you had nothing left.

My phone sat on the bench beside me, but I ignored it. It often lit up with messages. From my boss. My bandmates.

But never Jewel. Of course, never her.

In the beginning, every time the phone rang, I'd hoped it would be her. But hope was something that she brought. I didn't know how to find my way to it without her.

Loss consumed me, an overwhelming deprivation I couldn't process. I didn't play my guitar. I avoided everything that reminded me of her. That meant avoiding everything in my life.

I couldn't look out my bedroom window at the farm. It was an empty frame without her beauty to fill it. I couldn't lie in the bed where she'd comforted me. I couldn't stomach the knowing glances from my brother, my sister-in-law, or Brad. I certainly didn't turn on the TV to watch the media pick apart the remains of my life as if it were carrion.

Desperate for a change of scenery, I checked into a hotel. Days turned to weeks as we did what needed to be done to put my mother's affairs to rest. Alone each night, there was no rest for me. I tossed and turned. Pretended I was over Jewel. Pretended I didn't miss her.

Yet whenever I closed my eyes, I could see her in my mind, taste her, smell her, *feel* her. Every minute with her had been an eternity to savor. Every minute without her felt like an eternity to endure.

All that I'd had with her had been a lie. But that lie was better than any truth I'd ever known.

44

Jewel

"Eat something." Cam frowned at me.

"I'm not hu—"

"Don't say it. I'm *sick* of you saying it. Sick of you sitting on that bed, acting like your life has ended."

I blinked slowly, focusing on her. Hands-on-her-hips mad, her green eyes flashing irritation, she was dressed up to go out.

"Where are you going?"

"To work."

"Alone?"

"Yes. One of us has to work, honey."

"But—" I glanced around at the things his money had bought, and only in that moment realized how many were missing.

"I sold the TV," she said. "The espresso machine, the electronics."

"What about the money I gave you?" The cash from my first night with him. That was the only money I'd accepted. I couldn't take any after that. It wouldn't have been right.

"It went toward last month's rent." Her brow creased in concern as she studied me. "Wanda raised our rate this month. Don't you remember me telling you?"

I shook my head. It felt stuffy, as though it were filled with all the tissues that littered the floor around my bed. Had she told me that yesterday? Or had it been the day before that? Time barely had any meaning when time was all you had left.

"She heard about all the deliveries. She's also seen me carry stuff out. I don't think she knows about you and him. But she's got the idea that we're flush."

"Let me get dressed." Trying to stand, I swayed and reached back for the mattress to steady myself.

Cam's frown deepened. "I don't think you're up to it. Maybe if you move around a little more. Stop thinking about him. Eat something."

"I don't—" I swallowed to moisten my dry throat. We didn't speak his name. "I don't think about him."

"But you do." She shook her head sadly. "You cry out for him in your sleep."

I dropped my head. Strands of my tangled hair fell forward, along with a couple of warm tears. How could I have any left?

"I'm sorry." I swiped through the wetness. "I've let things slide."

"It's okay, Jewel. I want to throat-punch him, but I understand how you feel. I've been there."

She opened her arms, and I fell into them.

"Softies, you and me. But we have each other, and we learn from our mistakes, right?" She squeezed me close for a moment, then stepped back to give me a searching glance.

"Yes."

"Good. While I'm gone, I want you to take a shower. Wash your hair. Maybe paint something."

I vehemently shook my head. The last thing I'd painted was him and me. My Christmas present to him.

Cam sighed. "You just can't sit around wallowing anymore. I need you. It's lonely without my best friend. When I get back, we'll talk some more."

A billowy scarf trailing down the length of her spine, Cam left the apartment. Her perfume lingered in the air long after she closed the door.

Feeling guilty about her worry for me, I did the things she suggested. And more.

I cleaned the apartment. It didn't take long, but I had to sit down to catch my breath. I'd let things go too far. I found some crackers and a jar of peanut butter, and made myself eat. But the food sat heavy in my stomach.

Over the next few hours, my stomach started to cramp, and Cam didn't return. I had a bad feeling. And then I got the phone call.

When I jumped up to pull on my clothes, the room spun, but I powered through the dizziness. I had to be strong.

I grabbed my purse and dashed out the door.

"I can't put off Timmons any longer," Brad said.

"Why the fuck not?"

In the driver's seat of his rental car, he cut the ignition, turned, and gave me his pissed-off look. "She's the boss, Rush. Even with her releasing the songs you recorded over the break as singles, you're bleeding money. You have to talk to her. We need to go back on tour. You know it, and I know it."

"I don't—"

"Stop it with the bullshit. It's over with Jewel. She's gone."

"But—"

"I can't even imagine what you're going through." He gave me a sad look. "But staying here and avoiding everything in your life isn't about your mom anymore. Not entirely. And you know it."

I glanced away. Snow was coming down hard. The trees in the front yard were covered in a heavy white blanket. It felt like I was buried in it, and without her, I couldn't see a reason to keep digging out.

"Thanks for driving me over." I had to force myself to reach for the handle. One step at a time, one breath at a time. Pulling in one, I glanced at the house.

Randy was going to hit me up for money I didn't have to save the farm. The reading of the will and the hashing out of the finances today with the lawyers and the family accountant would detail the bleak situation.

"Want me to go inside with you?"

I shook my head. "It's family stuff, not work."

"Okay. Call me when you want me to pick you up."

I nodded and got out, slammed the door, and trudged up the steps.

On the porch, a flurry of memories hit me . . .

My dad pushing open the screen door to greet me, my mom tucked under his arm. They'd always met me together at the door as soon as they heard my car come up the drive. But not anymore. The things that had seemed inconsequential, the ones I'd taken for granted, were now the things I missed the most.

"Hey," Randy said, looking harried as I stepped inside. "They're in the dining room."

The Christmas tree was gone, the presents removed. Mine from my mother had been opened at the hotel—a leather-wrapped journal for lyrics I no longer felt inspired to write.

"Where's Brenda?" I followed him through the barren living room of the house that meant little to me anymore. The woman who'd made it a home for all of us was gone.

A murmur of voices rose as I approached the formal space where we'd celebrated so many holiday meals.

"She's at her parents' place," he said.

"Shouldn't she be here?"

The lawyers in expensive suits and the bespectacled accountant glanced up as we entered the room. Papers were strewn all over the glossy surface of the mahogany table.

"I sent her away." Randy ran a hand through his hair, avoiding my eyes. "We're separating."

Stunned, I took a step back. "Why?"

"I didn't know, Rush. It's on Brenda why she did what she did. But for what it's worth, I'm sorry."

"Sorry for what?" My nostalgia faded, replaced by a sour feeling in my gut.

Randy's bleak gaze finally met mine. "They found a cash discrepancy. Twenty thousand dollars in the farm account that never should have been there. I'll let them explain."

45

Jewel

Getting Cam back to the apartment from the hospital was no easy task. She was groggy from the pain meds, and I was weak from letting myself go and letting my best friend down.

Sitting on my bed, I glanced over at hers.

"No. Stop," she mumbled, agitated as she rolled over, even in her sleep.

My stomach clenched, knotted tighter by guilt. I stood and leaned over. With twin beds instead of cots, there was less than a foot between us. I reached for the comforter that had slid to her waist.

"It's okay, Cam." I pulled up the comforter and tucked it around her, avoiding her broken arm.

Tears pricked my eyes. The matter-of-fact accounting she'd given the hospital staff made my heart break for her, a heart I'd thought couldn't break any more.

I stroked a long strand of her hair back from her forehead and pressed a gentle kiss to her brow. "I'm so sorry," I whispered to her, vowing to myself as I'd already sworn to her out loud that I would make this right somehow.

Bone weary, I shuffled to the bathroom and took a shower to scrub off the grime, not only from the hospital, but also from weeks and weeks of just going through the motions.

Afterward, I gripped the sink to catch my breath, then picked up a comb. Working a tangle from a long russet ribbon of my hair, I stared at myself. *You've got to toughen up, Jewel.*

Cam had rescued me. She'd been the strong one. This time, it was my turn.

Back at my bed, I drew a sleep shirt over my head and settled against the padded headboard.

The furniture and decor Brad had chosen was stylish. Driftwood nightstands, comforters in soft teal, accents in ebony. Problem was, the luxury was out of place in our apartment, much like I'd been out of place in Rush's life.

As I reached to switch off the pretty crystal lamp, my gaze stopped on the portrait of my gran.

"Hey, Gran." My eyes filled as I whispered to her in the quiet shadowed room. Her beloved features wavered in my watery gaze. "I miss you so much."

A lump formed in my throat, keeping me from saying more for several long moments.

"I messed up with you," I said after swallowing through my regrets.

I'd messed up with him too.

Rush's accusing gaze at the church had been so much like hers. Even though I hadn't done what he accused me of, I'd withheld information from him. Maybe if I hadn't, he would have believed my denial.

I dropped my chin to my chest. A warm tear trickled down my cheek.

What was done was done. Being sorry didn't change things.

I lifted my head and met my gran's sympathetic gaze.

Before I could be a woman worthy of being believed and loved, I had to fix things. I had to fix *me*.

A wish, certainly. A seed of desire. A dream that required action.

Another tear fell, slipping down my cheek and sliding between my lips.

"I'm sorry, Gran, so sorry for what I did. Most of all for how my doing wrong hurt you. I can't take back what I did. I can't even hear you accept my apology. But I hope you can forgive me, that you can love me anyway."

I pulled in a shuddery breath.

"But I think you would, because that's the type of woman you are. You showed me time and time again by your example how I should be. Caring. Forgiving. Generous. Loving. Hardworking."

I lifted my chin and swiped the wetness away with the back of my hand.

"It's time for me to be like you."

"*Enchanté*, beautiful." Dwight smiled as he crossed the guitar shop to greet me.

"Hi. Thanks for agreeing to see me." Shifting my weight from one foot to the other, I stood inside the doorway of Norman's with the handle of my mother's guitar case clutched tightly in my grip, trying not to cry.

"Is that it?" His gaze dipped to the instrument. He didn't comment on my watery eyes.

"Yes."

"I can't wait to have a look at it." He turned. "Come on back."

He gestured for me to follow him. Bypassing the rows of guitars, he led me to the practice room where I'd last seen Shaina, War, and Bryan. It seemed like a lifetime ago.

Inside, I placed the case on the bench and let Dwight unlatch it.

"She's a beauty," he said, glancing from the guitar to me. "You even have a picture of your mom and the guitar with Dylan in here. That'll increase the value dramatically. But are you sure you want to sell?"

"Yes."

I had to. In the shelter Cam and I had been forced to move into without the money for rent, it would only get stolen, and I needed cash to take care of Cam. I needed cash to make things right.

I had an idea. A hope, a small one.

But one step at a time.

For now, I just needed enough cash to get us out of the shelter. Cam and I couldn't stay there. She was in no shape to watch my back.

I had her back, though, and I wouldn't let her down again, but I couldn't protect her there 24/7. When I left her today to take the bus here, my stomach had churned with anxiety the whole way.

She wasn't safe there.

We weren't safe.

Rush

"Don't tell me you can't find her." My grip tightened on the phone. "That's not what I want to hear."

I'd been trying to find Jewel since the meeting at the farmhouse with the lawyers, but had been stonewalled at every turn. Jewel's cell number was no longer active. Cam's phone was out of service as well. Their apartment had been vacated.

"There's more you're not going to want to hear," Brad said. "Where are you? You driving the Porsche?"

His serious tone made the fine hair at the back of my neck stand on end. My gut churned.

"No. I'm just getting ready to enter the condo."

My key was in the lock, my old guitar case on the floor of the hallway, the only thing I'd wanted to take back to LA after the settling of my mother's affairs. That and the T-shirt Jewel had worn the last night she'd still been mine. Only I wore it now.

"Do I need to be seated?" I opened the door, and it hit me like a punch. Her peach scent still hung in the air.

"There was a hospital visit."

I staggered in the entryway.

"Her best friend."

"Camaro?"

"Yes, she was beaten up. Her arm's broken, and she was sexually assaulted."

"No." I dropped the guitar case and sank to the floor. "Jewel?"

"Not involved. But an aggressive collection agency is after both of them for emergency-room charges. The landlord suggested I check the shelter on Peach."

"I'll meet you there." I pushed to my feet.

"Already checked. They were there, but they're not anymore."

"Fuck! Do you have any good news for me?"

"About Jewel?"

"Yes, of course."

"Not about her, no. I'm at a dead end."

I didn't like his choice of words, didn't like them at all. Switching the phone to speaker, I raked my free hand through my hair as I tried not to completely panic.

"Look, I've got a private investigator on it," Brad said, his voice soothing as he tried to reassure me. "We'll find her. You should call him. I'll text you his number. He wants you to give him all the information you can remember. But there's other good news . . ."

My phone bleeped with the texted info, and I said, "I'll call him right now."

I stood up, and when I reached the living room, that's when I saw it.

The painting. Her painting of us on the porch, sitting on the lounger together.

My guitar beside us. Her easel. The sunset over the Pacific. My expression. Hers. So much emotion. I could practically hear the melody to the song I'd written that night, listening to the crashing of the waves.

My throat closed. Then I saw the note and the stack of money beside it.

I rushed over and snagged the note, avoiding looking at the cash because I knew what it was—every single cent I'd given her for the time she spent with me here. I didn't need to count it to know that.

Bad news, knowing she could use that money.

But it gave me a glimmer of hope to know that from the moment she had crossed the threshold of my home, I'd been more than just a business transaction to her.

Remembering that Brad was still on the line, I held the phone to my ear. "Hang on a second."

He didn't know what I had seen.

The painting. And the note.

Even when today and tomorrow are over,
you will always be in my heart.
Merry Christmas.
Love, Jewel

I pulled in a breath and my chest expanded, but not only with air. With light, like only she could bring. Hope where there had been none.

That reminded me.

"Wait . . . you mentioned good news," I said to Brad. I'd take all that I could get.

"Just that I got an email alert from Norman's. They got a signed Martin in on consignment this week. One with a photo and a cool backstory."

"From Tennessee?" I held my breath.

"Yeah. How did you know?"

I exhaled. "It's her mother's guitar."

"Whose?"

"Jewel's mother's." My next breath came easier. "I'll call the shop. They should have a contact number for her."

46

Rush

Shaina answered the door.

"Is she here?" My heart hammered inside my chest. It had been in my throat on the drive over.

"Yes, they both are. They're in the back. I moved into the main house so they could stay in the garage apartment. But I told you on the phone, I don't know if she'll see you."

I had to see her. "I'll knock on the door. Can't we let fate decide?"

"She told you that?" Shaina raised a blond brow. "I don't know if it'll be fate in your instance. You screwed up badly. What you need is a miracle."

"I know I do. I believe in those. She's one of them. I'm here to make amends."

I was here to get her back.

Today. Tomorrow. However long it took.

"You can try."

"I plan to." I gestured to the driveway. "Can you open the gate so I can walk around back?"

"You can come through the house." Shaina stepped aside to let me enter.

When I was already halfway through the living room, she called my name. I stopped and glanced back.

"I'm sorry about your mom."

The pain was still so raw, my eyes burned. I nodded once and got moving again.

I had my free hand on the sliding-glass door handle to the patio when she said, "Do you love her?"

I froze, my voice low. "She's my world."

"Then I won't wish you luck. All you need to do is simply convince her what you feel is real."

Yeah, simple. I clung to that possibility the way Jewel had once let me cling to her.

My throat tight, I left the main house, crossed the patio and the lawn, and stepped onto the deck to the apartment. Ignoring my racing heart, I knocked, and was surprised when she answered.

"Jewel." I breathed out her name, drinking her in.

Her hair was loose. She wore cutoff shorts and an art T-shirt that said MY PAINTBRUSH IS MY SWORD. In other words, she looked perfect, and I took the first right breath I'd taken since I sent her away.

Her gold eyes widening in shock, she stepped back and slammed the door shut in my face.

"Jewel, please." I knocked again.

The door opened again and a fist came flying at my face. It wasn't Jewel's, and lucky for me, it didn't make the intended contact.

"Let go of my hand, you fucking shit!" Cam's green eyes were nearly as dark as her expression as I released her fist. "Go away and don't ever come back."

"I can't do that."

"You *so* can."

"I love her, Cam. I made a mistake."

Her entire body trembling, she shouted, "Your mistake nearly killed her!"

I absorbed that blow. It hit deeper than any punch could have.

"I can't take back the hurt, but I'm here to say I'm sorry. I made a mistake. I'll try, if you'll let me—if *she'll* let me—to make amends."

"There's no amending. What's done is done." Touching her fingers to her bruised cheek with the hand that wasn't encumbered by a sling, Cam glared at me, her eyes holding shadows that spoke of deeper, more significant injury than I could see.

"What's done is done?" I repeated, and she nodded. "Bullshit."

She flinched.

"I used to think like that. I let years pass by with my mom that I can never get back because I didn't make the effort to change things. It's a matter of trying. It's taking that first step. To make amends with the people you love, no distance is too great."

"Those are just words."

"It starts with words. My mom knew. Jewel knows. She was there when we all talked about it. She just has to believe."

Cam scoffed. "You want her to have faith in you after what you did?"

"I want her to have faith in us. In herself. In me. How right we are together. How wrong we are apart."

She shook her head. "That's never going to happen."

"It will. I won't give up. If she won't talk to me today, I'll be back tomorrow. And the day after that."

"Jewel goes to work in the daytime. And you're crazy if you think she'll listen to you. Delusional."

"I'm in love with her, Cam."

Something flickered in Cam's eyes before they hardened again. "Love doesn't change anything."

"It does. It changes *everything*. Jewel knows. She's the one who showed me. It's my turn now." I set the guitar case down. "I bought this from Norman's, and I'm gifting it to her."

Money was in an envelope, the same amount that I'd paid for the instrument. I set that down too.

"What's that?" Cam's eyes narrowed.

"My Christmas presents for Jewel, a little late. I have another one, but I'm saving it until she talks to me personally. I saw her present today. Tell her that. Tell her the painting blew me away. This is just me trying in a small way to reciprocate."

Jewel

"Aren't you going to peek in the envelope?" Cam asked.

I shook my head, sure it was all there.

Cam gave me a searching look. "Just want to throw it and your mom's guitar at his handsome head, huh?"

"Yes and no."

"He seems pretty determined."

I shrugged. "He's a lot of things." The most important thing wasn't the return of my mother's guitar, and it certainly wasn't the cash. It was the motivation behind those things.

"He said a lot."

"He did."

"You believe him?"

"I do."

Cam's tension seemed to fade away. "Then maybe you should stop him before he gets away."

"You hate him."

"I do. I'm the best friend. It's my role to look after you. But with him coming here, and the things he said, I realize I don't know him like you probably do."

Confused, I looked away. "He broke my heart."

"I know that. I was there to watch it shatter." She touched my arm gently. "I guess what you have to decide is if you can put it back together without him."

47

Rush

"Rush!" Jewel came flying down the driveway, her hair streaming behind her like a coppery banner. "Wait!"

Stunned, I didn't know whether to laugh or cry. So I went with what felt right.

I jogged to meet her halfway and swept her into my arms. Her body molded to mine, I could feel her heart racing.

"It's okay, baby. I'm here," I said, stroking my hand up and down her spine. Soothing her settled me too. "I was only going back to the condo. I planned to come back tomorrow."

"I wasn't sure." She stiffened, putting her hands on my chest, and tried to wiggle free.

I didn't allow her that freedom. Now that I had her back in my arms, it was all I could do not to crush her to me. "I told Cam I'd be back. I thought you heard me."

"I heard, but I wasn't sure how long you were staying in town."

"I'm here until I fix things with you."

"But the tour?"

"Postponed until I give the okay to restart it."

"You hurt me." Her expression darkened, and so did her eyes.

"I know I did. I'm sorry. I hurt me too."

She sighed. "I'm sorry I missed the funeral."

"Not sorrier than I am that you weren't with me."

"Did your Aunt Shea sing?"

"Yes. 'Amazing Grace,' like you suggested. It was moving."

"Was it difficult saying good-bye?" Moving her hands to my forearms, she leaned back to search my gaze. "It was for me. I fell apart when they lowered my gran's casket into the ground."

"Before that, I think I was in denial." I swallowed, knowing I still hadn't come to terms with my mom's passing. "I reached for you, Jewel, so many times. After I tossed the dirt in, I completely lost it."

"Oh, Rush." She wrapped her arms around me and laid her cheek on my chest.

I changed my mind. It wasn't her scent that was a balm. It was her.

"I missed you so much." I kissed the top of her head. "I'm sorry I made a terrible mistake. Sorry I didn't believe you."

"Was it Brenda?"

"Yes. The accountant found the discrepancy when they merged the farm accounts. Randy confronted her. They're separated now."

"Good."

"Better for him, for sure. How did you get back to LA?"

"I flew."

"Like a bird?" I said, trying to inject some levity.

"On American Airlines."

"Wasn't that expensive? You left all the money I gave you at the condo. How did you get by?"

Had she been with anyone else? It would be my fault if she had, but just the thought made me sick.

"Cam sold the stuff you bought us, but it wasn't enough without me working. She went out by herself and got hurt. She was sexually assaulted, but she won't go see a counselor. She pretends like it's not a big deal, but it is. And it's my fault."

I pulled Jewel close, squeezing her tight. "It's not."

"I should have gone with her," she murmured against my chest.

"Then both of you could've been hurt. Who would've taken care of her then?" I shook my head, angry with myself. "I wish I'd handled things differently."

Jewel pulled back, her expression fierce. "It takes two to keep up a misunderstanding. We're both responsible for not mending the distance that Brenda's lie put between us."

"Your part was minor."

She shook her head. "I should've tried harder to convince you to believe me. I should've told you a long time ago about the money I took."

"I had a crisis of faith. I know your heart. I should've trusted you."

"I left you alone in a dark place. I should've stayed."

Pulling her close again, I said softly, "Where do we go from here, baby?"

"I don't know, Rush."

"I don't want to be without you. What can I do to make things better?"

She was quiet for a moment, and when she spoke, her voice was low. "I need to know that you'll keep me safe. That I can trust you. That you trust me."

I'd lost her love. I had to regain it.

Leaning back so she could see how much I wanted this, I said, "Come back to the condo with me."

"I can't." Her gaze pleading for my understanding, she said, "I have Cam. She's important to me. I neglected her before. Besides, you have your band commitments. Your bandmates. Your brother. We can't go back to stealing borrowed moments of time outside our real lives anymore."

"You're right," I said, and she was.

I needed to merge my life with hers.

I needed to make adjustments.

I needed to show her I was committed to us.

Jewel had shown me the way in Indiana, blending in so effortlessly with me and my family, though Brenda denied it.

"Love isn't two separate existences," I said, meaning every word. "It's being together. It's sharing hopes. It's combining our dreams and helping each other achieve them. It's being each other's sure foundation to ride out any storm."

Jewel

"There's another delivery on the deck for you," Cam yelled.

"I'm running late," I shouted from the bathroom. "I still need to brush my teeth. Can you get it?"

"No."

"Cam . . ." I used my best wheedling tone. "C'mon."

"All right," she grumbled, stomping down the hall. "But if it's that pain-in-the-ass manager bringing more flowers, you're putting them in water, not me."

"They were irises, white irises." I smiled, thinking of the Van Gogh and our special day at the Getty Museum.

"They made me sneeze," she said.

They'd made me cry.

I heard the front door open and hurriedly brushed my teeth. Once I'd wiped my mouth, I snagged my bus pass from the counter and sped down the hall.

Cam blocked my way, standing in the doorway to the living room. "You're going to have to take this delivery yourself," she said, then stepped aside.

"Good morning." Rush straightened from the couch.

Like the day before, he wore jeans and the shirt I'd had on the last night we spent together. Heat hit my cheeks at the memory, and at the way the tee stretched tight across his broad shoulders and clung to his pecs.

"I'm on my way to work." I held up my bus pass.

Rush gave me a heart-stopping smile. "Thought I'd swing by and take you, spend a little time with you. Maybe shorten your commute."

The warmth from my cheeks spread through my entire body. "Oh. Yeah, sure. Thanks."

"My pleasure, baby."

He leaned in and pressed a kiss to my cheek. My knees buckled.

"Where we headed?" he asked, a grin in his voice as we left the apartment.

"Taix."

A stutter-step interrupted his usual smooth glide, and he gave me a curious look.

"I called Gustav. He hired me based on your recommendation, even though I told him about my record, my former occupation, all of it."

"How long you been working there?"

"Not long."

"Bussing tables?"

"Waitressing."

"How are the tips?"

I shrugged. "They make up for the minimum wage."

"I bet they do. I'll ask to get seated in your section tomorrow."

“You coming for business or pleasure?”

Rush gave me a serious look. “Jewel, anytime you’re around, it’s pleasure. But I’m meeting my boss. She wants to go over some things about the album, rescheduling tour dates. I want her to know about me and you, and where I feel like I am and want to go with my career.”

“Sounds serious.”

“It’s important. After my dad and mom, after losing you, I want to make the most of every day, every chance.”

“To do what?”

“To do things right.”

48

Rush

I waited for Jewel in the parking lot, leaning against the driver's side of the Porsche, my gaze glued to the back door. When she finally emerged, I straightened. Her hair was loose, blowing in the breeze.

Maybe not *the* answer blowing in the wind, but definitely *my* answer.

She was talking to another waitress. They paused to remove the long aprons Gustav insisted the waitstaff wear while working.

When she saw me, she smiled. The girl with her said something that made her nod, then Jewel came toward me. I moved to meet her.

"Hey, you," I said once I had her in my arms. "How'd your day go?"

"Long. My feet hurt. But Linda says I'm doing well. I might get a chance at a dinner shift."

"Linda, the girl who just left with you?"

"Yeah."

"That all she said?"

"No."

"Did she notice my entourage?"

The paps were tailing me. Opportunists, they knew their chances were high to snag a celebrity in the city. Around the high-end restaurants, clubs, and hotels, they were hard to avoid.

"She noticed you."

"Oh yeah?" I grinned. "What'd she say?"

"That you come in to Taix often. That you're good-looking and kind."

Surprised, I raised my brows at that last part. "Do you think I'm those things?" To me, Jewel's opinion was the only one that mattered.

"I told her you're much more."

"I'm going to take you to the condo, and you're not going to say no, but first I'm going to kiss you." My eyes broadcasting my intent, I tightened my grip on her arms. "I've been thinking about it all day."

Truthfully, I'd been thinking about a whole lot more, but we'd start with a kiss.

"Here?" she asked.

"Here. Now. I want the world to know you're mine, Jewel."

"Am I?"

"You are. You will be if you'll give me that privilege. There's no other for me but you. But we can try to keep it secret. We might manage it for a while. There's a circus that comes along with my life and being a public figure. It's intrusive and a pain, as you know, but there are also perks."

"You."

I grinned big. Her saying that lightened the weight that had crushed me since she left.

Her gaze fixed on my mouth, she reached up and traced my lips with her thumb. Desire roared in my ears, and love for her thundered in my heart.

"From the beginning," I said, my voice low, "you made me feel like I mattered. Just me."

"You made me feel the same way." Smiling softly, her gaze locked on mine, she lifted onto her toes.

I framed her face and lowered my head. A bolt of intense emotion jolted me as our mouths connected. Plunging my hands into her silky hair, I cradled her head gently while I ravaged her delicate mouth. Deep, deep, I sipped from the well. Tasting her. Reveling in her. Showing her without restraint that she was the center of my world. Then I pulled back, swiping my tongue gently across the lips that were swollen from my passion.

Withdrawing my hands from her hair, I lifted my head to stare in awe at the beautiful woman I held. Her lids fluttering, she opened her eyes, and it seemed her expression contained the same sense of wonder.

Jewel

"Where's the TV?" I asked, my eyes wide as I stared at my painting on the wall of his condo. He'd hung it where the flat screen had been.

"You didn't watch it. And I don't really." Holding me from behind, he linked his hands across my abdomen and softly kissed the side of my neck.

Warmth flowed through me. Comforting warmth, but other warmth too. It simmered beneath his hands. Even through the denim of my jeans, I registered the press of each of his fingers into my skin. The tips pointed to where I already ached.

"I'd rather sit outside," he said. "Play my guitar while you paint, and talk to you. And I want . . . I mean, I hope that soon you'll consider inviting Cam to come to the condo and stay with us."

"Rush." I spun in his arms and searched his gaze. "What are you saying?"

"That I want you to live here with me." He pressed a finger to my parted lips, his eyes glowing with intensity. "Don't say it's too soon. If I hadn't screwed up, you'd already be here."

"You don't know that," I whispered beneath his fingers.

"I do. And so do you. It's there in your painting, how we belong together."

It was. He was right. I didn't argue.

He moved his hand to cup my cheek. "I had a Christmas present for you too, that I never had a chance to give you."

"What was that?"

"A key to the condo. Move in with me, Jewel. Share my life."

My eyes burned with the pressure of tears, along with the desire to give him what he wanted. What I wanted.

"I'm not ready," I said softly.

"All right." His eyes darkened in disappointment, and he dropped his hand to my shoulder. "I understand."

"Maybe you don't. I love it here with you. I want to stay. I just need to consider more carefully before I take that leap."

"You're afraid. Because of what I did."

"Yes, because of what it did to me. Because of what you mean to me. I love you, Rush. I can't turn it off. I can't stop it."

"Neither can I, baby. The difference between me and you, though, is that I don't want to stop it."

He framed my face, his thumbs stroking my cheeks. The pads were rough against my skin, his silver ring cold. The contrasts were more than soothing. They felt familiar. They felt right. He felt right, but I truly was afraid.

The way I felt about him was big. Wild. Consuming.

And he seemed to read my mind.

"I want to crank up the heat. The passion. Will you let me, Jewel?" His eyes searched mine. "Will you let me make love to you?"

"Yes," I whispered.

There was no way to stop the way I felt. With him, it had gone one way the entire time. Falling. Fast.

I hadn't looked for a safety net before. Shouldn't I look for one now? Demand it?

"Rush, I . . ."

"You said yes, baby. I want you, so badly." His gaze dipped to my mouth. "Don't you want me too?" Raw need was clear in his voice, in his face, begging me not to reject him.

I don't do well with rejection, he'd told me before.

I didn't either.

In his darkest hour, he'd been deceived into believing my affection for him was a lie. And yet here we were, together again, and there was no place I would rather be.

Was love demanding? Could I insist on a guarantee?

No.

Love was giving. Receiving. Accepting. But more than anything, love was forgiving.

"I want you. Just you." I lifted my hands, pressing his deeper into my skin. "Make love to me, Rush. Please."

"Done."

The heat of his breath touched my mouth, then the delicious pressure of his lips sealed the deal. He kissed me like all we had was today. This moment.

And it struck me, after all that had happened, that a moment was the only guarantee anyone was given.

Wrapping my arms tight around his neck, I jumped into his arms. He caught me, his large hands cradling my rear.

"Baby, baby," he said against my mouth before stroking his tongue between my eagerly parted lips.

I returned his passion, kissing him like he kissed me. Making him feel what he made me feel. That this was it, that he was it for me.

Today. Tomorrow. Always.

I raked my fingers through his thick hair, then slid them under his shirt and on his skin, running my hands over every inch of him I could reach. Up over the ridges of his abdomen, across the contours of his pecs, around the flat crowns of his nipples. Grabbing the hard slabs of his shoulders, I shivered with want when his warm hands dove into the back of my jeans.

He broke the kiss and turned us so fast, my head spun. The walls of the hall disappeared for a second as he whipped my T-shirt over my head. His fingers immediately hooked into the back clasp of my bra. It hit the floor at the foot of the bed, right before my ass hit the mattress.

"Lay back," he said, his gaze dark.

While I scooted backward in the bed, kicking off my flip-flops, he undid the button on my jeans. Watching me, he slowly lowered the zipper.

Rush bent over me, shirtless? His warm fingers skimming my silk panties?

I nearly came. Only knowing how much better it would be with him inside me staved the need.

"Rush, I'm close. It's been so long."

"I lie awake in the night, remembering how you feel. How you sound." His gaze hot, he tugged off each leg of my jeans, leaving me naked on the bed except for a scrap of silk.

Wet silk. And me underneath throbbing as I watched him unhook his belt and unbutton his jeans.

"I remember too," I said. "I feel so empty. I ache. I ache so much, it hurts."

"Does it hurt now?" He dropped his jeans and boxers, his focus now on where I throbbed, and put a knee to the bed and his hands on my thighs. His grip was warm and firm.

"Yes."

When he cupped my pussy through the wet silk, I hissed and lifted my pelvis into his palm. He rotated it, grinding, the way I would around his cock if he were inside me.

Past the point of caring, I begged. "Take them off."

"Gladly." He lowered his head.

He licked a wet path along the top edge of my panties from one hip bone to the other, then took the silk between his teeth and yanked it down my legs. Panting, I reached for his cock, even as he spread apart my thighs and positioned between them.

"Guide me home, baby."

He bucked in my hand as I wrapped my fingers around his hard cock, already sheathed.

"Jewel . . ." He exhaled my name on a breath that lifted the hair around my face as he filled me, his weight on his hands dipping the mattress on either side of me. "So good."

He pulled out, whispering, "You're so good." Then he pushed in. "You feel so good."

"You feel better than good."

Digging in my heels, I lifted my hips, savoring the back-and-forth glide of his cock and the brilliance of how perfectly he filled me. His weight bearing down on me, his chiseled chest to my breasts, he moved in and out, his rhythm steady, his strokes deep, our damp skin sliding together.

"Baby, open for me." His mouth lowered to mine as he moved.

When I parted my lips, his tongue slipped inside. He fed me his passion, and I gave him my need. Harder, he pumped his cock into me. Deeper and faster, his tongue lashed mine.

I surrendered to it all . . . to him, to us.

My hips lifted and my fingers dug into his tight ass as his hands tunneled beneath mine to absorb the shock of each penetrating thrust. Again and again, until I turned my head to cry out it was so good.

"Jewel!"

He roared my name, stiffening inside me, the razor edge of his need slicing over the fine edge of my desire.

I came. I came so hard, and he was right there with me. The one who had the power to shatter me also had the power to put me back together.

Rush

"Stay tonight," I said, coming up behind Jewel after we showered together, and she nodded.

I draped my arms around her, liking the way we looked in the mirror. Her with one of my towels twisted into a knot between her lush breasts, me with mine knotted at the waist. Her here with me.

"I hate that bed without you," I said as my reflected gaze met hers, watching her lips lift and her golden eyes sparkle. "I missed that mouth."

I gently turned her head so I could kiss her. Tasting myself on her tongue gave me a surge of satisfaction. She was mine. Right now, she was mine.

Day by day, hour by hour, I would convince her. Every day was what I was after.

"You gonna do that lotion thing?" Moving my hands to her hips, I squeezed, frowning at the thick cotton that kept me from feeling her warm, silky skin. "Put on one of my shirts."

"I will." Her face broke out into a full smile that tilted the ground beneath my feet. It had been tilted with me sliding more and more under her spell from the very start.

"I'll pull on some jeans." I gentled my possessive caveman tone. "Grab a guitar. You get your paints. I'll meet you outside on the porch."

Within a few minutes that seemed too long, she joined me with a canvas under her arm. She set it on the easel that remained where she'd left it, in limbo like me without her in my life.

"Good one." I nodded, approving of her shirt choice.

"You ever see Dylan live?" she asked.

"Once." My tone turned reflective. "Once was all it took. I think I got the bug back then. Or maybe everything just coalesced in my mind."

I strummed my guitar, putting the pieces together while her brush moved on her canvas.

"The Gaelic melodies from my mother's side of the family. The structure of my dad's religion. R&B I've always been drawn to."

"I hear those influences in your music."

"I can see them in your brushstrokes." I inclined my head. She had her canvas angled so I could see it.

"Maybe so," she said, her head cocked like it did whenever she pondered a matter analytically.

An idea that had been percolating in my head came to the surface. I leaned over to scribble a few words in the journal my mother had given me. The first ones I had written in it.

I turned to Jewel to share. "Your art represents my music perfectly."

"That's a big compliment."

"It's the way it is." I shrugged. "Would you think about something?"

"What?" She paused with her brush dipped in indigo blue, poised over the already colorful canvas.

"Having one of your paintings be the cover for my next album."

"Oh no. I don't think my art is worthy of your music. I'm not trained."

"I'm not formally educated in music. I think the best art comes from your heart, not from instruction."

Her head tilted. "You might be right."

"I'm always right." I gave her my cocky grin, and she rolled her eyes. "I'm right about us, Jewel."

She didn't speak, didn't refute my claim. The setting sun over the water set fire to her hair.

My heart spilled into my eyes and out of my mouth. "I love you."

"I love you too."

Pleased, I nodded. Getting there. We were getting there.

"My Christmas present is the one I want to use. I've got a photo of it in my phone. I'll show it to Timmons tomorrow."

"How are you holding up?" Mary Timmons asked me from across the table, a table in Jewel's section of the restaurant. Her eyes were narrowed in concern.

Weeks later, the mention of my mom's passing still had the power to thrust all my emotions to the surface. Pushing them aside and keeping my expression impassive, I said, "I'm processing. Missing her. Trying to honor her memory to be a better me. Basically, I'm holding on."

"She's helping you." My boss inclined her head to where Jewel hovered nearby, a stainless-steel carafe at the ready to refill our coffee.

"She's helping me hold on."

"I thought that was the way you two were leaning the last time we met." Mary steepled her fingers and eased back in her chair. Whether behind the massive desk in her office or across a linen-draped restaurant table, she was ever the CEO, always in the know and always in charge.

"They aren't just leaning. They're there. I love her, and until I convince her that we're solid, I stay here."

Mary turned her head, glancing more fully at Jewel, who steadily returned the exec's gaze. She swiveled back. "I'd say she's already convinced."

I'd say so too. But tonight, I hoped to make it official.

"I'm glad to know you have someone to help you process. Losses like you've sustained cause most to lose their way."

I nodded, recognizing the truth in that. "She's helped me find it."

"That's my assessment. You're a different man than you were the last time we spoke. And your music . . ." As she shook her head, her straight brown hair skimmed her shoulders, the only part of her that seemed free and easy. "It's taken a turn I really like. In fact, it's incredible."

"Thank you." Dipping my head in response to Mary's praise, I pulled in a breath as my heart raced with excitement. I looked to Jewel, eager to share.

"Would you like her to join us?"

"Yes, I would. I have something I'd like to run by you that involves her."

"And I as well." Mary turned her head with her finger raised. "Jewel, could you sit with us a moment? I'll explain to your manager that it was at my request. No need to worry."

My girl skillfully refilled our cups before taking a seat beside me. Her hand trembled, and I clasped it in mine before she could put it under the table.

"Jewel's an artist." I slid my cell toward Mary. The display revealed the painting of the two of us.

"Stunning," Mary said, lifting her gaze.

"I want that to be my next cover."

She nodded, considering. "It would certainly mesh well with your new sound."

"And maybe a different one for the wrap for the vinyl?" I asked, hoping I wasn't pushing my luck.

"Artists of her caliber are expensive." Mary focused on Jewel. "Would two thousand be too little for the sunset? An additional two for an original for the wrap?"

"Too much." Jewel's eyes were wide and more beautiful even than the gold in her sunset. "It's a gift. He's done far too much for me already."

"There are no scales, Jewel," I told her. "Just me and you and the love that's between us."

"Those are the words you wrote in your journal last night," she whispered.

"If you want it to be a gift, I won't rob you of the joy of giving," I said firmly.

"You remembered."

"I remember everything when it comes to you."

Before we sank too deeply into each other's eyes, my boss cleared her throat.

"So two thousand for a commissioned piece of art, as yet to be determined." Mary drummed her manicured nails on the table. "Now to my proposal. We need to get you back on the road."

I held up a hand. "But—"

"You may take her with you, Rush. A larger private bus for the two of you can be arranged."

My jaw dropped. That was a big expense. I knew then for certain that Mary really liked the new songs. She liked Jewel too, I suspected. Though that was understandable.

“I can give you a couple of weeks in LA since I still have a few logistics of my own to iron out. There’s a new talent I want to bring in to open, Logan Black. I’m pairing you with 2 Rows Back. You’ll be co-headlining with them, of course. They have a new sound, a new direction, similar to yours.”

Surprised, I leaned back in my chair. “Wow.”

“Precisely.” Mary glanced down her nose at me, pausing in a manner that told me it wouldn’t be smart to comment on the matter further. “We’ll make the announcement at the Palladium tonight. Tempest has a show, a charity event. I want you to close it.”

She lifted her napkin from her lap and set it on the table. It was decided.

“And, Jewel,” Mary said as she stood. “Send me your contact information. I’ll forward it to my VP in charge of marketing. If you have any other pieces you’d like to sell, I’d like to have first option to purchase.”

50

Jewel

"Wow!"

Cam's eyes widened. We were on the couch in Shaina's apartment after Rush dropped me off.

"Two thousand a painting is a lot of money, a lot more than you're making waiting tables." She reached for my hand. "So, are you going to do it?"

"I already contacted her VP."

"No, not that. The other. Are you going to move in with Rush?"

"I'm not sure." I gnawed on my lip.

"C'mon, Jewel." Cam tilted her head, and when her long black hair caught in the top of her sling, she muttered and tugged it free.

"Would you be comfortable in his guest bedroom?" I winced, still feeling guilty about staying away all night.

"Not indefinitely. But short term, and condo-sitting if you go out on tour with him? Absolutely."

"I didn't say yes."

"Not in so many words, but you're happy with him. You're painting again. You love him, Jewel."

"I do."

Cam gave me an approving smile. "You don't do superficial. You're all in—loyal, encouraging, self-sacrificing with those you care about."

"That's the way you love too."

"Maybe. With you, for sure. It's not hard to love you."

"Thank you." I covered her hand with mine and squeezed.

"No argument, and accepting a compliment? Are you finally realizing your value?"

"I'm getting there. Seeing things differently, myself included, with his help."

"So, you're moving forward with him? Not backward anymore?"

I nodded. "Yes."

"Great."

"You like him too."

"I like his effect on you." She stood. "So, we need to pack up our things to give Shaina and War their apartment back, and then move into Rush's condo. But those can wait until tomorrow. We have more important things to decide right now."

"What's that?" I grinned, picking up on her lightened mood.

"What to wear to this concert Rush is closing tonight."

"You should go with the dark silver one," Cam said. She'd been adamant about that gown since I first tried it on.

I gestured to the gowns Shaina had located for us within hours of finding out we were attending the black-tie event.

They were Lace Lowell originals. The girlfriend of the Tempest lead guitarist was a fashion designer.

"If you wear the black one," I said, pointing at the one laid out beside the silver one next to us on the bed.

Cam shook her head and lifted her arm, still enclosed in a cast. "I'm not going. Not like this."

"You have to go with me. This is a big deal. And you're my best friend." I tilted my head, studying her. "This has nothing to do with your arm. You're worried about Brad being there."

She lifted her free hand, inspecting her nails. "Him? *Pfft*. Why would I care if he's there?"

"He seems to piss you off."

"He's arrogant. Stuffy and rude."

"He's also really cute."

Cam sighed. "And he has a girlfriend."

"Aha!"

She narrowed her gaze. "What's that supposed to mean?"

"You didn't bat on eye when I said he was good-looking. You only mentioned a deterrent."

Cam's gaze dropped to the black gown, and she plucked absently at the silky fabric. "A guy like him would never go for a girl like me, even without the deterrent."

I took her hand in mine. "Any guy would be fortunate to have the interest of an amazing and beautiful woman like you, Camaro Montepulciano." I squeezed and released her hand. "Don't you ever forget that."

"I hear you."

The front doorbell rang, and Cam hopped off the tall four-poster bed.

"I'll get it."

"All right." I slid to the floor too. It was time to get ready.

"Yo, best friend!" Cam yelled from the front door. "You have another delivery."

My heart started racing. I wasn't expecting him. I was supposed to meet him at the venue. But I also knew he liked to surprise me.

"Rush?" I left the bedroom and hurried down the hall.

"Nope." Cam sneezed. "More flowers."

My eyes widened as she handed me the florist box holding a crown made of white irises. I set it on a table, then opened the windowed lid and lifted out the floral ring.

"Put down your crown," she said. "I don't want you to crush it. It has a note too."

I returned the crown to the box, and she passed me an envelope. I slid out the card.

I hope it matches your dress.
Love, Rush

I blinked to clear my eyes.

"Don't get all teary. There's more."

"What?" I tried to peer around her back. She was hiding something.

"This." She whipped her hand from behind her back. A turquoise-colored jeweler's box lay in her outstretched palm.

"Oh shit!"

"You weren't expecting it?"

I shook my head.

"Aren't you going to look inside?"

"This is crazy."

"It might be, but I think I like his kind of crazy. Open it, Jewel."

She thrust the box into my hands. When I lifted the lid, tears flooded my eyes.

It was perfect for me.

Like him.

Rush

"I can't go out there."

Brad shook his head at me, looking like the Daniel Craig version of James Bond in his tux, but younger. "You don't want to go out there."

"I wanted her to be here already," I said. "Plus, I was nervous about the ring. I expected her to call once she received it."

"She'll come."

"But she's gonna miss the song."

The ring. The song. I was pulling out all the stops.

"Jack and Ben are already in place," Brad said. "You got your guitar. All you need to do is step onstage and sing. It's time."

He was right. Tempest had done their set. Now it was my turn.

I nodded to my bass man and made eye contact with my drummer. Huge screens behind him, projecting his image and making him look larger than life, Jack clacked his sticks over his head to set the beat.

I stepped out onstage. Beneath the crystal chandelier, a hush descended over the full-capacity audience of four thousand in the Hollywood Palladium.

At first, my guitar was the only instrument. My fingers strummed the strings in the simple but complex rolling rhythm inspired by the waves, and Jewel. At center stage, I put my lips to the mic, the first word poised to slip from my lips . . . when I saw her.

As if it were meant to be, Jewel crossed the stage to join me. The silver satin dress she wore hugged her curves as if custom fitted. Her coppery-brown hair fell in soft waves around her delicate shoulders. A white iris crown atop her head, she was as regal as a princess, and her golden eyes glittered like the treasure she was to me.

I didn't have a sight line to see the magnification of her on the screens above the stage, yet in my eyes, she was a goddess of epic proportions.

Taking her hand, I caressed her soft skin with my thumb as I drew her into the center spotlight with me to start the song. In her other hand, she carried a cordless mic, ready for her part of the chorus.

No time onstage had ever felt more right. No other partner was more perfect.

Somehow got lost
Along the way
Forgot all the things I knew
Didn't dare to dream
Or so it seemed
Until I found you

You started a fire
Rekindled desire
Now in your light I see

Whatever I want you to be
Whatever I need you to be
You're so right for me
So tonight you'll be my only one

Caught up in chaos
Trapped in a storm
A tempest of my mind
Out of control
Body and soul
No reason and no rhyme

But you cut through the noise
Gave me my voice
Brought me the calm I need

Whatever I want you to be
Whatever I need you to be
You're so right for me
So tonight you'll be my only one

Jewel

I knew as soon as I stepped out onstage and his eyes found mine that I'd made the right decisions.

Getting in the Porsche with him that first time.

Agreeing to our arrangement.

Deciding to forgive him.

Arriving at this moment right now.

Our coming together was like a fairy tale, meant to be. Like his parents after two dates. Like my gran after one dance with my grandfather. Despite my own self-doubts, the ones that had kept me down, stifling my spirit for so long, I had implemented the wishes of my heart.

The fancy gown and the platinum heels and all the accoutrements I wore made me feel like a fairy-tale princess. But those were just superficial things, not truly important. Deep inside, I felt like a princess because of his love. He was the other half of a love that made the two of us complete.

Once the concert was over, we were alone, sitting on the edge of the stage. The seats were all empty. The post-show meet and greet was over. The remaining fans had gone home or relocated to the VIP reception at the hotel, where his bandmates and our friends waited for us.

This moment was just for us.

He took my hands, and I grinned at him.

"How come the rock stars don't have to do tuxes and finery like everyone else?"

"I have on a shirt, darlin'. This *is* me dressed up." His hair fell forward as he glanced down at our joined hands. "How come you aren't wearing the ring?"

"I thought we should talk first."

"About?" he asked carefully.

"About us." I slid my hands from his and slipped off my high heels. Arranging the silver satin around my crossed ankles, I reached in my pocket and handed him the turquoise box.

When his face fell, I hurried to explain.

"I'm certain of my answer. I'm certain with you. I was certain before we left for Indiana, and I'm even more certain now because of the care you've shown me."

A relieved breath whooshed from Rush, and I smiled.

"You're all the things a good man should be. You're gentle with me. You listen to my concerns. You're kind. You change your plans for me. Limelight or spotlight, highlights to celebrate or challenges to endure, it's you I want, you I need. It just didn't seem right to put the ring on without you saying what it means to you for me to wear it."

He scanned my features, the love shining so bright in his eyes, it sent a bolt of warmth straight through me to my toes. Rush brushed a lock of hair from my shoulder, then gently grasped my chin and tilted my face up to his.

"It means you're the one, Jewel. It means you'll always be the one. You see me, the real me. You don't look at the photos online or the stuff on YouTube or the magazines to try to figure me out. You look in my eyes and listen to my words. You understand my heart. You understand *me*."

When he paused, I said with every bit of certainty, "I'm ready."

I stretched out my hand, fingers splayed, and he slid the ring on. Thrilled, I held it up for a second, admiring the emerald cut of the diamond with the micro slim platinum band. It twinkled under the stage lights. But lifting my gaze and looking into his eyes and seeing his love for me blazing within them was what made the moment priceless.

I gave him my biggest smile. "I love you, Rush."

"I would give anything, do anything, be anything for one of your smiles." He put his arms around me, drawing me into his embrace.

"It's the perfect place." I rested my head on his shoulder, feeling a whisper of magic swirling around us and knowing Gran was watching us from heaven.

"The Palladium?" he asked.

"No, right here with you. When you open your arms and I step inside them, I am where I want to be. Where I'm meant to be." I touched his cheek and said softly, "I'm home."

Epilogue

Jewel

Six years later

"I'm not tired." Snuggled into her narrow bed on the tour bus, the little girl could barely keep her golden eyes open.

"It's late. You'll fall asleep as soon as the bus pulls away from the venue." Jewel tucked the blanket she'd brought from home around her daughter, marveling how much her young Helen resembled the photos of her gran as a child.

"I like being on the tour bus with Daddy."

"I like it too, precious one."

Jewel thanked her lucky stars once again for the benefits that came with Rush's success. Unless she had a showing at her gallery, they went as a family wherever Rush's career took him.

"Will he come kiss me good night?"

"You know he will. Right after the encore."

"'Spend Your Hours Wise.'"

"Yes, he likes to end every performance with the song about your grandmother Moira."

"Can you tell me a story until he gets here? Like Gran used to tell you?"

"A fairy tale with magic?"

"Love is the real magic, and music gives it a voice," a deep voice said, resonating in the back space of the tour bus almost as nicely as it did inside a concert hall.

Helen

"Daddy!" Helen sat up in bed.

"Hey, precious." Her daddy's silver eyes shone with love for her, like they always did when he looked her way.

"Mommy was just getting ready to tell me a story."

"Was she now?"

Helen nodded, and her halo of reddish curls bounced.

"Then I'll come get my kisses before I go shower, since I know how much you love them."

Entranced, Helen watched her daddy draw close to her mommy. She thought he was the most handsome man on earth, and that her mother was the prettiest woman she had ever seen. But even better than all that was the beautiful life they all shared, as wonderful as any fairy tale.

"I love you." Daddy stopped in front of Mommy and framed her face. He kissed her on the lips and then pulled back to stare into her eyes for a long moment, as if making sure those very important words were absorbed.

Her mother tilted her face up to her father, her skin aglow as his warmth and love settled deeply inside her heart. Maybe deeper still where another baby grew. If it were a girl, they planned to name her Moira. If it were a boy, they would name him Ronald. Her parents firmly believed in making those they loved a forever part of their lives.

"I'll see you in our bed in just a bit," Daddy said to Mommy.

"I love you," Mommy said as Daddy tucked a long strand of her brown hair with the coppery threads behind her ear. She laid her hand over his, and they exchanged a long meaningful glance before she shifted sideways so he could get by her to see Helen. "She's been waiting for your kiss."

"Yes, she knows that I'm the handsome prince, and that my kisses are magical." Smiling, her daddy moved to Helen's side, smoothed her hair that had more fire than her mother's behind her ears, then bent and tenderly pressed his lips to each of her soft cheeks.

"Your whiskers tickle." She giggled delightedly. "And you're all sweaty, Daddy.

"I came right from the stage." He straightened. "I didn't want to risk missing saying good night to my girl."

She beamed at him, thrilled at the attention. "Good night, Daddy."

"Good night, precious."

As soon as he scooted past, her mother exchanged places with him at Helen's side.

"Can I feel the baby?" she asked as her mommy took a seat beside her on the bed.

"Of course you can." Mommy placed Helen's hand on her rounded belly. "So, which story will it be tonight? Cinderella? Snow White?"

"No, tell me about you and Daddy."

"That one again."

"Yes, it's my favorite."

"I know it is." Mommy smiled.

Helen smiled back just as brightly. "Everyone knows real love stories are the very best."

Acknowledgements

To my hubby for being the inspiration for everything romantic

To my boys, every day I have with you I consider a blessing (Hope lead the way home)

To my best friend Lisa Anthony (My Indie Author Fix) who is the best of all of us

To my best friend in Chicago. Michelle Warren. I call her sunshine for that is who she is

To Rock Chick. Teresa Marsh Jensen. You are the inspiration for the music, and my heart of hearts, I love you

Pam "Fairy Godmother" Berehulke for seeing my vision, for understanding where I was going and getting me there

To bloggers who tirelessly promote books and share the love of reading. To Brandee Price and Lexxie Lin of Un Conventional Bookworms and Brandee Veltri of Brandee's Book Endings, thank you for being extra special encouragers and friends

To my Rock All Stars. My positive support and encouragement group. You guys are the BEST!

To all readers and lovers of books. You are my peeps. Stay in touch. I love you all. Slumber party if I get to see you at a signing. Let's talk about books all night. Hugs and love forever.

Other Books

Michelle Mankin is the *New York Times* bestselling author of the Black Cat Records series of novels.

Fall in love with a rock star.

Love Evolution, Love Revolution, and Love Resolution are a **BRUTAL STRENGTH** centered trilogy, combining the plot underpinnings of Shakespeare with the drama, excitement, and indisputable sexiness of the rock 'n roll industry.

Things take a bit of an edgier, once upon a time turn with the **TEMPEST** series. These pierced, tatted, and troubled Seattle rockers are young and on the cusp of making it big, but with serious obstacles to overcome that may prevent them from ever getting there.

Rock stars, myths, and legends collide with paranormal romance in a totally mesmerizing way in the **MAGIC** series.

Get swept away by temptation in the **ROCK STARS, SURF AND SECOND CHANCES** series.

Romance and self-discovery, the **FINDING ME** series is a Tempest spin off with a more experienced but familiar cast of characters.

ROCK F*CK CLUB is a girl-power fueled reality show with the girls ranking the rock stars.

Once Upon A Rock Star Series is sexy modern-day fairytale retellings.

When Michelle is not prowling the streets of her Texas town listening to her rock or NOLA funk music much too loud, she is putting her daydreams down on paper or traveling the world with her family and friends, sometimes for real, and sometimes just for pretend.

BRUTAL STRENGTH series:
Love Evolution
Love Revolution
Love Resolution
Love Rock'ollection

TEMPEST series (also available in audio):
SOUTHSIDE HIGH
Irresistible Refrain
Enticing Interlude
Captivating Bridge
Relentless Rhythm
Tempest Raging
Tempting Tempo
Scandalous Beat
The Complete Tempest Rock Star Series, books 1-6

The MAGIC series (also available in audio):
Strange Magic
Dream Magic
Twisted Magic

ROCK STARS, SURF AND SECOND CHANCES
series (also available in audio):
Outside
Riptide
Oceanside
High Tide
Island Side
The Complete Rock Stars, Surf and Second Chances Series, books 1-5

FINDING ME series (also available in audio):
Find Me
Remember Me
Keep Me

Girls Ranking the Rock Stars series (also available in audio):
ROCK F*CK CLUB (Girls Ranking the Rock Stars, Book #1)
ROCK F*CK CLUB (Girls Ranking the Rock Stars, Book #2)
ROCK F*CK CLUB (Girls Ranking the Rock Stars, Book #3)
ROCK F*CK CLUB (Girls Ranking the Rock Stars, Book #4)
ROCK F*CK CLUB (Girls Ranking the Rock Stars, Book #5)
ROCK F*CK CLUB BOX SET BOOKS 1-5
ROCK F*CK CLUB (Girls Ranking the Rock Stars, Book #6)

Once Upon A Rock Star series:
The Right Man
The Right Wish
The Right Wrong

STAY CONNECTED

For cover reveal, flash sale, and release alerts
Text ROCK BOOK to 33777
Follow Michelle Mankin on Bookbub
Receive exclusive content. Sign up for the Black Cat Records newsletter (http://eepurl.com/Lvgzf)
Hang out with me in my reader group. Join the Rock All Stars.
Be an Author Michelle Mankin VIP.
www.facebook.com/groups/1673519816224970//

FOLLOW AUTHOR MICHELLE MANKIN

On Facebook
www.facebook.com/pages/Author-Michelle-Mankin/233503403414065
On Instagram @michellemankin
Twitter @MichelleMankin
Website www.michellemankin.com

Made in the USA
Coppell, TX
07 January 2023

10572348R00219